The People Next Door

ANNA WOIWOOD

for those who seek pleasure

"I desire
And I crave.

You set me on fire."

-Sappho

Chapter One

The moving truck had been parked in the driveway all morning.

Madelyn watched through the window, steaming cup of coffee in hand, as items were taken from the back of the yellow and red truck and escorted indelicately into the home next door.

It was a simple house. A mirror image of their own.

A large enough living room and a simple kitchen on the main floor. Upstairs would be two smaller bedrooms and one larger main room overlooking the backyard. It was nothing large or boisterous, like the homes across town, but it had been good enough for Madelyn and Arthur since they'd moved into the neighborhood in 1930.

She presumed their new next-door neighbors might be young, based on some of the more lavish pieces of furniture she'd noticed; a minibar, an interesting set of chairs, a rather theatrical lamp with golden leaves.

She wondered if there would be children.

The neighborhood had grown old with Madelyn and Arthur, but she had noticed an influx of younger couples in the years after the last war. Because it was an older development, house prices in the area had held steady, making them affordable and attractive to the younger couples just starting out fresh again.

"I always suspected you were a voyeur," the voice startled her, and she nearly spilled coffee on her freshly pressed white button-up.

"Really, Arthur." Madelyn sighed, wiping at the non-existent stains.

"What's so fascinating out there?" her husband asked as he took his seat at the kitchen table, picking up the paper she'd placed on the table for him. The pages were already wrinkled from her early morning perusal.

"The new neighbors." Madelyn turned away from the window, moving to pour a cup of coffee for him.

"Ah, yes. The Coopers."

"You've met them?" She settled the cup before him.

"No, that Johnson fellow who sold the house was out front the other night when I was watering the shrubs. He said they were young. No children."

Well, she thought as she leaned against the counter, that answered that question.

Her eyes returned to glance outside the window, and she watched as a large mattress was carried from the back of the truck.

She sipped her coffee and peered at her wristwatch. It was nearly eight thirty. "Would you like a ride to the college?"

Arthur shook his head. "Not today. There's a provost meeting this evening, so I thought I'd putter around the house until my eleven thirty seminar."

"So, you won't be home for dinner?" She reached for her jacket on the back of her chair and put her arms through the sleeves, buttoning it tightly in the front.

"Just as pretty as the day I met you." Arthur had been looking at her over the top of his paper.

She blushed and waved him off. "You didn't answer the question."

"No, darling, no dinner for me this evening. I suppose you'll have to dine alone. I know you're terribly disappointed."

She smiled and leaned down to kiss his cheek. "Devastated."

Affixing a hat to her head with a hatpin, she collected up her satchel – bursting with corrected student essays – and the keys to the car.

"Perhaps you should make those world-famous cookies of yours for the new neighbors and we could take them over this weekend," Arthur suggested before she walked out the door.

"All right, dear," Madelyn agreed as she went out the door.

She paused at the door of her car, watching as a dark green chaise lounge was removed from the back of the truck.

She thought it slightly absurd. All their items on display for anyone to peer into their lives.

She got into her car and started the ignition. A sleepy ballad came over the radio.

She backed out of the driveway as the movers removed a dressing table that looked like it was from the 1930s from the back of the van.

She angled the car away from the house next door and drove down the street to the main road that would take her across town and to the sprawling lawns and historic buildings of the college.

She pulled into the faculty lot and went to the space near the corner beneath a shady tree. The lawn was freshly cut, and she could smell the razed grass as soon as her heel touched the pavement.

A male colleague called out to her from the other side of the parking lot, "Good morning, Professor Turner."

"Professor Knight." She waved back to the middle-aged man who had once been her pupil.

She continued down the familiar path to the arts building, delighting in the tree lined sidewalks, the neatly cut grass, the young bodies that littered the lawn, huddled together in groups, talking to one another animatedly, so alive with thoughts and feelings and things that urgently needed to be expressed.

She delighted in their youth but did not wish to be young again.

They looked up at her as she walked by.

"Morning, Professor Turner."

"Heya, Professor Turner."

"Good morning, Professor Turner."

She waved to the young men and women as she went by.

Her heels clicked on the concrete stairs that led up to the imposing art building. She had always admired its classic façade, its pillars, the ivy that crawled up the sides.

She pushed open the main door and listened as her heels clicked upon the marble of the floors.

"Hello there, Professor."

"Good morning, Professor Turner."

The students smiled as she went by.

She addressed each by name, greeting them kindly, cordially.

She ascended the marble staircase, turning down a hall to retreat to her office, shaking her keys in her hand as she neared the door.

She was not surprised to find a tall, soft brown-haired girl pressed against the wall beside the door.

"Good morning, Professor Turner."

"Good morning, Ruby." She smiled at the young woman as she stuck the key into the lock and twisted.

"You look well today," Ruby commented as she hovered in the doorway, watching Madelyn as she settled her satchel atop her desk before unpinning her hat and hanging it carefully on the coat rack.

"Why thank you," Madelyn accepted the compliment. "I'm sure you're anxious to know how your paper came out."

"Oh, yes." Ruby colored a deep shade of red that could match her name.

Madelyn smiled at the girl, touching her hand slightly as if to console her. "You mustn't tell the others, but I was particularly impressed with your comparison of Pollock and O'Keefe. Quite an intriguing comparison really. You did a very nice job. Very nice indeed." Madelyn smiled and sat at her desk.

The next class would begin promptly at nine and she had intended to go over her notes one last time on architecture in the twenties to the forties. Though she taught the same classes year after year, she never tired of preparing. The world of art was always changing; the history rewritten every year.

But the girl was still standing near her, as if waiting for something.

Madelyn looked up and caught Ruby staring at her oddly. An expression that Madelyn had never seen before on a woman. A hunger that quite shocked her, made her feel as if she shouldn't be looking at the girl at all. It was far too intimate.

Ruby looked down at her saddle shoes, cheeks pink. "I'm sorry, I... "

"Ruby," Madelyn called out to the girl, but she'd turned on her heels and was off down the hall.

Had she praised her too much? Had she frightened her off?

She had grown very fond of the girl, was quite taken by her intellect. She wanted to guide her, but the girl would run away at the slightest compliment.

It was the strangest thing.

Madelyn couldn't puzzle it out.

She glanced at her watch again and realized she only had a few more minutes before she would be expected at the head of the lecture hall.

The slides were all prepared and ready for the projector. Her notes were typed up and coherent.

She reached for the pile of papers in her satchel.

"Morning, Professor Turner."

She was startled at the sound of the young man's voice. "George, my hero. Would you mind helping me carry these things to the lecture hall?"

"Not at all, Ma'am." He tipped his head, adjusted his satchel about his chest, and then picked up the slides and papers.

"Thank you." She smiled at him as they walked out of her office. She closed the door and locked it behind her, before they continued down the hall toward the lecture hall.

"I hope my paper wasn't plain rotten. I really struggled with it," he admitted bashfully.

She recalled his paper. It had been littered with grammatical errors, but he had made quite an interesting point about Henri Matisse. However, she quite wondered if he'd just been taken by Matisse's nudes. "Well, it was certainly a valiant effort," she assured him as they approached the hall.

He smiled slightly and held the door for her.

She slipped past him.

The students in the hall quieted at her entrance; sat up a bit straighter in their seats.

"Good morning class," she said as she came to stand at the podium in the center of the room.

They parroted her greeting, "Good morning, Professor Turner."

She smiled and began her lecture, delighted in the way the students hung on her every word.

Chapter Two

The moving truck was gone when she pulled into the driveway that evening.

The only indication that anyone might live there now was a newer looking maroon Ford in the drive and a light that shone from the living room window.

The light had not been on since Frank and Carole had moved away half a year before. Frank had taken Carole away to retire in the South.

Madelyn missed Carole.

There had been phone calls and a few letters with pictures of them in front of their new house near a beach.

But it was not the same as being able to walk next door and share a drink and a chat.

The light threw her, made her feel as if she could go over and open the door and be invited in for dinner. Which had often happened when Arthur was working late at the college.

Madelyn put the car in park and realized that she could not go over to the house because she did not yet know the Coopers. She supposed they would be like the other younger couples who moved into the neighborhood. Not interested in their elders.

She reached for her satchel and got out of the car.

The evening air smelled of the approaching autumn. She inhaled greedily as she walked to the house, unlocking the back door.

She flipped on the lights and kicked off her heels, unpinned her hat and let it drop carelessly atop the bench in the mud room. She unbuttoned her jacket and moved into the kitchen, turning on lights as she went.

She opened the refrigerator and peered in at its contents.

There would be no need to prepare anything intricate. It would only be her for dinner.

She had always hated cooking and so she refused to do it if she did not have to.

There was some sliced meat and bread.

She reached for the lettuce and tomatoes and some mayonnaise and a beer in the ice box.

Taking off her jacket, she tossed it onto the back of a chair and rummaged about for a bottle opener. The lid popped off and she drank back the beer and placed two slices of toast in the toaster.

Taking the drink in hand, she began unbuttoning her white shirt as she walked through the house and up the stairs, loosening her skirt from about her waist.

Her feet hurt from standing in classes all day.

She drank another sip from the bottle and sat it atop her bureau.

Pushing her skirt to the ground, she sat on the edge of the bed to remove her panty hose.

Little blue marks, freckles, stretch marks were uncovered as she rolled the silky material down her legs. The tells of age, all hidden away behind nylons.

She rubbed the soles of her feet, rolling her neck about.

She could smell the toast down in the kitchen.

She removed her shirt the rest of the way and tossed it in the basket for dry cleaning then reached into her closet for a simple house dress. She buttoned up the front buttons and slipped into her moccasins.

She picked up the bottle and drank again before lifting her skirt and hanging it in the closet before picking up the nylons from the floor.

She longed to have the luxury of leaving things strewn about, but who would clean up after her?

As she passed by the window in the bedroom, she paused.

She had never really noticed it before.

Perhaps because Frank and Carole had always kept the blinds and drapes firmly shut.

But there, across the driveway and lawn that stretched between, a light shone out from the window that mirrored her own.

There were no drapes, no blinds.

She had always been farsighted, so it was not hard for her to make out the form in the window across the way.

A sleek, young masculine body. From the waist up. Nude.

He was talking and gesturing with a burning cigarette between his teeth.

His face was full of mirth and youth. He was laughing at something.

Or someone.

A woman came into view but all she could see of her was dark, dark auburn hair and the thin strap of her bra.

The man grabbed her up in his arms and put his mouth on hers and she wrapped her arms about him.

Madelyn was warm.

She had unknowingly pressed the cold beer to her feverish forehead.

The couple disappeared from sight, and she could only imagine what it was they were up to.

An old, familiar ache shot through her center.

She drank back the beer.

The phone was ringing, startling her.

She tossed the nylons still grasped in her hands onto the bed and moved through the house, down the stairs to the ringing phone.

"Hello?" Her voice seemed higher than normal. She could tell that her cheeks were flushed.

"She's at it again," his voice growled over the phone.

"Oh, Mitch." Disappointment shot through her. A cold pail of ice water dowsing out her fever instantly. "I'll be over as soon as I can."

She hung up the phone.

She went back up the stairs and put on a pair of slacks and a simple button-up shirt. She put away the food in the kitchen, scribbled down a note for Arthur telling him where she was going, and then reached for her car keys.

The drive across town felt like an eternity.

They had offered to help Mitch and Rose move into the house next door, but Rose had been adamant about not moving.

She had said that the house was too small.

Madelyn knew it wasn't as nice as the place Mitch had them in across town.

And apart from that it would have been an admission that something was wrong, and Rose certainly did not think that anything was wrong.

Madelyn pulled into the driveway and killed the ignition.

She held the steering wheel in her hands, pausing to take several deep, steadying breaths.

It was never pleasant being called over by Mitch.

The front door opened before she could knock, and little Russell appeared. "Grandma!" he exclaimed and wrapped his arms tightly around Madelyn's legs. "I'm glad you're here," he said looking up at her seriously.

She ran her fingers through his sandy-blond hair. "Where's Charlotte?"

"In her room," Russell whispered.

"Good. Why don't you go on up to your room and I'll bring you both some dinner in a bit?" she insisted, pressing her lips to his forehead.

He smiled at her sadly and raced off up the stairs.

Mitch appeared from around the corner. Features tense and upset. "She's in there." And then he collected up his coat and brushed past Madelyn on his way out the front door.

She could smell the cigarettes and booze before she rounded the corner to the den.

The only light was the flash of a television in the corner. A staticky, garble of words hummed low.

"Rose." Madelyn moved toward the rise of smoke that came from a chair in the corner of the room.

The younger woman startled, messy blonde head rolling blearily to peer up at Madelyn.

"Why the hell are you here?" she slurred.

"Mitch called." Madelyn took the nearly smoked cigarette from her daughter's hand and put it out in the already too full ashtray. She hated seeing her like this. "Come on, let's get you to bed."

"Get your hands off me," Rose protested, batting Madelyn's hands away.

Madelyn straightened. She hadn't the energy to fight her like this.

Rose curled into herself. "I'm awful," She kept mewing over and over.

They had been here far too many times for Madelyn to count and she hadn't a clue what to do anymore. She had tried every tactic. Begging, pleading, crying, yelling, whispering, comforting.

She let Rose cry until her body stilled and she allowed Madelyn to help her up. She leaned against her as they walked through the house to the bedroom where she sat her down on the side of the bed.

Rose clung to her tightly, tears streaming down her cheeks. "It hurts."

"What hurts, sweetheart?" Madelyn sat on the bed beside her.

Rose shuddered. "Everything."

Madelyn rubbed soothing circles over her back. "It isn't fair, doing this to yourself when the kids are watching you."

"Don't yell at me," Rose whined.

"I'm not yelling," Madelyn said evenly. "But you need help."

"I don't need help," Rose parried and then grasped at Madelyn. "I think... I think I'm going to be sick."

And Madelyn eased her up and helped her into the bathroom, making it just in time for her to vomit into the toilet.

"You're making yourself miserable," Madelyn scolded as she cleaned her daughter up like she used to when she was little.

Only now she was thirty-six and should be able to care for herself.

"I don't want to hear it," Rose spat after Madelyn made her wash out her mouth.

"It was a long time ago, Rose. I wish you could get over it instead of letting it affect you like this. You have two beautiful children now and they need their mother," Madelyn chastised as she helped Rose back to her bed. She helped her beneath the covers and tucked her in.

"I can't just let it go."

"Then go visit her," Madelyn said.

"I can't," Rose spoke softly, ashamedly.

Madelyn filled a glass of water and placed it beside Rose's bed along with two Aspirin tablets. "Go to sleep then."

And then she left the room in darkness and went back out to the den where she turned off the television and went about emptying the ashtrays and pouring out the bottles of beer and the hidden stash of liquor bottles underneath the sink.

Putting on an apron, she peered into the refrigerator and pulled out some ingredients for egg salad with radish and asparagus. As she cooked, she felt someone watching her and looked up to see Charlotte, hovering in the doorway. Her gorgeous fifteen-year-old granddaughter. All long, dark hair like her father and tiny, tanned limbs.

"Is she okay?" Charlotte asked shyly.

Madelyn nodded. "She will be in the morning."

"I'm worried about her."

Madelyn sighed. "You shouldn't have to be worried about your mother." And she felt as if she had failed as a mother.

The way her daughter acted.

Had it been her fault?

Madelyn remembered when she'd caught Rose smoking at thirteen.

How she'd caught her sneaking out with boys at fifteen.

How she'd taken her to that doctor who had been impossible to find to have him perform that procedure when she was sixteen.

Only for her to drop out of college two years later to marry Mitch and have a child.

What had she done wrong?

Charlotte wrapped her arms around Madelyn. She was crying into her shirt sleeve.

Madelyn held her close.

Chapter Three

Arthur's car was in the driveway when she arrived home, and she could see the lamp through the blinds of the window upstairs.

There was a light still blazing in the front window of the house next door.

The image of what she had witnessed before came back to her in full force and she felt her knees weaken. Her hand went to the warm hood of the car, steadying herself.

She did not look up to see if the light was still on in the window upstairs.

She pushed into the house, tossing her keys onto the bench, kicking off her shoes.

She was no longer hungry. She retrieved the open beer from the refrigerator and poured it down the sink. Disgusted.

She went up the stairs to the front bedroom.

Arthur was looking up at her from the chair in the corner.

He was sitting in silence.

"How is she?" He looked worried.

Madelyn wiped at her brow. "Not good." She looked Arthur over and saw the pain in his eyes. "Did you take anything?"

14

He waved her off. "It's only a little headache."

She left him and went to the bathroom for the Aspirin.

"It's no fair to you, you know?" Arthur called to her from the room.

"Well, what am I supposed to do?" She returned to him with two pills, reaching for the water by his bedside table.

He gratefully swallowed the pills before pinching the bridge of his nose.

"How was the meeting?" she asked, sitting on the edge of the bed.

Arthur shrugged. "Nothing of great importance to report. Just budgets and schedules for the upcoming term."

"I see." She caught sight of the clock on the bedside table. It was half past nine.

"You ought to get some sleep. You look exhausted, dear," Arthur chided her.

"You don't look much better." She pulled herself up and went to Arthur, leaning down to press her lips to his forehead.

"Goodnight, darling," he said as she turned out the light and left the room.

She went across the hall to her bedroom and closed the door.

She slid from her pants, removed her tear-stained shirt, tossing both in the hamper. She unclasped her bra and stood staring at her figure in the full-length mirror propped up in the corner of the room.

In the dim light of her bedside lamp, she could almost see what she had once been.

But when she peered a bit closer, she could see all the lines and marks and indications of her sixty years.

She felt foolish and pulled on a nightgown.

She moved into her bathroom and went about washing her face, brushing her teeth, applying lotion to her skin in careful, upward motions, and then she washed out her nylons in the sink and hung them in the bathtub. She unpinned her hair from its clips and let it fall down around her face.

It was only then that she peered into the bathroom mirror again.

Her gray hair was dyed blonde every other week at the salon.

She kept it long.

It brushed against her shoulders, curling from where the pins had held it.

She mindlessly twirled a strand of it around her finger.

Her eyes were her eyes and yet she recognized so little else.

She turned off the light and went to the bed, pulling back the bedspread.

But she did not get into the bed.

She went to the window.

Peering out, she looked across the space between her house and the house next door.

The bedroom window was black.

She backed away from the window and got into the bed and put out her light.

In the darkness, the feeling returned to her.

Instead of thinking about Rose, she thought about what the couple next door might be doing just then in their new bedroom.

She could see the man vividly in her mind, embracing the red-headed woman, kissing her as he had taken her to the bed.

And then what would he have done?

She let her mind race with possibilities of the happenings in the room that Frank and Carole had once inhabited.

She knew, from Carole, that she and Frank had sex once a week. Usually on Wednesdays, for some reason. As if Frank needed a morale boost to make it through the work week.

Carole had always looked more relaxed on Thursdays.

This new, younger couple, however, looked to have much more sex than just once a week. It was only Monday, after all.

Would they still be having sex, or would they be asleep?

It was ten.

Madelyn turned on her side.

She couldn't sleep.

She was wired.

She turned onto her back and stared up at the ceiling.

The man had been very handsome, from what she could tell. Dark hair, defined chest. Different from Arthur and his soft blond, now gray, hair.

The man across the yard looked to be in his late twenties or early thirties. Not old at all. Far too young for her to be thinking about or looking at.

She twisted and her nightgown came up.

Her underwear was damp.

She rubbed her legs together.

She thought, for some reason, of Ruby and how she had flushed such a brilliant red earlier that day, at her mere compliment.

The girl was always blushing around her.

She wondered if the girl touched herself.

Then she stopped herself, because she was crossing a line, thinking about a student in such a way.

And so, she returned to the man next door and let her fingers slip between her legs. She thought of how he would touch the red head, of how he would get her ready and then he would put himself inside of her.

She rubbed furiously, unashamedly until she gasped around her release.

She lay back in the bed, slightly sweaty and warm and loose and panting.

She laid like that until her breathing evened out and the sweat cooled on her skin, chilling her.

She curled onto her side, pulling the bedsheets up around herself.

She drifted off to sleep.

Her dreams were littered with lewd, awful, terribly wonderful things.

She awoke to the screaming of her alarm and the ache from the night before.

But as light filtered in through the blinds, she was reminded of the day before. Of being called to Rose's. Of putting her back together and taking care of her grandchildren. She thought of her classes that day, of all the little things she needed to take care of.

She rose from the bed, performed her morning stretches and light calisthenics, and then wrapped a dressing gown about herself.

She went to the bathroom, washed her face, brushed her teeth, staring at her bare, blank face in the mirror.

She walked down the stairs, wrapping the robe tightly about herself. She unlocked the front door and stepped out into the cool, crisp air of morning, inhaling the scent of dawn. The birds were chirping in the trees.

She walked with bare feet over the cracking cement of their front walkway.

The newspaper was at the end of the path.

She bent down to pick it up, scanning the headlines. Western Germany seeking to rearm themselves, Eastern Germany pleading for reunification, conflict breaking out in Korea.

War, war. Always war.

Madelyn glanced up and was caught off-guard to see the dark-haired man emerge from the front door of the house next door, placing a hat on his head, juggling a briefcase and what looked to be a piece of toast with jam. He looked jovial as he bit off the edge of the bread.

Madelyn wanted to hide. She felt naked, exposed, barely dressed as she was and without her face on.

It was not the first impression she wanted to make.

But he had seen her.

He held up his hand in a welcoming wave, a wonderful, boyish smile illuminating his face.

She found herself waving back.

He looked as if he might say something, but Madelyn tucked her head down and pretended to be fascinated with the newspaper. She hurried inside, closing the door before leaning up against its surface.

She hugged the newspaper against her chest, trying to catch her breath.

She was being utterly ridiculous.

She peeled herself away from the door and went to the kitchen, catching sight of the man getting into his car through the windows at the side of the house. She could see him as he finished his toast, brushing the crumbs off his shirt, before starting up the ignition. He was backing out of the driveway by the time she reached the kitchen.

He was gone when she started the coffee.

She was too old to have such foolish feelings, she reasoned as she watched the water heat on the stove.

It was an escape, she reasoned, as she got out the bread to make herself toast. An escape, something outside the norm. Something apart from teaching and looking after and worrying about Rose and taking care of Arthur.

As she spread jam and butter over the toast, she thought of the pile of mail she had forgotten to look at the previous evening. Perhaps there would be a letter from Carole.

Biting into the toast, she moved to the table beside the front door, to the pile of letters that had accumulated.

It was there beneath a bill.

She took the letter and returned to the kitchen. She sat at the kitchen table with her toast and coffee and opened the letter. As if Carole could restore the equilibrium.

... Frank bought a new boat with some of the money from the sale of the house. He's enjoying his 'retirement' well enough.

... We go with this set in the neighborhood, but to be

completely honest, I find the other wives rather dull. Margaret is nice enough, but she always seems to side with her husband. She can be expressing her opinion and then he says something completely opposite and she agrees with him... It's all rather dreadful.

... Tell me about the new neighbors! I'm anxious to hear about them. Frank said they were young. No children?

... As always, I miss our chats. Shall we talk on the phone soon?

XO, Carole

Chapter Four

It was the simplicity, she thought as she stared at the stairway of Jacques Doucet's townhome, that she liked the most. It was the ease of shape and contrast of color. How bold it was and yet how elegant it remained. So different from everything that had come before.

She could get lost in the lines of Cubism, in the idea of how the art movement had morphed and shaped itself into three-dimensional architecture, influencing all the decadent art deco that came after.

That it had happened in her lifetime confounded her. From the rigid Victorian structure to the decadence of deco. How it had changed the lives of everything and everyone and then had led them straight into depression and war.

But her war had begun before the second one, after the first.

She didn't like to reminisce like this.

The architecture pulled her away from the ugliness of the first world war. *La Maison Cubiste* of 1912. Its perfect symmetry a balm.

Her watch said it was nearly noon.

Arthur had asked her to join him for lunch.

She placed the slide back into the canister and closed the lid, removing her glasses from her tired eyes. She rubbed her forehead.

Pinning her hat into place, Madelyn reapplied a fresh coat of lipstick and then reached for her pocketbook. She stepped out of her office and turned to lock the door but was startled by Ruby's presence outside her office.

Had she been hovering there the whole time?

She looked just as startled as Madelyn felt.

"I... " The girl looked down at the ground. "I didn't want to interrupt."

"There was nothing to interrupt." Madelyn locked the office door. "Walk with me to the cafeteria."

Ruby's cheeks turned crimson.

She fell into step beside Madelyn as they walked down the hall before descending the stairs.

"Hello, Professor Turner." Several young men nodded to her as they passed by.

She smiled back.

Ruby remained quiet at her side.

They pushed the front doors open to the fresh air and bright sunlight of the day.

Ruby held her books tightly against her chest. So tight that her knuckles turned white.

"Is everything all right?" Madelyn asked after the silence had extended past the science building.

"Oh," Ruby mumbled. "Yes."

"Did you come to see me about something?" Madelyn inquired, glancing at the girl, wishing she could make this all easier for her somehow.

"I suppose I wanted to... to discuss the next essay. I wondered if perhaps I could... well if you might help me with it."

Madelyn laughed a bit. "Of course, but what help might

you need? Your last paper had one of the highest marks in class."

Ruby smiled shyly at this. "Oh."

"I do think you should apply for the fellowship."

"Oh, no. I couldn't." Ruby shook her head.

"Why not?" Madelyn insisted.

"No, my parents wouldn't like that very much."

Madelyn stared at her curiously. "Your parents? But they sent you here to get an education, didn't they?"

Ruby did not look at her. "They sent me here to get married."

Madelyn stared at the path ahead. "All the more reason you should go for it."

Ruby was glancing at her then. A little smile playing on her lips. "You really think I have a chance?"

"More than a chance. I happen to know the dean who makes those decisions. I'll put in a good word," Madelyn assured.

And then Ruby had her arm about Madelyn, hugging her awkwardly on the sidewalk in front of the cafeteria. "Thank you," she whispered.

Madelyn patted her back gently, stiffly.

The girl pulled herself away, embarrassed.

Madelyn stood looking at Ruby, twirling her keys about in her hand. Absently.

"I should go," Ruby stammered and turned to walk away, down the path. Head bent forward, staring at her feet.

Madelyn watched her go. What an odd girl, she thought before turning to enter the stately dining hall. It smelled as it always smelled, of roasted vegetables, meatloaf, and fried potatoes.

Arthur was sitting by the window. He waved her over.

She never understood why he insisted they eat at the cafeteria.

She preferred the little counter down the road that hardly

any students frequented. A young man in a white hat named Ken would always greet her and make the egg cream she liked.

"That Sorrell girl certainly admires you," Arthur said as she sat across the table from him.

"What do you mean?" She looked down at the salad and meatloaf Arthur had gotten for her.

"The way she was looking at you. I'd say she's got one hell of a crush." Arthur winked before taking a bite of his meatloaf.

"Oh, Arthur." She rolled her eyes to the ceiling. "Ruby is shy. She probably hasn't any friends to confide in. She sees me as a confidant."

Arthur smiled. "Just because she's a woman like yourself doesn't mean she can't have feelings for you like that Mason boy over there." He nodded toward John Mason who, when Madelyn followed Arthur's gesture with her eyes, found that the boy was watching her.

"Christ." Madelyn looked back to her food. "Not everyone is vying to get me into bed, Arthur. I'm old enough to be their mothers. Probably grandmother really."

Arthur was laughing at her, delighted by the candor. "It doesn't help that you don't look a day over thirty."

"Oh, sure." Madelyn could have believed forty, but Arthur was being ridiculous.

Arthur sipped his iced tea. "By the way, the Coopers invited us to dinner Friday."

Madelyn looked up at her husband. "The Coopers?"

"Yes, darling. The new next-door neighbors. I ran into the wife on my way out this morning and she invited us over."

Madelyn's palms felt warm and moist. Her appetite lost.

Dinner with the Coopers in the house that had once belonged to Frank and Carole. Sitting across from the gorgeous young couple, radiant and glowing. At the beginning where Madelyn and Arthur were at the end.

Would she be able to meet the man's eyes when he spoke?

Would he know what she had seen and what she had done?

"What's the matter with it? I think it will be good for you. You've been moping about ever since Carole left. Why not give them a chance?"

Madelyn's mouth was dry.

She drank back her iced tea. "Of course," was all she could say.

She had a one o'clock seminar.

She immersed herself in the Renaissance art she was teaching.

She tried not to think of Friday or the Coopers or Ruby or John Mason or Ken.

When the class concluded, she went to her office and gathered her things for the day. She drove home and thought to stop at her daughter's house, but she was a coward and could not face her that day.

Instead, she stopped at the grocery store and purchased items for dinner.

When she pulled into the driveway, she saw that the car next door was in the driveway. His car. He would be inside.

She went inside her home, settling the grocery bags on the table, tossing off her hat and jacket.

She opened a beer and walked up the stairs and, without turning on the overhead light, went to the bedroom window and stood in the shadows.

She could see clearly into the room, could make out the art deco make-up table in a corner, the posters of a bed.

But the room was empty.

She changed into her house dress and went back down to the kitchen to sort out a meal.

Arthur arrived home at the perfect moment.

When he came back from changing, she had set the table and was sitting at her end with a fresh beer. She never drank two, but something about that night made her feel as if she needed it.

Arthur took his seat and surveyed the feast. "Looks delicious, darling."

"We'll see how it tastes." She winked.

They ate in relative silence, Arthur complimenting the food as he tried a bit of everything.

She did not feel hungry but ate half a plate.

Arthur drank his beer and watched her from across the table.

"What?" she questioned him.

"It's been a while, hasn't it?" The conversation from that afternoon was lingering.

She picked at the label on the beer bottle. "I'm all right."

"You seem on edge," Arthur noted. "When I joked about Ruby Sorrell earlier..."

"Oh, you and your Kinsey report. Suddenly thinking everyone's a queer. Honestly," she dismissed him.

"It wouldn't hurt for you to..."

"I'd rather not, Arthur."

He let it drop.

She began to reach for plates, to clean them up, suddenly exhausted.

"Mitch called me today," Arthur said as he drank his beer and watched her motions at the sink.

Her heart skipped a beat.

"Said Rose seemed better. She took the kids to school and picked them up and doesn't smell a bit like liquor."

Madelyn raised an eyebrow. "We'll see how long it lasts this time." She accidentally let a plate clash against another in the sink.

"You don't seem to have much faith in her."

"She doesn't seem to change." Madelyn wiped a strand of hair from her eyes.

"She's had a rough go of things," Arthur conceded.

"We've all had a rough go," Madelyn corrected.

She felt his hands about her waist. The contact warmed her, made the stress melt away for an instant. She wanted him to press himself against her, to pull their bodies tight.

But he lightly kissed her cheek and told her he was heading to his study to take advantage of his clear head.

She finished washing the dishes, cleaning off the table, the counter, putting everything back into its place.

And then she went up the stairs to her bedroom.

The light in the bedroom across the yard was on.

She did not turn on her overhead light.

She peered inside the other room and saw the man standing near the window. He was smoking a cigarette and talking to his unseen wife. With the cigarette in the corner of his lips, he began unbuttoning his shirt.

Madelyn swallowed.

She watched as the shirt fell away to reveal his smooth, naked chest, watching as his hands moved down to unbutton his pants.

She watched him smoke and slip his hand inside his boxers to remove himself.

The redhead appeared in profile, reaching for him, pulling him close, the duo toppling out of sight.

Madelyn got into her bed in the dark and touched herself.

Afterwards, she peered out across the yard and was disappointed to see that the light was off.

She forced herself to get up, to go to the bathroom to take care of her nightly routine. She could not meet her own eyes in the mirror.

She slipped into her nightgown and laid in bed.

She thought that she should write Carole.

Chapter Five

What could she write to Carole?

The man is very handsome. We're going to have dinner with them Friday.

Did you know that I could see your bedroom window from mine?

They don't have blinds, so I can see them having sex sometimes.

She stared at the blank letterhead before her.

She decided not to write to Carole until after the dinner on Friday. She would have a better impression of the Coopers then.

She let the pen in her hand drop and pulled out the textbook she had been leafing through. The early work of Picasso, a series of nudes. So different from the Renaissance hyperrealism she was examining in her classes just then.

Picasso took the human form and showed its rough edges. The hints of motion, striping everything down to the essentials.

Homme nu assis caught her attention. The dark hair, broad shoulders, his eyes downcast leading the viewer to the limp dick between his legs. It was defeated, the colors lonely, isolated.

She hadn't a clue why it arrested her more than the realistic nudes of the Renaissance. It somehow seemed more immediate, more intimate.

Her eyes returned to the space between his legs.

The phone in her office rang.

She closed the textbook and picked up the receiver. "Hello?"

"Mother," the deep voice that she hardly recognized anymore spoke steadily on the other end.

"How are you feeling, Rose?" She sat back in her chair.

"I suppose... I suppose I should apologize. For the other evening. Charlotte told me you came over."

So, Rose didn't even remember any of it.

"Yes, Mitch called."

Rose lightly huffed. "It's not like it was."

Madelyn pinched the bridge of her nose, checked her watch. Her seminar would begin soon.

"Why don't you come to dinner. I know Daddy works late Wednesdays," Rose was insisting.

Madelyn had been looking forward to an evening alone. But she knew an olive branch when it was being offered. And the children would be happy to see her. She could make it through dinner, pretend that everything was fine, and then be home. "All right," she heard herself agreeing.

"I'll see you at six." And then the line went dead.

The warm feeling from before dissipated.

She gathered together the items for her class and looked up to find Ruby hovering in the doorway. "I can help," she insisted.

Madelyn let her take the canisters and she took her notes.

"I decided to apply." Ruby looked sure of herself that day.

"That's wonderful." Madelyn applauded as they walked side-by-side down the hall. "I'd be happy to help you with it."

Ruby was smiling but not looking at Madelyn. "Thank you."

If only Rose could have been more like Ruby.

Ruby helped Madelyn set up for class and then left with an appointment for Monday afternoon to review her start on the essay for the fellowship application.

Madelyn felt a warmth return as she looked out at the students seated before her. And the day slipped by.

There would be nothing to drink at Rose's that evening. She would feign that she hadn't anything. Mitch did his drinking at bars. Madelyn had a feeling he was stepping out on Rose, but she didn't want to add insult to injury.

The table was set nicely. The children looked groomed and tidy when they greeted her with hugs.

Rose greeted her with a kiss to the cheek. The house did not smell of smoke.

Mitch was in the den in front of the television. He grumbled his greeting.

They all sat down at the table to a feast of turkey and vegetables and some jiggly Jell-O concoction. "I saw it in a magazine." Rose shrugged and laughed at it.

"Grandma, I got an A on my spelling test today," Russell announced.

"That's very good," Madelyn complimented him.

Charlotte picked at her food, staring surreptitiously at Madelyn, as if trying to tell her something. She was uneasy, Madelyn could tell.

They all were.

Rose seemed fine.

Madelyn helped her wash dishes afterward.

"I made a plate for you to take home to Daddy," she said instead of the things she needed to say.

Madelyn leaned against the counter. "Have you thought more about..."

"No, Mother." A crack in her happy homemaker façade.

"It might do you some good."

Rose pulled off her rubber gloves and reached into a cabinet for a pack of cigarettes. She lit one. "Why do you have to do this? Hmm? I was having a good day, and you have to bring it up."

"You don't get to blame this on me." Madelyn had heard it too many times. The excuses. The reasons.

Rose puffed out a stream of smoke. "I'm sorry I'm not the perfect son you wanted."

Madelyn took a deep breath and steadied herself. "Thank you for dinner, Rose. But I do think it's time I leave."

Rose grabbed her before she could turn, holding her tight. "I'm sorry, Mother. I'm sorry." And her eyes held a world of pain that pierced Madelyn.

Madelyn wrapped her up in her arms and held her tight. "I know you're stronger than this, Rose. Don't let it win."

Rose was crying against her chest. Crying like when her closest friend had told a lie about her to the rest of the class. Crying like when she'd lost her favorite toy on a family outing. Crying like when she'd scraped her knee playing outside with the neighbor kids.

But Madelyn couldn't make this better with a Band-aid.

Rose let her go and slunk away from her, lifting the cigarette to her lips.

Charlotte was standing near the front door before she could leave. There were tears in her eyes. Madelyn reached up and stroked her cheek. "I know it's hard, but you'll be okay. Trust me." And she kissed Charlotte's cheek.

Charlotte gave her a sad little smile.

Russell came tearing out of nowhere. "Are you leaving?"

"Yes, but I'll be around. All right?" She ruffled his hair, and he wrapped his arms about her.

She made it out to her car with the dinner plate for Arthur. And then she managed to back out of the driveway and head toward the main road before the tears came.

That she had created this. That she had done this to her daughter.

No.

She was not to blame.

She could not get sucked down this rabbit hole again. One of the doctors had told her she should not feel responsible. That it was Rose's own doing. Her own decisions. Her own problems.

But Madelyn couldn't help the feeling that it was she who had failed her somehow. Her own ambition, her own drive had blindsided her. She had chosen a career over staying at home with her child and that was probably the whole of it.

Rose had felt abandoned by her.

That was the very reason Rose had given when Madelyn had come home one day to find Rose, aged fourteen, drinking straight out of a bourbon bottle.

They didn't keep alcohol in the house after that.

Madelyn had dried her tears by the time she arrived home.

Arthur was already there.

The man's car was parked in the driveway of the house next door.

She looked up to the neighbor's back bedroom window before going inside. The light was on.

She unbuttoned her jacket, ridding her feet of their heels, put the plate of food on the stove for Arthur and got a bottle of beer out of the fridge.

His bedroom light had been off.

She went to his study and found him rubbing his temples and marking papers.

"It's hurting today." She leaned against the frame of the door.

Arthur looked up at her and smiled. "Only a little."

"Take the pills," she insisted. "Your daughter made you dinner. It's on the stove."

Arthur sat back in his seat. "Everything all right?"

Madelyn drank the beer and shrugged. She stared at the reproduction La Fresnaye *Homme assis* that hung on the wall behind Arthur's desk. She had chosen it for the room.

The flash of pink was unexpected, the confusion of blindness in the otherwise tidy man of the image captivated her. His face reminded her so often of Arthur after the war.

"She's fine for now, but you know how that goes."

Arthur shook his head. "Perhaps I'll try to talk to her again about that place."

Madelyn shrugged. "You can try it." She stifled a yawn. "I'm going to bed."

"It's early."

"I have a book waiting," she said.

"I do hope you'll tell me about it." Arthur smiled at her. "Sleep well."

She unfastened her skirt as she went up the stairs to her bedroom. She did not turn on the light. She went to the window with her shirt untucked and her skirt slipping to the side.

She could instantly tell that the mood was different.

The man's face was hard, angry. He was yelling, pointing his fingers with a cigarette between them in the direction of his wife, somewhere out of view from the window.

Her heart pounded in her chest, frightened.

His shirt was half un-buttoned.

Arthur never yelled.

The wife came into view, in profile. He grabbed her.

Madelyn thought that perhaps she should call the police.

But she couldn't move.

The wife was saying something, and the husband responded harshly, looking angrier than before. The wife was yelling. He put the cigarette between his lips and grabbed her by the shoulders.

Words flew between them before the wife took his cigarette and crushed it out in an ashtray and he grabbed her arm and turned her around and then their lips were crushed together in a tense kiss.

They were laughing, they were petting one another. His shirt came off.

They disappeared.

Madelyn pressed herself against the wall, drinking back the last of her beer.

Her face was hot.

It was only a matter of seconds before she was undressed and lying face down on her bed, hand between her legs rubbing furiously until she came undone.

Chapter Six

To say that she was unnerved was an understatement. Arthur was in a nice vest and bowtie. He had taken care to freshen himself up.

She could not decide between a simple black dress or a slightly more eye-catching blue.

"You always did look nice in blue." Arthur had poked his head in the room to see what was keeping her.

She chose the simple black dress.

She pressed perfume to her pulse points, half-glancing into the mirror so she could see herself slightly obscured. Her blonde hair was twisted up at the back of her head neatly. Only a few tendrils escaped about her face. She had applied a muted red to her lips, a slight blush to her cheeks.

She affixed a pearl necklace that Arthur had given her for their twentieth wedding anniversary around her neck.

It would soon be forty years and Madelyn could not fathom the number. Forty when they had only been able to share two of those years as a proper husband and wife.

She twisted the simple gold wedding band about her finger.

"We're going to be late," Arthur called up to her from the front hall.

"I'm coming," she said and put out the bathroom light.

She fastened a black capulet over her head. Arthur complimented her as he helped her into a jacket. The compliment made her feel uneasy.

She reached for the plate of cookies she'd made that afternoon and arranged neatly on a plate and then they went out the front door together. Arthur locked the door before putting his arm through hers. They walked down the walkway and onto the sidewalk that connected their home with the Coopers'. "You act as if you're going to a funeral," Arthur mused.

Madelyn clung to his arm, too afraid to admit her fear.

"They seem like nice enough kids," he assured her. "If you hate it, though, you can always give me a signal and I'll feign a headache."

"Oh, Arthur. What signal would that be?"

"If you touch your right ear," he whispered conspiratorially as they went up the walkway to the once familiar home next door.

Madelyn couldn't remember the last time she'd passed through the front door. She'd always let herself informally in the side door that led into the kitchen.

Would the new neighbors have changed everything?

Carole had always had such good taste, but it was probably aged and tired to the young couple.

Arthur put his arm about her waist and rang the bell.

There was the sound of someone approaching from within. Her heartbeat sped up.

She expected the wife to answer, but as the door opened it revealed the man.

Up close. Personal.

He was tall, much taller than she had imagined. He had

smooth, soft looking skin and piercing eyes. His hair was slicked back carefully, and he smelled of expensive aftershave. His shirt was buttoned up and he wore dress pants.

"Thank you for coming. You must be Arthur." The man held out his hand to Arthur. "I'm Pete. Pete Cooper."

Arthur took his hand. The men shook.

Madelyn did not want Pete to look at her. Madelyn wanted to be invisible.

But he did look at her.

"This is my wife. Madelyn." Arthur held her out, as if an offering.

Pete looked her over. From head to toe. "Madelyn, it's a pleasure." And he extended his hand to her. "Are these cookies for us?"

She felt lightheaded when their hands touched. It was a gentle handshake. His hands were soft and warm.

"Y-yes." Madelyn nodded, then had to mechanically make herself hold them out.

"They smell delicious." Pete smiled, winsomely. He took them from her as he held open the door. "Come in, come in. My wife's around here somewhere. Honey!" He called out as Arthur and Madelyn stepped inside the front foyer. He disappeared around the corner and into the kitchen.

Madelyn looked about. The walls were cream. The furniture had changed, arranged about the rooms in a different way than it had been before. It was a strange sensation of both knowing the space and not recognizing it at all.

This was no longer Frank and Carole's home.

She wanted to go home then, until her eyes fell upon the entranceway to the kitchen.

The wife.

Perfectly set auburn hair, wide, brilliant eyes, bright red lips, cheeks flushed and full. Her dress was green. Her eyes were locked on Madelyn.

"My, what a handsome couple you are," the wife stated without taking her eyes off Madelyn. "We're thrilled you could make it." And she moved with a dancer's grace to clasp Arthur's hand and kiss his cheek and then she was clasping Madelyn's hands, her lips close to her cheek. "You smell delicious. What are you wearing?" Her breath was warm against Madelyn's skin.

But it was she who smelled delicious. Something warm and vibrant with a hint of spice.

She kissed Madelyn's cheek and then squeezed her hands.

"Where are your manners? You haven't even introduced yourself." Pete was laughing at his wife. "Arthur, Madelyn, this is my wife. Billie."

Billie playfully shoved her husband. "That's right. I'm Billie because my mother had the audacity to name me Wilma."

Arthur laughed with her.

He was captivated by her.

She was captivating.

Madelyn tried to recall the way she looked in the bedroom upstairs in her bra, clasping at her husband. She had not seen her as clearly as she could see her now.

She swallowed roughly, nearly coughed.

Billie was smiling at her.

"But really, where are my manners? Can I get you a drink? Gin, whiskey, you name it, we probably have it." Billie ushered them into the well-lit living room. There was the minibar that Madelyn had seen being brought in. It sat perfectly in the corner as if the space had been intended just for it.

"Billie makes a mean martini." Pete collapsed into a chair in the corner.

Madelyn and Arthur sat side-by-side on a modern looking couch.

"Sounds good to me." Arthur smiled politely.

Billie was mid picking up the martini shaker when she

glanced again at Madelyn. "And what about you? Would you also like to try one of my world-famous martinis?"

Madelyn felt her voice disappear. "Yes." She forced the word to form. "Yes, thank you." It was barely a whisper.

Arthur looked at her strangely.

She felt her cheeks flush.

Pete lifted a box of cigarettes. "Care for a smoke?"

"Oh, no. No, I don't smoke," Arthur declined congenially.

Pete was looking at Madelyn again with his strong, assured gaze. As if pleading with her to smoke with him.

She had never found it appetizing, but something in the way he held the box out for her made her almost want to try it. "No. Thank you," she politely declined because she felt Arthur's curious gaze on the side of her face.

Pete shrugged and placed a cigarette between his pink lips. He pulled out a lighter and with practiced ease lit the end of his cigarette. Madelyn watched each motion, intrigued by his movement. He was like an actor in a movie.

He looked at her as he exhaled a cloud of smoke.

She startled at having been caught staring.

What was wrong with her?

"How long have you been in the neighborhood?" Pete asked.

"Oh, I'd say about twenty years. Isn't that right, Madelyn?" Arthur said, as if trying to get her to say more than 'yes' or 'no' or 'thank you'.

"Yes, that's right," Was all Madelyn could say.

"Twenty years. Well, isn't that something? We haven't lived anywhere more than a year," Billie said as she moved toward them, a martini in each hand.

She had used a generous portion of gin in each, Madelyn noticed. She would be gone after a few sips.

"Well, let me know how it is." Billie smiled, watching them as they each took their first sips.

"Delicious," Arthur said after a swallow.

Billie looked to Madelyn for a compliment. "Yes, wonderful," she said after she swallowed.

It burned down the back of her throat and she felt her eyes water. She hadn't had a real drink in ages. The second sip made her feel warm.

Pete's lips wrapped around the edge of his martini glass, and she thought of his lips crushing against Billie's.

Billie sat on the arm of Pete's chair. Pete put his arm on the small of her back. Intimate. Billie sipped her martini and then removed the lid of the cigarette box to fish for a cigarette. Pete leaned forward to light it for her.

They were talking about something, but the alcohol made it sound like there was cotton in Madelyn's ears. Arthur had asked what brought them to the area. Pete was talking about his business.

"... they keep moving me up, but every time they open a new factory I have to relocate. Billie hates it. She's always preferred the city, but I'm trying to make an honest woman out of her now."

Pete poked at Billie playfully.

Madelyn thought of how angry he had appeared those nights before. How they had yelled at one another before his body crushed against Billie's passionately.

Madelyn's thighs squeezed tightly together.

"Oh, stop it." Billie batted his hands away. "It is true, though. I never thought I'd leave the city, but I've enjoyed getting to know these quaint little towns with their quaint people. Perhaps, you could give me some pointers on what there is to do around here." She was looking at Madelyn, holding her cigarette between her red-tipped nails, thumb rubbing ever so against her pinky finger.

Madelyn wasn't sure if she'd meant quaint as an insult or a compliment.

"It's a college town. There's always something to do

around here if you look hard enough," Madelyn found herself saying.

"Hopefully I won't have to look too hard." Billie winked.

Had she winked at Madelyn?

Was Madelyn drunk?

"Shall we have dinner?" Billie stood suddenly with youthful grace.

The dining room was painted a light rose. The color led the eye to a reproduction of a Henri Matisse painting. A woman standing at the window, staring out on a pink-hued sunset.

Madelyn, in her hazy mind, realized at that moment that Matisse had painted a number of windows. Someone always looking out. As if he preferred the confinement of four walls to the world outside.

The woman's hand was raised, as if waving to someone. A lover gone, a sadness in her expression.

"It's the sunset that I love. Reminds me of the coast." Billie had caught her curious gaze.

"But the woman… " Madelyn trailed off.

"Do you think she's sad that the person's coming or going?" Billie's shoulder – though higher than Madelyn's - brushed against Madelyn's arm. "That's what I always wonder." And she smoked at a fresh cigarette and stared.

"She's trapped," Madelyn said suddenly.

Billie regarded the image a bit more closely and then shrugged. "Perhaps that's why I like it." And she smiled at Madelyn. "Are you a painter?"

Madelyn shook her head. "No. I teach art history."

"You're a teacher?" Pete had appeared at his wife's side, staring warmly at Madelyn. As if this were the most interesting thing he'd ever heard in his life.

"Yes, a professor at the college." She nodded and sipped her martini, watching as Pete's arm went about his wife's body so easily and yet his eyes were still on her.

"Maybe you could teach me a thing or two." He smiled.

Was there a hint of mischief in his eyes? She couldn't tell around the alcohol she'd consumed.

Billie made fresh martinis midway through the meal.

Madelyn watched as Billie's hand slid beneath the table, and she could only imagine where it was that it landed on Pete's person. The little intimacies of married life.

Arthur did not seem to notice. He continued to eat and compliment Billie's food and speak of his work in the philosophy department at the school. Pete called them a couple of intellectuals, but admitted he'd taken a philosophy course himself in college.

Madelyn could not look away from the couple.

And the more she looked the more she began to notice things. How Pete's face was still smooth with youth where Billie had wrinkles about her eyes and her lips.

Madelyn drank and found herself captivated by Billie's amused smile, the way her eyes focused upon whoever was speaking, how attentive she was.

Madelyn drank a bit more and found that Pete was very charming. She liked his easy laughter, the way he would look at Billie when she was speaking.

It was intimate. The way they handled one another.

A wash of loneliness overcame her.

"Are you all right?" Arthur was leaning into her, whispering in her ear.

She wasn't sure.

She'd had too much to drink and needed to relieve herself. She excused herself from the table. "Don't worry, I know where the bathroom is. Unless you moved it in the past week," she said, an attempt at a joke. She heard Pete laugh.

She hadn't a clue if she was drunk or not, but she felt for the wall to steady herself as she went down the hall. The bathroom was there on the right. It had not changed much. There was a Matisse companion hung up on the wall, a rose on a windowsill. She stared at it as she sat on the toilet. It could have been in the same home as the lonely woman at the window hanging in the dining room.

After she washed her hands, she opened the door to the darkened hallway and fell right into Pete's chest.

The aftershave was pleasant so near her nostrils.

He grabbed her elbows, laughing. "Pardon me," he said gaily.

She looked up and he down and she thought he might kiss her.

She fell backwards against the wall and then was laughing herself. "I think I'm drunk."

He smiled. "I'd say so. Billie always makes 'em too strong." He put his arm about her, and she offered no resistance as he led her into the living room where Billie and Arthur had retired. "I found her stumbling about in the hall." He laughed and released her down into a chair.

She missed the contact of his large arms about her smaller person.

Arthur was smiling at her over a coffee cup. "She never was able to hold her liquor."

"Shh." She laughed again. Suddenly everything was hilarious.

"Here, have some coffee." Billie handed her a cup. "Pete's trying to find an umbrella."

"But it's bad luck to open one inside," Madelyn exclaimed.

"It's raining, darling." Arthur laughed.

She hadn't noticed the sound of rain hitting the window.

"I found it." Pete appeared with an oversized umbrella.

"Thank you for a lovely evening." Arthur was saying.

The parting was a bit of a blur to Madelyn.

"You're awfully handsome," she'd said, staring up at Pete. And they'd all looked at her with varying shades of amusement.

Arthur clasped her arm tightly, holding her and the

umbrella up, as they walked away from the house that had once been Frank and Carole's.

Her ankles were soaked from the rain.

Arthur helped her up the stairs.

They fell on her bed together, laughing about something.

It was the first time in years that Arthur fell asleep beside her.

Chapter Seven

They had us over for dinner. The wife, Billie, makes a mean martini. I was gone after the first one - you know me. I probably made a fool of myself. The husband, Pete, is young. Very young and very handsome. Probably half my age.

She rubbed her forehead. The Aspirin hadn't quite kicked in, but she felt as if she needed to absolve her sins to someone. Had she truly told Pete that he was handsome?

She was mortified.

She was sitting in her nightgown at Arthur's desk, her hair wrecked, head pounding.

They painted the dining room pink.

She thought Carole would like that.

I'll be free Tuesday evening if you're up for a call. I miss hearing your voice.

XO, Mad

"Who are you writing, darling?" Arthur appeared in the study doorway.

"Carole," she said as she folded the letter and slipped it into an envelope. She wrote the address from memory on the front.

"How are they getting along?"

"Oh, well enough." She shrugged, pulling open a drawer to rummage for a stamp. "I think the other ladies bore her, but Frank seems content."

"I always knew it would take getting out of here for him to be happy."

"He wasn't so miserable." She affixed the stamp to the corner of the envelope.

"You didn't have to talk to him every time we went over there," Arthur pointed out.

Madelyn smiled.

"I think I prefer Pete. He's very amicable," Arthur went on, coming to sit in the chair in the corner of the room.

"Yes, he was very friendly." Madelyn agreed, warm.

Arthur was looking at her strangely. "You seemed to like them."

Madelyn frowned. "Of course, I liked them."

Arthur smiled. "He's quite striking. I could see how women would fall for him."

Madelyn flushed. What was Arthur going on about? "Well, he's a married man and I happened to like Billie a great deal."

Arthur nodded. "I could tell."

Madelyn held up the envelope and pointed at her husband. "I don't know what you're getting at, but I'm not sure I like it."

"I wasn't implying anything." Arthur held up his hands in mock defense.

"You have a twisted mind, Arthur Turner." And she got up, tightening her robe about herself and made her way to the front door. She pulled the door open and let the fresh air of the day wash over her. Her head felt clear for the first time that morning.

She walked toward the mailbox.

Just because they had a somewhat unconventional marriage did not mean that the whole world did.

"Good morning, Madelyn!"

She startled at the sound of the voice, nearly dropping the envelope in a puddle of rainwater.

She looked up to find Pete standing in his driveway. Also, in a robe. His chest bare beneath, a cigarette hanging out the side of his mouth.

She pulled her robe tighter about herself and gave a little wave. Her voice lost.

He was striding toward her.

She put the envelope in the mail and, drawn to him, walked to meet him between their driveways. "Thank you for having us last night," she thought to say.

"Oh, we certainly enjoyed it, especially getting to know you," he said, looking down at her.

She wished he wouldn't look at her so closely. She was not done up in the least. She'd slept in her make-up so that her pillow was stained with lipstick and mascara. She'd scrubbed at her face that morning and hadn't taken the time to comb out her hair. She was not fit to be seen, to be looked at.

And yet he was looking at her. "Here's your paper." He held it out for her.

"Thank you." She hadn't realized he'd picked it up for her.

"You remind me of someone," he said suddenly.

"Who?" She pushed hair from her cheek.

He shook his head. "I can't put my finger on it." He smiled boyishly.

She found herself smiling in return, pulling her robe more tightly about herself as his hung loose, his chest revealed to her. She felt much too exposed standing with him out in the open, in front of John and Louise across the street. Would they be looking out the window?

"Thanks for the paper," she said quickly and turned from

him. "Why don't you two come next Friday and I'll make dinner," she found herself saying.

"We'd love to," Pete called back.

"Then it's a date." She turned and smiled at him before making her way back up the path to the house.

What had she done?

She tossed the newspaper on the table and poured herself another cup of coffee. She took the cup up the stairs and drew herself a bath.

She felt a wave of arousal overcome her, but she steadied herself. She slipped out of her robe and nightgown and then into the water. She drank her coffee, settling the cup on the ledge before sinking down into the warm watery refuge.

The thought of Pete's chest floated about in her mind.

She wondered what Billie would have looked like that morning. Her hair all curled wildly about her face; eyes rimmed with sleep. She would still be more beautiful than Madelyn even in that state.

And yet Pete had looked at her so carefully...

She was too old to be fantasizing like this.

Had they had sex the previous evening? She'd been too far gone to peer out the window. Arthur had been beside her.

The bath water went cold. She shivered as she toweled herself dry.

She went through the motions of dressing for the day. She let the improper thoughts swirl down the drain with the bath water.

Arthur was washed up and waiting for her at the table. "We can take my car."

She sat in the passenger seat and stared over at the house next door.

Arthur drove them down the street, away from their home and the home next door.

"I wish Rose would come with us." She sighed, uselessly.

Arthur hummed.

It was a long drive. Out of the town and down a winding road. They drove through the town over and then further on.

The institution rose out of the trees. It had once been lovely, but now felt haunted, lifeless, abandoned. With vines winding all about the exterior. It reminded her so much of the college, but it gave her the creeps.

Her chest constricted as they made their way up the drive and to the parking lot.

There were very few other visitors making their way toward the building. Everyone walked in near silence, as if they all felt the same trepidation.

The nurse at the front smiled at them when they entered. "It's nice to see you both," she greeted them congenially.

"How is she?" Madelyn asked tentatively.

The nurse gave her a gentle smile. "Well, there were a couple of outbursts this week, but she seems happy today. She knows you're coming."

Madelyn smiled, relieved that it wasn't any worse than normal. Arthur took her arm, and they went down the familiar, antiseptic smelling hall. "I don't know why it has to be so dismal around here," she whispered as they walked past rooms where they heard the cries of children.

"They do the best they can," Arthur offered as they went up the stairs, the same path they took every Saturday.

The room was at the end of the hall. Painted a cheerful shade of pink.

Betsy did not look up when they entered, but the crayon in her hand stilled. As if she knew. She was wearing a bow in her hair. She looked very well.

There was a nurse standing near her. She leaned close to Betsy, letting her know that her grandparents had arrived.

Betsy did not look up.

"Hello, Betsy. It's your grandmother. Madelyn," she spoke gently but did not hug the girl. Betsy did not like hugs.

The thought depressed Madelyn.

"How are you today, sweet girl?" Arthur chimed in at her side. "It's Grandpa Arthur."

Betsy did not look at them but began to move a bit up and down, as if pleased by their presence.

"You look very beautiful today." Madelyn smiled as she sat at the foot of the bed. "What are you coloring?" She looked down to see a somewhat abstract rendition of a garden. Greens, reds, pinks, purples. "Is this outside?"

The girl made a noise of affirmation.

"It's beautiful." Madelyn stared in awe at it.

"You should see the paintings she's been working on." The nurse was smiling.

"I would like to see them." Madelyn smiled at Betsy. Proud of her abstract mind that created a plethora of beautiful images.

The nurse went away to collect the paintings as Arthur came to look at the drawing the girl had gone back to with a new fervor. As if showing off for them.

"I wish I could know what was going on in that head of hers," he said, admiring the artwork.

"I wonder if we could get her a show," Madelyn was saying seriously.

"I doubt Rose would approve... ," Arthur cautioned.

Madelyn smiled at the girl. "We could do it anonymously. She's so talented, Arthur. All the talent I wish I'd had."

Arthur laughed at her. "You sound like a stage mother."

Madelyn laughed at her foolish idea. "Perhaps."

The nurse came back with several larger canvases. "We don't usually let them have such big canvases, but we thought she might enjoy having more space to cover."

Madelyn looked at the art and was astonished by it. One was dark as night, but there was a brilliance of colors spattered about the surface. The other was as blue and clear as a stream in nature.

"Oh, Betsy. Look at what you've done," Madelyn exclaimed.

The girl was smiling and clapping but did not seem to see what she had done.

"They're beautiful. Can I take one?" Madelyn asked.

The nurse shrugged. "What do you think, Betsy? Can your grandmother have one of these?"

Betsy rocked back and forth then bounced up and down.

"We hardly have space for everything she does." The nurse was smiling.

"I can take them." Madelyn smiled. She wished she could reach out and stroke the girl's cheek. To hold her close, but instead she sat on the edge of the bed – as close as she would allow – and marveled at the girl.

And, after an hour of visiting, with the two canvases tucked beneath their arms, they made their way from the facility. And she felt deflated, exhausted, and sadder than when they had arrived.

"What will we do with these?" Arthur asked as he carefully loaded them in the trunk.

"I'm not sure. Perhaps put them up in Rose's old bedroom. Or I might take the black one for my office." She thought, glancing at them again. But how might she explain the spectacular imagery and the mastermind behind it?

They drove to the diner in the town over where they usually stopped.

They ordered coffee. Arthur ordered an egg with bacon and Madelyn ordered toast with butter.

Madelyn fiddled with a packet of sugar. "I hate it."

"You say it every time we leave. But you know it's better this way," Arthur carefully coaxed her.

She sighed. It was better.

Chapter Eight

There was an informal monthly faculty dinner that evening.

Madelyn wore her simple black suit with a dark green silk button up beneath the jacket. Her hair was twisted and neatly tucked at the back of her head. She stared at her reflection in the mirror.

It was the same woman she saw every day and yet she did not recognize herself.

She dragged a drop of perfume down the skin behind her ear.

Arthur was sitting in the living room with a book on the philosophy of Ernst Cassirer.

He looked up at her when she stepped into the room, and she could see in his eyes that she was somehow different.

She did not want him to acknowledge this difference in her.

She noticed an umbrella propped up against the wall in the main hall. "Where did that come from?"

Arthur laughed. "You certainly were smashed last night, weren't you? Don't you remember? It was raining when we walked home."

Madelyn laughed, fragments from the night before coming back to her in fragmented bits and pieces. The rain. Arthur sleeping beside her. Pete's strong arms wrapped around her. The spicy note in Billie's perfume. "I should take it back before we go." She decided, glancing through the windows on the side of the house, noticing that Pete's car was in the driveway.

"We're expected soon," Arthur was saying, but Madelyn had collected up the umbrella with the promise that it would only take a second.

She walked out the front door and down the walkway to the sidewalk.

There was an adolescent flutter of nerves that settled in her chest.

She tried to reason with herself that she was being foolish. She was simply dropping off an umbrella, it was not life or death.

She walked onto the front porch of the home next door and rang the bell, tapping the umbrella anxiously against her heel.

There was a flurry of footsteps and then the opening of the front door to reveal Billie – all done up to the nines.

Her beauty was shocking to behold again accompanied by a rush of her perfume.

Madelyn looked away.

Billie was smiling at her. "Why, you didn't have to bring that old thing back. I think Pete keeps about ten of them stored away in the closet." She was laughing. "But I'm certainly glad you stopped by. You look lovely this evening." Billie was ushering her inside, pressing air kisses to her cheeks.

A record player was playing something jazzy and upbeat.

The room was smoky with perfume and aftershave.

A chaos erupted forth from the house.

Madelyn was enthralled.

"Oh, no. I shouldn't come in. You look as if you have somewhere to go and we're expected... "

"Oh, come in for a moment. Perhaps you can help us solve Pete's little conundrum." She winked at Madelyn, pulling her inside. She took the umbrella from her but left it forgotten in the hall. She linked their arms together as they came to stand at the foot of the stairs. "Honey, come show us the shirt you like and then the one I like," she called up the stairs, patting Madelyn's arm. "He never believes me, but I know he'll listen to you if you tell him."

"Who's 'us', darling?" Pete's voice called down from the top of the stairs.

"Madelyn's here!" Billie called back.

Pete appeared with a cigarette in the corner of his mouth wearing what, Madelyn, presumed was his choice of shirt. Despite the awful color, he still looked handsome.

"Madelyn, well aren't you looking well this evening." Pete kissed her cheek. He was freshly shaven. "Well, what do you think?" He held out his arms for her to examine him.

"I'd have to see the other one to compare." She found herself playing along.

"I'll be right back." And he went scampering back up the stairs.

"It's awful, isn't it?" Billie leaned into Madelyn conspiratorially.

"Yes." Madelyn could feel the blush creeping up her cheeks.

She had missed having a female companion the past few months. Carole had always been there to talk. She had been her confidant; someone she could tell anything to. And Carole would listen, only the slight widening of her eyes would belay her shock and surprise at the things Madelyn might confide in her, but otherwise there was never a secret kept between them, nor judgment passed.

It was refreshing to have Billie coaxing her along, grasping her arm.

"Would you care for a drink?" Billie steered them toward the living room.

"Oh, no. No, no. I couldn't possibly after last night."

Billie laughed. "I'm a bit of a heavy pourer, aren't I?" She left Madelyn standing in the doorway. "Where are you two headed this evening?" Billie asked as she refreshed her cocktail.

"A faculty dinner. It will be a rather boring evening, I'm afraid," Madelyn found herself confessing.

"Perhaps a shot might do you some good." Billie poured out a thimble of whiskey and held it up.

Madelyn shook her head. "I really shouldn't... "

Billie winked. "It will make it bearable." And she returned to Madelyn's side with her drink in hand and the shot in the other.

Madelyn was being reckless.

But Billie, with her big, kind eyes, had a fair point.

Madelyn downed the shot, coughed a bit, and then looked up to find Pete standing on the stairwell in a very attractive blue shirt. He was looking at her. His expression unreadable. A small smile gracing the corner of his lips.

"It compliments your eyes better," she said over her thickened tongue without thought.

Pete's chest seemed to puff out at the compliment. He smiled in earnest. "All right then, it seems you women win this time." He took his wife's drink and sipped it, and she, in turn, took his cigarette to smoke before crushing it out in a nearby ashtray. The little habits of a marriage.

"I should... I should be going," Madelyn said, feeling as if she were intruding upon something she should not be.

The thought of walking back to her quiet home to find her quiet Arthur reading a book, awaiting her to return so that they could go to Professor Milton's home to sit quietly sipping wine and discussing worldly things seemed suddenly terribly dull.

Billie and Pete both walked her to the door and saw her off.

She felt strangely as if they were both watching her as she went down the path and back to the sidewalk. She walked deliberately. Carefully.

Arthur was waiting for her in the driveway.

They stared at one another.

"We'll be late." He opened the door for her.

She slid past him, but he caught her briefly before she could climb into the car.

"Having a little aperitif?"

She moved out of his grasp and got into the car.

He walked around the front of the car and slid into the driver's seat. "Should I be worried?"

"It was a sip, Arthur. A thank you, I suppose."

"For returning the umbrella."

"For returning the umbrella," she confirmed and leaned back against the car seat. She looked at the well illuminated home beside their dark one.

She envied Pete and Billie's night out together.

Pete had said they were going dancing in the city.

But then she thought better of it. She would not want to be pressed up against so many bodies, the room heavy with alcohol and clouded with smoke. The music would be too loud, the chatter even louder.

No, she was too old to enjoy such a night out.

The faculty dinner was more manageable. More appropriate for someone like her.

The daydream faded as they approached the Milton's home several neighborhoods over.

Jane Milton, always the perfectly buttoned up hostess and perfect professor's wife, greeted them at the door cordially, inviting them in.

She made sure to let them know that they were late. That they were the last to arrive and everyone was already in the sitting room.

Arthur seemed embarrassed by this.

Madelyn felt woozy from the whiskey she'd downed.

She ate hors d'oeuvres to try and sober herself.

"Well, well. Madelyn Turner. You look radiant this evening." Bill Braxton appeared at the hors d'oeuvre table, smiling down at her from his towering height and expansive stomach.

"Bill, it's so nice to see you." She scanned the room, looking for his wife. "Where is Lillian?"

"She couldn't make it. Our son wasn't feeling well."

"What a shame." A shame because Lillian Braxton was the only person who made things bearable for her at these functions.

While Madelyn was a respected professor at the college, these dinners remained a boy's club. The women would be holed up in one room and the men in another and rarely did the two mix.

However, Madelyn noticed the man she wished to speak with sitting in the corner. "Will you excuse me?" she begged off from Bill and made her way through the crowd, saying her hellos as she went, before sitting down beside Richard Stillwell.

"Madelyn, how are you this evening?" He looked her over, but his gaze was not the dress down it so often was amongst the other men in the room. He regarded her the way he regarded anyone else.

She had always appreciated that about him.

She never wanted to believe the rumors that circulated around him. How it was strange for him, a man nearing his fifties, to remain a bachelor. So, what if he enjoyed his solitude? Madelyn could not fault him for that.

"I wanted to talk to you about one of my students. She would be an excellent candidate for the fellowship."

"Has she submitted the application?" he asked.

"She's working on it. I'm meeting with her on Monday. Oh, you must shortlist her, though. She's terribly brilliant."

"You sound quite passionate about her."

Madelyn smiled. "She deserves it. She has a mind I haven't seen in years."

Richard smiled a little and adjusted his thick-rimmed glasses on his face. "She's lucky to have you in her corner."

Madelyn laughed modestly.

"What's her name?" he asked.

"Ruby. Ruby Sorrell."

"Ruby. I'll make sure to push her through. Don't you worry." He smiled amicably at her.

They sat side-by-side, looking out at the crowd together.

"God, these dinners are dreadful," Richard whispered under his breath.

Madelyn broke out into laughter and quickly covered her mouth with her hand when several older gentlemen glanced her way. "I couldn't agree more."

<h1>Chapter Nine</h1>

The house next door was dark when they arrived home at a quarter past nine.

A migraine had overcome Arthur at the party. Madelyn had driven them home and Arthur had gone directly to his bedroom to lay in darkness.

Madelyn made him an ice pack and took it up with his medicine.

She sat quietly on the side of his bed and helped him to swallow down the pills and then undress. She put him beneath the covers and placed the ice pack over his forehead.

She left him in the dark.

She went into her room and turned on the bedside lamp. She slipped out of her skirt and jacket and put her shirt in the dry-cleaning hamper. A late-night burst of energy overcame her at the prospect of an evening to herself.

She put on a nightgown, washed her face, and then padded back down to the kitchen to make herself a cup of tea.

She stood at the kitchen window, staring out absently, waiting for the water to boil.

The house next door was still dark. The car still absent from the driveway.

59

She thought to call Carole, but then decided she would be out with Frank somewhere. Probably with their new group of friends who bored Carole to death.

They had often sneaked out during the night together to sit on the deckchairs in the backyard, sharing a bottle of wine and talking about everything and nothing.

The kettle whistled and Madelyn quickly removed it from the heat so as not to disturb Arthur.

She poured the boiling water over a teabag, put out the lights, and carried the mug back up the stairs.

She closed the door and surveyed the room.

She thought of how Arthur had slept with her the previous evening. His body had been warm pressed against her own.

But he had been gone that morning when she awoke.

She sighed, putting on her glasses before selecting a browning magazine from a shelf in the corner of her room.

Arthur had collected *Hesser's Art Monthly* magazines in the 20s. Madelyn had taken a liking to them, finding the female form infinitely spectacular. The way Edwin Bower Hesser had captured the young starlets' bodies was both provocative and yet tasteful. They were not like the tasteless men's magazines that littered newsstands nowadays.

These were well captured images. The lighting exquisite, the women sensually photographed.

He used sheer sheets to cover and uncover the female body. To reveal a breast, the curve of a hip, the outline of a waist.

She hadn't a clue why she'd thought to return to these magazines. She wasn't even sure why she had kept them, but there was something arousing in the forms, in the promiscuous positions.

She sipped her tea and felt aroused.

She peered out the window, but the house across was still dark.

They would still be out dancing.

She turned the page and stared at the backside of a woman laying on her side.

She mindlessly traced the curve of her behind with her index finger.

She turned the page again and landed on an image that reminded her so terribly of Billie.

Billie's large, wide eyes. Her dark auburn hair. The curve of her breasts.

Yes, Billie had evoked the image into her memory.

Madelyn lay back in the bed and stared at the ceiling.

The craving to touch herself overwhelmed her, and yet she did not move.

Instead, she stared up at the ceiling, working out the form of Billie's body beneath her attractive dresses. She would have luxurious hips and ample thighs. Her waist was trim, her breasts large and giving.

She could feel the weight of Billie's arm linked through her own. The way the woman had pulled at her, inviting her in as if she had known her a thousand years.

Carole had always been so tentative with Madelyn. They would exchange a brief hug when greeting and parting. She had never clasped at Madelyn the way Billie had.

Madelyn moved her legs together.

Carole had always been rather modest. Always quite buttoned up, somewhat reserved in her sexuality.

Billie oozed with it.

Madelyn could very well see why Pete would wish to rip her apart night after night. Their bodies vibrated on the same frequency, complimenting the others' wants.

But Carole was not without her own allure. Her body had hummed with something, perhaps repressed, but there. A radiance that Madelyn envied and appreciated.

Madelyn suddenly recalled that one time they had gone

away together on a trip with Arthur and Frank. The only time that Madelyn had seen Carole naked.

Madelyn had woken up early one morning to use the bathroom only to find Carole showering behind a somewhat sheer glass pane. Her outline had been like one of Hesser's models. Her breasts pert despite having had two children, her hips curved delicately, her behind sumptuously round.

Madelyn had watched her shower before realizing what she was doing.

Guiltily, as if she'd crossed an unspeakable line, she'd closed the door quietly. Unable to breathe until she'd made it back to bed. The image burned into her mind until she'd quietly touched herself with Arthur lying asleep beside her.

It was not an absolution of guilt.

For the rest of that day, each time she looked at Carole, she could see her naked form. She thought of the pinks of her nipples, blurred through the shower pane.

She supposed it lingered long past that day, but never at the forefront of her mind as in those following twenty-four hours. She remembered how Carole had caught her staring that evening at dinner and had given her the strangest look.

Madelyn sat up and stared out the window.

The light was on next door.

She shut out her light and stood by the window. Just out of view, just in case.

Billie was laughing.

It seemed an invasion of privacy now that she knew them. Knew their names.

And yet she could not look away as Pete kissed Billie's neck, her ear.

They were drunk. She could tell.

Billie stumbled and Pete caught her.

They peeled away their clothes and Madelyn watched as Pete's mouth enveloped Billie's round, pert breast.

And for a brief second Billie seemed to look in her direction.

It was as if their eyes met and yet Billie continued to hold Pete close to her until her head rolled back and her eyes closed.

Madelyn's heart was beating wildly.

She stepped back, further away from the window, embarrassed and pink in the cheeks.

Had she been caught?

No, Billie couldn't possibly have seen her.

The couple disappeared from view.

The light went out not long after.

Madelyn sat on the edge of the bed. Warm, worried, aroused.

She sank back onto the bed, too far gone to touch herself.

The embarrassment returned. Shame.

And yet if Billie had seen her, she hadn't seemed to mind. Had kept right on going, as if she liked having an audience.

No, Madelyn was being ridiculous.

Billie had not seen her.

She turned on her bedside lamp and got up to put away the magazine so as not to wrinkle the pages. She tried to read the novel she had been working on, but the words all jumbled together.

She put out the light again and laid wide awake in bed.

And her school-aged Billie seemed to look in her direction.

It was as if their eyes met and, yet, Billie couldn't direct her gaze to her aunt but head rolled back and her eyes closed.

Madelyn's heart was beating wildly.

She stepped back further away from the window, afraid, and paid in the chest.

Billie couldn't possibly be expecting...

The couple disappeared from view.

The girl wouldn't be long after.

Madelyn sat on the edge of the bed, worried, strained.

She sank back into the bed until she could barely make herself comfortable.

Chapter Ten

Ruby sat across from her; hands tucked beneath her thighs.

She could feel Ruby's eyes watching her from beneath her lashes.

Madelyn did not raise her gaze, afraid that their eyes would meet.

She kept her head bowed as she read through the typed pages.

It was hard to focus. Ruby's gaze was so innocently intense.

She hadn't a clue what she could do to a person with that gaze.

"Perhaps I could take this home with me and go over it more thoroughly," Madelyn spoke before lifting her head.

Ruby bashfully looked at her lap. "Is it... is it that awful?"

"Awful? No, it's wonderful. I just thought if I could take my time with it, I could give you better feedback."

Ruby nodded.

Madelyn stacked the pages into a neat pile and paper-clipped them together, settling them at the edge of her desk in her "to take home" pile.

"You really think I have a shot at it?" Ruby worried her pouty pink lip.

Madelyn wondered if the girl had been kissed. She seemed so terribly pure.

And then she felt ashamed at the thought.

"Of course, I do." Madelyn tried to smile. She looked at her watch. Some excuse to leave before she began to think of more preposterous, lewd things. "I'm so sorry, but I do have a meeting."

"Oh." Ruby looked snubbed but tried to cover it with a smile. "I really appreciate your help."

Madelyn smiled. "A mind like yours would be a terrible thing to waste. We'll put it to good use."

Ruby shuffled out with her head down, as if afraid to look at Madelyn.

Such an odd girl.

Madelyn sighed.

She did not have a meeting. Nor a class for another two hours.

She grabbed up her hat and jacket and decided to walk to the drug store up the road. It was a nice day. The sun shone overhead but it was not too warm. Her heels clicked pleasantly on the pavement. She eyed the store windows as she passed by, staring idly at the displays.

The drug store was on the corner.

She went in and smiled at Ken behind the counter, who smiled back at her in turn.

"Howdy, Professor Turner." He nodded his head at her.

She sat at the counter, placing her jacket on the seat beside her.

"Would you like your usual?"

"Yes, thank you." She smiled and watched him as he put in her order with the kitchen before making her an egg cream.

There was a young couple seated on the other side of the

room. Several older gentlemen pouring over their newspapers as they picked at their food.

She enjoyed the quiet solitude of the place.

The door opened behind her.

She glanced up in the mirror above the soda fountain and felt her heart stop.

Pete.

Pete, with his hat in hand and jacket over his arm, had walked in.

He happened to glance upward, and their eyes met in the mirror.

He smiled.

He walked toward her. "Is this seat taken?" He leaned in close enough for her to smell his after shave.

She smiled and removed her jacket. "Now it is."

It sounded like bad movie dialogue.

He sat down beside her.

Ken returned with her egg cream, eyeing the man now sitting beside her curiously.

"Can I take your order?" Ken asked Pete.

"Well sure. I'll have the minced ham omelet," Pete said after eyeing the menu. "And one of whatever she's having." He was looking at her egg cream.

Ken looked Pete over again and then turned to start on his egg cream with much less enthusiasm than he had with hers.

"What brings you here?" Madelyn asked.

"The factory's down the road. I thought I'd venture into town and see what the fare was like around here."

"Well, it's nothing fancy, but it's better than the cafeteria food at the college." Madelyn raised an eyebrow conspiratorially.

Pete laughed with her. "You come here often?"

"Oh, maybe three times a week. Whenever Arthur has a class at noon." She fiddled with the paper she'd torn from her straw.

"I'm glad I ran into you then. I always hate sitting alone in places like this," he admitted.

She found she liked the easy way he had about him. How he could admit such things so readily.

"Sometimes I enjoy the solitude," Madelyn confessed. Though she did not want to admit that she had a great deal of solitude.

"Is it hard? Being a professor?" Pete asked.

"Hard? I never thought of it as being hard. I suppose tedious at times, but rather rewarding as well."

"I'll bet your students love you," Pete said, graciously accepting his egg cream. She watched him eagerly put his straw into the concoction and sip it.

"Why is that?" Madelyn dared to ask.

Pete coughed a bit and laughed again. "You're quite riveting. Your students like that."

"Riveting?" Madelyn smiled.

Pete shrugged nonchalantly. "Captivating."

"Captivating?" Madelyn was smiling wider.

Pete's cheeks flushed.

He bowed his head and toyed with the egg cream glass. "I had one of those teachers, you know, that everybody loved. She was really something."

Madelyn eyed him.

Ken sat her plate of home style chicken stew rather roughly before her before going to greet a new customer.

"Does every young man want to sleep with his teacher if she's female?" she asked, picking up her roll to butter it.

Pete sputtered at the statement. "Gee, I didn't say... "

"You didn't have to." Madelyn tore off a piece of the roll and dipped it in the stew.

Pete looked at her again. "That's who you reminded me of," he said shyly. "The other morning when I couldn't remember who you reminded me of. It was a teacher I had."

Madelyn felt her cheeks go red. She did not look at Pete.

"I hope I didn't... "

"No." Madelyn shook her head and smiled at Pete.

Pete smiled back at her. Bashfully.

She asked him about the factory. He talked to her about the odds and ends of his job, apologizing for boring her. But he was easy to listen to and she liked the way his eyebrows rose when he made a point.

He caught sight of his watch. "My, how time flies."

She looked at her own watch. She had a class in thirty minutes.

Pete pulled out his wallet and left enough to cover both their lunches and a nice tip.

"Oh, you don't have to... "

"I insist." Pete placed his hat atop his head and hung his jacket over his arm. "I'm certainly glad I ran into you here. Perhaps we can do this again soon."

Madelyn nodded. "I'd like that." She kept her tone even, hoping she had not betrayed her eager enthusiasm at the prospect.

He tipped his hat at her, thanked Ken, and then went on his way.

Madelyn sat at the counter for a moment more.

She daintily wiped at her lips with a napkin. She extracted her lipstick and mirror and delicately put her face back in order.

"Thanks for lunch, Ken," she said to the boy.

He listlessly nodded in her direction.

She wondered what had gotten into him as she collected up her jacket.

She walked back to the college. A thrill racing down her spine. Something inexplicable that made her smile, made her float her way through the following seminar with the first-year students who normally were not as pliant as the others. And yet they seemed more attentive to her that day. Drawn to her, hanging on her every word.

She arrived home and made dinner.

Pete arrived home around five-thirty. She watched him spring out from his car with a cigarette between his teeth. He was so handsome in the dimming light of day.

Arthur came home at six-thirty.

They ate at the kitchen table.

"You really outdid yourself tonight, Madelyn." Arthur smiled at her over the food.

It tasted better than anything she'd made in a long while.

Arthur went to his study.

Madelyn cleaned the kitchen before taking a beer to the living room. She pulled Ruby's paper from her satchel and sank to the ground in front of the couch. She poured over the pages with a red pen. She found herself perfecting already perfect phrases. But it would have to be exceptional. Even if Richard would pass it along at her insistence, she still wanted it to be worthy of its own merit.

She sank back against the couch, dropping the red pen on the table beside the paper once she's gone through the paper two times. She drank at her beer.

The house was calm, quiet.

She wondered what Pete and Billie would be doing just then. Would they have music blaring as they had the night before? The room shrouded in cigarette smoke, sharing a glass of bourbon with one another?

Madelyn caught sight of the clock on the wall.

It was nearly eleven.

Time was speeding up.

She shoved the paper into her satchel and put out the lights.

Arthur was still in his study. She peered in and found him lost in thought.

He opened his eyes and smiled at her.

"I'm going up to bed," she whispered.

"Good night, darling." Arthur yawned. "I'll be headed up soon."

"Sleep well." She smiled and closed the door again.

The beer made her feel drowsy and warm. She did not turn on the light when she went into her bedroom.

She peered out the window and saw that the light in the room across from her own was on.

The Coopers hadn't had sex the past few evenings, as far as she had been able to tell. So, she wondered if this night would be different.

She could see into the room and yet no one seemed to be about.

It was when she glanced into the lower floor's windows that she saw Billie standing at the kitchen sink in a rather revealing slip. She was drinking something out of a cup, holding a burning cigarette between her fingers. There was a strange look on her face, as if she were contemplating something.

A movement in the upstairs window caught her attention and she looked up to find Pete standing in the room. He was only wearing the shirt he had been wearing that day, unbuttoned. And nothing else.

She could see his dick hanging limply between his legs as he smoked.

She wondered if she had already missed their evening copulation.

Had they done it in the living room?

Madelyn watched him take off his shirt and toss it somewhere in the room. He put out his cigarette and moved toward the adjoining bathroom.

Madelyn looked down and found that Billie was on the phone with someone. She was blowing smoke from between her lips and nodding.

Madelyn turned away from the window, wondering if she should not be watching the couple next door so closely.

They were like any other couple. They fought, they got upset, they had disagreements, they had sex, they laughed, they loved one another.

All the normal things Madelyn imagined a couple to do.

They were not above the banalities of married life.

They were also not machines. Made to make love nightly. Least of all for her enjoyment.

She went into the bathroom and turned on the light. She brushed her teeth, combed her hair, lotioned her face.

She put out the lights again and pulled back the sheets of her bed.

But she did not get in.

She went to the window one last time.

The downstairs light was still on, but Billie was nowhere to be seen.

The bedroom light upstairs was off.

The phone rang sometime after seven the following evening.

Madelyn felt a little thrill race through her as she lifted the receiver in the kitchen. "Hello?"

"My goodness, it feels like ages since I've heard your voice."

Madelyn smiled and leaned against the wall. "Well, you could call more often then."

"I probably should."

"You got my note."

"I got your note in the post today. It seems you have a lot to catch me up on."

"Not *so* much."

"From the sound of it, it appears you enjoy your new neighbors more than the old ones." Carole was laughing.

Madelyn missed her laughter.

"Oh, yes. That is precisely what I said." Madelyn smiled, wishing that she could stare the woman in the face for this conversation. But Carole was so terribly far away now. "Tell me everything about you first."

"What's to tell? Frank joined a bingo group and goes out

fishing most of the day."

"What the hell are you doing?"

"Oh, you know. Lunching with the women here. Organizing events. It's all rather mindless."

"It sounds dreadful," Madelyn said before she could stop herself.

Carole was laughing again. "Oh, it's not so terrible. It gives me something to do anyway." But her voice sounded lackluster, dull. Madelyn could tell she was not happy.

Madelyn resented Frank for taking her away. So far away.

"What's this about the attractive new neighbor? I wish there was anyone under fifty around here to look at," Carole admitted and then there was the sound of a lighter on the other end of the phone that piqued Madelyn's curiosity.

"Are you smoking?" she lowered her voice.

There was a cool rush of air on the other end of the phone followed by Carole's laughter. "Oh, don't get all on your high horse."

Madelyn felt a strange twist of pain and pleasure in her chest. Imagining Carole's lips curled around a cigarette. She had never imagined it before. Carole had always been the perfectly put together wife and mother next door. She'd had it out with her son when she'd caught him smoking one afternoon, had come crying to Madelyn and they'd shared a bottle of wine over it. And now here she was. Smoking herself.

"You must really be bored out of your mind."

"Well Frank took up hobbies, so why shouldn't I?" she protested. "Besides, it's only one here and there. Frank hates it, banishes me from the house." Madelyn could tell that she was smiling at that, that she was proud of her rebellion.

Madelyn felt strangely loose and warm. "I suppose you deserve some little protest." She was not certain if she liked or was repelled by this new development.

"So... tell me about the Coopers," Carole prodded.

Madelyn flushed. Having forgotten all about the Coopers at the sound of Carole's voice.

"Well, the Coopers are... quite something." Madelyn drank her beer.

"You said he was handsome."

"He is." Madelyn's throat was tight.

"Sounds like you have a crush." Carole could always tell.

"Carole." Madelyn sighed.

"You can tell me," Carole assured her gently.

Madelyn took another sip of her beer and stared out the kitchen window, out to the backyard. She did not want to look at the house next door.

Carole knew. Had known for some time. She was the one person that Madelyn could confide in about such things. She would not judge her as others might.

"I ran into him at the drug store counter yesterday. We had lunch together." She felt excited and daring for admitting it.

"My goodness." Carole laughed pleasurably. "He's young though?"

"Oh, maybe mid-thirties at most which, mind you, makes him half my age!"

"Do you think he's interested?"

"I hardly know him." She sighed. "He's our neighbor now, for Christ's sake." Madelyn wrapped her lips around the beer bottle top.

"Yes, I suppose that might be an issue," Carole agreed. "But, Mad, how long has it been?"

Madelyn twirled the wedding band about her finger absently. She had not thought about the last time for a long while.

The last time had been sometime past her fiftieth birthday. A hotel room somewhere near the city.

She chose not to think about it because it was an impossibility for that to ever happen again.

"That's what I thought," Carole was saying on the other

end. "Well, if not him I'm sure there are plenty of other eligible men if you'd like."

"As if it were so easy," Madelyn bristled.

"I sometimes wish... " But she did not finish the sentence. "Well, it doesn't matter." Carole laughed at herself and then asked about Betsy.

They spoke for what felt like ages. Saying everything and nothing. Madelyn did not mention her new awareness of the windows that once had opened onto Carole and Frank's bedroom.

She did not mention how she drove herself wild thinking about Pete inside of her. That she had begun to think of Billie's naked body and then Carole's own body.

Instead, they spoke about mundane things that did not matter. But it did make Madelyn happy to simply speak to Carole. About her life, about her children, about the boredom she felt with Frank, about the awful women she had to contend with. And they spoke and spoke until Arthur put his head in the door and waved to say he was going off to bed and said to say hello to Carole because he seemed to know she was on the other end.

It was nearing ten in the evening when they finally, reluctantly ended the call – Frank had been on the other end, calling Carole to bed.

Madelyn felt a great sense of loneliness overcome her after they hung up with one another.

The house was silent.

She tidied up the kitchen and went up to bed.

The lights were out across the way. There would be no show that evening, and she felt guilty for expecting one.

She washed her face, brushed her teeth, went about her nightly routine, but felt somehow different.

She laid in bed and wondered about what it was that Carole had wished for before stopping herself. Was she so discontent with Frank? They had never seemed particularly happy and yet they had always been very compatible. They, like Madelyn and Arthur, hardly fought. Frank was quiet, kept mostly to himself. He did not like mindless chatter. Madelyn could understand if Carole were to wish things differently. From what she had once told her, Frank had been her one and only sexual partner.

That had once been true of herself with Arthur.

She twisted onto her side, finding herself wired from the call.

She could hardly sleep a wink. She laid, staring at the ceiling, recalling the pertness of pink nipples through the shower pane.

She slipped her hand between her legs and rocked against it until she couldn't stand to not touch herself and her thoughts shifted to Pete and his penis standing erect.

Chapter Twelve

Arthur had stopped by her office that day to let her know he was helping with a forum that evening and not to expect him for dinner.

She was relieved as she drove home. Only a slight nagging feeling remained at the thought that she could get a call from Mitch at any moment, letting her know that Rose had gone off the wagon again.

But she pushed the thought from her mind as she pulled into the driveway a little before four that afternoon.

Pete's car was not in the driveway next door, nor did she expect it to be. He would be at work, the usual business hours of a businessman.

As she got out of the car with her satchel and purse, she glanced up and saw Billie headed right in her direction.

She was wearing slacks and a tightfitting sweater, her auburn hair done up in curls about her pretty face. She did not look as she had the night before at their first meeting and yet she was almost more radiant in this casual attire. Her kitten-heeled feet skipped toward Madelyn, a hand held up in a wave.

Madelyn raised her hand to wave back.

"Madelyn! I'm so glad I saw you pull in. Have you got anything to do this evening? Pete's working late and I'm just dying to see that new Lana Turner movie. He always hates going with me to women's movies. He's such a bore sometimes." She rolled her eyes as if to stress her point. "Oh, say you'll come with me!"

Madelyn hadn't been to a movie – least of all on a school night – in ages.

Billie's big, wide, pleading eyes were beguiling. "It'll give us a chance to get to know one another better. We can just be girls together without the men. Please, say you can," she was speaking as if she and Madelyn were the same age, which made Madelyn feel strangely giddy.

"As a matter of fact, Arthur's out late tonight, too."

Billie clasped her hands together excitedly.

"What time is the movie?"

"I checked the listing. There's one at five and one at seven thirty."

"How about the one at five and we can get dinner after. Would you mind if I change?"

"Not at all."

Madelyn looked Billie over and smiled. "Would you care for a beer before we go?"

"I'd love one." Billie followed her inside.

Madelyn dropped her satchel, aware of Billie behind her as she unbuttoned her jacket. "The house may be in disarray."

"No, it's marvelous." Billie glanced about her covertly, smiling at Madelyn when she turned to hang up her jacket.

Madelyn felt strangely pleased by Billie's nearness.

She turned away, leading them into the kitchen and pulling out two beers from the icebox. "What do you get up to when Pete's out working all day?" Madelyn asked as she opened the bottles, handing one off to Billie.

They ceremoniously clinked their bottles and drank. Billie's eyes stayed on Madelyn's face. "Not too terribly much.

I've become a bored housewife, I suppose." Her eyes sparkled mischievously as she spoke, as if it were not entirely true. "I used to be like you, working. Until I met Pete. The Goddamn kid got under my skin. Do you know I was working before he'd even started college?"

Madelyn looked at her and, again, saw the signs of age that she had detected before yet were not obvious upon first viewing.

"That's right. I'm older than you'd think." She shrugged. "He likes them older." She fluffed her hair and drank back her beer and Madelyn flushed. "I didn't think it'd work, but here we are. Nearly three years married." She laughed.

Madelyn could see that they weren't bored at all. She thought to ask Billie to follow her upstairs while she changed, but then thought of the clear view to Billie's bedroom window.

Madelyn felt instantly ashamed, covering by putting her lips to the beer bottle.

"He likes you a great deal, you know," Billie said as she picked at the label on the bottle.

Madelyn smiled. "And I like him." Oh, how she did.

They looked at one another and Madelyn saw something that was not jealousy or even fear, but a sincere fondness in Billie's gaze.

She was warm all over again. "I'll just be a second..."

Billie nodded, leaning against the counter as if she owned the place.

Madelyn liked the way she was not self-conscious. She envied her.

Madelyn retreated up the stairs and went about undoing herself. Hanging up her skirt, tossing away her hose and shirt and undergarments. She put on a simple skirt and sweater. She unpinned her hair and brushed it out to pin it at the side of her head.

And then she heard a record start up downstairs and knew

that Billie had been going through their record collection. She smiled to herself as she reapplied a fresh shade of lipstick, something muted and simple.

Billie was examining their bookshelf when she came down the stairs to Duke Ellington playing "Take the A Train."

Madelyn watched Billie as she swayed to the music, reminded of what it was she looked like at night when she was in Pete's arms.

Billie seemed to sense her presence. She turned and her eyes drank Madelyn in. "You look real swell."

Madelyn tugged at her sweater. It was only an old outfit. She didn't think it was so swell. "Thank you." She found herself shy.

"I hope you don't mind that I put on some music." Billie was smiling.

"Not at all." Madelyn found herself at ease with Billie.

They let the record player go on and finished off their beers in the kitchen. Madelyn felt her tongue growing loser with the help of the alcohol. She liked Billie and the easy way she had about her.

"We should be going," Billie said as she sat the beer bottles on the drainboard. "The movie will start soon!" Sse exclaimed and then insisted that she drive them.

They walked back to her house, and she ran inside for her purse and scarf and then the garage door opened to reveal a gorgeous convertible that Madelyn did not remember seeing.

"He just bought it for me on our second anniversary," she exclaimed. "Get in!"

And Madelyn got into the gorgeous machine.

Billie lit a cigarette before starting up the engine and then they were off down the road together into the fading clear skies of dusk.

They headed downtown and Madelyn wondered if she might see any of her students. She wondered what they might think of their professor seated in a convertible with an attractive, mysterious woman at her side.

She strangely liked the idea of being seen.

Billie was a good driver. She pulled into a spot a few stores down from the movie theater. She insisted on buying their tickets to *A Life of Her Own* since Madelyn had been such a good sport about coming along with her.

They sat side-by-side in the dark movie theater. She could feel the heat of Billie's thigh. Madelyn glanced about, half expecting to recognize someone. Yet, she didn't recognize any of the faces.

One young couple sat off to the side, already necking with one another before the lights had gone down all the way. She thought she saw him slip his hand beneath the girl's skirt before the credits began to roll. She wondered if the girl enjoyed the attention or not. She did not seem to protest.

"These kids nowadays," Billie's whisper was warm against her cheek.

Madelyn flushed.

She had seen it, too.

The movie started and they moved closer to one another, Billie leaning against the arm rest, smoking cigarettes as she stared up at the silver screen. Madelyn liked the way her perfume mixed with the smoke of her cigarettes.

She liked the story that unfolded on the screen before them, as well. She liked the strength and beauty of Lana Turner's character, but somehow found she sympathized with Ray Milland's character more.

It was nearing seven by the time the movie ended.

"That Lana Turner's really something, isn't she? Poised and sexy as hell," Billie said as they stepped out of the theater.

Madelyn found that she liked how Billie talked about Lana Turner. Found that she liked it even more when Billie put her arm through her own and led her down the sidewalk. "Where shall we dine this evening?"

"There's a spot around the corner, just here." Madelyn led her to the steakhouse that she and Arthur went to once a month.

They were seated in a booth in the middle of the room. It was oddly full that Wednesday evening. They ordered high-balls and a shrimp cocktail to share.

"Would you have walked away if you'd loved the man?" Billie was asking about the movie.

Madelyn considered it. For how could she tell Billie that she was in a similar predicament to the characters they had watched on screen? That she was Steve and Arthur his para-plegic wife, Nora. No, it wasn't as awful as all of that. "I suppose it would depend. Steve really does love his wife. Even if she can't give him what he needs."

"Lord knows a man like that would find it where he could whether Lily stayed or not." Billie winked as she tapped off ash from her cigarette. "Sometimes I think men don't deserve women at all."

Madelyn looked down at her lap.

Billie was studying her silently.

She felt the other woman touch her arm lightly. "Oh, hey. I didn't mean to upset you."

Madelyn shook her head. "No, it's only… " It's only that Arthur doesn't sleep with me anymore and what am I to do?

No, she couldn't tell that to Billie. Not now. Not just yet. Perhaps not ever.

Yet, the woman was looking at her curiously.

Madelyn tried to shrug it off. "It's nothing. Nothing really. Tell me… tell me about your job, before Pete."

Billie smiled again. "I met him on the job. I was a secretary at the firm, and he came in as a junior executive." Her lip quirked upwards as if she were letting Madelyn in on some big secret. "I was off men at the time," she said it casually. Madelyn nodded as if she understood. "I didn't think they were worth my time and here he comes. Waltzing in, asking me out to dine, to dance, to drinks. And the sex... well... " Billie shook her head.

Madelyn glanced about the room, wondering if anyone else might be listening to them. But the room was crowded and loud and she didn't think anyone else had heard.

"I thought it'd just be a fling, but he went and fell in love with me." Billie tapped ash off before lifting the cigarette to her lips. Her eyes took Madelyn in as she inhaled. "Am I embarrassing you?"

Madelyn could feel herself flushing. "No."

"You're as red as the seat." Billie was laughing at her.

Madelyn shook her head. "No, I'm just not accustomed to..."

"I'm sorry," Billie apologized.

But Madelyn didn't want her to think that she was a prude. "It's not... I'm just not used to such frank conversation."

Billie toyed with her highball glass. "If I'm saying too much..."

"No, please." Madelyn looked up at her seriously. She could feel the warmth of the alcohol, knew that she was on her way to drunk. "I may be older than you, but I'm still human."

Billie's lip was curling up in the corner again.

Their food came and their conversation shifted into something tamer, as if Billie sensed Madelyn needed a reprieve.

Madelyn had to lean into Billie as they walked back to the car. Billie helped her into the seat and Madelyn could smell her perfume, her body so close to her own. And then they were driving home.

Madelyn could see Arthur's car in the drive and Pete's in the driveway next door.

"I forgot to leave a note," Madelyn exclaimed guiltily.

Billie laughed. "I'm sure he hasn't sent out a search party yet."

They stood in Billie and Pete's driveway. As if neither

wanted to part. Madelyn felt high from the alcohol, but steadier on her heels.

"Thank you. Thank you for tonight." Madelyn held out her hand and Billie clasped it.

"It was my absolute pleasure." She lifted Madelyn's hand to kiss the back of it.

They laughed at the strange pleasure that passed between them. A new familiarity.

Billie was not Carole, but she might just help replace the Carole shaped void in Madelyn's life.

"I hope we can do it again. Soon," Billie called before Madelyn tottered onto her own driveway.

"Me, too," she responded, wondering again what John and Louise across the street might think if they were to look out their windows now and see Madelyn stumbling home drunk after a night out with the new neighbor's wife.

Arthur was in his study. He looked rather amused when Madelyn poked her head in.

"I went to the movies with Billie."

"And a bar after, I presume."

"Gordon's," she amended.

"I'm not sure if the new neighbors are a good influence on you," he said playfully, but she felt an angry pull at the words.

"I'm not Rose."

"I never said you were, darling." Arthur was before her. "I'll help you up to bed."

"I can do it myself." But he had his arm around her, and it felt safe and warm.

She kissed him when he sat her on the edge of the bed.

He did not pull away from her. His lips were soft and pliant.

They hardly kissed anymore.

"I'll draw you a bath," he said and then moved away from her.

She missed his presence. But, as she peered out the

window, realized that perhaps it was not his lips that she sought.

She could blearily make out the outline of two bodies together, illuminated by the light of the room across the yard. She thought that if she could stand, she could see Pete undress Billie.

But Arthur soon returned and told her the bath was waiting.

She abandoned the window for the sobering bath waters.

Chapter Thirteen

She did not go to the drug store counter thinking that Pete would be there. She suspected that he might have found another place to take his lunch.

But when she walked inside the following afternoon, head slightly pounding from the too many drinks his wife had gotten into her the previous evening, she found him seated at the counter. As if waiting for her.

He removed his jacket from the seat beside himself and motioned for her to join him.

Ken gave her a strained smile and politely asked if she'd like her usual. She nodded and removed her gloves daintily from her fingers.

Pete was smiling at her. "I heard you gave my wife a good time last night. I certainly appreciate it. She couldn't stop going on about you and Lana Turner."

Madelyn laughed at the statement. "I didn't know I was in league with Lana Turner."

Pete laughed handsomely. He was very attractive that day. "My wife really likes you. Thinks you're really swell." He crushed out the cigarette he'd been working on.

"I think she's real swell," Madelyn said thoughtfully.

Because she found she did like Billie. She liked Billie a great deal and she was beginning to feel strangely speaking to the two of them separately like this. Since they all liked one another so terribly well.

"She's got a darn good crush on you." He laughed again as Ken placed their steaming lunches on the counter before them without glancing Madelyn's way.

Madelyn felt her cheeks go red at his offhand comment. As if it had meant nothing, and yet it was rather queer. To speak so freely of a spouse's crushes. As if it were so banal.

"I have to admit," he leaned a little closer to her, "so do I." And he sat back and winked at her.

She narrowed her gaze at him.

The smile slipped from his mouth. "Oh, I didn't mean to embarrass you."

She shook her head. "No, I just find it curious. How free you both are with your affections. Perhaps I'm too old to understand it all. Too far behind the times." She toyed with her soup. "You can't really mean it, can you? You do know I'm old enough to be your mother," she pointed out.

Pete was laughing again. "I don't believe it."

"Believe it," she insisted. And then she remembered what Billie had said about Pete's preference for older women and turned back to her food.

"Oh." Pete lightly nudged her. "I'm serious about it, but I don't mean any harm." He bowed his head a bit as he ate. His forehead wrinkled in contemplation. "I suppose Billie and I forget a bit when we move to a place like this."

"Forget what?" She broke apart the roll but found she was not hungry.

"Formalities. Decorum. The way of things." He ate a bite of his mashed potatoes. "It wasn't like that during wartime. It got all mixed up." He was lost to a distant memory.

Madelyn folded her hands beneath her chin. "You were in the war?"

He was still lost but nodded. "I graduated college and ended up drafted. War is hell on earth. A fucking nightmare if you ask me. I hope it never happens again." He held up his hand a bit. "Sorry for the language."

Madelyn waved him off. "I couldn't agree more."

Pete eyed her.

"Arthur fought, in the first war," she spoke shyly, as if revealing something she shouldn't.

"Ah." Pete wiped his mouth politely with his napkin and reached for his cigarettes. He offered one to her, but she declined. "Then you know what a war does to a person."

"Sure." Madelyn nodded. "Senseless. All of it. And for what?"

Pete shrugged. "At least we liberated the concentration camps, but I'll tell you what. Those boys on the American side should've been fighting for Germany for all I could tell. It wasn't about saving people; it was something else."

Madelyn marveled at his words. The United States of America was supposed to have been the ideal of the world, but she'd heard the talk, the lies, the little slights against the Jews, the blacks, the outsiders.

"I didn't mean to get all morose." Pete's smile had returned. "Say, won't you let me walk you back to campus? I'd like to see where it is you work."

Madelyn was startled out of her reverie.

Pete was already paying for them. He grabbed up his coat and held hers up.

She allowed him to help her into the sleeves, grabbing her gloves from the counter where she'd left them.

He took her arm when they stepped out on the sidewalk.

"Lead the way." He laughed heartily.

She wondered if it might look strange to be seen walking down the road on his arm.

She thought of the previous night when she'd been on the arm of his wife. The way she smelled... Madelyn thought that perhaps she could smell hints of Billie in the threads of Pete's jacket.

"It'll be Halloween before long," Pete was saying.

"What will you go as?" Madelyn needled him.

"Oh, well I was thinking perhaps a scarecrow. Or maybe I'll go as an esteemed college professor."

"The costume would be too simple, I think," Madelyn said straight.

Pete laughed with her.

They came apart when they walked up the road to the campus.

"That's where Arthur's office is."

"Shall we see him?"

"Oh, no. He has a class just now." Madelyn smiled. "There's the science hall. English over there. The library. I've always loved the library." She marveled at its grandiosity. She liked to watch Pete as he looked it over. "And here is where I work." They came across the art building.

Several of her students rushed by, smiling at her, glancing curiously at Pete.

She nearly took his hand, but, stopping herself, motioned for him to follow her instead.

The halls were cluttered with students. Most of whom smiled and said hello to her. She nodded to them as they passed, going up the stairs and down the hall to her office. She slid the key in the lock and pressed the door open.

She could feel the heat of Pete's body behind her.

She looked around the room and saw it as Pete would see it, taking it in as if for the first time.

Her desk was in a state of disarray. But she had not been expecting anyone.

She moved to shuffle some of the papers into some semblance of order before turning to watch Pete as he moved about her office. He inspected every little detail, his fingers running curiously over spines of books or the miniature sculpture of the goddess Nike. It was intimate being in this familiar space with this rather unfamiliar man. He smelled of his tobacco and aftershave.

She leaned against her desk and thought of what he looked like beneath his clothes.

She thought about the necessity of clothing and then also the unnecessity of clothing.

She envisioned Billie in his arms but then herself enveloped in his embrace.

He looked up at her and smiled. As if he could read her thoughts. "You've got quite a collection here."

"Yes." She half-set atop her desk.

He had come to stand before her. His dark eyes peering down at her. Mischievously.

She thought that if she were to reach out, he might lean down...

There was the sound of something falling.

They both turned toward the door.

Ruby, bright red, was leaning over to pick up the pencil that had slipped from her hand.

"Ruby... " Madelyn stood up from her desk.

"I'm sorry, Professor Turner. I... I didn't mean to interrupt."

"You didn't interrupt, sweetheart." Pete said, smiling. "In fact, I must be on my way back to the factory. I'm glad I ran into you at the counter. Perhaps tomorrow?"

"Oh, no. I can't tomorrow, but Monday."

"Yes." Pete bowed to her and placed his hat back on his head. "Billie and I are looking forward to tomorrow evening," he said before he parted.

Madelyn had nearly forgotten her promised dinner. "Yes," she choked. "Tomorrow."

Pete smiled at her, nodded to Ruby, and then left.

Ruby was looking at her strangely.

Madelyn straightened out her skirt and tried to smile at the girl. "Can I help you with something, Ruby?"

Ruby's cheeks seemed flushed. "I – I'm finished with the edits. I thought perhaps you might give it another look before I submit it next week," she said quietly, embarrassed.

She had nothing to be embarrassed for.

Madelyn went to her and took the proffered essay from the girl's slightly trembling hand.

She gazed upward at the girl, smiling ever so. "You didn't interrupt anything." She gave her a careful smile, trying to reassure her.

Ruby nodded. "I... I have another class. I must go." She thanked Madelyn again before turning to leave, and Madelyn frowned after her.

What had changed to make her demeanor sour?

It had been nothing. Nothing at all. That Pete had been there, touching her things, talking to her. So closely.

It had been nothing, but she thought that perhaps it had been something.

But she let it go and gathered her notes for the next class.

Chapter Fourteen

She had forgotten to tell Arthur. In the mess of it all.

He wasn't feeling well when she got home with a load of groceries to begin preparing the meal.

He came into the kitchen holding his head and she looked up at him and realized that she hadn't said a word about it.

"Someone's coming for dinner?" He looked over the plethora of food.

"The Coopers. I invited them... I... oh, Arthur. I forgot to mention it. And you're not feeling well. I'll call to cancel."

Arthur waved her off. "I'll take the pills and it'll be just fine."

"But it's no bother if I cancel," she protested, because she wasn't sure how the turkey would come out and if she would remember how to create an elaborate meal to match the one Billie had made. Billie had been a much better chef from what Madelyn could hazily recall.

Arthur shook his head. "No, let's go on with it. I'll have a little rest before they arrive if that's all right."

"Of course." She smiled helplessly at him as he left her to go up the stairs to his room.

She felt guilty. As if she had been neglectful of him. Ever

since the Coopers had arrived, it felt as if he were the furthest thing from her mind.

She washed her hands and tried to put it out of her head. Arthur would have told her to cancel if he really wasn't feeling up to it. And he liked the Coopers as much as she did. So, he would soldier through the evening.

She put the turkey in to roast with the potatoes and then went upstairs to take a shower and change into something less formal. She chose the blue dress. It cut downwards in the front, just ever so. And she was fond of her still smooth chest. The skin had not wrinkled and freckled like others her age.

She pressed perfume into her pulse points and then went down to the kitchen to finish up the last of the meal and prepare some bowls of snacks for the coffee table.

Arthur would make drinks for everyone. It was his specialty, so she left it to him.

And at the last moment, she reached into a back cabinet for the ashtrays she kept about for her guests who smoked. She wanted the Coopers to feel comfortable in her home.

She glanced up at the clock and realized it was nearing seven thirty. They would be over at any moment.

She went up the stairs to check on Arthur.

She was surprised to see him up and changed and combing his hair. He smiled at her.

"How are you feeling?" she asked him.

"Right as rain." He winked at her.

But she knew he did not feel well. She could see it in the downward slope of his eyes.

"Thank you," she whispered.

He moved toward her and put his arms about her waist. "You seem different." He said and she wanted to push him away.

"Oh, nothing's changed."

He kissed her on the cheek so as not to smear her freshly painted lipstick and released her. "You're radiant."

She waved him off.

They both heard the doorbell downstairs.

She went off, down the stairs, to open the front door.

Billie and Pete were standing on the other side, holding out a bottle of wine and a little cake on a platter.

"Oh, how thoughtful!" Madelyn smiled and took the platter from Pete.

They both kissed her on the cheek, just where Arthur had, as they walked in.

"Why it's a mirror image of our place, isn't it?" Pete marveled as he looked around.

"But they have a better record collection than we do." Billie winked at Madelyn.

Arthur had come down the stairs and greeted Billie and Pete warmly. "Would you care for a drink?"

Arthur fixed them highballs and Pete chose a Jackie Gleason record.

The men took up a conversation – Madelyn half listened to them speak but was pleased that Arthur seemed engaged with Pete – and Billie and Madelyn sat down beside one another on the couch.

Billie was done up that evening. It was a simple black dress, but with her hair piled up and her make-up more prominent, it seemed to transform her into a movie star. The scent of her perfume lingered in the air around her.

"I hear you saw my husband the other day," Billie said, and Madelyn's easy smile dimmed, wondering if there was an accusation behind her words. But the woman simply smiled and went on. "He goes on and on about you, you know. He likes you so well. Said he was very impressed by your office."

Madelyn smiled at the memory of him there at the school with her. Where he did not belong. "It seems to me that he rather likes teachers." Madelyn laughed.

Billie smiled. "He did always have a thing for them," she agreed. "Who wouldn't though?"

"And what do you find so appealing about them?" Madelyn sipped her highball, curious to know what all this nonsense was about teachers. They were only people, after all. They lived their own lives, performed the same functions as anyone else.

"I suppose it's the not knowing that's so attractive about it. You see the person almost daily for a week, and they're talking to you, but you don't really get any sense of what they're like outside the classroom," Billie said after some thought.

Madelyn grinned. "Shouldn't we have some privacy?"

Billie smiled and twirled a curl about her finger absently. "Have you ever been attracted to a student?" she asked conspiratorially.

Madelyn rolled her eyes but was not offended by the question. Probably because the highball was working its magic and making her feel quite loose. "Goodness no."

But it was a lie.

There had once been a very attractive graduate student. They had kissed late one night in her office and then he'd taken her home to his little one room apartment.

But that had been the extent of it. She'd ended it before it could become too messy for her, for him, for Arthur. He'd understood. He had been hurt, but he had walked away like a gentleman.

It had been a horrible lapse of judgment. She was not proud of it.

Even if she had enjoyed it a great deal.

Billie was looking at her curiously. As if she didn't believe it. As if she could see right through her. "I see," she finally said and a little smile broke out on her full lips. Lips that kissed Pete.

Goodness, Madelyn couldn't be drunk already, could she?

"Shall we have dinner?" Arthur was asking. He wanted the

evening to progress so that he could get off to bed. Even if he was enjoying Pete's company.

Pete who sat handsomely in the chair in the corner, listening intently as Arthur discussed something of interest.

"Oh, yes. It should be ready." Madelyn stood, a little unsteady on her feet.

"We'll go out to smoke before the meal."

"You're welcome to smoke here if you'd like." Madelyn pointed to the ashtrays.

"Oh, no. We wouldn't want to dirty up the place." Billie shook her head as if she wouldn't hear it.

The Coopers went out to the back porch and spoke in hushed tones to one another as a couple might as clouds of smoke swirled around their heads.

Madelyn could see them from the window in the kitchen as she plated everything. Arthur came in to help her.

"Are you feeling all right?" she asked him.

"Yes," he confirmed with a little smile.

He helped bring the things to the dining room table and Billie and Pete returned smelling of tobacco and their distinctly pleasant scents.

Pete sat across from Madelyn. He spoke to her as they ate, asking about the type of artwork she preferred. He said they were contemplating getting something for their room, and wondered if she might have an idea, or might even like to come along to the city to pick something out.

She said she would and was pleased at the idea of such an outing.

They enjoyed the meal very much and Madelyn felt relieved that she hadn't botched it.

Afterward, Arthur excused himself.

He could only make it so far with the migraines. He apologized profusely and insisted that their guests stay on in his absence.

He went up the stairs and Pete went out back for a smoke.

Billie helped Madelyn clear the table, bringing things to the kitchen with her.

"You don't have to help me clean up," Madelyn said.

But Billie insisted.

She offered her an apron so she wouldn't soil her dress and they went about washing dishes.

"Is Arthur all right?" Billie asked, rather forwardly.

"Oh." Madelyn scrubbed at a dish. "Yes. He gets migraines. He fought, you know, in the first war. There was an accident and it left him with these lingering headaches now and again." She tried to explain it as nonchalantly as possible.

"Thank God he came out of it alive!" Billie exclaimed. "I'm sure that was rough on you when he came back."

Madelyn nodded, not used to anyone caring about what it had been like for her when Arthur had come back all bandaged up and in pain. Calling out in the night, waking up after night terrors, no longer able to sleep in the same bed as her...

"Yes," she said simply.

"Would you like a hand with those dishes?" Pete appeared in the kitchen.

"As if you would know how to wash a plate." Billie rolled her eyes at Madelyn and the tension was dissolved. "Why don't you make us some coffee? Do you think you can manage that, darling?" Billie asked.

"If Madelyn points me in the right direction, I'm sure I can." He took off his jacket and rolled up his sleeves.

Madelyn tried to protest, but they insisted that they help her, that she relax.

"Besides, the cake is better with some coffee," Billie insisted.

And so, Madelyn took out the things for coffee and allowed Pete to take over. To make the coffee and Billie slipped out to smoke, leaving the two of them alone.

Madelyn wiped at the plates, watching like an anxious

mother, as Pete measured the coffee grounds into the filter and boiled the water. He was rather good at it, she realized as she watched his confident, practiced motions.

"It was a very lovely dinner. You're quite the cook," Pete said as they stood near one another.

"Oh, no. I can't say that I am. I know about two recipes that will do for nights like tonight."

"Well, it was delicious." He smiled his boyish smile at her.

She liked the way his hands looked as he poured the water over the coffee grounds. So assured and strong. She thought of his arms wrapped around Billie again, touching her firmly, confidently.

Madelyn could see Billie standing outside, smoke billowing from her lips.

She felt a strange confusion overcome her. Something she had not yet felt before.

She liked both of them.

But it was foolish, wasn't it? And Billie was a woman.

"Have you got the mugs?" Pete broke her from her thoughts.

"Y-yes. Here." And she stood up on her tiptoes, but he was beside her, his body warm and large as he grasped the mugs for her. "Oh." She stepped away from him, not sure of herself.

Pete was looking at her softly. "I'm sorry," he apologized with a smile and went about pouring the coffee into the mugs.

"I'll cut the cake," Billie announced from the doorway and Madelyn startled at the sound of her voice.

She turned away from her, as if afraid that whatever she had been thinking would show on her face, and pulled the cake from the fridge. Billie neatly split the cake into equal slivers for each of them, carefully plating them.

They carried the plates to the table in the kitchen and sat around it. It was very informal and not proper, yet none of them seemed to care.

Carole had shared meals with Madelyn at the kitchen table when Frank had been away too late.

Madelyn wondered why she had thought of Carole. She forgot that a letter had come from her. She would have so much to say when there was a moment to write back to her.

The cake was a decadent chocolate affair that was not too heavy and tasted of vanilla. It melted on her tongue, and she found that it paired perfectly with the coffee. "It's delicious," Madelyn raved. "You'll have to send me the recipe."

"I'd be happy to. It was Pete's mother's recipe, in fact." Billie winked at Pete.

"I bet you grew up well fed." Madelyn looked at him.

He patted his taut stomach. "Sure did. But I had to have my mother teach Billie here how to cook so I could keep on the weight."

Billie shoved him in the arm. "I was a fine chef before I met you, Peter Cooper."

Madelyn smiled at their playful banter. She found them charming, easy with one another.

She could see them alone in their room, going on like this, until Pete would undress Billie and kiss her...

"We should be on our way," Pete said after glancing at his watch.

"But it's..." Madelyn wanted to protest yet caught sight of the clock on the wall and realized it was well past ten.

She did not want them to leave, but Arthur would sleep better without the sound of guests, and she didn't want to keep them any longer. They would want to be alone.

"We can help with the rest of the dishes," Billie offered. As if she, too, did not yet want to leave.

"No, no. Go on," Madelyn insisted. And she walked them to the door.

They were sober as they stood in the foyer.

Billie put her arms around Madelyn.

Her lipstick had faded over the night, but she still looked

fresh and beautiful. And Madelyn liked the way she embraced her. As if they had known one another for years.

"It was a lovely evening. And I do hope Arthur feels better in the morning," Billie said and then leaned in. Madelyn thought to offer her her cheek, but Billie pressed her lips to the corner of Madelyn's mouth. "You're so lovely," she said.

"You're hogging her all to yourself." Pete was pulling at his wife so that he could embrace Madelyn gently and kiss her cheek. "Thank you for the evening."

And she found she liked his embrace but was still stunned by Billie's forward kiss.

"We'll have you and Arthur over soon. Very soon." Billie smiled.

And Madelyn watched them go, closing and locking the door behind them as she had done a thousand times before after guests left, only it felt strangely different that evening.

She was taut with some unfamiliar feeling.

She cleaned the kitchen in a state of confusion and then went up the stairs to look in at Arthur, who was thankfully sound asleep in his bed, and then went to her own bedroom.

She kept the lights off and undressed and stood at the window and stared out at the bedroom across the lawn.

The light was on.

Billie was smoking a cigarette at the window.

It startled Madelyn.

Could she see her?

But Billie turned away and said something to Pete. And then Pete was behind her, helping her out of her dress. He kissed her shoulder blade as the zipper descended.

Madelyn sank onto the bed and pressed her hand between her legs. No longer certain of what or whom she was fantasizing about but needing... needing a release.

Chapter Fifteen

Carole had nothing new to report in her letter but asked about the new neighbors, particularly Pete.

Madelyn was thinking particularly about Billie.

She had awoken, bothered by dreams of Billie.

Billie kissing her. Billie lying beside her. Billie doing any number of unspeakable things to her.

So, Madelyn stared at the blank page and could not think of what to write back to Carole.

She left the empty page on Arthur's desk and went to the kitchen to make another cup of coffee.

Arthur was at the kitchen table with the paper. He shook the pages and peered over the edge at her. "You enjoyed the Coopers last night?"

Madelyn thought of Pete reaching over her for the mugs and found that her body was still warm. "Oh, yes," she replied, pouring the coffee into her empty mug.

"I'm sorry I didn't make it to the end."

Madelyn waved him off. "I felt awful that you weren't feeling well. Is it better today?"

Arthur nodded. "All better."

"I'll shower before we leave," Madelyn announced, gathering her nightgown more tightly about herself.

Arthur nodded and went back to his paper.

She went up the stairs and closed the door to her bedroom. She settled the coffee cup on her bedside table and collapsed on the bed.

She laid there and let the thoughts dance around in her mind.

She couldn't go see Betsy feeling the way she was feeling.

It felt wrong, somehow.

So, she pressed her hand between her legs and stifled the cry of her release when it came.

She got up and went to the bathroom and turned on the shower. She let her nightgown fall to the ground at her feet before stepping beneath the steamy water. She let it pour down upon her skin, washing away the thoughts that had come over her.

Arthur was dressed and sitting in the living room when she came down later.

They got into the car and drove to the institution.

Betsy appeared happy to see them. She bounced up and down and clapped at the sound of their voices.

They sat and talked with her until she began to get restless, and then they said goodbye to her, Madelyn longing to put her arms about the girl and hold her tightly.

They went to the diner in the town over and had lunch.

They returned home and Arthur went out to tend to the lawn and Madelyn sat again at his desk, staring at the blank sheet of paper.

Pete is very kind, very handsome. But I could never cross a line with him. I like Billie so wonderfully.

She kissed me the other night.

She struck out the line and tossed the sheet of paper into the wastebasket and pulled out a fresh sheet.

She cursed at the third draft and thought to simply pick

up the phone and call Carole, because she was certain she wouldn't spew out the whole of it on the phone but glancing at the clock, she knew that she would be busy with a party. The couples in Carole's new community met up every Saturday evening.

Madelyn tossed down her pen and stood up.

Arthur was raking leaves in the backyard.

She made up a glass of water and took it to him.

"Thank you." He sipped it and surveyed the lawn. The same lawn they'd looked at for thirty years. Always perfectly manicured and taken care of by Arthur. Occasionally, Madelyn would grow flowers, but they were all dead now with the approach of Autumn.

"You look restless." Arthur was eyeing her.

"I can't think of what to write Carole." Madelyn broke off a browning leaf from the nearby tree and twirled it in her hands.

"You two never have a problem finding something to say," Arthur said.

Madelyn felt her lip quirk up. "No, no. We never do. I thought I'd run to the grocery store to pick something up for dinner. Anything you'd like?"

Arthur nodded. "Anything you'd like would be just fine."

She crushed the leaf in her hand and let the pieces scatter across the drying grass at their feet. "All right then. I'll be back soon."

She went into the house for her purse and hat. She noticed that Pete's car was absent from the driveway next door. She wondered what Pete and Billie would be up to that day. Probably out somewhere exciting in the city. Meeting with friends, doing any number of things that young people did.

She got in her car and drove down the streets mindlessly, aimlessly.

She ended up off in the country. Down a winding road that led to a lake.

The water was sapphire blue, illuminated in the fading light of day.

She stood beside her car, keys clutched in her hand, staring out at the water.

She closed her eyes and breathed.

It was the scent of nature all around her, the quiet murmur of the fishermen down by the water, the wind in the trees overhead.

And Billie's lips pressing to the corner of her mouth. As if on purpose.

The feel of Pete's body pressed against her own.

It was a painful longing agony that shot through her, driving her to open her eyes, to try and find her bearings again. She stared out at the calming water stretched out to the other shoreline and the beating of her heart slowly subsided.

A dark cloud opened up and rain began to descend from the sky. She jumped back into her car and watched the droplets hit against the glass of the windshield.

She waited, waited and watched it pour until it let up and then she started up her car and turned back toward town.

She went to the grocery store and purchased items to make the casserole Arthur liked.

Arthur was playing Debussy's *Prélude à L'Après-midi d'un faune* on the record player when she returned. He had fallen asleep in the armchair by the window. The prelude always reminded her of Monet's *Poppy Field*. Of the way the sun beat down upon the people strolling through the field, the sky bright, the poppies lush and vibrant. The movement of the piece always stirred her.

She listened as she quietly went about making dinner. The sun set out the window over the sink.

The lights did not come on in the house next door.

As she waited for the casserole to bake, she peered in at Arthur still asleep in his chair.

The music had stopped.

She tip-toed to the record player and began the prelude again.

She opened a beer and went to Arthur's office. She sat at the desk and looked down at the note she had begun to Carole.

They were over for dinner. They seem to enjoy us well enough. They stayed very late; Billie brought a wonderful cake. Arthur had a migraine and went to bed early. They helped clean up. Pete even made coffee!

I like them both so well. I don't know what it is that they see in me. I'm only a rather dull woman who lives next door.

I couldn't possibly imagine that they mean the little flirtatious things they say. No, I'm reading into it because I'm bored. I'm impossibly bored without you.

You'll call me sometime this week, won't you? Let me know how you are.

XOXO, Mad

She sealed the envelope and caught a whiff of the casserole. It would be overdone. She went to the oven and rescued it before it could burn.

The phone was ringing.

She felt a wave of panic well inside of herself.

She lifted the receiver. "Hello?"

"She's at it again," Mitch's voice was low and upset.

"I'll be over."

"No." He stopped her. "She's not here. She went to the store at noon and never came back. I haven't a clue where she is," he said sullenly.

"I see." Madelyn had an idea of where she might be. "I'll find her."

And she hung up the phone.

She looked in again at Arthur. He was still out like a light.

There was no use in disturbing him, so she went upstairs to change, covered up the casserole and put it in the oven. She left a note on the off chance he'd wake up and wonder where she'd gotten off to.

She went out the side door with her purse and keys, steeling herself for the task she would have to accomplish.

She got in the car and turned over the ignition, but it wouldn't catch.

The car wouldn't start.

She tried it again, but it sputtered and fizzled out.

"Damn," she cursed and hit the steering wheel.

And her car was blocking Arthur's so that she couldn't easily take his car.

"Damn, damn." She sighed and leaned back in the seat.

She took a deep breath and cursed her daughter.

And just as she was about to get out of the car to go wake Arthur, two headlights shone brightly in her direction.

Chapter Sixteen

"Car troubles?" Pete asked when Madelyn stepped out of her car.

Billie climbed out of their car, laughing about something. "Hey there, Madelyn!" She called, tipsy.

Her cleavage was spilling out over the top of her tight black dress.

"It's nice to see you." Madelyn's throat was dry.

Pete looked more sober than Billie. He was coming around the hedge to her driveway.

"It won't start." Madelyn sighed, rubbing her forehead.

"Let me give it a try," he said calmly.

She handed him the keys. He got behind the wheel and tried to turn the engine over a time or two before announcing that it was a problem with the ignition coil.

"Where were you headed?" he asked.

Madelyn felt her cheeks flush. "My daughter. She's in a bit of trouble and I..."

"I'll take you," Pete said.

Billie smiled at Madelyn, holding herself up on the side of their car. "He's not as far gone as I am."

Madelyn shook her head. "Oh, no. I couldn't… "

"It's all right. Come on," Pete insisted.

She saw no other way, short of making Mitch come get her, but she knew he wouldn't be very happy about that.

She gave in and followed Pete.

Billie kissed Pete, a bit enthusiastically, and then turned to Madelyn. "I hope things are all right." And she kissed her lightly on the cheek. She smelled distinctly of her tobacco and perfume and liquor. "I'm headed off to bed before I collapse. Get her home safely, Petey."

Pete held the door open for Madelyn and she felt strangely as if she were doing something she shouldn't.

He was a careful driver, and she could sense he really wasn't as far gone as Billie.

"I didn't know you had a daughter," Pete said as they sat at a stop sign.

"Go right here," Madelyn said, and then added, "Yes. I have grandchildren as well."

Pete turned right and looked at her. "That's marvelous. How old are they?"

"Well, the eldest is seventeen, Betsy. And Charlotte is fifteen, and the youngest, Russell, is ten," Madelyn distractedly explained. "Left here."

Pete turned left. "And what about your daughter? What's she like?"

Madelyn laughed deep in her throat. "I suppose you're about to find out."

"Is she… really in trouble?"

"Depends on what she's up to." Madelyn sighed. "Right here."

"You get along?"

"When she's in the right mood, sure we do. She was a very strong-willed child. Always had a mind of her own." Madelyn's hands were balled into fists in her lap. She could feel Pete watching her. "Have you and Billie ever thought about children?" she asked without thought and then regretted having asked.

Pete smiled though. "Sure, we've tried. It never worked out."

Madelyn turned to look at him.

He put a cigarette between his teeth and lit it at a stoplight.

"I'm very sorry."

He shrugged. "Quite all right."

Madelyn thought of Billie trying to get pregnant. She suddenly felt very sad for her, at the thought that she could want a child and not be able to have one.

"I think it's simpler this way. We have more freedom," he offered.

Madelyn nodded. "Yes." And she felt the old guilt that crept up now and again when she thought of her own fear at getting pregnant when she had been younger. She had wanted her life, her career, and then Rose had been born.

There had been several pregnancy scares along the way. And she had always been relieved when the test had come back negative.

He nearly drove past the turn off and she was shaken from her thoughts.

"Pull in here." She sat forward.

He brought the car to a stop in front of the grungy tavern on the edge of town.

"Are you sure this is the right place?"

"I'm sure." Madelyn nodded and moved to get out of the car.

"I don't think you should go in there alone," Pete was saying.

"I'll be all right."

"I'm going with you." Pete was out of the car and beside her as they walked to the entrance.

Madelyn felt strangely calm as they entered through the front door that squeaked on its rusty hinges.

The music coming out over a jukebox in the corner was far too loud.

Madelyn looked around the room, hoping that Rose wasn't there.

But she had noticed a car that looked like Rose's parked in the parking lot. And, when she looked a bit further, she saw a tipsy, laughing blonde woman sitting atop a barstool, and naturally a young man was leaning into her. His hand halfway up her dress.

"Do you see her?" Pete had to lean into Madelyn to be heard. His body was solid against hers. She felt relieved and frightened at his presence there with her.

"There." Madelyn pointed and then moved through the crowd.

The men jeered at her.

"Whatcha doin' in a place like this, lady?"

She ignored them and went to Rose.

Rose sensed her presence, her eyes coming to meet her mother's head-on.

However, Rose did not move away from her paramour of the evening. She continued to allow him to caress her, continued to laugh at whatever it was that he was whispering drunkenly in her ear.

"Rose." Madelyn was standing directly beside her, but her daughter wouldn't even look at her. "It's time we get you home."

The man was leaning in close to Rose, his hand traveling further and further up her thigh.

"Rose." Madelyn watched the way he touched her daughter and felt horror and something else that she should not.

"She ain't goin' nowhere, lady," the man said firmly.

"Yeah, what he said." Rose laughed.

"Rose, you must get home. Your husband is looking for you and if he finds you... "

"I don't give no shit about a husband. He can come fight me himself," the guy was saying, his hand still up her skirt, his mouth pressing against Rose's neck. She laughed at it.

"Listen up, Buddy. You've gotta let her go." Pete was standing beside the man now.

He turned and looked up at him and laughed in his face. "What're you gonna do about it?"

Pete pulled back his fist and slammed the guy in the face, forcing him backward.

"Pete!" Madelyn cried.

Rose let out a horrified cry and then was laughing. "My savior. My fucking hero."

"Pay her tab and I'll get her out of here," Pete said to Madelyn.

Madelyn opened her purse and pulled out what she hoped would cover the drinks her daughter had consumed and then followed Pete - who had her daughter, yelling and screaming, tucked beneath his arm – outside.

"Who the hell are you?!" Rose was pounding at his chest as he gently maneuvered her into the backseat of his car.

As Pete drove them, Madelyn giving him directions, they listened to Rose drunkenly rant on about how they'd ruined her night, how awful Madelyn was, how horribly mistreated she was.

And then Rose sunk down in the seat and passed out.

It was silent for a while.

Madelyn, staring straight ahead, said, "I'm sorry."

Pete shook his head. "Please, I'm happy to help."

Madelyn chuckled, darkly. "You didn't have to punch the guy."

"He was asking for it." Pete uncurled and then curled his hand around the steering wheel, and she could tell it was hurt from the force of the punch. "But you're probably right. I apologize if it was untoward."

Madelyn considered it. All the times she'd found her daughter in such a position. How she'd wanted to do the same. "No," she finally said. "Thank you."

They arrived at Mitch and Rose's home.

There was a quiet uproar in the house. Mitch angry with Rose, Rose falling down drunk, Charlotte and Russell watching from the stairwell, Mitch asking about Pete...

Finally, Madelyn got Rose washed up and in bed, put the children back to sleep, and then she and Pete took their leave.

They drove down the tired, nighttime street.

"Thank you," she said again. "You didn't have to... "

"I'm glad to have helped," he offered.

"Your hand... " She looked at it. "Does it hurt?"

"It'll be okay," he tried to assure her.

But when they pulled into Pete and Billie's driveway, she took his hand in her own and examined it beneath the street-light. It was red and angry. "We should ice it."

"Yeah?" Pete gave her a crooked smile.

"Are you hungry? I made a casserole before all this. I could get you some ice, a beer... "

"Sure. I'd like that." Pete followed her up the drive.

She noticed their bedroom window was dark in the night. Billie would be asleep.

There wasn't a light on in Arthur's room upstairs either. She could see from the front of the house. There was still a light in the kitchen, so she thought that perhaps he would be there, waiting for her.

She unlocked the back door and Pete held it open for her.

"Hello?" she called out.

But no one responded.

The dishes had been neatly cleaned and put away and the casserole had a piece taken out of the corner but was otherwise neatly covered.

Arthur was asleep upstairs.

"Should I go?" Pete hovered in the doorway.

"No, it's all right." She reheated the oven and put the casserole in.

She told Pete to sit at the table and got him a beer and filled a washcloth with ice. He held out his hand to her and she could see it better in the kitchen light. It was turning purple. She pressed the wrapped ice against the skin.

Pete was watching her.

He didn't flinch a bit.

She could hear the beat of her heart in her ears. Louder than the ticking of the clock. Faster too.

She could not look at him.

With his unharmed hand, he tentatively reached out and touched her arm. His fingers trailed down the sleeve of her dress.

"Pete," she whispered.

"It's all right," he said, taking her hand in his.

She reasoned that it was only because he felt bad for her.

That it was his way of reassuring her somehow.

She leaned down and he tilted his head back. They kissed.

His lips were large and gentle. It sent a shock through her.

She pulled away from him and went to check on the casserole in the oven.

She fixed a plate for him, because she was not hungry, and they sat across the table from one another. Pete looked at her. She looked back but could not meet his eyes. He ate the casserole.

"I have a friend who could come around and take a look at that ignition coil tomorrow. I'll call him first thing," Pete said after the silence had stretched on.

"No, I don't want to inconvenience you any further. You've done enough."

"Nonsense," Pete dismissed her.

She made up a plate of food for Billie and sent it home with Pete.

They stood in the doorway. She thanked him again for his help and then they kissed. More passionately than before, but careful of the plate of food between them, and then he took his leave.

She went upstairs feeling dizzy. She couldn't bring herself to touch the arousal that had pooled between her legs.

Chapter Seventeen

Pete stood in the driveway with Arthur.

Billie was in the kitchen helping Madelyn with the coffee.

"... I can't believe he actually did it. I would've liked to have seen it. Are you listening to a word I'm saying?" Billie bumped against Madelyn's hip, knocking her line of vision out to Pete.

"Hmm?"

"You're a million miles away today." Billie was looking at her and her eyes were so beautiful.

And Madelyn had kissed her husband.

"Do you want to talk about it?" Billie's smile slipped, concern clouding her brow.

She did not want to talk to Billie about kissing Pete. And how his mouth had felt moving against her own and how she'd wanted him to stay, to climb the stairs with her and sleep with her the way he slept with Billie in the room across the yard.

She began to wonder if she'd dreamt it all, if the kiss had even happened.

"Your daughter..."

"Oh." Madelyn looked away, turned back to pouring the black liquid into four cups. "Yes."

"Is she always like that?" Billie poured a bit of sugar into one of the mugs.

"No," Madelyn answered absently and then shook her head. "I suppose it depends. But rather often than not, yes."

Billie sipped her coffee and rested her lower back against the countertop. "It's hard on you."

Madelyn felt as if she might cry and then felt foolish. She rubbed her cheek on her sleeve and smiled at Billie. "Yes, I suppose."

Billie gave her an encouraging smile. "I hope it was all right; what Pete did."

Madelyn laughed dryly. "More than all right."

"I'm awfully sorry," Billie was saying, looking at Madelyn.

Madelyn did not want Billie to feel sorry for her. She felt sorry for having kissed Pete.

Pete had hardly looked at her that morning, he'd smiled at her when they'd come over to see about helping with the car, as if they hadn't kissed the night before.

And it was making Madelyn wonder if he regretted it.

A car pulled up in front of the house and another man got out. He looked young, around Pete's age. They shook hands. He was holding some sort of car part. Arthur spoke to them.

"That's Harry." Billie was standing at Madelyn's side; both of them stared out the window. "Isn't he handsome?"

Madelyn did not find Harry handsome. She marveled at Billie.

"What? I'm married, not dead." Billie winked. "Shall we take them coffee?"

Madelyn held two cups and Billie followed with a third.

Pete looked up when they walked outside.

His eyes met Madelyn's, turning upward in a smile.

She smiled back.

Perhaps he didn't regret it after all.

Billie took the coffee to Harry, kissing him on the cheek. The two chatting as if they were the dearest of friends.

Madelyn handed a mug to Arthur and then the other to Pete.

"My wife's a terrible flirt," Pete said, as if just to her.

She smiled as they both watched Billie laugh and lightly touch Harry's arm.

The men worked on the car and Madelyn and Billie sat on the back porch, overlooking the backyard. Madelyn watched Billie blow smoke into the clear sky above, eyes shielded behind large sunglasses.

She was sitting in the chair that Carole used to curl up atop in the late evenings.

If Carole was there now, would she be smoking a cigarette as Billie was?

Suddenly, Madelyn wanted to speak to Carole. As if Carole might untangle the mess she'd gotten herself into.

Madelyn wanted to turn to Billie and tell her that her husband had kissed her, but when she looked at the woman – sitting with her legs crossed so casually, smoke curling from between her contented red lips – she couldn't bring herself to say a word.

They spoke about everything but what Madelyn was thinking.

Madelyn told Billie that yes, Rose was their only daughter. She spoke of her grandchildren and felt terribly old.

"My sister in Kansas has three children. I couldn't imagine it, myself," Billie conceded.

Madelyn watched her put out her cigarette. "Do you want children?" She remembered the candid conversation she'd had with Pete in the car the previous night. She was curious about Billie's side of the story.

Billie shook her dark head of hair. "Perhaps it's bad of me to say, but no. I don't really want children." And she shrugged, sipping her cooling coffee. "I suppose for a time, when I was younger, I thought I would end up with a whole hoard of them, but when Pete and I finally decided to try," she shrugged, "it just didn't work." She turned and smiled at Madelyn. "I think it's better this way. We can do what we want, you know? Be who we want to be."

Madelyn nodded. "I can understand that." She leaned back in the chair, peering at the sky above. "I never would have thought I would still be taking care of her after all these years." She shook her head.

She felt Billie's hand come to rest atop her hand.

Her eyes shifted to watch the youthful hand covering her own age weathered hand.

Billie's skin was warm and soft.

Billie's red-tipped fingers wrapped lightly over her own so that they were holding hands.

Madelyn heard the snap of a twig underfoot.

Billie shifted; her hand removed from Madelyn's.

"Harry managed to fix the coil," Arthur spoke.

Madelyn felt dizzy. "Oh," she managed to say.

Billie lit another cigarette.

Madelyn got up to look at Arthur. He was standing half on the back porch, his fingers skimming over the leaves of a nearby branch. He was looking at her.

"That's wonderful. Will it run?" she managed to ask.

Arthur nodded. "It will run. I'll take it for some more gas. You let the tank get awfully low, dear."

"Thank you," Madelyn said and then looked down to find Billie smiling up at her through her sunglasses.

Pete and Billie went home after Harry left.

Madelyn made lunch for Arthur before going to his study to grade essays from the week. He went up the stairs to nap.

However, as she sat trying to grade, she found that her mind was a million miles away.

She stared at her hand.

Lost for what felt like an eternity.

And then she lifted her hand and pressed her fingers against her lips.

The phone rang.

She dropped her red pen and a small mark bled onto the essay before her. She cursed and got up to pick up the phone in the corner of the study.

"Hello?"

"Madelyn, I just wanted to hear a familiar voice. I'm glad you picked up," Carole said.

Madelyn smiled and curled into the chair by the window. "It's nice to hear your voice." She wanted to tell her everything, but she hadn't a clue how to begin. "What is it? Is something wrong?"

"No, nothing's wrong. Frank went out this afternoon and I thought I might call you. See what you're getting yourself up to."

Madelyn laughed under her breath. "Well, I certainly wouldn't know where to begin with that."

"What happened?" Carole's voice held caring concern. Madelyn longed for her to be in the same room.

She wondered if Arthur was still awake, if he would pick up the phone and listen. And she was suddenly afraid and did not want to say the things she so desperately wanted to say.

"Rose."

"Oh dear."

"Yes. I found her at that bar... "

"The awful one outside of town?"

"Yes." Madelyn absently let her finger run along her lower lip. "My car wouldn't start. It was blocking Arthur's in, so Pete had to take me." *And then he kissed me. Or I kissed him.* But she didn't say that.

Carole's breathing changed on the other end of the line. There was a pause. "You went alone with Pete?"

"Yes." Madelyn twirled the phone cord around her finger.

"I see." Carole was asking for more.

Madelyn looked out at the doorway, straining to see if she could hear Arthur up and about in the house, but it was only the clicking of the clock.

"When we got there, a man had his hand up her skirt and Pete punched him in the face." Madelyn smiled at the memory of it.

"My God."

And then we kissed in the kitchen.

But she didn't say it.

"And... " Carole could hear the words.

"I don't know, Carole." Madelyn inhaled shakily. His wife's hand had lingered on hers only hours before, but she certainly could not tell Carole that.

"She needs a center. I've heard of them. One of the women here got sent off to one a few years ago. Her husband moved them away, but I suppose it does some good," Carole went on.

Perhaps she could write it all down to her. Perhaps she could try and untangle these feelings in a letter. It would be easier, safer to write it down than to say it.

Chapter Eighteen

The lecture hall felt as if another world entirely. A world she understood. She was assured, in control. She delighted in the feel of the student's eyes on her when she spoke. She had watched other professors speaking and had noticed that the students did not seem to pay as much attention as they did when they were in her class, listening to her. The thought made her feel powerful. Assured.

It was her domain. No one could touch her here.

She was completely in control until she walked back to her office and found Pete standing outside the door, hat in his hands.

Two separate worlds colliding.

Her heart beat faster in her ears.

He smiled at her and then offered to help with the slides and things she was carrying so that she could get her key into the lock.

"What are you doing here?" she asked as he followed her inside the office.

He closed the door behind them.

He wrapped her up in his arms and pressed their lips together.

"I couldn't stop thinking about the other night," he whispered against her hair.

And she, too, could not stop thinking about the other night.

But they couldn't carry on like this. Not here.

"Pete." She moved away from him, running a hand over her hair to smooth it out again.

"It's lunchtime, isn't it? Let me take you somewhere," he offered.

"No, I don't think... " But she wanted to go with him. She would have gone anywhere in that moment with him. "What do you want with me?" she whispered, staring down at her desk.

Pete touched the space above her right hip, and it sent a jolt through her.

She wondered if she would regret it. If she would be able to face Billie again. If she could do this and then go on and act as if she had never done it. As she had done so many times before.

But Pete was so young and his want for her was overwhelming. Surprising. Because she had not thought it possible now at her age.

And she wanted it.

"Let me get my hat," she said queasily.

He took her by the arm.

They walked past the building where Arthur was teaching.

Pete lit a cigarette at a crosswalk and then took her arm again.

He led her to his car and ushered her inside.

He drove them away from the town.

"Do you do this often?" she asked.

He looked at her briefly. "Do you?"

She looked down at her lap. "Occasionally," she admitted because there was no reason to hide it now.

"I had a feeling," he said and drove toward the city.

"You didn't answer the question," she said.

"Yes," he said finally.

She felt a terrible stab in her chest at the thought that he had done this before. She felt bad for herself and worse for Billie.

"Does Arthur know?" he asked her.

She felt her heart pound at the mention of her husband's name. At his shame around all of it, but how forgiving he was, how considerate he had always been of her. "Yes," she finally admitted.

Pete lit another cigarette.

"Can I have one of those?" She watched him put it between his lips and inhale.

He held it up. "You sure?"

She nodded.

He handed the cigarette to her, and she inhaled. Coughed. Inhaled again.

"And Billie?" she said as a cloud of smoke escaped from between her lips.

He nodded. "Sure, she does."

It did not sound convincing.

She wanted to ask if Billie did the same. If she saw who she wanted. If she had the same freedoms he had.

But they pulled up to a hotel.

"Wait here," Pete told her.

She waited in the car.

He went into a lobby and spoke with the receptionist. It seemed all very cordial and polite.

She smoked but did not inhale, yet still felt lightheaded.

She crushed out the cigarette in the car ashtray when Pete returned with a key.

She had been to this hotel before.

He drove them to a room around the corner and they went inside.

The curtains were drawn. The room was dark when the door closed.

Pete began to undo his jacket, his tie.

Madelyn stood, frozen, struggling to reconcile reality with fantasy.

She suddenly wanted to call Carole. To tell her that the young man next door was now undressing in front of her.

Pete laughed and came to Madelyn, taking her purse from her arm, undoing the buttons on her jacket. She allowed him to do so.

She unfastened her skirt and let it fall to the ground.

He worked the buttons on her silk shirt.

She undid his trousers and put her hand down between the zipper and felt his hardness through his boxers.

He kissed her intensely.

He pushed off his boxers as she removed her nylons and then her underpants, unclasping her bra, and he pulled her onto the bed, kissing her exposed skin.

His large hand cupped her breast, adept fingers rolling over a nipple, and then his hand was between her legs, touching her.

And she could feel her unbidden arousal.

She spread herself open to him and he entered her, and she moaned in appreciation, having wanted it so terribly, to feel his dick inside of her.

Working in and out of her, the same way he would do with Billie.

And she felt a rush of fresh arousal at the very thought that he did this very thing with Billie.

And then she was thinking of Billie beneath Pete's body, and she could not stop the rising sensation that was about to overtake her.

Her whole body tensed, and she felt sounds emitting forth from deep in her throat. Something primal and overwhelming.

She grasped at Pete's back, surprised by the orgasm that overcame her.

He pressed into her and then she felt the warmth of his orgasm. He slid out of her and rolled onto the bed beside her.

The liquid pooled between her legs and all she could do was lay beside him. Both of them breathing heavily.

"You're goddamn gorgeous," Pete said. "I don't know if you know it, but you're impossible not to notice. I wasn't sure you'd go for it, but Jesus." He leaned over the bed to fish his cigarettes from his jacket pocket.

She hadn't had such an overwhelming orgasm for decades. Not with another person anyway. She wasn't sure if it was him or this need she had. Or the thought that he did this very act with his wife whenever he wanted. Did he make her come as he had Madelyn?

"It's all right?" he asked, laying back on the sheets, blowing smoke from his cigarette.

She nodded. It was more than all right and also not right at all.

He passed the cigarette to her.

She inhaled this time and then passed it back to him.

She sat up and got out of the bed to go to the bathroom, closing the door so that she could have a moment away. She thought that perhaps she would begin to feel guilty, feel some sort of remorse, but she felt nothing as she sat on the toilet.

She turned on the shower and carefully washed herself.

Pete came in while she was still in the shower and got in behind her.

She was embarrassed, but he touched her gently, kissed her neck, her shoulder.

They dressed and then he took her to a nearby diner and bought her lunch before returning her to the college.

They did not kiss in parting.

"Will I see you again?" he asked and she realized he was nervous.

She took a deep breath, hand on the car door handle. "Yes. I'd like that."

He smiled.

She got out of his car and walked back toward the campus.

Chapter Nineteen

She realized that writing it down would not work. Writing it all down would be too incriminating. Anyone might see.

Her fingers hovered over the phone, tempted to take it off the hook and dial the number she had memorized.

She heard the backdoor open and close and retracted her hand away from the phone.

"Are you home?" she heard Arthur call from the kitchen.

She moved from the study and walked toward his voice.

He was standing, looking through the mail that she'd tossed on the kitchen table earlier.

"I'm here," she said, leaning against the doorway.

He didn't seem to notice her, until he looked up and then he stared at her. As if he had not seen her before. And she wondered if he knew.

He smiled at her. "You look as beautiful as the day I met you." And he came toward her and pressed his lips to her cheek. "I've got a headache. I'm going to lie down." And he left her with a small bundle of letters under his arm.

She wanted to call Carole, but instead, she went through the mail, dealt with several bills, and then began with dinner.

Occasionally, she glanced out the window to see if Pete had arrived home, but his car did not appear.

It was after they had sat down to dinner that headlights turned into the drive next door.

Madelyn's heart pounded in her ears.

Arthur looked at her. "Are you all right?"

She must have looked strange.

She tried to smile. "Of course."

But after dinner she avoided going upstairs.

Arthur sat in his study with his papers and books, and she cleaned the kitchen from top to bottom. Every nook and cranny sparkled with a renewed vigor after she'd finished with it.

Peering out the window, she noticed the lights of the house next door were still on, so she went into the living room and took down the book she had been reading and feigned reading while absently staring at the house on the opposite side of their home. And she did not go upstairs.

At one point she felt Arthur shaking her and she realized she'd fallen asleep reading.

It was dark.

She could tell it was very late.

"I'm going up to bed," Arthur was saying.

"Oh." She passed a hand over her face, pulling off her reading glasses. "Of course."

"Seems as if you should be headed there, too." Arthur sat on the edge of the coffee table.

The only light in the room came from the hallway. It filtered in hazily. She could barely make out Arthur's features in the night.

She had lost her spot in the book.

"I came by your office," Arthur spoke in the dark room.

"You did?"

"Someone said they'd seen you going out with a dashing young man," Arthur said.

She leaned forward. "Pete came by. He took me for lunch." She toyed with a cuticle on her nail.

The visceral sensation of Pete inside of her that very afternoon overcame her at the mention of his name. It was so real to her that she felt a slight moan settle in the back of her throat.

"He's showing you a good time, is he?" Arthur knew. He always knew.

"I suppose so," she murmured and wanted to go up to her bedroom.

Or to kiss Arthur, to arouse him as she had once been able to. But he would remain flaccid and unmoved by her. She had long ago learned to live with this.

Arthur leaned forward and pressed his lips to her forehead. "He has a wife... "

"I know that." She sighed.

Billie. Beautiful Billie.

"Well then." Arthur stood up. "I'll be off to bed."

Madelyn rubbed at her eyes, settling her book on the coffee table before her. "Good night, Arthur," she said and listened to him climb the stairs.

She contemplated sleeping on the couch. So that she would not see the light on or the couple just across the lawn.

But after she stretched out across its surface, she found that it was not as comfortable as she had imagined.

She stared blankly at the ceiling and the image of Pete above her returned. And she was aroused by the memory of it.

She closed her eyes and listened to the silent house around her.

Arthur would be finishing up his nightly routine and soon he would climb into his bed and be out like a light.

And the image of Pete naked and aroused swirled around in her mind until, in the still quiet of the evening, she slid her hand beneath her house dress and then beneath her underwear.

But it was not Pete who tormented her thoughts as she touched herself.

If she closed her eyes tightly enough, she could peer through the window upstairs and she could see Pete kissing Billie. It all twisted around in her mind. Pete inside of her and then inside of Billie and then she found herself imagining what it would be like to press herself into Billie and it was the wildest sensation that overcame her. It sent her falling right over the edge for the second time that day.

She covered her mouth with her hand and lay with her eyes wide open on the couch, staring blindly up at the ceiling.

She couldn't move.

A revelation.

But what did it mean?

She was not a man.

She went over it again and it made her feel strangely intoxicated thinking about what it might feel like.

She twisted on the couch, curling herself around a pillow.

Imagining her arms wrapped around Billie. As Pete would do.

It felt strangely comfortable, beautiful even.

She dozed off in this hazy daydream where she was not man nor woman but simply a being that existed with a woman in its arms.

Until her back began to hurt on the rigid surface.

She strained to see the time on the clock across the room, but it was a blur.

She got up and walked into the kitchen to wash her hands, to pour herself a glass of water, and to see that the house next door was now in darkness.

The lights were off.

She went up the stairs and went about her nightly routine and then put herself to bed and tried not to think about what she had thought about.

Chapter Twenty

The Johnson's down the road hosted a party that Friday evening.

Nancy loved to host elaborate evenings. Everything always in place, the hors d'oeuvre carefully plated, the ash trays always promptly emptied, the alcohol flowing seamlessly. Madelyn had tried to watch the way in which she accomplished all of this, but she had never been able to figure out her secret.

Madelyn was not surprised when Billie and Pete arrived, rather late.

They caused a commotion at the door, a flurry of greetings and questions put to the newest couple of the neighborhood.

Madelyn sat on the sofa by Ralph Lewis who lived the street over. He appreciated art and they would end up deep in conversation about the new artists cropping up in the bigger cities.

But Madelyn could not follow whatever it was he was saying about a new young painter in New York who was throwing paint on a canvas and calling it post-war art, because Billie was pressing her bright red lips to Nancy's cheek, but her eyes were on Madelyn.

Madelyn was warm all over.

"Are those the new neighbors?" Ralph followed her line of sight.

She realized she had not responded to something he had been saying before that.

"Yes." She drank back the scotch Arthur had brought for her earlier. The glass was empty, and the room was hazy.

A crack in the sea of people appeared and she could make out Pete clearly.

She squeezed her legs together.

"You've gotten to know them? What do you think of them?" Ralph was asking.

Madelyn wished she'd had another scotch. "Oh." She didn't know what to say.

She wished that Carole was there. She wanted to call her right away, to run from the party and not face Pete or Billie.

The throng of people thinned out, losing interest in the newness of Pete and Billie.

The women seemed to find Billie too showy and Pete very handsome. Madelyn could sense this in the room.

Billie was whispering something to Pete. An intimate exchange. He slid his hand to the small of her back.

Madelyn recrossed her legs.

They were coming toward her.

She was unsteady as she stood up to greet them. Ralph braced her arm as he stood at her side.

"Hello there." Pete was beaming down at her, pulled her close and kissed her cheek.

She flushed deeply.

"You look radiant this evening," Billie slurred, and Madelyn could tell she was already tipsy. They kissed cheeks.

"Well, hello. I'm Ralph Lewis." Ralph was extending his hand to Pete.

"Yes." Madelyn realized she'd forgotten her party companion. "Ralph lives just behind your house."

"So nice to meet you." Pete shook his hand. "I'm Pete and this is my wife, Billie."

"How do you do?" Ralph shook Billie's hand.

Billie responded absently.

She had not seen either since her encounter with Pete. To be so near to him and Billie was overwhelming.

"Shall we get these ladies a drink? I wanted to steal you away and ask about the factory," Ralph was saying to Pete.

The men walked away from them, and Billie smiled at Madelyn, happily collapsing onto the couch beside her. "I always hate these overcrowded house parties. It feels like everyone's always trying to size everybody else up," she said as she fumbled with her cigarette case.

Madelyn did not think Billie should be so kind to her.

She was not sure how they could make such intimate conversation with one another now.

Billie's thigh was warm where their legs brushed against the other's. Billie was so close to her.

She thought of putting her arm around Billie, to pull her closer, and then flushed at the ridiculous thought.

Pete and Ralph were talking near the bar. The women and drinks seemed forgotten.

Pete was laughing.

"I suppose we'll have to get our own drinks if we expect to get any this evening," Billie hummed, also looking at her husband.

And where was Arthur?

Madelyn had lost him in the crowd of people.

She wondered if he might have sneaked out and would be asleep in his bed. But she noticed him sitting in a corner, speaking with George and Edward. They always ended up in some deeply complicated social political conversation. She could tell, however, that it did something for Arthur. That his eyes lit up in a way she rarely saw.

"You're terribly quiet this evening." Billie blew a stream of smoke away from Madelyn. Her piercing eyes were upon her, staring her down.

"Sorry." Madelyn toyed with her wedding band.

"Pete said he's been enjoying your company at lunch. I must admit, I'm jealous he gets so much of your attention," Billie said it so matter-of-factly.

Could she know?

"It's only now and then." Madelyn tried to correct. For they had only met once that week and he had taken her to the hotel...

"What do you do on Saturdays?" Billie was asking.

Saturdays were Betsy's day.

"We visit our granddaughter," Madelyn said absently.

Billie looked at her over her cigarette. "Does she live far away?"

"No. A few towns over."

"Is she in school?" Billie was tapping her foot, body fully turned to Madelyn's body. No one else in the room mattered.

Madelyn shook her head. "Something like that."

"I got you another scotch." Ralph had reappeared, Pete on his heels.

Pete handed Billie a drink, their lips meeting in a brief kiss.

"My wife has a headache, so I must be off, but it's been lovely catching up," Ralph was apologizing.

"Lovely to see you," Madelyn said as they kissed cheeks in parting.

She looked over to see if Arthur had seen, but he was not looking at her. He was deep in contemplation about something George was saying.

Pete came to sit beside Billie on the small couch.

The action pushed Billie closer into Madelyn's side.

Billie put her arm on the couch behind Madelyn to balance out the shift.

"Darling, I'm not sure this couch is large enough for the three of us." Billie laughed.

Pete shrugged her off. "How are you, Madelyn?" He leaned over Billie to ask.

Madelyn smiled politely, relishing the feel of Billie's arm around her. "Oh, just fine."

Pete smiled and took his wife's cigarette to puff at the end of it. "You look more than just fine this evening."

Billie swatted his thigh and then kept her hand on the large spans of his leg.

Her arm was still around Madelyn.

"I was just telling Madelyn how unfair it is that you get to take her off to lunch and yet I have no time alone with her." Billie pouted as Pete put out her cigarette and then pulled out two from his pack.

"Well, honey, I'm certain she wants to spend some time with you, too. Don't you, Madelyn?" He smiled slyly at her as he placed both cigarettes between his lips and lit them.

A party trick.

Madelyn did not want to be in the midst of this party having such a strange conversation with a man she'd slept with and his wife who had her arm wrapped around her.

Would Billie remove her arm if she were to know what had transpired between her husband and Madelyn?

She was far too old to be caught in the middle of this.

"I would like to spend time with you, Billie," Madelyn assured her.

And the woman smiled and pulled her closer. "I was going to propose we drive into the city for that artwork together. But it seems you're otherwise occupied on Saturday."

"I'm free in the afternoon," Madelyn found herself saying.

"Can I take you with me, then? Just the two of us? I want to get you all alone so that Pete can be the jealous one."

Madelyn felt her stomach knot.

Was it some kind of a trap?

Could Billie know about what she'd done with Pete? Would want to confront her?

But there wasn't an angry look to her at all. She was smiling, looking hopefully at Madelyn.

"I would like that. I have a friend with a gallery. I'll call him first thing," Madelyn said, rearranging her dress.

Billie smiled at her. "I can't wait."

The party shifted, pulling Pete away at one moment and then Billie.

Madelyn needed the restroom.

When she stood, she found that she was quite tipsy from nervously sipping her scotch.

She used the wall to pull herself toward the hallway.

No one seemed to notice her, and she was relieved.

She opened the wrong door and stumbled across a couple making out in the dark. It was too blurry for her to see their faces, but she could tell that it was some sort of illicit kind of affair that was not between husband and wife.

They called out and she promptly shut the door behind her and went to the correct room down the hall.

The bathroom lights were far too bright, blinding her.

She had to carefully lower herself onto the toilet seat.

She closed her eyes, trying to make the room stop spinning.

She needed water. Her bed.

She would be alone with Billie the following day.

She flushed the toilet and washed her hands, only looking briefly in the mirror to smooth over her hair, to see how flushed and rosy her cheeks were.

She opened the door and ran right into Pete's chest.

Just like she had all those nights before.

He took her by the arm and led her back into the bathroom.

He cupped her cheek and kissed her, and she put her arms around him.

"We shouldn't... " She thought of the other couple she'd

walked in on. It was getting late. Everyone was hammered, but anyone might see...

"I've wanted to kiss you all night," Pete whispered.

Madelyn fell back against the wall. Pete caressed her side.

"Billie... "

"Billie adores you." Pete traced the line of her jaw.

"But... "

"Shh." Pete kissed her again. "Can we meet again? Wednesday, perhaps?"

Billie adored her.

"Please." Pete kissed her neck.

"Yes," she whispered.

They kissed again and then he went to relieve himself as she stood at the sink to make sure her make-up wasn't smeared.

He made her leave and told her he would follow after.

She left him washing his hands.

She ran into Billie in the living room.

"Have you seen Pete?" she asked over the big band music playing in the background.

"The bathroom," Madelyn said.

"Ah." Billie nodded and then smiled. "You really look nice this evening." And her eyes darted from Madelyn's eyes to her lips, as if she knew.

Madelyn needed to leave.

"It's late. I think that I should be going," Madelyn said, suddenly.

Billie smiled. "But I'll see you tomorrow?"

"Yes." Madelyn nodded.

Billie pulled her close and pressed her lips dangerously close to Madelyn's.

Madelyn made her escape and went to fetch Arthur who actually looked reluctant to leave his friends. He usually found the parties so terribly dull, but he seemed alive that evening.

They walked home in the crisp evening air.

She was more sober than she had been in the Johnson's house.

The sky was littered with stars, and she thought of kissing Pete in the bathroom and wanted to sink between her sheets and touch herself.

"You had an enjoyable time?" Arthur asked.

"Yes, and you seemed quite happy."

Arthur smiled. "It was a riveting discussion."

"I could tell." Madelyn wrapped her arms about herself.

"It seemed you were enjoying your own riveting conversation."

She felt her cheeks go red and was grateful for the night around them. "I suppose."

He let them into the side door, then kissed her on the cheek and went up the stairs to his bedroom.

She was suddenly wide awake, unwilling to go up the stairs to her bedroom. It felt lonely knowing that Pete and Billie were still at the party down the street.

She could have stayed longer, but being near them...

She went to Arthur's study and sat down on the chair in the corner.

Disregarding the time, she lifted the phone receiver and dialed the familiar number.

The phone rang in her ear. Over and over. And she began to regret the decision, and was almost about to hang up, when the phone picked up on the other end.

"Madelyn?" her voice sounded so hopeful.

"Carole." Madelyn breathed. "I'm sorry, did I wake you?"

"No. I was out on the back porch." She had been smoking. "Frank's asleep," she said. "Is everything all right?"

Madelyn took a deep breath. Was everything all right? Well certainly not. "I've done it," she whispered.

"Done... what?" Carole asked.

Madelyn took a deep breath. She wanted another drink.

"Pete," she finally said shakily.

"Oh," Carole said.

"Yes."

"And... ," Carole led.

"I like his wife," Madelyn said.

"Well, you know how men are. They step out whenever they can... "

"But they're different. There's something different about them," Madelyn whispered.

Carole sharply inhaled on the other end of the phone. "What do you mean?"

Madelyn hadn't a clue. "It feels like... she knows. Somehow, she knows."

"Does she hate you?"

"She wants to take me to the city tomorrow. She wants some artwork. In their bedroom." Madelyn rubbed her forehead.

"So, she likes you," Carole said.

Madelyn nodded and longed for Carole to be there in the room with her. To help her puzzle out all the feelings and emotions all jumbled inside of her.

Billie liked her.

Perhaps...

"I met a woman once," Madelyn realized. "She was married to a man but she... " Madelyn paused, wondering if Carole would think it odd. "Well, she occasionally slept with other women."

Madelyn felt her throat go dry, her heart pounding away in her chest.

She knew about this sort of thing. She stared at the images throughout history of naked women entangled together. Described as 'friends' in the history books. She had read Sappho. She had seen several girls in her classes get closer and closer and knew that they were doing things behind closed doors. She remembered back to her own college years, hearing about such girls.

It felt so far from her, from who she was.

"Why are you telling me this?" Carole's voice was low.

"I... ," Madelyn began to protest, but then closed her mouth.

Silence settled on the line between them. Something taut and strained.

"Perhaps she's like that, too," Madelyn suggested, the idea making sense in her mind.

"It's late," Carole said abruptly. Madelyn had shocked her.

"I'm sorry," Madelyn said.

"No, no. There's nothing to be sorry about." Carole sighed on the other end. "I suppose I'm not as progressive as you."

And something in her voice made Madelyn remember the naked outline of Carole's body in the shower. How she'd stood there watching her.

She wondered what would have happened if Carole had seen her watching. Would she have laughed it off or allowed her in?

"I should let you go," Madelyn said, suddenly nervous.

Carole laughed on the other end. "Sleep well, Madelyn. Please, call me anytime. I mean it." The awkwardness dissipated between them.

They hung up and Madelyn went up the stairs, undressed messily, and climbed into her bed and let her mind run wild.

Chapter Twenty-One

Betsy was not in a good mood when they arrived. She yelled and threw whatever was nearby.

Madelyn and Arthur were escorted from the room until they could calm her down and Madelyn thought, while sitting out on a sun patio, that the girl could sense her roaming mind. She was protesting because Madelyn was already hours ahead with Billie and not present there with Betsy.

Betsy had calmed considerably when they were allowed to return to her.

Madelyn sat with her on the bed, told her about the beautiful artwork she was teaching that week while Betsy let her brush her hair. Madelyn told her she was a beautiful girl and Betsy beamed with pride at this.

They left but did not stop at the diner in the town over.

They drove home and Madelyn made sandwiches but could hardly touch hers.

Arthur was looking at her oddly.

"You're going into the city then. With Billie?"

She nodded. "I put in a call to Philip. We're going to his gallery. I think he'll have something she likes."

She went up the stairs and freshened up.

She heard the doorbell and felt her heart leap in her chest.

She heard Billie and Arthur exchanging words in the front foyer as she descended the stairs.

Billie looked up at her and fell silent.

Billie, who looked like a movie star in a black dress and black and white plaid swing coat, lips dark red, looked dangerously attractive.

Madelyn felt underdressed in her simple slacks and button-up shirt.

"You look beautiful today," Billie commented.

"Perhaps I should change." Madelyn touched the back of her neck where her hair was pinned up.

"Please, let's go!" Billie exclaimed.

"Don't keep her out too late." Arthur laughed, kissing Madelyn on the cheek after she collected up her jacket and slipped into her shoes.

"I promise I'll take good care of her." Billie saluted Arthur as she looped her arm through Madelyn's.

She escorted her, laughing and chatting away to her waiting car. Pete's car was missing. He was away with friends just then, Billie explained.

They got in the convertible and Billie lit up a cigarette before backing out of the drive. She drove sturdily. Madelyn liked the way she sat confidently, handling the car beautifully. Madelyn admired the way her legs moved and shifted as she changed gears expertly.

When they got near the city, Madelyn gave directions down the cluttered roads and soon they were near the warehouse that Philip worked out of. Billie parked across the street. They walked together and when they got to the gate, Madelyn rang up. The door opened and they took a large service elevator up to the third floor.

Philip was waiting for them with open arms. "Hello, darling! I'm so glad you called me." He reached for Madelyn and pressed his lips to each of her cheeks. "And who is this gorgeous creature?" He looked Billie up and down.

Billie smiled, flattered.

"Billie Cooper. My new neighbor. She wants some nice artwork, and I knew you'd have just what she was looking for," Madelyn found her voice.

Philip kissed both of Billie's cheeks as he had with Madelyn. And Madelyn remembered that he was a gay man.

"How large are you thinking?" Philip asked Billie and soon the two took up an animated conversation with the other, Billie laughing away at Philip, both entertained and enamored by each other.

Madelyn looked over the canvases he had littering every surface. His colorwork was beyond comparison. The abstract images came to life in different ways whether she stood up close or walked a bit further away. As if he were painting two different things. One to be seen, the other whispered to those who dared to get close enough.

There was a long, naked body painted on a canvas in the corner. A woman. Her breasts round, a Y between her legs.

Madelyn stared at its perfect symmetry.

"You like that one?" Philip was behind her.

She flushed, startled. "It's beautiful."

"A commission. For a fellow I know. He wants it in his bathroom, can you believe it?"

She could believe it.

She turned to find Billie also admiring the painting and wanted to know what she thought of it.

"I'm happy to report that your friend has wonderful taste!" Philip exclaimed. "She chose one of my favorite pieces. I call it *The Isle Without Man*." Philip motioned for Madelyn to follow and took her to the painting.

An abstract of blues and lush greens. And the nude of bodies.

"I think it's the perfect bedroom piece, don't you?" Billie came to stand beside her.

"It's magnificent." Madelyn inspected it closer and could make out that the figures were all women.

"I can have it wrapped up and shipped to you next week." Philip was saying to Madelyn, who was lost in the painting.

It would soon hang over Pete and Billie's bed.

Billie wrote him a check. They thanked him and walked out of the studio together.

Madelyn was pleased that Billie had liked the artwork as much as she did.

But then being alone with Billie again made her nervous. As if there had been an ulterior motive to this outing. As if Billie might turn on her at any moment and say, "I know what you did with my husband."

But Billie only went on about how much she had enjoyed meeting Philip and how she loved his artwork and thanked Madelyn for sharing him with her.

"I'm starving. Would you care for a bite?" Billie asked hopefully when they got into the car.

Madelyn was too nervous to eat, but she wanted to stay a moment longer in whatever this was. "Of course. There's a marvelous little place just up the road."

They parked out front and went inside. They were seated at a little side table and the waiter brought them drinks in tiki cups, which Billie found adorable. "This is a great little spot, isn't it?" She sipped her Mai Tai. "And this is delicious."

Madelyn drank her drink and felt warm and toasty by the third sip. It was stronger than she'd remembered. But she had scarcely eaten that day.

Billie ordered wontons and pineapple chicken to share.

Madelyn's head buzzed from the drink and Billie ordered another round before she could protest.

Madelyn wondered if this was Billie's ultimate plan. To get

her drunk and then weasel out the details of her liaison with Pete.

But she didn't bring it up.

"Did you enjoy seeing your granddaughter today?"

Madelyn had forgotten all about mentioning Betsy the previous evening. "Yes. At first it was a little difficult, but once they calmed her down it was a lovely visit."

Billie was looking at her intensely. "You see her every weekend?"

"Every weekend we can." Madelyn nodded.

Billie tore off a piece of a wonton. "Is she... all right?"

Madelyn shifted in her seat. It was not something she was particularly ashamed of, but it was not something she shared casually with just anyone.

Though she supposed Billie was not just anyone.

"My daughter got pregnant rather young, married before she was even twenty." She rolled her eyes. "The baby, Betsy, was born and immediately the doctors knew something was wrong. Her features were off, and she had so many health issues. My daughter was too young to deal with it. She wanted nothing to do with her." Madelyn toyed with the edge of the napkin on her lap. "I took off from work to nurse the baby, to look after her, but she was terribly fussy. Then without Arthur or I knowing, my daughter's husband made arrangements for Betsy to be taken to a home where they could take care of children with disabilities. I hated the idea, but I suppose it has been better this way. Only Rose won't go see Betsy. She acts like she doesn't exist most days. She's drinking herself into oblivion to forget, I suppose." Madelyn went on and then looked up to find Billie enraptured in her tale. "I think she blames me."

"How could she blame you?" Billie scoffed, blowing smoke from her freshly lit cigarette.

"Well." Madelyn sipped her drink and realized it was nearly gone. "When she was very young, she got pregnant and

I... " Madelyn felt she shouldn't be sharing her daughter's personal life with this woman she barely knew.

Yet something in the easy, caring way that Billie had, made her feel as if she could unburden herself.

Billie clasped her hand in her own atop the table. "It was the right thing to do," Billie insisted.

Madelyn looked up to the ceiling, willing herself not to lose control of her emotions. "Yes. It was. It was the right thing to do."

"And anyway, you can't blame that procedure on what happened to Betsy. Believe me, I've known many women who had healthy babies after," Billie said resolutely, squeezing Madelyn's hand in her own.

Madelyn smiled.

Billie ordered another round of drinks, despite Madelyn's disapproval.

Her hand was removed from Madelyn's when the waiter appeared at their table.

Madelyn missed the contact.

Billie insisted she pay the bill as thanks to Madelyn for connecting her with Philip.

Madelyn was tipsy as they walked outside.

She leaned against Billie, inhaled the perfumed tobacco scent of her.

It was dark out. Madelyn hadn't a clue what time it was, but she suddenly did not want to return home. To Arthur and the quiet house.

She wanted to stay with Billie, like this.

They got into Billie's car. Billie put the hood up because it was getting chilly.

Billie looked at her watch. "Is Arthur expecting you home?"

"No," Madelyn said.

"There's a drive-in movie theater, just off the interstate on the way back. There's a show at 8:30 if you'd like... "

"Yes." Madelyn smiled and Billie turned the car back in the right direction.

They found a spot not too far but not too close from the screen. It had been ages since Madelyn had been to a drive-in.

Madelyn could see the cars parked near them in the dim light flickering from the screen. She looked over and saw a young couple already lip-locked and heavily petting one another before the movie had even begun.

She shivered.

"Are you cold?" Billie asked and Madelyn's heart leapt into her throat.

"No... "

"I brought a blanket. Pete makes me keep it in the car, you know just in case something happens." She got out and went to the trunk and returned with a soft plaid quilt. "Scoot over," she commanded of Madelyn, motioning for her to come closer.

They met in the middle of the front seat and Billie draped the blanket comfortably over their laps. Their legs were touching.

"Mind if I smoke?" Billie asked, fiddling with her cigarette case.

"No." Madelyn shook her head.

Billie smiled and placed a cigarette between her lips, flicking a golden lighter that burned the end of the paper. She inhaled and exhaled out the partially rolled down car window. Her arm went about Madelyn as the credits turned into the beginning of the film. A film noir. A world of black and white playing on the large screen before them and Madelyn hadn't a clue what was happening or who the actors were because Billie's arm was wrapped around her and their bodies were so close. As if they were on a date...

Just as it had been those nights before at the Johnson's.

As comfortable as if they always did this together in the dark of a drive-in. Where no one was paying them any mind and they were far enough from their neighbors to not be noticed.

Two women alone in a car, wrapped up in a blanket.

Billie's eyes were trained on the screen. She smoked carefully as she watched, red lips wrapped about the white of her cigarette.

She crushed it out in the car ashtray, her arm momentarily removed from Madelyn's person.

Billie's eyes returned to the screen when she straightened back up, her arm going back around Madelyn.

The movie went on.

Madelyn could feel her heart pounding in her chest, in her ears, reverberating everywhere in her body and she wondered if Billie could feel it as well.

"Is this all right?" Billie whispered.

At first, she wasn't sure she had been talking to her at all. Perhaps it was a voice from the film. But when she looked at Billie, she saw that the woman's eyes were on her.

She had asked her the question.

They were so close to one another. Closer than they had ever been and as alone as they had ever been in such a precarious situation.

It was the slight glint of fear in Billie's smiling eyes that enthralled Madelyn. That she could not be as confident as she appeared. It was intoxicating to see.

Madelyn's eyes fluttered to Billie's red lips.

The drinks they had shared earlier had lost their potency. She was more sober now and yet...

Their lips met, tentatively at first. Then again.

Billie tasted of beeswax and cigarettes and booze.

Her tongue darted between Madelyn's lips and Madelyn inhaled sharply.

Billie turned into Madelyn, pulling her closer in the dark car cabin.

Madelyn was young again. Her whole life a blank before her, and Billie's lips the only thing that mattered.

She had wanted to kiss her since the first time she had seen her.

It suddenly all made sense to her and yet it frightened her all the same.

She hadn't a clue how long it went on, but soon Billie sat back, a bit breathless, and smiled as she lit a cigarette. "Well, well, well." She sighed out a stream of smoke. "I thought so, but I wasn't... "

Madelyn straightened herself out.

"It's okay?" Billie noticed this shift and looked a bit frightened, uncertain.

Madelyn nodded up and down, glancing down at her lap. "I think so."

Billie smiled bashfully, happily. "That's good. That's... I'm glad. I wanted... but I wasn't sure... "

"It's all right. I... yes." Madelyn looked at Billie. She reached up and cupped her cheek, let her fingers graze over her soft skin. "I wanted it, too."

Billie smiled, kissed the pads of Madelyn's fingers.

She pulled Madelyn closer to her and they watched the end of the movie distractedly and then Billie drove them home.

Madelyn's head spun when Billie walked her to the backdoor and pressed her against the side of her house so that she could kiss her again in the dark of the night.

"I hope we can do this again," Billie whispered.

"Yes." Madelyn's chest heaved up and down. "I hope so, too."

She watched Billie walk away, and then turn to wave at the end of the driveway.

Madelyn waved back and went inside.

The house was deafeningly silent.

Chapter Twenty-Two

She twirled a loose strand of hair thoughtlessly about her finger as her eyes scanned the paper before her. She crossed off a word, scribbled a note in the margin, and then twirled her hair again.

A knock at the door caused her to leap in her chair, her heart pounding roughly in her chest.

"I didn't mean to surprise you, Madelyn." Richard Stillwell was standing in the doorway.

"Oh, no. You didn't." She capped her red pen and motioned for Richard to come in.

He took the seat against the wall. "I just wanted to tell you that your girl has been selected for the fellowship. The official list will be released next week, but I thought you should know. It was a very fine essay. I suspect you had a hand in it."

"Well," Madelyn gave him a quick smile, "it was all her. I just offered some advice." She sat forward. "I'm really happy for her. I hope she'll accept."

"What do you mean?"

Madelyn fiddled with her pen. She had not seen Ruby in days. She hoped the girl was all right. She realized just how distracted she had been. "I think it's a matter of her family. They don't think a girl needs a real education."

Richard sat back in the chair and rolled his eyes. "It's terribly old-fashioned."

"I remember when women were really studying in the thirties because there were jobs opening up to them. But then the goddamn war had to come along and mess it all up again." Madelyn sighed. She'd watched it happen again and again in her lifetime. The memory of obtaining her own right to vote and then the war that had sent women right back home. Then a new freedom had blossomed only to be curtailed by the end of the second world war. She was lucky to have had the job she had for so long. Though it had not always been so easy for her. There had been a time that they wanted to push her out.

Arthur had saved her. By being married to her.

"It's a shame," Richard agreed with her. "Well, I hope you'll talk to her. Help her see that she should accept."

"Believe me, I will," Madelyn promised.

Richard nodded, looked at her for a moment. "Is everything all right with you?"

She felt her cheeks grow hot and warm and wondered if he could see it there on her face.

What would he think of her if he knew that only a few nights before Billie had...

"Yes," she said before the thought could arise and overcome her completely.

Richard smiled at her. "I'll be on my way. But it's always a pleasure speaking with you, Madelyn. You let me know if you need anything. Anything at all."

Madelyn nodded. "I believe it's I who owes you the favor, but I'll keep that in mind."

Richard left her office.

She stared down at the student essay before her and could not make any sense of it.

She gave up.

Tossing down her pen, she collected up her coat and hat and headed out across the campus, toward the cafeteria.

Arthur was sitting at the table inside with his lunch and a book propped open before him.

There was a comfort in knowing that he was there, as always. And he was handsome, and she was proud to be married to him and to no one else as she gazed at him. This man who had been by her side for over forty years.

He looked up and met her gaze, smiling at the sight of her.

She wondered if, after all she put him through, he still thought kindly of her.

It had not always been so amicable, the agreement between them. But the years had changed them.

She put together a salad at the bar and then took her seat across from Arthur.

"I wasn't sure if you were coming or not," he said, smiling at her.

"I had to get out of my office, stretch my legs," get *her* off my mind.

"I can understand that," Arthur agreed.

She poked at the salad. "What are you reading?"

"*The Concept of Mind.*" He held it up and she saw the title. "Ryle's opposed to Cartesian dualism."

"I haven't a clue what that means, but I bet you find it terribly fascinating." Madelyn smiled.

Arthur laughed and settled the book back atop the table. "I'm not sure I follow his conclusions, that the body and mind could exist so separately from one another, as if in their own realms entirely."

Madelyn laughed. "He thinks the mind doesn't lead the body to act in a physical way?"

"Seems so."

She pondered this, "I suppose one can live a whole life inside one's head without ever expressing it in the physical world."

"And Ryle would then say that we don't know another's internal world."

"And how could we?" Madelyn mused. If only she could know another's mind.

Suddenly, Arthur was coughing, gasping for air, a low rumbling noise that she had heard some nights before.

"Drink some water." She was practically standing, attempting to hand the glass to him.

He managed to suppress the cough and drink the water back.

"Are you all right?" she asked, concern knitting her brow.

Arthur waved her off with a small laugh. "As good as ever. It's nothing, Madelyn."

"It's been going on for some time," she pointed out.

Arthur's brow furrowed. "Not so long."

"I can hear you at night. Coughing."

"It's nothing, darling," he dismissed her concern.

She did not like the way it had sounded, how violently it had overtaken him.

He wiped the corner of his mouth and put his napkin neatly atop the table. "I must be going. I have a seminar soon."

"Arthur..."

"Please, Madelyn. I'm all right," he assured her, leaning down to press his lips chastely against her temple.

She let him go off, the book tucked beneath his arm.

She finished her lunch alone and then made her way back across campus.

But as she went, she noticed her student, George, sitting on the stairs of the history building. He smiled at her over the top of his textbook.

"Heya George," she said.

"Hi, Professor Turner," he responded. "It's a nice day out."

She pulled her coat a bit more tightly about herself. "A little chilly, I'd say."

"Care for a smoke?" He held out a pack and she recognized the brand. The same Pete smoked. "It'll warm you."

She stared at the packet.

Confused.

She glanced around and saw a few groups of students huddled together as they went off to their classes. No one was nearby.

She nodded and George smiled wide, handing a cigarette to her, placing one between his lips.

She sat down on the stoop beside him, and he leaned in, cupping his hand close to her cheek to keep the wind from blowing out the light. The cigarette caught and she pulled on the smoke but did not inhale.

She watched as George lit his own cigarette, inhaling deeply, content.

"Seems like you needed a break," he said.

She laughed and toyed with inhaling.

It smelled of Pete.

"You could say that."

They sat in silence, smoking and staring off at the campus colored for autumn.

"You did rather well, you know, on the second essay." Madelyn turned to George. She knew he had worked carefully on it, as if he had wanted to impress her.

"Oh, really? Gee, that's great. My parents will be relieved that I'm not completely flunking out of school." He laughed.

She turned to him. "Are you?"

"No. It was a joke." He winked.

She wondered if he wanted to sleep with her. The young boy who wanted to sleep with his teacher. The same scenario that played out a thousand times. She could see how easy it might be. To see him on campus some evening and he would invite her somewhere, perhaps some dive bar, and he'd get handsy with her and then she might allow him to put his hand up her skirt.

She thought of Arthur and his book and the power of the mind.

All the lives she could lead. All the things she was careful not to do.

But now she'd slept with Pete, and she'd kissed Billie.

Billie.

She accidentally inhaled the cigarette and found herself coughing up a cloud of smoke.

"Whoa, whoa!" George patted her on the back.

She stubbed out the cigarette and stood. "You know, smoking isn't very good for you." She brushed her hands over her skirt.

They looked at one another and smiled.

"I'll see you in class, George."

"Professor Turner." He nodded to her.

She pulled her coat around herself and inhaled the tobacco scent.

She was grateful that she could submerge herself so easily into her role as a teacher for her afternoon class on Medieval art. At least in teaching there was some sense of normalcy.

Chapter Twenty-Three

A call came through for her in her office that morning before class.

As if he had memorized her schedule.

"I'll meet you at your office at a quarter to noon," he said.

"It's better if I meet you somewhere," she said.

Pete laughed on the other end. "I see."

"Too many eyes on campus."

He told her to meet at the diner on the corner and they would go from there.

The call was still replaying in her mind as she stood in the darkened classroom; a slide of John Singer Sargent's *The Portrait of Madame X* projected on the wall.

"What is it that is so evocative about this piece?" she asked and stared out at her fourth-year pupils and noticed the males sitting at the edge of their seats with rapt attention.

"It's the lighting."

"No," she responded without looking at the boy who spoke.

"The blackness of her dress? That's challenging to make look like fabric."

"No." Madelyn looked at the red of the model's hair. The

156

woman's name was Virginie Gautreau, so history stated. She had been an attractive young woman.

"Is it the pose she's in?" A female's voice asked tentatively.

Madelyn's attention snapped to the young woman. "Why yes, Laura. It's very daring, isn't it? He turned her face away, almost as if to make her seem modest and yet her body is fully on view. As if asking us to see her. You would agree, Warren, that it's rather hard to look away?" She eyed the young man in the fourth row who was on the edge of his seat.

"She's quite a looker," Warren called out, falling into laughter that the other boys took up as if they were all in on some joke.

The seminar ended, and when the lights came on, Madelyn felt a nervous energy course through her veins.

She walked the slides back to her office, went through some errant paperwork she had put off, but then caught sight of her watch and knew she would be late if she did not leave soon.

She thought of Virginie Gautreau as she drove out of town, down the side streets. That red hair and sharp profile.

Pete was leaning against his car, smoking a cigarette when she pulled into the diner.

"You hungry?" he asked when she came closer to him.

"No." She shook her head.

He opened the car door for her and then got in on the driver's side. The motel was just down the road. He paid for the room while she waited in the car and then they went around to the room.

She followed him inside.

She watched him put out his cigarette before turning suddenly, bracing her up against the door, his lips hungry upon her lips.

She thought how very unlike Billie he kissed. He did not have her finesse, the gentle way she had pulled at her lips, asking for entrance instead of demanding.

No one had ever kissed her like that.

But Pete was hungry for her.

He released her from the door, smiling sheepishly at her. He looked so terribly young to her and uncertain and she liked this about him.

They undressed carefully and then found their way to the bed.

He kissed her as she touched him and she thought of how Billie would touch him, how Billie would straddle him and take him inside of her. Her kisses became more feverish, and Pete soon positioned himself over her and she opened herself to him. She lay back as he moved inside of her. She imagined red curls and red lips. When she opened her eyes, she saw Billie on top of her and she called out.

Pete grunted and she felt his release inside of her.

He rolled onto the bed beside her, fishing out a cigarette, his breathing uneven.

She stared at his limp dick between his legs and longed to touch herself again, longed for Billie's fingers...

Pete eased back in the bed, and she sat up. She could feel him watching her as she got up to collect her clothes and walk across the room to the bathroom.

She was glad when he did not join her in the shower.

He was partially dressed when she came out. "Everything all right?" he asked, as if he could sense something was different in her.

She nodded yes.

Pete smiled. "Would you care for some lunch then?"

She let him take her to the diner and they shared a meal and before they parted, they kissed up against the side of the building, careful to be out of sight of any passing onlookers. Pete seemed to like that.

"Will there be a next week?" he asked hopefully.

She smiled. "Same place?"

"Same time," he confirmed.

She got in her car and drove away, watching as he lit another cigarette before climbing in his car.

She drove and drove but did not go immediately back to the college. Instead, she headed out to the nearby lake and parked in a shady alcove and let her hand go up her skirt, stroking herself to orgasm. The thought of Billie's lips on her lips bringing her over the edge.

She straightened herself out and went back to the college.

She was grateful that she had laid out the items for her following class before having left, for when she reached the art building and climbed the stairs to her office, she noticed the form of a young woman standing outside her door.

"Ruby?" she asked, having not seen the girl for days.

The young woman turned to her, eyes wide and afraid.

"Are you all right?" she asked as she moved closer.

The girl shook her head, remaining frozen in place.

"Come here, come in." Madelyn unlocked her office door and ushered the girl inside. "Sit down." She closed the door behind her.

The girl sat.

"Is everything all right?" Madelyn leaned against the edge of her desk.

Ruby shook her head. She covered her face with her hands and began to sob.

"What's the matter?" Madelyn moved toward the girl.

Ruby could only cry, so she wrapped her arms about her, rubbing gentle circles against her back.

"It's all right. You can tell me."

"It's awful." Ruby sobbed.

"What's awful?"

"Me... it's me. I'm... I'm pregnant." Ruby spoke the words in disbelief, as if it were the first time she'd uttered them out loud.

Madelyn stood back. "What?"

"They're making me... I have to... I can't continue... I'll be married soon... I can't... " Ruby cried.

"Oh, Ruby. Ruby." Madelyn wanted to offer her something, anything.

Ruby stood up and clung to Madelyn, holding her tight. "I love you, Professor Turner. I love you," she whispered passionately, wildly.

Madelyn fought back the surprised tears that welled in her eyes.

The girl looked up at her through her watery eyes and then pulled her close, crushing their lips together.

Madelyn stepped back.

The girl's eyes went wide and then she covered her mouth, her cheeks coloring with shame. "I'm sorry, I'm so... I'm so sorry... " And before Madelyn could reach for her and pull her back, the young woman turned and raced from the office. Disappearing.

Chapter Twenty-Four

She sat on the edge of the barstool, a cool glass of watered whiskey pressed to her warm forehead.

The room was noisy about her, a cacophony of the human voice and music from a pianist fighting for space in the corner.

It all jumbled together in her second glass haze.

She thought that she should call Arthur, to let him know she was okay. That she was *not* doing what their daughter Rose did and going off on a bender. No, it had only seemed necessary after the shock of the afternoon.

She had made it through a Renaissance art course with half a mind and then she'd driven to the piano bar in the town over where there wouldn't be students.

She settled the glass back down atop the bar and stood up. Her legs felt loose. She used the back of the barstools to make her way to the hotel lobby the bar was attached to. There was a wall of pay phones. She went into a stall and placed a nickel in the machine, lifting the receiver.

She placed her call and listened as the phone rang.

"Hello?" A feminine voice inquired.

Oh.

"Billie?" Madelyn laughed incredulously. She'd dialed the wrong number.

"Madelyn? Is everything all right?"

Madelyn leaned her head back against the booth's wooden surface. "'s fine. I'm fine."

"Where are you?"

Madelyn told her.

"Don't go anywhere, I'll be there in twenty minutes." And then Billie hung up.

Madelyn stared at the phone that was echoing a dial tone back at her.

She should call Arthur.

She hung up the phone.

She went out of the booth and back to the bar, back to her seat atop the barstool and ordered another whiskey and water.

It was nearly thirty minutes later that she looked up to find Billie, wrapped up in a delectable black fur, red hair curled about her face, lips a brilliant red, standing in the doorway, eyes searching the room.

Madelyn realized this beautiful creature was searching for her.

Their eyes met. Billie raised her hand to wave.

Madelyn could feel everyone's eyes on Billie as she swept inside. A porter took her coat, and its removal revealed a dazzling black dress covered in an emerald and pink floral pattern. She took the seat beside Madelyn and ordered a martini.

"Nice place you found here," she leaned into Madelyn to whisper.

Madelyn smiled bashfully.

"Don't you worry, I left word with Arthur of where you were. I told him I'd take care of you." Billie raised the martini glass the bartender handed her in a salute and then sipped the clear liquid.

"Thank you," Madelyn whispered.

"Now what's all of this about?" Billie turned so that all of her was facing Madelyn.

Madelyn toyed with her nearly empty glass. She knew she wouldn't be able to handle another. "A student." Madelyn sighed, turning her eyes upward to the tin ceiling above.

Billie nodded, encouragingly.

"I really believed in her." Madelyn's tongue was thick. "I stuck my neck out for her to get a fellowship. She's b-brilliant, you know? R-really smart." Madelyn rolled her neck to the side. "She was always hanging around, all the time just appearing out of nowhere, I thought she was... different. I thought she really wanted it." Madelyn pursed her lips. "Maybe I pushed her too hard. Maybe it was... too much."

"What happened?" Billie toyed with the olive in her drink.

Madelyn looked at Billie and then was laughing at the preposterousness of it all. "She's pregnant."

Billie's big eyes went wide, rolling up to the heavens. "Jesus."

"Exactly." Madelyn lifted her glass and saluted the sky and then downed the rest of the whiskey. "But the worst part of it," she slammed the tumbler back down, "the thing that doesn't make any sense to me, is that I think... well, I don't get the idea that she particularly *likes*... men." Madelyn lowered her gaze, turning the empty tumbler in her hands.

"She's not even boy crazy?" Billie's elbow came to rest on the bar. She was leaning in so terribly close to Madelyn.

Madelyn shook her head. Her eyes darted to the other patrons sitting nearby.

No one seemed to be paying her any mind. She caught the occasional glance in Billie's direction, but no one seemed interested in whatever it was they were talking about.

The piano was still playing loudly in the corner, some tune she recognized but couldn't name.

"She kissed me." Madelyn bit her lip.

Billie sucked in a breath of air. "I see." She fumbled for her cigarette case.

"I didn't know what to do... I just let her run away."

Billie's hand came to rest gently on Madelyn's shoulder. "I'm sure just believing in her was enough. It's a rotten thing sometimes, to be born a woman." Billie removed her hand to light her cigarette. A man beside her turned and offered her a light, but she refused him. Rather abruptly. He looked peeved with her. She turned to Madelyn and rolled her eyes as she lit her own cigarette. "They always think we're so helpless." She laughed as she exhaled a cloud of smoke.

Madelyn thought Billie was impossibly beautiful just then.

"Can I get you another?" The bartender had appeared before them.

Madelyn shook her head. She couldn't fathom another drink. "A coffee. Decaf, please," she said.

Billie tapped off ash and looked at Madelyn. "What do you think it is about you?"

Madelyn's lip curled in question. "What do you mean?"

"That makes everyone want to kiss you." Billie was smiling playfully.

Madelyn felt her cheeks flush. "Oh, now. I'm sure not everyone wants to kiss me. I mean the moment you walked in everybody's eyes were on you."

Billie laughed at that. "Well, I'm certainly saddened to hear we lost another brilliant mind to the evils of marriage and family life." Billie sighed.

Madelyn eyed her as the bartender sat a cup of steaming coffee before her. "What about yourself?"

Billie blew out a stream of smoke. "Well, I wouldn't have married Pete if he didn't accept me for who I was." Who was she, Madelyn wondered. "He knows all of me and that's what matters. And no pregnancy forced my hand." Here she laughed.

Madelyn eyed her. Did she know everything about Pete?

But she could not bring herself to ask. She did not want to upset whatever this was between them.

"You were working before you met Pete, weren't you?" Madelyn cupped the warm cup of coffee between her hands.

"Of course! I supported myself for years. It was a kind of relief, though, when Pete came along and told me we were moving, and I couldn't keep on at that incestuous company. You know my boss tried to put his hand up my skirt just about every day." Billie smiled lopsidedly.

Madelyn was horrified, but not surprised. There had once been a provost who had made her sit on his lap a time or two. She had been disgusted when they had promoted him to vice president of the college. She had never told anyone, but she had been glad when he'd died of a heart attack.

"Terrible." Madelyn grimaced.

"But don't you worry. I keep myself occupied." Billie winked.

Madelyn glanced at her. "Occupied?"

It was Billie's turn to lower her gaze and glance about. "You know those terrible little nothing books you can buy for a quarter at the store?"

Madelyn recalled the salacious covers. The times she'd seek out the ones with two women instead of the hunky man and woman. "Yes."

Billie leaned in close to Madelyn. "I write those."

Madelyn's eyes went wide. "What?"

Billie was laughing. "Yes, under an assumed name of course."

"What name?" Madelyn insisted.

"If I told you then you'd know all my secrets." Billie stirred her drink and sipped again.

Madelyn very much doubted that. "I want to know."

Billie laughed. "Oh, they're just silly. I'm sure it's nothing like what an esteemed college professor would read."

"I've read a few," Madelyn insisted.

Billie's lips were adorable when she smiled the way she was smiling. "All right then. Dominique Lawson."

Madelyn laughed at the name.

"I didn't choose it," Billie added.

"It's wonderful. Very serious. I have to read something you've written. You'll let me?"

Billie shrugged. "I'll think about it." But Madelyn knew she would. "Shall we get you home?"

They collected their coats and Billie put her arm about Madelyn's waist as they walked from the hotel and out into the chilly night air. Madelyn was not drunk. She could feel everything. Her thoughts were crystalline.

Billie escorted them to her convertible, the cloth top securely up against the oncoming cold weather. Once safely inside, beneath its cover, they found one another.

"You were the most beautiful woman in that room," Billie whispered as she reached out to cup Madelyn's cheek, to pull her closer.

They kissed.

Billie drove her home and walked her to the door. They might have kissed again, had Arthur not opened the door and welcomed Madelyn home. As if a relieved parent.

"I'm all right, darling," Madelyn said to him and kissed his cheek.

"I brought her back in one piece," Billie said.

Madelyn turned to her. "Thank you."

Billie winked and turned on her heel to amble back down the driveway, back toward her house, to Pete...

Madelyn watched her go until she felt Arthur's hand on her back. He pulled her inside, looked her over.

"It was all right." She sighed. "It was only a drink or two." They walked to the kitchen where Arthur made them both a cup of tea and Madelyn sank into the kitchen chair. Exhausted.

Chapter Twenty-Five

The phone rang sometime after she got home the following evening.

Arthur had a late seminar. The house was quiet.

She picked up the kitchen phone as she stirred the soup she'd started for dinner. "Hello?"

"I haven't heard your voice in ages," Carole admonished on the other end.

Madelyn pressed the phone between her shoulder and ear so that she could turn down the heat of the stove. "It's wonderful to hear your voice." She smiled at the thought of the woman on the other end of the phone. But then she remembered the strange tension in their last phone conversation. The slight disapproval in Carole's voice when Madelyn had mentioned Billie, about women who might like women.

How could she tell her what had happened?

"I was afraid... " Carole started, but then chuckled. "Well, you must be busy then."

"I have been." Madelyn wiped her hands on her apron and grasped the phone in her hand. "But never too busy for you."

"Well, I haven't got any exciting news to share, I just assumed you might," Carole said.

Madelyn sighed. "You're very nosey, you know."

"Oh, come on. It's not as if anything ever goes on around here. Sure, I think Norm might be stepping out on Shirley and Barbara is very frigid with her husband Mort, but I'm not close enough to them to hear the real ins and outs of their lives. And, frankly, they don't seem half as interesting as you. All these wives seem totally braindead."

"So, you only like me because I'm a scholar, then?"

"Sure, that's it." Carole laughed and Madelyn realized how much she missed her laughter.

Madelyn felt her stomach flutter with nerves. What to tell Carole? It felt too raw, too intimate to share things. Especially knowing how Carole felt about two women...

"I saw him again," Madelyn said instead.

"Oh, really?" Carole preened.

"Yes." But she had also kissed his wife in her car the same evening and that had felt delicious.

"Is he... good?" Carole asked quietly.

Madelyn smiled. "Yes."

"Have you seen much of his wife?" Carole asked quietly.

Madelyn swallowed, peering out the window that opened to a view of the home next door. "We went to the city. For a painting and ended up at a drive-in movie."

"A drive-in movie. Just the two of you?"

"Yes, the two of us," Madelyn conceded. "Just the two of us."

"I see."

Madelyn did not want to share more.

"Is she very beautiful?" Carole prodded.

"I suppose, yes." Madelyn tried to sound non-committal to the glamorous beauty the woman possessed. As if it might hurt Carole somehow.

But how could she hurt Carole when Carole possessed her own breed of beauty?

Carole was quiet on the other end. Distant.

Madelyn took a deep breath and sunk back against the counter again. "Oh, Carole. I don't know what I'm doing. And on top of that, I'm worried about Arthur." She knew it would be best to change course, to move away from Pete and Billie and their flirtations toward her... Something about it irked Carole.

And Madelyn could not lose Carole.

"Arthur? What's the matter with Arthur?"

"He's been coughing. He says he's fine, but he has these attacks. He won't go to the doctor. He's so stubborn." Madelyn sighed.

"It could be nothing."

"It certainly doesn't sound like nothing," Madelyn hummed.

"Perhaps you could tell him you're taking him to some lecture in the city but end up at the doctor's instead," Carole suggested, knowing Arthur as well as Madelyn.

Madelyn chuckled at that.

She heard a car come to a stop outside and looked out the window to see Pete stepping out of his car. She watched him as he moved, jacket tucked beneath his arm, up the driveway. His broad shoulders, that she had touched and caressed, moved beneath his crisp white button-up.

Would he see Billie when he went inside? Would he kiss her hello? She could envision Billie's pliant lips welcoming his greeting.

"Where'd you go?" Carole was asking.

"I'm right here." Madelyn closed her eyes, all mixed up.

They spoke of everything and nothing until Arthur came home. It was stilted because it felt as if they were both avoiding speaking about the elephant between them.

Madelyn did not like the distance in Carole's voice. Her disapproval.

She tried not to think about it as she greeted Arthur. He looked exhausted.

They ate dinner across from one another and then Arthur, coughing, went to his study.

"Don't you work yourself to death," Madelyn warned.

Arthur gave her a dark smile.

She went to work putting the kitchen back into order. As she stood at the sink, she peered out and saw the lights on in the house across the yard. She could make out a feminine figure in the kitchen. Billie. Smoking a cigarette and talking to someone, probably Pete, as she moved back and forth at her own sink. Her red hair was piled atop her head, she had glasses on. Thick, black frames.

Madelyn did not remember having ever seen her in glasses, but she quite liked the way it made her appear.

Billie was laughing.

Madelyn turned away from the window and collected the essays she had to grade before heading to the living room. She put on a Frank Sinatra record and curled around the coffee table.

She graded until her body felt tired and heavy and the stack had receded, and the album had been changed over to Gene Autry, Glenn Miller, and finally Erik Satie.

She put the papers away in her bag, went to the kitchen sink to pour herself a glass of water, and stared out the window to find that the light across the way was out.

Would they be in bed?

She felt a horrible thrill race through her.

Placing her cup by the sink, she went to the stairs, passing by the study where Arthur was coughing. She thought to tell him to go on up to bed but knew he wouldn't budge until he had to. His head wasn't hurting that day. He would take advantage of this.

She went up the stairs and into her bedroom. She did not turn on the light.

She went to the window, as she had not for the past few weeks. Not sure who or what she was more afraid to see.

Looking out across the yard, she could make out that the light was on. But there were no figures in the window.

Only the light.

She stood there for some time. Staring out through the dark evening. Seeing nothing.

She began to feel depressed and foolish.

Turning on the bedside lamp, she slid from her house dress and went to the bathroom where she drew herself a bath. She sank down into the water and looked down at her naked body. The hair between her legs, blonde and gray, the way her breasts floated upward to the surface of the water, the pink tips of her nipples pert from the warmth of the water, from the warmth of what she was feeling.

Her eyes slid closed, and she thought of how Pete felt inside of her and how Billie's lips felt every time she kissed her.

Her eyes came open, surprised by what she had become tangled up in. This couple who seemed to give in to her every strange desire, her every whim... how could they know? What were they after?

She was just the old woman next door, after all. It was improper and yet she had already yielded to their advances...

She wanted to get out of the tub, to run to Arthur and tell him all that she had done, to ask him what he thought of it, yet it would be breaking their unspoken rule. She did as she pleased, as long as it didn't affect him, and it was swept under the rug.

But this was different from all the other times before.

There was no precedent for this.

She got out of the bathtub and dried herself off. She cleaned her face, moisturized, brushed her teeth, reset her hair.

By the time she'd slipped into her nightgown, the bedroom across the yard's light was out.

She settled beneath her sheets, putting out the light on her bedside table.

It was late and yet her mind raced. As she thought of Billie and Pete. Asleep in their darkened room. So near and yet so far from her.

Chapter Twenty-Six

Betsy applauded at the art prints Madelyn had brought for her to look at. She held each, seemed to examine them as an art critic might, and decided she liked the one of the field best. She hugged the paper to her chest, crushing it.

On their way out, an administrator caught up to them.

"Excuse me, Mr. and Mrs. Turner."

They turned to face the woman.

"Would you mind if we spoke in my office?"

Madelyn looked at Arthur. He nodded.

They followed the woman, who introduced herself as Ms. Jane, into her office. She shut the door behind them and then took her seat behind the desk.

"It has been brought to my attention that Betsy's birthday is coming up soon."

"Yes, November twenty-fifth." Madelyn smiled.

Ms. Jane smiled, but the smile did not reach her eyes. "Yes. And she will be turning eighteen."

"Yes, she will." Arthur was not smiling.

"As you know, our facilities are for children. Betsy has done very well here, but as soon as she turns eighteen, I'm afraid we will not be able to keep her here. You see? She will need to be moved to another facility."

Madelyn should have thought of it. She should have remembered that such a thing could happen.

"She'll legally be an adult, I'm afraid, and the state has very specific rules when it comes to such matters." Ms. Jane smiled sadly.

Madelyn looked to Arthur. "I forgot… "

Arthur rubbed his forehead. She wondered if a migraine was coming on.

"I also understand that you are not her parents. Is that correct?" Ms. Jane was looking between them.

"That is correct," Arthur said.

"I would suggest that if you would like to remain in charge of Betsy's care that either of you accept guardianship over her. Legally. Or, if you think it might be appropriate, I suggest asking her parents," Ms. Jane calmly explained.

Madelyn folded her hands in her lap.

Betsy's parents were not fit to be guardians of her. Her mother hadn't laid eyes on her since she was six years old. "No. I think we shall seek guardianship."

Arthur was looking at her. "Perhaps it's best, darling, if we speak to Rose… "

Madelyn shook her head. "What good would it do? We've been there every step of the way… "

"And maybe it's time we let our daughter take care of things."

She saw, in that moment, something in Arthur that she had not seen before.

He looked exhausted. His eyes pale, his features thin and tired. He was aging before her.

It frightened her.

Madelyn turned to Ms. Jane and smiled tightly. "Thank you for letting us know. We will certainly take it up with Betsy's parents."

Ms. Jane nodded, handing them over several brochures for adult care facilities in the area.

Madelyn felt as if she couldn't breathe until they made their way out of the place and into the mid-afternoon air. She inhaled the fresh air, greedily.

She could hardly look at Arthur when he sat across from her at the diner in the town over, eating his eggs and toast. She sipped coffee and picked at her omelet.

She felt Arthur's hand cover her own.

A tear slid from the corner of her eye, and she felt embarrassed for crying in public.

The waitress came by, and Arthur's hand was removed and her coffee was topped off.

She excused herself to go to the bathroom.

Leaning against the tiled wall, she closed her eyes and took deep breaths, trying to steady herself.

Once the world stopped turning so horribly fast, she went to the sink and wiped away the smear of mascara and fixed her face before returning to the table.

"I'll call Mitch," Arthur said as he finished his coffee. "Don't you worry about it."

Madelyn took a deep breath and nodded.

They went home.

They hardly spoke a word to one another.

Pete's car was missing from the driveway when they arrived, and Madelyn wondered if they would be off to some weekend soiree in the city.

She felt upset by their absence, as if just knowing they were there might make her loneliness diminish.

Arthur went up to bed – his head was hurting - and she kicked off her heels and went to the kitchen. She uncapped a beer, reached for a blanket, and went out to sit on the back porch. To stare at the leaves in all their autumn glory.

The beer made her feel morose.

The house next door was still and empty.

Arthur would be upstairs, probably asleep.

She needed something...

Moving back into the house, she slipped into her moccasins, tip-toed upstairs to check on Arthur – he was asleep – then grabbed a jacket and slipped out of the house. She drove down the suburban road, desolate on a Saturday evening. People would be at home or off to parties, to the piano bar in the town over, or simply out to dine.

And she was as alone as she usually ended up being.

She took the road out of town, heading toward the town over. Then the one over from that, across a bridge and a little river.

The sun was slowly setting around her, casting a glowing yellow light on the fall foliage clinging to the trees as she passed.

The small downtown strip rose to greet her. Several people strolled down the main drag, taking in the store front windows, idly passing their evening. A rush of teens raced from the pharmacy, nearly knocking her over.

"Sorry, ma'am," One young man turned to apologize, blindly.

She made her way into the pharmacy and was glad to find it filled with patrons. So that no one paid her much mind as she meandered amongst the shelves, searching without seeing anything. She reached for some toothpaste, she was nearly out after all, and then some hand lotion.

The paperbacks were in a rack near the door.

Madelyn scanned the covers, seeking...

She spun the rack and glanced over the images of nearly naked men and busty women in negligees. She spun the rack again and felt warm all over when she found two women seated beside one another, the older one touching the younger's hand.

Below it a woman standing over a nearly naked woman laid out atop the bed.

The author's name jumped out at her.

Dominique Lawson.

She was not sure if she should be surprised or not to find the name on a cover with two women.

Madelyn looked up, glancing about the store. But no one was paying her any mind.

Her heart pounded in her chest as she reached for the copy.

She wondered what the young man working at the register might think of her. She wished she could simply tuck the book into her purse and not lay it out for him to see, for him to think, to know...

But she had never seen him before, and he had never seen her before and so she took the toothpaste and the lotion and the book to the counter.

The boy looked at the book, eyed her, and then carefully rang up the items. "That'll be $1.50," he said, slipping the book along with the other items into a brown paper bag.

She handed over the money and took the bag from him without looking him in the eyes.

Her face burned, but the shame was no match for her curiosity. It overtook her. That the novel should be about two women.

She wanted to open the book, to scan its contents as soon as she was safely back inside of her car, but instead she drove straight home.

She hoped that the lights would be on in the house next door, but as she approached, she found them off and Pete's car still missing from the driveway. They would be gone for the night, she reasoned.

She carried the items into the kitchen and was somewhat relieved to find the house quiet.

Arthur was still asleep.

She opened another beer and took the bag up the stairs, moving quietly over the parts of the stairs that she knew would creak if she stepped too heavily. She walked past Arthur's room, listening to hear if he might be awake, but it was silent on the other side of the door. She went to her room and closed the door and kicked off her shoes and slipped into a nightgown and sat on the edge of the bed.

She pulled the book from the bag and leaned back into her pillows, staring at the cover.

She felt naughty, as if she were not supposed to be seeing the book. As if she were not supposed to know that Dominique Lawson was a nom de plume.

Turning on her nightstand light, she opened the page as if it were the most sacred, holy book she had ever read.

Chapter Twenty-Seven

"There's no place in this world for women like us." Rita crossed her legs atop the divan. Her robe was slipping from her shoulder and Peggy wanted to press her lips to the exposed skin.

"What do you mean?" Peggy whimpered.

"Women who love women." Rita's eyebrows rose in mock amusement at the statement.

Peggy reached for the back of a nearby chair, trying to steady herself.

Couldn't Rita see how much she wanted her? How she had wanted her since the first day she'd seen her in the hat shop? Had the way Rita's hand grazed her so brazenly at that bar, those lingering looks meant nothing to her?

"You don't want me." Rita flicked ash angrily from her cigarette.

Was she dismissing her? Just like that?

"You're better off with that Johnny you've been running around with." She crushed out her cigarette.

"I don't love him." Peggy's cheeks were bright red, anger curling into her hands so that she clenched her fists.

Rita laughed. "Darling, it's impossible to love another

woman. Believe me," Rita stood from the chair, moving to Peggy. *"I've tried it."*

Peggy swallowed as Rita drew nearer to her. The older woman's eyes narrowed as she came closer and closer.

Rita's finger moved beneath Peggy's chin, drawing her face upward to look into her eyes. "You'd better get out while you can."

Peggy couldn't move. The smell of Rita's perfume invaded her senses. She wanted to kiss the other woman and yet she was afraid of her.

But it was the slight tremor in Rita's hand that made Peggy realize that perhaps she was bluffing. That maybe she wanted it just as much as Peggy did.

Peggy leaned forward and pressed her lips against Rita's lips. They were soft and supple. Rita gave into her, her hand snaking its way about Peggy, pulling her close to her, opening her mouth to Peggy, as if begging her for more. And Peggy wanted to give her more. Peggy wanted to give her everything.

Peggy's fingers worked at the buttons on Rita's shirt.

Rita's hand clasped at her hand. "You don't know what you're doing to me."

Peggy was breathless, a strange, animalistic desire welling deep inside. Peggy pushed Rita's hand away and tore at her shirt. They tumbled through Rita's Washington Square apartment, falling into chairs and walls until Peggy pulled Rita into the bedroom. With the lights off, they fell to the bed. Rita's kisses were rough and searing and Peggy fought against her, until Rita's breathing softened, and her body became passionate.

Rita transformed before her, taking over, pinning Peggy to the bed. She caressed the girl, making her shudder with inexplicable pleasures she did not know could exist.

Once it was done, she knew she was not the same. Nothing would ever feel the same as it had before because she now knew the love of a woman.

Madelyn stared at the ceiling.

Burning.

That Billie had written these things, that Billie could know...

Well, Billie had kissed her. Certainly, she would know.

Madelyn was not so naïve that she had not considered this before, but... what about Pete? The passion they shared... she had watched it unfold across the yard, through the window.

The window, when she managed to sit up in bed and peer through the blinds, remained dark. The couple had not come home the whole of the evening.

Madelyn glanced at the clock and realized it was nearing three in the morning.

She groaned, not tired and yet delirious at the words on the page.

She knew how it ended. She had devoured the story in a matter of hours but had returned to the moment the line had been crossed, wishing it might have been the ending.

She fell asleep clutching the book and awoke to find it had fallen to the floor.

The morning sun was blinding and at first she did not register where she was or who she was.

There had been dreams of the city, of bars and women and soft lips and gentle caresses.

Something had come to life inside of her. She had never seen it expressed in print the way Billie had written it. There were no novels, no other stories that she had come across before that allowed two women to find one another in such a way and lead them to the bedroom.

It existed, didn't it? Love between two women.

There was a knock at her bedroom door. She sat straight up in bed, her back groaning at the sudden motion.

"Darling, it's nearly ten," Arthur's voice came from the other side.

Madelyn leaned over the bed to pick up the book, to slip it beneath the cover. "I'm awake. You can... you can come in."

Arthur turned the handle on the door and appeared before her with a cup of coffee. "Tired?" he asked, coming to her with the mug.

She yawned as she accepted the coffee. "Thank you. Yes, I suppose I stayed up too late last night."

Arthur sat on the edge of the bed. "You're exhausted, darling." He patted her hair gently.

"No." She shook her head. "Not really." She smiled and sipped the coffee. Just the way she liked it.

"I've had a talk with Mitch. We'll take them to dinner this evening," Arthur broke the news.

Madelyn groaned. "Does Rose know?"

He shook his head. "I only told him a little of it."

"God." Madelyn sighed.

Arthur took her hand, squeezing it gently. "It's time she faces it."

Madelyn nodded but found Arthur far too optimistic.

Arthur went to do his stretches and to work on his papers. She had grading to do, but she made the bed, washed her face, reset her hair, and slipped into a house dress, before making herself some toast and eggs.

She looked across the way to the house next door. It still looked vacant.

She wished that she might be able to go over, to ask Billie about what she had written, but she also felt embarrassed at having read it.

She took a fresh cup of coffee to Arthur and settled in the living room with her own cup and went about her grading with Doris Day, followed by Jo Stafford playing on the record player in the background.

The papers distracted her mind from wandering to Peggy ripping Rita's shirt open.

When the imagery crept up, she'd stand up to go to the kitchen, to make herself a cup of tea, to nibble at something from the fridge, to make her body forget the unknown sensations.

When the grading was done, she swept and vacuumed the house, her mind humming. Nerves and arousal clashing as she dusted all the surfaces and wiped down the woodwork and mopped the kitchen floor.

When the chores were complete, she went up the stairs and showered and changed into a skirt and sweater.

Arthur was waiting for her in the living room.

"Beautiful as always." He smiled at her, kissing her cheek.

As they left, she noticed that Pete's car had returned to its place in the driveway. The couple were home.

Madelyn stared wistfully as Arthur drove them to the restaurant near the campus. She was not sure why she was so afraid to face her daughter. Her own daughter. Whom she had birthed and loved and taken care of. Her daughter, who used to crawl into bed with her in the night and curl her little arms around Madelyn's stomach and hold her until she fell asleep. She had been such a darling little girl.

And now, at the restaurant, Madelyn sat across from Rose. Watching as she lit a cigarette and refused to meet her eyes fully.

"... so, you see, she'll need a new facility," Arthur was explaining.

Rose shifted in her seat; an annoyed look formed in the corner of her eyes. As if Madelyn were doing this to her on purpose.

"And to be frank, she needs someone to file for guardianship. After she turns eighteen, she will be a legal adult, but we all know she can't function as one." Arthur was using his teaching voice. The voice Madelyn knew made Rose livid.

The fights they had had when Rose had been younger...

"What do you want us to do about it?" Rose tapped off ash from her cigarette angrily.

"I think you need to file for legal guardianship," Arthur said.

Rose rolled her eyes. "The doctors said she wouldn't live to be ten."

Madelyn flinched at the animosity Rose had toward her own daughter. "You listen here, Rose... "

"Madelyn... " Arthur put his hand upon hers in warning.

"Your daughter is a beautiful young woman. Sure, she doesn't look like other teenagers, sure she doesn't act like them, but she's special, Rose. She is very special."

"Special is the right word." Rose blew smoke irritably from between her lips.

Madelyn wanted to shake her daughter. "We won't be around forever to care for her, Rose."

"I wouldn't have given birth to her if I'd known... "

Madelyn would have slapped her were they not in such a public place. A professor she knew was dining a table over with his wife and a dean was not too far off.

"Honey, I'll handle things." Mitch had placed his hand over the top of Rose's. "We can talk to a lawyer, have her moved somewhere else. All right?" He looked from Arthur to Madelyn.

Madelyn was furious.

They would simply put another bandage on the situation without making an attempt to know the wonderful young woman they had created.

Madelyn stood up. "I can't do this." And she grabbed up her purse and her jacket.

"Where are you going?" Arthur called after her.

"I'll walk home." She tossed over her shoulder, carelessly, nodding blindly at the professor who was now looking at her strangely.

She pushed her way out of the smoky restaurant and into the fresh autumn night air.

She pulled on her jacket and walked down the tree-lined street, leaves crunching beneath her heels.

She hadn't a clue where she was headed, only that she could not stay there a moment longer, listening to her daughter say such awful things. Her own daughter.

She walked, head slightly bent against the cooler evening air, so that she did not see the man standing before her. Their paths collided and he clasped her shoulders to keep her from falling.

"Whoa there," it was a familiar voice.

When she looked up, she found Pete's face above her, smiling his charming smile.

"Where are you off to in such a hurry, Madelyn?" He laughed.

"Oh!" She stepped back and smoothed a hand over her skirt, having not expected to run into him like this.

"Is everything all right?" A familiar female voice inquired, and Madelyn turned, finding Billie was only a step away from Pete. She looked glorious in the fading light of day and Madelyn was suddenly bashful in her presence.

Madelyn looked down at the ground, shaking her head. "Dinner. With my daughter and her husband," she explained quietly. "I couldn't... I left."

"We were just about to have some dinner at this dive. Join us." Pete insisted.

"Oh, I shouldn't... " But it was so much more appealing than the dinner she had just left.

Madelyn glanced behind her, to see if Arthur had followed. But she knew how winded he got and knew he would not come racing after her. She assumed he would stay at the restaurant and try to talk sense into Mitch, ignoring Rose as she drank herself into a stupor. So, she would have time.

"All right." She nodded.

Chapter Twenty-Eight

She was seated between Pete and Billie.

She could smell Billie's perfume.

"Will they take on guardianship of Betsy?" Billie was looking her over, a careful concern etched in her brow.

Madelyn nodded, turning the glass of Coke before her about in her hands. "Oh, I suppose they will. But I don't trust that it will change anything. You should have seen the look on her face... I don't know how I raised her to act like this."

"I don't always think it's the parent's fault," Pete said optimistically.

Madelyn laughed deeply. "That's kind of you to say, but she certainly enjoys blaming me."

"It's an easy way out," Billie said as she tapped her pack of cigarettes against her hand. Everything about her was ridiculously intoxicating in that moment. Every slight gesture made Madelyn's mind space out for a moment and she forgot who she was and where she was.

Billie placed a cigarette between her lips and winked at Madelyn. Could she know?

Madelyn wanted to tell her that she had read her story. But did Pete know what it was she wrote?

"I had a dreadful mother, but I don't blame her. She was simply doing her best with what she was given. An abusive husband and too many children." Billie laughed and Madelyn glanced at her, wondering what her life had been like growing up. She knew so little about her. "At least your daughter had a loving mother and father. I know that that is true. Sometimes it's simply a matter of personal character. She's embarrassed," Billie said so nonchalantly. As if she'd worked it all out in her mind.

The words struck Madelyn.

Perhaps she was going about it all wrong with Rose.

"Yes, I think that might be it." Madelyn sipped her Coke.

Billie was smiling at her, that dazzling smile.

Pete had put his arm around the back of the seat, brushing her shoulders. She could feel the heat from it on her back.

She wondered what it was they looked like to the world around them. A couple taking their mother out for dinner, Madelyn decided. Though she certainly did not feel maternally toward either of them.

Pete ordered some hamburgers and fries for the table.

"Oh, and I want a milkshake. Strawberry," Billie piped up.

The waiter, a young man, stared at her with delighted amusement before nodding and then went off to put in the order.

"Where did you two get off to this weekend?" Madelyn toyed with loose hair at the base of her neck. Embarrassed as soon as she asked. As if she were keeping tabs on them and now she had revealed herself.

"Oh, our friends had a party in the city. We drank a bit too much and slept on a horribly uncomfortable pull-out." Pete said without batting an eye.

Billie was smiling at him as he spoke. A knowing, familiar smile. "It makes us sound like we're lushes," she teased.

"Well, that's what happened, darling." Pete shot back.

Billie smiled at him and then turned back to Madelyn. "What about you?"

Madelyn felt a blush rise to her cheeks. "Oh, just... nothing." She shrugged and thought again of Peggy ripping Rita's shirt off.

Had Billie really written that?

Billie's forehead creased. "Why are you looking at me like that?" Her lips wrinkled into a playful smile.

Madelyn looked down at her Coke, shaking her head. "It's nothing... nothing, I... " But she couldn't say it. "I read something rather interesting. Last night. Was all."

Billie was looking at her with the most curious gaze. "My goodness."

Madelyn shifted uncomfortably.

"She's read the women's one." Billie said to Pete. "Madelyn, I would have given you a copy! You went out and bought it?"

Madelyn felt the blush growing redder. "I hadn't... well... "

Billie nudged her gently. "Well, what did you think of it? Am I an embarrassment to the literary world?"

"Oh, no. I wouldn't say that." Madelyn looked at her quickly and then saw something in her gaze that made her lower her eyes again. "It was... gripping." She decided carefully upon the adjective.

"Gripping until they made me kill Rita off. The censors are ridiculously rigid. There's only been a handful of them published this way, you see, and they think that if the women's lives end terribly then they can do whatever they want. I would have also told you that some of those things were added in by some Steve or Dick in their editing department. You know, like how Rita is always warning that there's something wrong with the two of them." Here Billie rolled her eyes. "I hate that they must do that to the women. I hope you saw when the story should have ended."

Madelyn glanced at Pete and found that he was raptly

listening to his wife. "Yes, I do think so. Right after that night... at Rita's."

Billie smiled and leaned forward to rest her chin on her hands. "Exactly."

Madelyn looked at Pete. "You've read it?"

Pete smiled. "Oh, yes. Billie likes to read to me at night." He winked at his wife.

Madelyn was warm all over.

"He gives me wonderful ideas," Billie said.

The waiter interrupted their repartee, placing a burger before each, a basket of fries in the middle and a strawberry milkshake before Billie.

Madelyn did not understand the sensation that rippled through her at the knowledge that Pete had also read the very words she had.

It had felt as if a secret, meant only for her.

But how could a published book be for only one person?

Naturally, Pete would have every right to the words, to Billie's process, and yet it felt terribly unfair.

A betrayal.

What would a man know about that kind of a relationship?

But what did Billie know about that kind of a relationship?

Madelyn lifted her head to watch Billie say something to Pete as she cut her hamburger delicately into smaller bites. She caught Madelyn looking at her and smiled.

Of course.

Billie would know that kind of love.

How many women had there been?

Madelyn felt irritable and flushed.

She was not hungry, but she made herself pick at the burger before she wiped at her cheek and excused herself to the lady's room.

Pete stood and offered her a hand, but she did not allow

him to help her from the booth. She stood and walked to the back of the diner and into the small, rather dingy, dimly lit bathroom. It smelled of stale cigarettes and cleaning products.

She stood at the sink, wondering just what had gotten into her. She was a married woman.

They were a married couple.

She had already cheated with Pete, and she had kissed Billie. What had she been trying to prove?

She did not fit into their lives. She was merely a neighbor, not some play toy, some amusement for them.

The bathroom door opened behind her, and Billie appeared in the mirror.

"What's the matter?" Billie stayed near the door. "Have I done something to upset you?"

"No." Madelyn ran the water as if to wash her hands.

"Well, something certainly changed back there. I didn't mean...well, I hope the story didn't put you off. I thought you might..."

"It's not about the story." Madelyn reached for paper towels, tearing them from the holder.

Billie looked stricken and confused. "Whatever it is, Madelyn, you can tell me."

Madelyn closed her eyes and leaned against the sink.

I slept with Pete.

"It's nothing," Madelyn said instead. "I liked your story. Very much. Perhaps too much."

Billie was smiling when Madelyn opened her eyes again.

"You find it strange that I share that side of myself with Pete, don't you?" Billie surmised.

Madelyn turned to face Billie. "Who am I to say anything about another person's marriage?" Madelyn laughed humorlessly.

"Arthur is devoted to you." Billie crossed her arms over her chest.

"Yes, but he... " Madelyn couldn't say the words. Not in this dingy bathroom. Not like this. "I only mean that I'm not one to judge how a relationship is carried out. It just took me by surprise that he would know... "

Billie nodded, a little smile playing at the edge of her red lips. "Pete and I have always been open with one another about who we are. Like I said, I wouldn't have married him otherwise."

Could she know? Or was she only bluffing? Was this her way of getting it out of Madelyn, making her fess up to her afternoons spent with Pete?

She couldn't do it. Not to either of them because she liked both of them so much. She would not want to hurt Billie or betray Pete or hurt Pete and betray Billie.

It was all so confusing. What was she doing here? With them.

"Relax, darling." Billie braced Madelyn in her arms. "Whatever it is, it's all right."

Madelyn exhaled.

They kissed.

Madelyn thought of ripping at Billie's shirt, but then thought of Pete waiting for them at the table.

"Come on. The food's getting cold." Billie released Madelyn, checked her lipstick in the mirror and then held the door open for them to return to Pete.

"Having a closed-door meeting without me, I see," Pete said as they all settled back into the table. But he looked at Madelyn carefully. "I apologize if I did something... "

"You didn't." Madelyn folded her napkin carefully in her lap.

They drove her home after dinner.

Arthur's car was in the driveway. A light was on in the living room.

She was almost thankful for the excuse to get away from

Billie and Pete. Pete and Billie. The couple was too complicated for her to puzzle out.

She kept thinking of Billie's words.

"Whatever it is, it's all right."

What could that mean?

Anything was fair game?

She looked from the back of Pete's head to the back of Billie's in the passenger seat and wondered what they might do if she were to offer them both a kiss good night in view of the other.

Instead, she thanked them both for the night out and bid them a cordial farewell.

"Oh, and Madelyn." Billie caught her before she could go. "We're having a little Halloween party the twenty-eighth. Please tell me that you and Arthur can come."

Madelyn tried to think up some reason why they couldn't but found none. "I'll check my calendar, but I think we're free."

Billie smiled. "Then we'll count you in." Her lips were red in the fading light of day and Madelyn thought of kissing them again.

But Pete had his hands shoved in his pockets, looking pleased as well that Madelyn had agreed to their party.

The thought of them going up to bed together made her flush. "G-goodnight," she said.

Billie and Pete waved her off and Pete put his arm about Billie's waist.

Which one was she jealous of? Billie or Pete?

She tried to clear her head on the short walk from their driveway to her own.

Arthur would be waiting for her.

Chapter Twenty-Nine

Arthur was on the couch in the living room listening to his favorite Thelonious Monk album. His head was tilted back, eyes closed, as if he could have a migraine, but she knew he was only listening to the music.

Madelyn slipped out of her heels and sat beside him on the couch, listening.

"Where did you get off to?" Arthur asked finally.

Madelyn tapped her foot to the beat of the drum carelessly. "I ran into the Coopers."

"Ah." Arthur nodded without opening his eyes.

They sat in silence as a piano melody took over.

"Mitch agreed to go see a lawyer next Friday. I offered to go along with him." Arthur folded his hands in his lap.

Madelyn let her hand come to rest atop Arthur's head, her fingers playing in the wisps of hair on his scalp. "Thank you."

Arthur relaxed into her touch.

Touch.

Something that only existed in small spits and starts in their relationship. Only so much and never too much. Not since...

And she had kissed Billie again in that awful diner bathroom.

And she wanted to rip Billie's shirt open the way Peggy had ripped Rita's shirt open. Would Billie like that?

She realized the pressure of her nails on Arthur's scalp had intensified and she relaxed her hand again.

"Was she all right?" Madelyn sniffed.

Arthur shrugged. "She drank a bit too much. Could barely make it out of the place. Refused to hear anything more about Betsy."

Madelyn sighed. "I'm sure she cursed me when I left. I just couldn't... "

Arthur patted her hand that rested on her thigh. "It's all right."

He was so kind. He was so patient with her. And she loved him in her own unconventional way.

Madelyn leaned back on the couch, letting her head rest on Arthur's shoulder. "Billie thinks she's embarrassed."

Arthur nodded. "You've told them then." It was not an accusation, merely an observation.

"Some of it." How could she have not?

Arthur considered this. "Yes. Rose probably is, but there's no reason to carry on the way she does."

"Well... " Madelyn shrugged. "We tried."

They sat that way until the record played itself out.

"I'll be off to bed." Arthur kissed the top of her head.

She slipped away from him.

As he rose, he fell into a fit of coughing.

She stood with him; concern etched in her brow as she went to fetch him a glass of water. "It's sounding worse," she admonished.

"It's nothing," he said when he caught his breath again. "Nothing," he repeated.

He took the glass of water and went up the stairs.

Madelyn stood in the middle of the living room and put her arms about herself.

Her heart raced a thousand miles a minute.

She went to Arthur's study and closed the door and sat down in the chair in the corner, then dialed the familiar number.

It rang and then rang, and she wondered if she would be out.

But then a breathless, tired voice picked up, "Madelyn, is that you?"

"Did I wake you?" Madelyn looked then to the clock and found that the hours had moved forward, and it was nearing ten-thirty.

"No, darling," Carole's voice was low and hoarser than Madelyn ever remembered it being. She was not sure why it was making her feel strangely. "What's the matter?"

Madelyn laughed. "Nothing and everything."

They spoke for an hour about Rose and Betsy. Carole listened astutely, inquiring when an inquiry was needed, suggesting when Madelyn asked for suggestions.

"Do you think she is?" Madelyn pondered aloud.

"Embarrassed?" Carole said around an exhale of smoke. "Certainly. No one wants to have a child that's different. That was incredibly difficult for her. She doesn't have the perspective you have, though. Betsy came from her, so she feels as if she's done something wrong."

Madelyn had thought this through a thousand times before. She'd had nearly eighteen years to ponder this, but she hadn't a clue how to approach her daughter about it.

"I should try and talk with her." Madelyn sighed, rubbing her forehead.

"Billie said that about her?" Carole seemed stuck on Madelyn's causal inference to the new neighbor.

"Yes," Madelyn affirmed and did not understand the slight change in Carole's tone when she spoke the name. Billie.

"You've gotten close," Carole mused.

Madelyn thought of kissing Billie again.

"Not so close." Madelyn twirled the phone cord around her fingers for the hundredth time, not liking the change in Carole's voice at the mention of the new neighbor.

"But she knows about Betsy." But not about Pete, went unspoken.

"Sure. She's a good listener." Madelyn felt as if she needed to defend her. "You know, I think you rather disapprove of the new neighbors."

Carole tsked on the other end. "How could I disapprove of them when I don't even know them?"

"Well." Madelyn fell silent.

What had come between her and Carole?

Was it that she could not vocalize to her the things that Billie did to her?

It was growing late.

Madelyn wondered if her neighbors would be asleep by the time she hung up with Carole and dragged herself up the stairs. She did not want to go to bed alone again.

If only Carole could be there, sitting with her.

It was nearing midnight.

"We kissed," Madelyn whispered. And then was horrified that she'd said it aloud.

But it had been her only recourse to relieve her conscience. To topple the wall that had come between her and Carole.

"Kissed," Carole repeated the word, sounding more alert than she had in the past half hour.

"Yes." Madelyn clutched at the phone cord.

"Billie... and you?" Carole dared to clarify.

Madelyn nodded her head up and down. At the memory of the drive-in movie theater – like they were teenagers – and then the stolen kisses in between.

"My."

"What does it mean?" Madelyn asked because she was

finally able to ask the question that had been haunting her since it had first happened.

"Do you think her husband knows?" Carole asked, riveted.

"I don't know. I don't know... " Madelyn closed her eyes and curled to her side on the chair.

"Perhaps you should ask her," Carole said it as if it were the easiest solution.

"Whatever it is, it's all right."

"Do you think... ," Madelyn whispered but couldn't fathom that Pete would know and that Billie would know and that they might know together.

"I haven't a clue about this sort of thing," Carole responded cooly.

The wall was still up between them.

Madelyn wondered if Carole judged her.

Though Carole had never judged her before. Carole had always been accepting of Madelyn and her alternative marriage arrangement. It had always been something avoided, a secret she had locked away inside of herself until she had reached out to Carole. And Carole had warmed to her, accepted, and understood it.

But what was it in the fact that she had now kissed another woman?

Would it change things?

They lapsed into silence again.

"Is everything all right, Carole?" Madelyn curled her hand more tightly around the phone receiver.

The silence stretched on.

She listened as Carole exhaled.

"Don't ask me that."

Madelyn wanted to grasp her, to shake her awake.

"I don't have what you have, Mad." Carole's voice was smaller when she spoke again.

Madelyn shook her head no, but Carole's words began to

seep in.

Madelyn had her own bank account. Madelyn made her own money.

Carole had always been Frank's wife and nothing more. She'd birthed him two children.

She was a wife and a mother.

Madelyn was a wife and a mother and a professor and...

"I wish you were here," Madelyn said instead.

Carole was quiet on the other end. "It's late."

Madelyn felt something painful in her chest at Carole's dismissal. She wanted to take back having told her about the kiss.

They said goodbye to one another and as soon as they hung up Madelyn immediately missed Carole's voice in her ear. She missed Carole's warmth, missed their connection.

She went through the house, turning off lights as she went.

She poured herself a glass of water at the sink and peered out the window.

The lights were out in the house next door.

They would be asleep.

She went up the stairs in the dark.

Arthur's room was quiet.

Madelyn took off her clothes, hanging her skirt in the closet, tossing the rest in the hamper. She went to the bathroom naked and started a bath.

She made it hot and sank down into its recesses until it went cold.

Getting up, she brushed her teeth, set her hair, lotioned her face, pulled on a nightgown, and slid into the bed.

It was a fitful night, devoid of sleep.

Chapter Thirty

He rolled to the side of the bed.

She pressed her legs together. Afterwards coursing through her veins. Content and confused.

Pete rummaged for his cigarettes.

She didn't think she could move just then, so she laid and stared at the muscles on his back.

She watched the smoke rise from his cigarette.

Since he wasn't facing her, she dared to ask, "You like the things that your wife writes?"

Pete froze amid reaching for his shirt. He turned to look at Madelyn with a smile on the corner of his lips. "Sure, I do."

She pulled the sheet around her naked body. She was fully aware of his gaze.

"She... has she ever... " But with him looking at her she couldn't ask the question that had floated about in her mind for days. Weeks.

Since the kiss.

Pete smiled. "You seem to be a fan of her writing."

Madelyn's cheeks warmed at the implication. "Oh, I... "

Pete laughed. "Billie's always been... free with her affections. I thought I'd marry her to straighten her out."

Madelyn eased up in the bed. "So, she has been... "

"With women. Sure, she has." Pete smiled then got up to walk across the room shamelessly to the bathroom. "You know," he called out to her, "she likes you a great deal."

She had kissed Madelyn. Was that what he meant by a great deal? She wanted to ask but couldn't bring herself to voice the question. Pete was Billie and Billie was Pete. It did not make any sense, and yet it did.

"Do you like that she... " Madelyn had pulled herself into a seated position by the time Pete returned to collect his trousers from off the floor.

"As long as she comes back to me... " Pete pulled his briefs over himself. "You're certainly curious today. Has she done something?"

Madelyn flushed again. "No." And she got up and went to the bathroom, closing the door.

So then. There was no knowledge between them. Billie did not know, and Pete did not know, and it was only she who knew.

And guilt crept in.

She did not take lunch with Pete. Instead, she kissed him in the parking lot of the diner and went back to campus.

The college students were wound up from the approaching holiday. They wore thicker sweaters and huddled together indoors.

Madelyn walked through the campus and inhaled the misty afternoon air. The scent of fall, of the change of season. The trees were golden yellow and crisp red, the campus greens now brown and crimson with fallen leaves.

How so much had changed in such a short period of time and yet it seemed as if nothing changed. But life was ever changing, ever moving forward from one season to the next. The cycle completed in perfect harmony. Predictable. Safe.

And yet, she was no longer who she had been.

The week drifted on.

Billie called to inform her that the Halloween party that Saturday was to be a costumed affair.

Arthur wore a Western looking shirt and some boots he kept in the back of his closet. Madelyn slipped into some black pants and a black turtleneck, wrapping a colorful scarf about her neck and a beret atop her head. She would be a painter in Paris and he a cowboy from the West.

The party was in full swing when they arrived that Saturday evening.

People Madelyn had never seen before littered the usually tidy suburban home. She could tell that it was not a party intended for the neighbors.

She looked without seeing the group about her – for there were no familiar faces to latch onto – and finally found Billie at the center of the living room, head of red hair thrown backward, laughing, accentuating her long neck. Her body was on display in a revealing little negligee that was passing as some kind of a costume. Her legs were encased in fishnets that left nothing to the imagination.

Madelyn wanted a drink.

Arthur appeared at her side with two tumblers of something green. He shrugged at her, and she sipped it and found that it was some kind of a gin cocktail.

"I don't recognize a soul," Arthur said beside her.

"Me either," Madelyn mused, her eyes locked on Billie and the young man standing beside her, hanging on her every word.

Except, Madelyn realized as she stared a bit closer, that it was no man at all.

It was a woman.

Passing as a man.

In a suit.

Hair trimmed neat and short.

It seemed like a very committed Halloween costume.

Billie's eyes landed on Madelyn from across the room. Those brilliant eyes lit up into a smile. Her hand landed on the man-woman's arm, something whispered to the person before Billie turned and was coming towards Madelyn.

"You came!" Billie exclaimed, wrapping her arms about Madelyn, kissing both of her cheeks. She was more than tipsy. "Arthur, you're quite something tonight. I didn't expect you to have a pair of genuine cowboy boots!" She kissed both of his cheeks.

Madelyn felt a hand at the small of her back and turned to find Pete standing beside her. His made-up eyes sober, smiling at her. "I'm glad to see you." He leaned down to press his lips to her cheek. Just where his wife had kissed her.

He was wearing a cape, all in black just as Madelyn. His eyebrows had been painted upwards into points, eyes lined so that they looked so beautifully clear and feminine.

"Isn't he a handsome vampire?" Billie clasped at her husband.

"Quite a look," Arthur commented with a smile.

Madelyn felt Billie and Pete's eyes upon her, as if waiting for her approval. She sipped the green drink again and smiled at them, at the way Pete had his arm around Billie. "Very handsome." She nearly choked out.

"You must meet everyone!" Billie clasped at Madelyn, pulling her through the crowd. She introduced her to nearly everyone they collided with. And at first Madelyn did not notice the difference in the people. They were all done up for Halloween. A man dressed as a woman, a woman dressed as a man, two men whispering close, a woman sitting atop another woman's lap. The drinks had been flowing, certainly it could explain all the merriment away. Couldn't it?

And then Billie pulled Madelyn to the man-woman she had first seen. "And this is my dearest friend, Liv."

The man-woman extended her hand. "And who might this enchanting creature be?"

"Madelyn," Billie said the name with great reverence.

"Ah, *the* Madelyn?" Liv had a knowing look on her face.

Billie laughed. "Yes, our new neighbor. Isn't she spectacular?" Billie turned to look at Madelyn. "You're absolutely gorgeous this evening. I like you in pants."

Madelyn felt her cheeks warming. To be praised and appreciated in this way. So openly.

She was not accustomed to it.

"Oh." She lowered her head, busying her lips with her drink.

She saw Arthur talking to another older gentleman in the corner. He was good at finding something to do with himself.

His eyes met hers and he offered her a familiar smile.

The party shifted. Madelyn ended up on a couch near Liv.

She could feel the other woman's eyes upon her, looking her over.

"So, you're the neighbor," Liv said after lighting a cigarette. "I bet you find Pete and Billie rather... eccentric. No one thought they'd end up in a place like this, "she spoke as if she thought the neighborhood was a dump.

"I rather like them," Madelyn said, a bit tipsy on her second green concoction. "I wouldn't say they were eccentric."

Liv scoffed at that. "Then you hardly know them."

And Madelyn felt as if she were an outsider. That perhaps she really did not know who these people were.

She had shared a bed with Pete, had kissed Billie, but what did she know of them?

These people around them were not like anyone she had ever met before. They were... colorful. A word her mother had once used to describe people when they did not fit in.

Madelyn looked around the room and began to grasp just what sort of party this was. Just who these people were.

It did not put her off.

It felt dangerously intoxicating.

The woman beside her was not wearing a costume. The woman beside her dressed as a man. The woman beside her was a woman who carried on with women lovers.

"I suppose I don't know them well enough." Madelyn sipped her drink and felt drunk.

Billie had floated toward them, she collapsed on the couch beside Madelyn, practically draping herself atop Madelyn's lap. Her arm went about her. "Is Liv playing nice?"

Liv huffed. "I always play nice."

Billie rolled her eyes and leaned across Madelyn to kiss Liv. Right on the mouth. "Perhaps you're jealous."

"Jealous." Liv sighed. "You're drunk."

Billie laughed at that, turning her big, sparkling eyes to Madelyn. Drinking her in. "Are you enjoying yourself?"

Madelyn did not fit in at such a party. She was accustomed to boring faculty dinners. The same Johns and Patricks and Janes and Judys. She was not accustomed to women dressed up like men named Liv.

Nor the pair of men in the corner who were now kissing one another with a surprising fervor.

"Certainly." Madelyn smiled.

Billie laughed, taking Liv's cigarette for herself. "I suppose it's not your crowd."

Madelyn shook her head. "No, it's... it's... it's very nice."

Billie pressed a kiss to her cheek and was pulled away again.

Liv cursed her for taking her cigarette. "You know," she said as she pulled another from a case. "I can't figure it out, but both of them are taken with you." She lit the cigarette and exhaled in a thin straight line.

"I certainly don't understand it either," Madelyn said.

They settled back on the couch.

Madelyn sipped her drink.

Arthur made his way toward her. A tired look on his face.

"Liv, this is my husband. Arthur," Madelyn spoke when he came to stand before them.

Liv reached out to shake his hand. "How d'you do?"

"Very well." But Madelyn could see that the smoke was bothering him. The migraine was coming on. "I think I might go on home, but don't leave because of me," he said.

"I won't be long," she said when he leaned over to kiss her chastely.

He stopped to say good evening to Pete, who was standing near the door, and then disappeared around the corner.

"Your husband is charming," Liv's voice held a hint of sarcasm and Madelyn wasn't sure if she resented it or not.

"He is," Madelyn decided to say as Pete came to sit beside her.

"Is Arthur under the weather?" Pete asked as his arm went behind Madelyn to rest on the back of the couch. His body was warm and large where it pressed against her.

Madelyn had not realized how keyed up she was until she shifted to re-cross her legs. "Headache," she said simply.

Liv was looking at the two of them. As if she knew something.

"Where's that wife of yours?" Madelyn asked, having not seen Billie since she'd been near the fireplace talking animatedly to the two queer men.

"She took over mixing drinks. She gets quite creative when she's three sheets to the wind. Should I refresh your glass?" he asked, noticing that she'd reached the ice of her cocktail.

"I'll go." Madelyn patted him on the knee and got up.

She had the need to get away from Liv's knowing glances and Pete's warm body.

But she could not fathom another drink. So, she stumbled her way down the hall to the bathroom. However, she ran into a line that extended dangerously long. Too many people waiting to get in to relieve themselves.

So, without thinking, she went around the corner and to the stairs, stumbling into two bodies that were wrapped up in the other. She realized, when they both turned to look at her, that it was a pair of women. Two beautiful women. They had just been kissing one another.

They laughed and moved out of her way.

She felt as if she were intruding, but she knew there was a bathroom up the stairs.

She pressed past the two women and clumsily pulled herself up the steps using the railing. The sound of the record player was muted on the second story of the home.

She turned down the hall and went to the bathroom but found that it was locked. Pressing her ear against the wooden door, she could hear the heavy breathing of an explicit act occurring on the other side.

So, she wandered again down the hall to the main bedroom.

Billie and Pete's bedroom.

The bed was made up neatly. The smell of Billie's intoxicating perfume permeated the space.

Madelyn closed the door behind her.

There was no light, save for the faded yellow that bled out from the windows down below. There was the bed against the wall. A chair in the corner. Bureau along the wall, a mirror.

She hadn't a clue what led her forward, but her hand reached out to caress the soft green quilt that covered the bed.

Her eyes traveled upward, and, in the dimness, she saw the painting that she and Billie had purchased.

It went remarkably well with the rest of the room.

Billie had chosen well.

She felt her legs carry her forward, moving towards the bureau across the room. Knickknacks were scattered out across the top of it. An errant pair of earrings, a necklace, a bottle of perfume – that she picked up and dabbed a spritz of it onto her wrist, inhaling the scent of Billie – a picture of a little girl – was it Billie? – and then a picture of an older couple with two children, an enamel cigarette box, a packet of matches.

She played with a golden bracelet, eyes suddenly shifting, glancing out the window.

She looked out across the lawn and saw the window that opened into her own room.

She froze.

She did not belong in *this* room.

What was she doing?

The sound of the door unlatching set her heart hammering away in her chest.

She had been caught. She was an intruder.

She turned at the sound of feet on the ground and instead of Pete or Billie, a couple stumbled in, lips pressed together, not paying her any mind.

"Oh!" she cried, dropping the golden bracelet atop the bureau, startling the couple as she did so.

"Oh ho! We didn't know this room was occupied, sorry!" the man said.

"It's... it's not. I was just... I'm... I'm going." Madelyn made her way quickly from Pete and Billie's room.

She went down the stairs.

She did not belong there. Amongst all these young bohemians. Who kissed who they wanted and made love during a party.

She should leave. She could make a cup of tea and finish the novel she'd started reading and she could forget the things she had seen. The way those two women had kissed one another on the stairs. The way that Liv had looked at her.

She moved for the foyer, but a hand caught her arm. "Where are you running off to?" Billie. More sober than before.

"I think... it's time for me to turn in. I'm an old woman,

you must understand." Madelyn was trying to sound steady, certain of herself.

"I'm sorry if... " Billie's brow furrowed in worry.

"No. No, it was a lovely party. Thank you. For inviting us." She patted Billie's hand and thought of the two women kissing on the stairwell again.

She left Billie staring curiously after her.

Chapter Thirty-One

They spent Halloween at Rose and Mitch's house. Charlotte was now too old to dress up like a little kid, but she wore a full skirt and a nice white shirt, and her hair tied up atop her head with a scarf. She was going to a party with friends down the road. When Madelyn pressed a kiss to her cheek, she caught a whiff of smoke.

Her heart hammered in her chest.

Charlotte was too smart to get caught up in her mother's vices.

The girl looked at her with wide, startled eyes, begging.

And Madelyn let her slip away from her grasp and out the door to her friend's house.

Russell was dressed up like Davy Crockett. He raced about the house pretending to shoot at everyone with his rifle.

Rose was in the kitchen checking on a pot of chili, smoking a cigarette.

She looked up when Madelyn entered with the plate of cookies she'd made the previous evening.

Rose's eyes seemed clear. She was not too far gone, so that perhaps she might be reasonable that evening.

"Mother," Rose said.

Madelyn sat the cookies down on the counter. She wanted to wrap her daughter up in her arms, but it would be impossible, wouldn't it? The woman did not want her near.

"I apologize," Madelyn said instead, leaning against the counter.

Rose turned to eye her again warily.

"For running out the other night. At dinner." Madelyn picked at a plate of crackers Rose had laid out.

Rose shrugged, looking back at the chili, taking a drag of her cigarette. Her hand shook. "It's just infuriating. And you haven't any idea how it feels," Rose said, as if they were in the midst of an argument already.

"Darling, you're right. I don't know. But I do know that I have been there for her since the beginning."

"Oh, don't act like you're some martyr," Rose shot at her.

"Would you stop this?" Madelyn said firmly.

Rose looked at her, startled.

"Madelyn, perhaps you'd like to go with Mitch on the trick-or-treat rounds with Russell and his friends?" Arthur's voice came from the kitchen doorway.

Madelyn took a deep breath. "I want to talk to my daughter, but she seems to make it impossible for the two of us to have a conversation."

Rose was looking at her like a stricken child.

"Dad, why don't you go with Mitch?" Rose said without looking at Arthur.

Arthur touched Madelyn's arm and then she felt him leave the room.

"Would you like a drink?" Rose asked without looking at her.

"Yes." Madelyn rubbed her forehead.

Rose opened the fridge and pulled out two beers. She uncapped them and handed one to Madelyn.

They listened as the voices of children and the two men

receded into the background. There was the shutting of the front door and then only the sound of the record player playing jazz that cut through the air between them.

"Well." Rose looked at Madelyn after stirring the chili.

"Why are you so angry with me?" Madelyn leaned against the kitchen cabinets. "You've been angry at me your whole life."

Rose laughed at this, lighting a fresh cigarette. "Maybe it's not about you." She sat at the kitchen table.

"Then what is it about? What can I do?" Madelyn grasped for something as she sat across from her.

Rose shook her head. "There's nothing you can do."

"You're hurting, Rose. You're hurting inside and you're hurting yourself and everyone around you."

"Don't tell me what I feel." Rose's walls were slowly slipping back up.

Madelyn sighed. It always felt like a dead-end trying to talk to her daughter. "There are facilities... "

"My God! You want to lock me up?" Rose looked at her, wide-eyed. "You're unbelievable."

"Well, what do you expect when you act carelessly, recklessly. Don't you see how worrisome it is?"

"I'm not reckless." Rose rolled her eyes.

"When I find you at that dive with those men... don't you think that's rather reckless? When you're drunk all the time... "

"Don't throw it in my face." Rose's cheeks had colored. She was ashamed. She picked restlessly at her beer bottle. "You have *no* idea. Not a single clue what it's like to be me. You've always had everything so perfectly figured out, haven't you?"

"No! No, I don't have everything perfectly figured out, Rose. I'm as human as anyone else." Madelyn cursed.

Rose looked at her as if she had never seen her before as a real human. Madelyn could feel this in her glance.

"Do you know how hard it is to always be on guard?

Always wondering if I'm going to find you alive and unharmed? I've been worried about you since the day you were born. I didn't want you to be perfect, but I wanted... "

"You wanted more *for* me," Rose stated. As if she knew. As if she had always known. She drank her beer. "Maybe *I* didn't want that for myself."

Madelyn took a deep breath. She had failed, hadn't she? She'd pushed her too hard, had wanted too much. If she could go back, would she have done it all differently?

She looked at Rose and shook her head. No. It could not have been different. Rose was bound to have always been the way she was.

Madelyn leaned forward, reaching her hand across the table to clasp Rose's. "I'm sorry it was so difficult for you. I'm sorry I wasn't there for you more, that I didn't... but you have to know I love you. No matter what, I love you."

Rose's eye twitched, her lips curled. She wiped beneath her eyes, turning away. Sniffing. She squeezed Madelyn's hand and pulled hers away. She stubbed out her cigarette in the ashtray and got up to check the chili again.

"It is difficult," she spoke quietly, staring down at the boiling pot. "To always live in your shadow." Rose said.

Madelyn felt her heart shatter.

It felt impossible to mend things. There had almost been a moment, but Rose had disappeared from her. Again.

The boys came back later. They all ate and then Madelyn and Arthur went home. Arthur went up to bed and Madelyn paced the living room anxiously.

She went to the kitchen and made a cup of tea.

The lights were off at the house next door. She wondered if Billie and Pete would have gone out that evening. She had not spoken to them since the party. She wondered if Billie was sore at her for some reason.

She took the tea up the stairs and drew herself a bath.

As she laid in the watery shroud, she closed her eyes. She thought of Rose, of how if she could only reach out and touch her, grasp her, then perhaps she might have been able to help her... but the woman did not seem to want any saving.

It made her sad to think about. Morose. And so, as she soaped her breasts, she found her mind wandering away from the pain, seeking an escape. Images that she remembered clearly from long ago came back to her. The illustrations she'd found tucked away in some of Arthur's things when they had been returned to him after the war.

He'd seen her looking at them and had apologized to her, but she had told him that they were beautiful in a way, and he had been startled that she should appreciate them.

But they were works of art as any other work of art was, weren't they?

She finished washing herself and pulled herself from the tub.

She dried herself off and pulled on a nightgown. With her hair wet, she padded down the stairs in her moccasins and flipped on the study light. She knew where it would be, up on the shelf in the corner. She pulled it down, careful with the old pages.

She turned on the light over Arthur's desk and laid out the illustrations, carefully flipping through the images of naked bodies. There were couples, but there were also images depicting rooms of people. All naked, the lines of their bodies connected by mouths, hands, penises.

De Figuris Veneris. The illustrations attributed to someone named Paul Avril.

She paused on one. IV.

A man atop a messily made-up bed of decadent green covers and red pillows. A woman straddled atop him, his penis inside of her, his hand near her behind. And another woman stood off to the side. Naked. Watching.

She sank atop Arthur's leather desk chair.

Warm.

She thought of the green of Billie and Pete's quilt atop their bed.

She thought of smoke swirling from Billie's cigarette.

She thought of Pete inside of her.

She put everything back in its place and shut off the lights as she made her way back up the stairs, back to her bed.

The lights were still off across the way. No one was home in the house next door.

She was restless.

She touched herself and slept fitfully.

The sun came up the next morning and she was still aroused.

The thought had seeped in through half-awakened, half-asleep imaginings.

She was to meet Pete that day and the thought propelled her up. She made coffee for herself and Arthur. She wrapped a robe about herself and went out the front door for the newspaper. The day was chilly. Winter was fast approaching now.

She reached the end of her walk and retrieved the fresh smelling newspaper. And just as she stood up to go back inside, she noticed Billie tottering out of her front door, robe slipping off her shoulder, cigarette clasped between her fingers.

They stopped moving as they looked at one another.

A slow smile crept its way onto Billie's face and she held up her hand in a wave.

She was unkempt and ridiculously beautiful.

They met at the place between their driveways, both pulling their robes about themselves to ward off the cold of the morning.

"I'm sorry," Billie said shyly, her voice low and slightly hoarse in the morning and Madelyn pressed her legs together.

"For what?" Madelyn tilted her head.

"The party... I shouldn't have... well, I wanted you there." Billie was smiling, arms crossed over her chest.

Madelyn could see a hint of her cleavage through the opening of her robe. A hint of the low-cut nightgown beneath.

"The party was very enjoyable," Madelyn said.

Billie smiled, bringing the cigarette to her lips. "You seemed uncomfortable," she said after she exhaled.

Madelyn shook her head. "No. I wasn't."

"I'm certain you're not accustomed to parties with... queers." Billie looked at her with an amused little tilt of her head. As if mimicking Madelyn's position.

Madelyn shook her head. "I may be older than you, but I'm not ignorant to the world."

Billie laughed. Pleased. "But let me make it up to you. Do you and Arthur have plans Friday? I'd like to have you over for dinner. Just the four of us, if you'd like."

"That would be nice."

Billie smiled wide. "Great. Then it's a date."

They looked at one another until Billie turned, half-hopping, half-racing back to the warmth of her home. She glanced back over her shoulder to send another smile in Madelyn's direction.

Madelyn returned to her own home. Only then realizing how cold she had been.

Arthur was sitting in the kitchen, sipping his coffee, and buttering a piece of toast.

She laid the newspaper before him and poured herself another cup of coffee. "Billie has invited us to dinner Friday."

Arthur looked at her and she felt the elation at the invitation begin to dissipate. "I have that meeting with the lawyer Friday. We may stay overnight; it sounds like there may be a hearing the following morning."

Madelyn let her hip fall against the counter. "Oh."

Arthur shook out the newspaper. "But don't cancel on my

account. You deserve a home-cooked meal every now and again." He looked at her from behind the newspaper and smiled.

She smiled back.

She went to him and pressed her lips against his cheek before going up the stairs to put herself together for the day.

Chapter Thirty-Two

Feeling the way she did, she surprised Pete by climbing on top of him and taking him inside of her.

He had liked that she had been in control.

She had orgasmed and then he had and then they had collapsed onto the bed.

"Billie likes it that way," he spoke as he lit a cigarette.

And she felt a fresh wave of arousal overcome her.

"I hope you don't mind if I talk about her... "

"No. Not at all." Madelyn let her hand fall across her sweaty forehead.

Pete grinned and leaned over to press his smoky lips to her own. "You're a marvel."

"Why is that?" she asked, slick and warm all over.

Pete shook his head. "You just, surprise me."

She showered and put herself together.

Pete was sitting on the edge of the bed with his hat in his hands when she emerged.

"I suppose I'll be seeing you for dinner Friday." He smiled at her.

"Yes." She checked her hair and her lipstick in the mirror. "But Arthur can't make it. He has to go into the city."

"Oh." Pete's expression was unreadable. "Then it will just be the three of us."

Madelyn's heart pounded in her ears. "Yes, I suppose it will."

Chapter Thirty-Three

There was a faculty meeting, a thesis review with one of her doctoral students, the usual pile of assignments to grade, classes to teach, and then there was Friday evening.

Arthur had left before she got home.

The house was quiet.

She put on the radio to fill the void and made a batch of cookies, putting them in the oven with a timer as she went up the stairs to shower away the day and look through her closet for something to wear.

What to wear?

She heard the timer on the oven buzzing.

She put on her robe and went down the stairs, pulling out the still soft sugar cookies. She had never messed up a batch of sugar cookies. She placed them atop the stove to cool and went back up the stairs.

She was nervous.

She contemplated her options. It would be casual, wouldn't it? There was no need to be formal. She disregarded her black dress and also the blue dress.

She opted for a nice, pressed pair of slacks. The perfect

autumn color with a matching shirt and cardigan. There. She looked very nice as she stood at her sink and retouched her make-up, her lipstick. She tucked her hair along the side of her face and pulled it into a low bun at the base of her neck.

Her hand shook ever so slightly as she wiped again beneath her lip.

When she stepped out of the bathroom, she caught sight of the clock on her bedside table.

She was almost late.

She went down the stairs and arranged the cookies atop a platter and covered it in cellophane. She slipped into her loafers and a coat. The night had grown cold.

She turned out the lights - save for one in the kitchen in case Arthur were to return that evening – and went out, down the drive.

Everything smelled of autumn, of chimneys put to work and leaves being burnt somewhere off in the countryside near town. It was sweet and nostalgic.

She walked to the house next door and went to the front door. Lights shown out on the front lawn. She could hear their voices talking to one another through the door, then footsteps moving closer when she rang the bell.

Her heart was pounding wildly in her chest when Billie opened the door.

She was wearing slacks and a sweater that stretched tightly across her chest. Her lips were a deep red that complimented her hair. She pulled Madelyn inside.

"You needn't look so frightened. It's only me." She toyed with Madelyn, pulling her into a tight embrace before leaning back, her eyes searching Madelyn's before their lips met for the briefest of kisses.

"You made it," Pete's voice boomed in the hallway and Madelyn stepped away from Billie. "Hasn't my wife any manners at all? Let's get you out of this coat." And Billie took the cookies from Madelyn as Pete helped her out of her coat, hanging it in their coat closet. Billie had disappeared into the kitchen and Pete escorted Madelyn into the living room.

He looked handsome in pressed pants and a knitted sweater.

"How about a drink?" he said, moving toward the minibar in the corner. "What'll it be?"

But Madelyn wasn't sure alcohol was the solution for this evening.

"How about a scotch, on the rocks," Pete suggested.

"Make that two." Billie appeared again.

They all sat apart from one another. Pete in his chair near the fireplace which crackled with glowing flames and smoking wood. Madelyn took the side of the couch and Billie sat down cross-legged on the ground, near both of them.

It was very casual, so very informal.

"... she'll need to have a guardian. Mitch could only make it work today, I suppose. It will be a process, I guess they're meeting with the lawyer again and then will have some opening procedure tomorrow, so they'll stay in the city. Arthur hates driving at night anyway." Madelyn was explaining her husband's absence.

It all felt so far away in Pete and Billie's living room. Another life entirely.

"It's wonderful that you care so much for her." Billie sipped her drink, her eyes not leaving Madelyn's face.

"I only wish my daughter might be more involved with her." Madelyn rolled the ice cubes about in her drink, watching as they tumbled about in the liquid. She felt nervous.

"Perhaps this will force her to get more involved," Pete suggested.

Madelyn shrugged.

She could not bring herself to look up. She could feel both of their eyes upon her. Watching her intently.

The fire was warm.

She was uneasy but there was no reason to be.

Was there?

"Well, we're certainly glad you could make it this evening," Billie said, as if trying to clear the air.

Madelyn glanced up at her.

What was this?

Billie sipped the last of her scotch and moved to stand. "Shall we eat?"

They moved to the dining room. The table was set so that Billie was on the end of the table and Madelyn was across from Pete. A triangle.

Billie served soup to each of them, a basket of warm bread sat on the table in the middle, candles flickered in a holder. Pete refreshed their drinks before he settled down in his seat.

The chatter was sparse, the alcohol frightening because it made Madelyn warm and hazy. Yet she still felt rigid, on edge.

"Do we make you uncomfortable?" Billie asked.

Madelyn looked up, shocked by the forward tone of her voice.

Billie's elbows were poised on the table, enchanting eyes gazing right at her. Almost seeing through her.

She could feel Pete glance from his wife to Madelyn.

"Billie." Pete sighed.

"Well." Billie sighed.

Madelyn let her spoon fall against the side of the soup bowl. "I'm not... I'm not uncomfortable."

"Then what is it?" Billie let her hand fall lightly on Madelyn's hand where it rested on the table.

Madelyn thought she should pull away, that it was inappropriate since Pete was watching them, but when she glanced up, she saw something curious in Pete's gaze.

"What is this?" she asked. "What is going on here?" Her voice was small.

Billie removed her hand, crossing her arms before her on

the table, leaning forward. She looked at Pete, who looked at her, and then turned back to Madelyn.

"Pete and I... " Billie, for the first time since Madelyn had met her, faltered momentarily. She fumbled for a cigarette from a pack that sat beside her. "Pete and I like you. A great deal."

Madelyn looked from Billie to Pete and then back. She lifted her hands. "Yes, you tell me quite often how much you both like me, but I... "

Billie lit her cigarette. She looked into Madelyn's eyes as she exhaled a cloud of smoke. Her pink tongue darted out to lick her upper lip. She looked down as she tapped off ash from the end of the cigarette. "Well, you see, it isn't fair." Her voice was low and smoky when she spoke.

"What isn't... " Madelyn's heart was beating rapidly against her rib cage.

Pete's head was bowed.

"That I'm left out every Wednesday afternoon." Billie's eyes met Madelyn's, a stream of smoke escaping from between her red lips.

Madelyn felt her cheeks flush, her throat dry. "I should go." She moved to stand, but Billie put her hand on her arm.

"Don't go."

Madelyn sat back in the chair. "I don't know what it is you want from me, but I... "

"We don't want anything that you're not willing to give." Billie was looking at her.

"You're frightening her." Pete took the cigarette from his wife's fingers.

Madelyn stared between the couple.

It had been there the whole time.

This thing amongst them, pulling them to this moment.

Madelyn drank back more of the scotch to steady herself.

"Madelyn, I'm not upset with you. Do you see? I only want," Billie swallowed, "I want to be involved."

Madelyn's cheeks flamed again.

"Do you understand?"

Madelyn did understand.

Billie's worried brow smoothed over and a smile curled her cheeks upward.

Pete was smiling. He seemed pleased.

Billie stood, hovering over Madelyn. She let her fingers trail down Madelyn's cheek, the perfume on her wrists was intoxicating so near. "Would you like that?"

Madelyn's breath was shallow.

She could tell that Pete was watching them. Her eyes darted to his and he gave her a reassuring grin.

Billie's eyes did not stray from her face, so that when Madelyn looked up at the other woman, she felt the wind knocked from her lungs. That look, both intense and intimate.

Billie wanted to kiss her.

And she wanted Billie to.

Billie leaned over, her lips whispering against Madelyn's, barely touching so that Madelyn had to strain, to pull herself upward, closer, closer until Billie's lips covered hers in a searing kiss.

Chapter Thirty-Four

They kissed. Drunk on each other's lips.

Dinner forgotten, fire crackling away in the hearth as they found their way to the carpeted living room floor, a hand up Madelyn's blouse, fingers fumbling over her nipple as her lips pressed against Billie's lips and it took a moment to realize that it was Billie's hand up her shirt and not Pete's and somehow her embarrassment in the moment was abated by the drinks they'd shared and the warmth of her body. Her lips came away from Billie's and she watched as Pete kissed Billie, while Billie possessively touched Madelyn, and Madelyn's eyes dropped to see Pete's arousal beginning to form in his pants.

And Madelyn's eyes felt wide as she regarded them together. So very near and intimate to her.

She was in the same room as them, not across the yard peering through the window.

Pete's hand slid up her thigh, pulling her back into the moment and then she felt Billie's eyes on her as Pete turned to kiss her. He pressed his tongue between her lips and she moaned at the sensation before realizing that Billie was watching them.

225

Madelyn pulled back, shy at her wants.

"Are you all right?" Billie asked.

Madelyn nodded, watching as Pete caressed Billie's back. Their intimacy and knowledge of one another was arousing.

"Can we undress you?" Billie crawled forward on her hands and knees slowly, pleadingly toward Madelyn.

Madelyn sat back, feeling the way her body shook beneath their gazes. Humming with fear and excitement.

"I haven't gotten to see you naked," Billie whispered as she pressed her lips to Madelyn's neck. "God, you smell so nice."

Madelyn felt her cheeks warm.

"I want... ," Madelyn stuttered.

"What is it?" Pete asked, concerned.

Madelyn looked from one to the other, still surprised that they had found their way here.

But hadn't she known?

But people didn't do such things, did they?

"Would it make you feel better if we were all naked?" Billie seemed to read her mind.

Madelyn nodded.

Billie smiled and reached down to the bottom of her sweater, pulling it up and over her head to reveal her bra beneath. Her hair got caught and mussed. She was a vision like that.

Pete was unbuttoning his shirt as Billie undid her pants, moving to slide them down her legs unceremoniously.

Madelyn watched them in the light floating from the fireplace, breathing difficult as they unveiled themselves to her in the warm light.

Pete pulled off his pants and his dick stood erect in his underwear.

Billie was wearing a lacy pair of black underwear.

Pete turned to his wife, kissing her as his arms went about her, unclasping her bra before bending down to suck at her nipple, Billie's eyes fixed on Madelyn.

Madelyn could feel the pulse of her arousal, watching.

They turned to her. As if on command, she began to unbutton her cardigan.

Billie smiled, watching, her breasts hanging beautifully, Pete straining in his underwear.

Pete crawled toward Madelyn, his hands going to the button and zipper on her slacks. Billie helped to remove her shirt.

She shivered before the fire, laid bare.

"Gorgeous, isn't she?" Pete marveled.

"Beautiful." Billie was staring at her intensely.

Billie shifted, came to kneel before Madelyn. Her fingers traced over Madelyn's cheek, trailing down her neck, until her fingers slid beneath Madelyn's bra to fondle her nipple as their lips met. "Very beautiful," Billie whispered.

Pete was kissing Billie's shoulder, embracing her from behind. Madelyn could feel Billie pressing back against him.

"Is this okay?" Billie cradled Madelyn's cheek.

Madelyn nodded bashfully, thinking about how she had them before her, practically naked and she realized she wanted to see what they did together.

She was comfortable with Pete sexually, but Billie was something else entirely. There was a fear, a panic that she hadn't a clue what it was she should do.

"What if we take this upstairs?" Billie suggested.

A bed sounded welcome, wanted.

Madelyn felt Pete's arm go about her as they went up the stairs, as they all crossed the threshold into the bedroom. It was Billie whose arms Madelyn found pulled her down to the bed, tucked her safely beneath her. It was Billie's fingers that freed her breasts from her bra and her lips that suckled delicately, deliciously at her nipples. Her legs shifted against one another and Pete kissed her lips and massaged her hip gently, thoughtfully. Their hands and mouths and tongues seemed to collide together on her person, worshiping her and her body hummed responsively, wantonly.

Billie looked her in the eyes. "Can I touch you?"

Madelyn nodded dreamily, rising to meet the fingers that slipped beneath the only remaining garment she wore.

Billie's touch was deft, practiced. She seemed to know the places that Madelyn knew. It was familiar and Madelyn's legs fell open, inviting her in.

She felt herself dissolve in their sheets, felt both more and less of herself.

Billie's fingers slipped into her, temptingly, teasingly.

Madelyn grasped at the sheets, at Billie's soft hip, wanting more, wanting her deeper.

But Billie slid from her and it was Pete who took down her underpants and climbed on top of her. Billie curved into her side, Pete's arms going about the two of them. He bowed his head to kiss Billie and Madelyn watched, hungry, feeling him strong and hard between her legs, wanting him to finish what Billie had started.

Pete settled back, as if reading her mind, and entered her, moving slowly inside of her, teasing as Billie had. Slow, slow at first.

"Kiss her," he commanded of his wife and Madelyn felt her chin being turned and Billie's lips on hers, tongue slipping inside her mouth as Pete slipped inside of her.

Gradually, he began to move more roughly against her, the speed increasing, the sensation gathering low and intoxicating between her legs. She grasped and moaned and then felt Billie's hand return to touch, to fill in the missing piece and then she was falling, overwhelmed, undone, so that she couldn't take him a second longer and she twisted away from them and fell back against the bed and watched as Pete touched Billie between her legs and then positioned her on her stomach and pulled her hips back to meet his still hard dick.

And Madelyn watched as husband took wife, rough and dirty and passionate.

The missing piece of the puzzle laid out before her. The thing she could not see from her window, being enacted before her.

She listened to Billie's guttural moaning. Sounds she'd never heard from another woman before in her life. It was so raw and beautiful.

And then Pete thrust and groaned and Madelyn watched Billie shudder in his grasp.

He let his hand slap against Billie's behind before extracting himself from her, falling down to lay on the bed. Exhausted, spent.

Billie's red hair was everywhere, and her cheeks seemed flushed in the low light of evening.

She was looking at Madelyn with bedroom eyes as she turned over to catch her breath, to pull Madelyn close to her. "That was all right?"

Madelyn let her cradle her in her arms, nodding up and down as Pete lit a cigarette on the other side of the bed.

Chapter Thirty-Five

She awoke aroused.

Her dreams had been of flesh and pleasure. A garden of earthly delights before the fall. Free.

Billie's face was resting next to hers when her eyes opened.

It was dark still. Night.

They'd somehow made it to the bedroom upstairs. Madelyn nestled between the couple. All naked still. Revealed to one another. As if nakedness were their normal state.

Billie's nipple was visible in the starlight.

Pete snored lightly beside her.

Billie's chest rose and fell, her arm carelessly thrown over her head.

Her nipple was erect.

Madelyn had never before desired a woman this way.

It was something new and yet it felt as normal as her desire for a man.

Two women lying in bed together. The intimacy that it evoked, that any two women together had always evoked. Madelyn was not afraid of this revelation about herself.

She reached out in the moonlit night, hand hovering over the rise and fall of Billie's chest.

The object of her imagination and desires. The woman who haunted her visits with Pete in the hotel room. Now lay beside her. Naked and bare.

But it seemed wrong to reach out, to let her fingers skim over the dark of her nipple.

"It's all right," Billie's voice floated to her, sleepy in the night.

Madelyn startled, her eyes shifting to capture Billie's. She was wide awake, watching Madelyn.

Madelyn shook her head, hand retracted.

Billie chuckled low in her throat. She took Madelyn's hand in her own, splaying it out over her breast.

Billie lay still.

Madelyn's hand covered the supple flesh and then released it, kneaded it gently in her palm, and then let her hand trail over the soft sternum, to the other breast that was laid bare for her. The motions continued again and again.

Until Billie's hand covered hers and led it over the spans of her stomach, downward. "Look at what you've done to me," Billie whispered as she pulled Madelyn's hand between her legs.

Madelyn inhaled sharply.

Her fingers collided with the slickness of Billie's arousal.

"Touch me," Billie hummed, shifting beside Madelyn, putting her arm about her.

Madelyn touched Billie the way she touched herself. And Billie rolled with her motions, her breathing shallow, Madelyn was transfixed by her. Astounded when Billie grasped at her as her whole body shook.

"Jesus," Billie said when she came.

Madelyn rolled to face her.

"Was that... " She was anxious to have pleased Billie.

"More than okay," Billie assured her.

Pete was still slumbering near them.

They stared at one another.

Billie let her fingers push an errant strand of hair from Madelyn's face. "You're marvelous."

And Madelyn felt wide awake.

With want, with a need she could not define or describe.

Billie kissed her gently before sliding away to sit up.

"Where are you going?" Madelyn whispered.

"The bathroom." Billie smiled.

Madelyn watched her as she moved across the dark room. Her body beautiful in motion.

Billie disappeared into the adjoining room.

Madelyn could hear her lift the lid of the toilet.

Pete shifted beside her. She looked at his flaccid dick between his legs then his boyish face relaxed in slumber.

There was the sound of a faucet in the bathroom.

Madelyn had to relieve herself. She was no longer tired, but still hanging on the edge of arousal.

Billie appeared in the bathroom doorway. She'd put on a robe.

Madelyn rolled away from Pete and stood from the bed, moving naked toward the other woman.

They kissed, Madelyn shy. Billie smiled at her.

"I'll make some tea downstairs. There are extra towels below the sink if you'd like to wash up." Billie whispered, pressing her lips against Madelyn's neck and then shoulder as she spoke. "I hope you'll join me if you aren't too tired," she whispered against her ear. "I left a robe on the back of the door for you."

Madelyn nodded and disappeared into the bathroom. She relieved herself and then started the shower. She stepped beneath the strong, hot spray and washed away the moisture between her legs.

When she was done, she wrapped the robe about herself and used one of Billie's combs to brush her hair back into some semblance of order. She used some mouth rinse, swishing it about in her mouth, then spitting it out.

Pete was still asleep when she emerged from the bathroom.

He'd shifted, one arm over his head, the other across his body.

She went out of the room and down the stairs.

Billie was smoking a cigarette with the radio down low, pouring hot water over a tea when Madelyn came into the kitchen.

"What time is it?" Madelyn realized she'd lost track of everything. It felt as if a year had transpired, but, as she glanced toward the clock on the wall, she realized it was not even eleven yet.

"Ten forty-five," Billie said.

"Is Pete..."

"He'll be out like a light for the rest of the night." Billie chuckled to herself.

And Madelyn suddenly felt self-conscious of herself.

That they were both standing in Billie's kitchen, naked beneath their robes. That they had just been naked with one another.

It was such a departure from reality.

"Hey." Billie caught her gently. "Are you all right?"

And Madelyn wondered if she should be going home. If she should leave, but she did not want to leave. "Yes."

Billie smiled. "It's all right that we... because I've wanted it. For some time now. Since I met you, I thought, but... well, I wasn't sure."

Madelyn sat down at the kitchen table. "I see." She clasped her hands before her.

Billie came with the teapot and two mugs.

"I never imagined... " Madelyn closed her eyes and laughed. "Well, I suppose I once imagined something like it."

Billie crossed her legs and stubbed out her cigarette in an ashtray on the table. "I thought you might have the mind for it."

Madelyn was not sure if she should be offended by the comment or not. "Is this something you do... regularly?"

Billie shook her head. "No, not regularly. Once or twice before, but certainly not regularly. Most of my friends are women who only like women. It's rare that Pete and I find a woman who likes the both of us." Billie smiled at the statement.

Madelyn toyed with her wedding band. "I hope you weren't well, I apologize. For going out with Pete."

Billie waved her off, "I encouraged it."

Madelyn looked at her incredulously.

Billie bit her lip in laughter. "Don't be cross with me. I had to know if you might be open. And I liked just how much Pete liked you."

"Did he... " Madelyn felt a bit betrayed, "... tell you about... "

"Some of it," Billie calmly admitted.

Then she poured the tea into the two mugs and placed a sugar cube in each.

But what did it matter? It had come to this. There were no more secrets between them. Not after she had laid bare before them. Both of them.

"But what about you?" Billie twirled a spoon about in her teacup, dissolving the sugar.

"What about me?" Madelyn asked warily.

"How is it that you go off with other people?"

The question did not surprise Madelyn.

She inhaled the aroma of the tea.

"Arthur is impotent." Madelyn sipped the tea. As if it were the most natural thing to admit about one's husband. "Since the first war."

Billie considered this for some time. "And so you... "

"He gave me... permission, I suppose. A gentleman's agreement of sorts." Madelyn exhaled.

Billie nodded, sipping her tea. "That was kind of him."

Madelyn nodded, eyes slipping downward. "He's my... my dearest friend, and I love him. I've always loved him, but I'm not a saint." She shrugged.

Billie smiled again. "He's very lucky to have you."

Madelyn nodded, rubbing her forehead. "And Pete... Pete approves of your... female relationships?"

Billie tapped a cigarette out of a pack. "He's known since he met me. I was with a woman the first time I saw him. I told him it would never work, so he gave me some concessions. Rather modern of him, isn't it?"

"And he... "

"He can do as he pleases, as long as I know about it." Billie smiled as she lit her cigarette. "It's better, I think. If I know."

Madelyn did not understand why she was aroused by this arrangement. Fortuitous that this couple should have happened to move in next door to her. "My." She sighed, lifting the tea cup. "The things people kept hidden behind closed doors."

Billie laughed at this, tapping off ash.

They sipped their tea and then their eyes met.

The arousal had not dissipated.

Billie's hand fell over Madelyn's. "As long as you're here, I hope you know that nothing is out of bounds."

Her fingers stroked the wrinkled skin of Madelyn's hand.

Madelyn laughed nervously.

"What's so funny?" Billie's lip curled upward in amusement.

"You do realize I'm a great bit older than you."

"Oh, I think that makes it even more thrilling." Billie winked.

"I'm serious."

"Well, I'm no spring chicken. I'll be forty in two years," Billie admitted and Madelyn considered that she had never known just how old the ageless women before her was. "What are you? Fifty-two?"

Madelyn laughed at that. "Sixty."

Billie just smiled. "Even better."

"I'm glad you find it so amusing." Madelyn huffed.

"Pete's a goddamn baby. You know he's only thirty-two," Billie whispered conspiratorially.

"Christ." Madelyn had had no idea.

Billie laughed. "Who cares, darling."

"I care," Madelyn cried, but then was laughing. For what did it matter now?

And then Billie had left her cigarette burning in the ashtray and was kissing her again.

They stumbled messily toward the living room, to the couch that Madelyn and Arthur had sat upon the very first night they had met Pete and Billie as a couple.

And Billie kissed a line from Madelyn's lips, down her torso, before disappearing between her legs.

"Oh."

Chapter Thirty-Six

"What did you get up to with the Coopers last night?" Arthur asked after snapping the newspaper in his hands.

Madelyn nearly dropped the coffee cup she'd just lifted from the counter.

Her mind raced with the images of the night before.

Watching Pete fuck his wife, what Billie had done between her legs...

"Oh, just... dinner," Madelyn faltered, sipping her coffee.

Arthur was looking at her over the folded corner of the paper. "Late, I suppose."

"Oh, not so late." Madelyn was looking out the window, out toward their house.

Arthur was sipping his orange juice. "You went to bed early, then?"

She could feel his eyes on her.

She turned to look at him, afraid of what she might see. Afraid that he could know.

He gave her the benefit of the doubt. "I phoned, but you didn't pick up," he said and she thought, in that moment, that he knew.

But he smiled at her and went back to the paper.

She had been in the shower when he'd come home.

Fingers pressed up inside of herself when she'd heard the door downstairs.

Only having arrived moments before. The timing somehow perfect.

They would go to see Betsy.

Betsy.

The lawyer had opened the case and would need to see Betsy. They were to speak with the facility that day about making the necessary arrangements.

And guilt seeped in because Madelyn's mind was a million miles away.

Gone to the bedroom with Billie and Pete.

Her body was burning beneath her clothes.

The things Billie had done to her...

She had not known it possible, and yet it seemed as natural as anything else.

The world fought so adamantly against two men or two women taking up together and yet...

"Shall we be going then?" Arthur had noticed the time.

Arthur drove and for this Madelyn was thankful.

She was distracted with the happenings of the morning. Of Pete waking up and kissing her leisurely as if they had all the time in the world and then Billie's hand on her hip. She had not been certain that she could take more, but her body surprised her.

She was deliciously sore. Arms tired, legs exhausted.

And she had stood at the door with them after, reluctant to leave, but knowing she had to. The question on the tip of her tongue. *What am I supposed to do now?* But she did not ask it.

They pulled up to the facility and Madelyn realized she had not been aware of the journey. Had not seen a single thing as they'd passed.

The building was cold, and unwelcoming and she hated that Betsy lived there. That soon she would not be allowed to live there and then where would she go? Would it be worse or better?

Betsy was not in a good mood. They were ushered away from her, which gave them time to speak with the warden. He was an imposing man. He did not suggest they take Betsy out of the facility, but have the lawyer send someone to interview her.

Madelyn felt as if Betsy were trapped. In this place. With nowhere to go and she wished she could help her but knew that she could do no more than what she was doing now.

It depressed her.

The previous night felt a strange exuberant luxury that she did not deserve to have enjoyed. Not when there were so many real things to be dealt with.

They went to the diner in the town over after saying goodbye to Betsy.

Arthur ordered an egg salad sandwich and Madelyn got chicken salad but was not hungry. She picked at the crust of the bread.

The sensation of the previous night overwhelmed her so that she bowed her head, least Arthur see, and closed her eyes.

"Is everything all right?" Arthur was watching her though.

She nodded. Up and down. Everything was fine.

Arthur looked at her for some time and then let it drop.

She stared out the car door window at the golden red trees as they passed by on the side of the road and thought about how intensely she had come to life at Billie's touch.

Pete had been one thing, but Billie was something else entirely.

A new door opened. A door that could not be closed.

They arrived home and Madelyn's eyes wandered to the house next door. Pete's car was gone from the drive.

Would they be away again?

She wanted to talk to Billie, but there was no reason to do so. Not that evening.

That evening was a faculty dinner.

One night had not been enough.

Her mind wandered back to the previous dawn, when she had not wanted to sleep, as awake and alive as she had been laying on the couch with Billie. But somewhere in the early morning she hadn't been able to keep her eyes open and Billie had been dipping in and out of consciousness. And Billie had suggested they go back to the bed that was too small for the three of them, but Billie had put her arms around Madelyn and had held her naked, her own back pressed into Pete.

Carole.

She thought that perhaps she could call Carole.

But what would she tell her?

She had sounded so distant those nights before on the phone.

A note had come, but Carole had barely divulged anything. Only that Frank was away quite often, and she was bored of Susie, or was it Sharon, who lived next door to her now.

Madelyn longed for her to live next door again. If Carole were still there then perhaps none of this would have happened and Carole would still be warm to her.

She was restless.

She slipped into another shower before putting on a smart suit for the faculty dinner.

She heard Arthur coughing in his study and paused to listen.

It seemed to be getting worse.

She felt guiltier listening to him.

She was remiss in her duties as a wife.

She had taken advantage of his absence.

Had she wanted him to leave her alone so that she might...

They drove to the neighborhood near the college, all lined with the decadently large homes of the previous decades.

She greeted the other professors and was happy to see that Lillian Braxton was there that evening.

She exuded glamor in the midst of academia.

She saw Madelyn and her big eyes lit up with happiness and she air kissed both of Madelyn's cheeks. "You look radiant this evening!" Lillian exclaimed. "What is your secret, you must tell me." She whispered conspiratorially as she looped her arm through Madelyn's and steered her towards a settee in the corner.

Madelyn grabbed for a cocktail as it passed, her cheeks flushed even before she'd had a drink.

Lillian was a straight woman.

And yet Madelyn was warm all over by their contact.

This had never happened before.

She did not trust herself, she moved slightly away from Lillian.

No, it could not be that she was now attracted to every woman she knew.

She glanced around at the other wives and found no one that piqued her interest and so she rest assured that it was only the way Lillian was looking at her, so raptly, so attentively that had made her flush this way.

She unbuttoned the top button of her jacket, sipping her drink.

The secret. Well, it was the sex she had had.

And the thought of it sent off another reel of images that she did not wish to relive in that moment.

Christ, she needed to get a hold of herself.

"... but you know how it is," Lillian was saying and then she was looking at Madelyn. "Are you even listening to a word I'm saying?"

Madelyn was lost.

Chapter Thirty-Seven

She picked up the phone and then settled it back in the cradle.

Arthur had gone up to bed.

She looked out the window to the house next door. It was still dark.

Pete and Billie had gone out.

Nervousness settled in the pit of her stomach. That she had done those things. As if it were nothing.

She was suddenly glad that they were not home.

Carole.

She wanted to tell Carole, but Carole could not possibly understand what she had done.

She stared at the phone.

What did it matter?

Carole was gone.

Frank had taken her away from Madelyn and she hadn't a clue if or when she would see her again, so if she told her...

She picked up the phone and dialed the number.

The phone rang and she hung it up, stepping away from the phone.

She went to the tea kettle on the stove, her mind still

buzzing from the too many drinks she'd consumed at the faculty party. She wanted to think straight, to stop the thoughts from racing through her mind.

As she lit the flame of the stove, the phone started to ring.

Her heart raced in her ears.

She let it ring again, afraid to answer.

But Arthur would find it strange if she let it go on.

The phone rang a third time, and she went to lift it off the cradle.

She heard noise on the other end and then a voice, far off and then nearby to her ear. "Madelyn? Did you call?" It was Carole. High, words slurred a bit.

She could not talk to her like this. "Yes... yes... I called, but... if it's not a good time... "

"It's a wonderful time! Hang on. Just hold on. Don't hang up!" Carole called. Madelyn could hear the clamor of a party in the background.

She waited, thinking she should hang up and call Carole again tomorrow.

But she did not hang up.

She heard the click of another line and then Carole's muffled voice calling for Frank to hang up the other phone.

The party died out in the background.

It was only Carole.

"What is it?" Carole asked, her voice crystal clear.

"I'm interrupting," Madelyn demurred.

"Nonsense. The party is dull. You've saved me from another drink and droll conversation with Larry." And then Madelyn heard a lighter on the other end of the line. "Well, what's the matter?"

Madelyn sighed, pressing her head against the wall near the phone. "I've... " But she couldn't say the words.

It felt oddly like a betrayal. To admit to it when she was still inside of it, living it out as if it were a prolonged fantasy.

Carole exhaled over the receiver of the phone. "What

happened? Is everything all right?" Her voice sounded more sober, worry etched around the edges.

Madelyn shook her head. "Everything's fine... everything's... " Was everything fine?

"Is it Arthur?"

"No." Madelyn choked, her throat suddenly dry.

The tea kettle was whistling on the stove.

She moved to turn off the heat, to pull the kettle away from the flame.

"Is it Rose?"

"No, Rose is... Rose... it's not... " Madelyn said absently as she poured the water over a tea bag.

"Oh, I see." A breath, a pause. "It's the neighbors, isn't it?"

Madelyn closed her eyes and leaned against the counter. "Yes."

"What happened?"

Madelyn bit her lip.

She rubbed a hand over her forehead.

She could not speak the words.

It would become real and not the ephemeral experience it had been.

"Did he hurt you?" Carole whispered.

"No!" Madelyn sighed.

"Well, Christ, Madelyn! Is this a game of charades? I'm afraid I'm a bit too far gone for that right now."

"I slept with them." Madelyn blurted the words.

There was silence on the other end.

For a moment Madelyn thought Carole had not heard her.

Carole exhaled. "Well, you... of course, you slept with the... what's his name? Oh yes, Pete."

Had she not understood?

Madelyn's hand was shaking.

She looked out the kitchen window, glancing out across the lawn. The house next door remained dark.

"What are you saying?" Carole asked. "What do you mean *them*?"

"You know what it means." Madelyn watched the steam come off the top of her teacup.

"Why... but why are you telling me this?" Carole sounded strangely very sober.

But her voice was that of a stranger's.

Madelyn felt as if she could cry.

"Madelyn," Carole's voice had changed again. "I'm sorry. You've caught me off-guard. I... well... so you've been with the both of them, then?"

"It's late." Madelyn did not want to go on about this with Carole.

"Don't... Madelyn, don't you hang up on me." Carole threatened.

"It just doesn't seem like a good time for us to..."

"It's a perfectly wonderful time."

"You're drunk." Madelyn said.

Carole huffed on the other end of the line. "You would be too if you were here."

Madelyn closed her eyes and leaned back against the counter. "I shouldn't have said a thing..."

"Perhaps not." Carole's voice was far too sober on the other end of the line.

Madelyn sank down into the kitchen chair with the tea. What had gotten into Carole? The woman she had once confided in about everything. The one who had encouraged her on several rather risqué conquests. And suddenly, it was all different because it had been a woman... or perhaps it was because it had been a woman AND a man?

She sipped its warm surface, her hand shaking. "I'm sorry I bothered you with it." Madelyn felt chastised.

Carole was quiet on the other end.

Madelyn could hear her breathing.

"I should go," Carole finally spoke, throat strangled.

Madelyn felt so far away from the other woman, from what they had once been. Had Carole become a stranger?

No, she couldn't lose her. Not now.

She would call her in the morning, apologize for the impromptu phone call.

"I'm so – "

"It's late – "

They said in unison.

"Good night, Madelyn," Carole said after a moment.

They hung up and Madelyn felt restless. Alone. Abandoned.

She longed for Carole to be there so that she could see her objection on her face, to understand it better.

She felt as if she'd lost her.

Perhaps the drinks had depressed her, perhaps if she were to reach out again it would be better…

Restless, Madelyn got up and peered out the window. The house across the way was still dark.

She did not think they would come home that evening.

So, she went up the stairs and made herself a bath and afterward she realized just how exhausted she was from her lack of sleep the previous night.

When she got into bed, the dreams and fantasies and realities all swam together in her head and she woke up tangled in her sheets having dreamed of Billie's lips and Carole's face.

Chapter Thirty-Eight

The heaters in the college always ran hot after the first of November.

She was warm beneath her too many layers.

Talking about the impressionist Paul Gauguin.

Without thought she had unbuttoned the front of her jacket and began shrugging her arms out of the sleeves as the words continued to come forth on the history of Gauguin's rather wild life that influenced and transformed his painting style throughout his career.

She had always found him fascinating, moving from place to place, abandoning his career as a stockbroker to pursue the poor life of a painter.

With the jacket removed, she was still too warm.

"... and so, he left his wife and children in Copenhagen to return to Paris... " So that his wife had had to take up the task of raising the children and procuring a job as a French teacher to make ends meet when Gauguin decided to run off...

She touched the buttons on her blouse, but suddenly felt self-conscious. She had elicited the stares of the students. A group of young men sat off to one side and she could feel their eyes on her.

Made freshly aware of her body, she felt ashamed.

And then aroused at the thought of being watched so closely.

The weekend flooded back to her as she slipped the next image into the projector.

She wiped a droplet of sweat from her brow.

It was much too warm.

"... in the 1890s he went to Tahiti and began to capture life there... " The naked women. The child bride of thirteen that he had idolized and then impregnated.

She heard whispering amongst the students. She turned to chastise them that they should not appreciate "The Seed of the Areoi" for its brilliant color palette and depiction of a Tahitian woman, with pert pink breasts – but realized that someone was standing at the door to the lecture hall.

"Professor Turner," it was Ms. Langley, the department secretary.

She had a panicked look in her eyes.

"What is it?" Madelyn turned the next slide about in her hands.

"A word, please. In the hall." Ms. Langley was motioning with her head for Madelyn to follow her, immediately.

Madelyn frowned before turning back to her class. "I apologize for the interruption. Please, excuse me for a moment." She reached for her jacket and moved toward Ms. Langley.

They stepped into the hallway and the younger woman worried her hands together as Madelyn closed the door behind her. "What is all of this about?"

Ms. Langley shifted feet. "It's your... it's Professor Turner."

"What about him?" Her heart began to beat wildly in her chest.

"There was an incident during his seminar. He just... stopped breathing and then... "

"My God." Madelyn exclaimed and then, brushing past

Ms. Langley, pulled her jacket about herself, and as fast as her heeled feet could carry her, she went clamoring down the stairs of the art building, down through the foyer and out into the crisp autumn day and down the sidewalks of the campus, up the small hill, and just there was the philosophy building standing tall and silent as if it all were some bad dream.

Her feet carried her forward, forward into the building.

Someone tried to grab at her, but she shoved the arm away.

She went up the stairs and came across the scene. The silence disrupted.

A tall, broad shouldered man caught her. "Ma'am you shouldn't be here now."

"I'm his wife, for Christ's sake." She pulled her arm with great force away from the man.

"Let her through, let her through," Richard Stillwell said, reaching for her, helping her through the tangle of students and campus personnel. So that she was rushed to the spot where Arthur lay.

His eyes were open. He was looking around with tired embarrassment.

"Arthur." She knelt, reaching for his hand.

His eyes found hers. He looked relieved at the sight of her.

"Arthur, what happened?" she whispered and knew her voice could not be heard over the noise around them.

"We have to get him to the hospital. He lost consciousness," a young man was saying.

"I'll take him, I'll... Arthur can you walk?" Richard was saying.

"I can take him," Madelyn insisted, but Richard shook his head.

"You'll come along."

And so several of the young men helped Arthur up, and Madelyn followed helplessly as they half-carried him outside to the faculty parking lot, to Richard's car.

It all blurred together, sitting in the back seat with Arthur slumped in the seat before her, Richard driving through stop signs and lights in a rush to get them to the hospital.

The intake, the lights, the beeping, the sounds of it all.

And all she heard was the pounding of her heart in her ears.

And she watched Arthur get rolled off down a hallway where she was not allowed, and a nurse was telling her to sit in the waiting room.

She sank down onto the sky blue, cushioned chair she was taken to. Unaware of the world around her. Everything fading away. No thought, no sound, nothing could reach her.

She sat like that for some time.

Blank.

Chapter Thirty-Nine

It was dark outside.

She could tell because the light behind the hospital curtains had faded.

The waiting room was quiet. People had come and gone so that there was only a young black woman sitting in a corner, rocking a baby, waiting for news of someone and an older white gentleman across the way, his hat in his hands, head bowed. And then there was Madelyn.

A door opened.

Madelyn looked up.

It was only a nurse.

She stopped at the reception desk and spoke quietly to the woman sitting behind it.

Madelyn sighed, settling back in the chair.

Her head hurt.

She rubbed her forehead.

She was exhausted and anxious.

The nurse was looking at her.

She sat up, watching as the nurse made her way through the empty chairs and came to stand before her. "Mrs. Turner?"

"Yes." Madelyn sat up straighter.

The nurse smiled. "The doctor would like to keep your husband overnight. He is responding well, but there are tests... "

"Tests?" Madelyn asked.

"Yes, tests that the doctor would like to have done. He would like to keep him overnight to monitor him and then in the morning... "

"Tests." Madelyn nodded.

"Yes, Mrs. Turner." The nurse smiled a little.

"But what is... what does the doctor... "

The nurse smiled again. "I suppose we will find out soon enough. But for now, Mrs. Turner, I'd suggest you go on home."

"Can I... can I see him?"

"I'm afraid he's sleeping just now." The nurse frowned. "It's best if you come back tomorrow, perhaps in the afternoon."

Madelyn wanted to throw a fit. That she had been left there uselessly without a word from the doctor as to her husband's condition and now she was being asked to leave. How dare they?

"Your husband is just fine, Mrs. Turner. Come back tomorrow," the nurse assured her.

Madelyn sighed.

She reached for her purse and realized she hadn't taken it in her haste to get to Arthur.

So, she stood, her body protesting as she unfolded herself to her full height.

The black woman in the corner eyed her enviously.

The nurse continued to smile at Madelyn.

"What about her?" Madelyn motioned to the woman.

"Hmm?" The nurse asked.

"Well, she's been sitting here since before I arrived without a word about her loved one."

"Don't you worry about her, Mrs. Turner. Go on home."
The nurse did not look at the woman.

Madelyn buttoned her jacket and looked apologetically at the woman.

The woman did not meet her eyes.

Madelyn walked toward the exit, but as soon as she got outside, she realized that she was stuck. Without a car. Without her purse. Without anything.

"Damn," she cursed.

Reaching into her jacket pocket, she was relieved to find some change. She scooped the coins out and looked at them, elated when she found a nickel.

There was a bank of payphones just inside the hospital entrance. She went inside of one, closing the door. She dropped the nickel into the slot and dialed.

The phone rang in her ear, and she felt a wave of nausea overcome her, fear gripping at her chest.

"Hello?" The question was asked with a playful laugh, the sounds of a record going in the background. Incongruous with her too bright, too dreadfully somber surroundings.

She shouldn't have called them. Her.

"Hello?" The voice asked again.

"Billie," Madelyn whispered and then cleared her throat.

"Madelyn? Is that you?"

Madelyn was sitting on the curb in the dark when headlights flashed in her direction.

A light rain had descended about her, but Madelyn had scarcely noticed.

Billie jumped from the car and took Madelyn into her arms and hugged her.

She smelled of her perfume. Warm.

Billie put her in her car and drove them away from the hospital, Billie turning up the car heater because Madelyn was shivering. So very cold all of a sudden. Not even the car heater could thaw her out by the time they turned onto the street they lived on.

"Have you eaten?" Billie asked, as they pulled into Madelyn's driveway.

"No. I don't think I could eat." Madelyn stared up at the dark house that lay before them.

It seemed so cold, abandoned, lonely.

"You should eat," Billie insisted. "Come on." And she got out of the car and helped Madelyn out and the duo walked together to the backdoor. "Is there a key?"

"Under the mat," Madelyn said absently.

Billie bent down to fetch the key and unlock the door, flipping on the light switch so that the blinding overhead light illuminated the kitchen.

The house was so quiet.

"Go get out of those clothes. You're soaking wet," Billie instructed. "I'll see what you have to eat around here."

And Madelyn was thankful that Billie was there. Glad that she had called her.

She went up the stairs, undoing her jacket, the buttons on her blouse, the zipper on her skirt. She let it all fall away from her, unrolling her pantyhose down her legs. She shivered in the chill of the evening before slipping into her flannel pajamas, rubbing rainwater from her wrecked hair, and then wrapping a robe about herself.

Something smelled delicious when she came back down the stairs.

Billie had created a feast out of what little was left in the fridge.

"Sit," Billie instructed and Madelyn took a seat at the table and a plate of food was placed before her with a warm cup of tea.

Billie sat down beside her with her own cup of tea, hands clasped about it.

"Are you all right?" Billie asked after a while.

Madelyn shook her head. "I don't... I don't know. They didn't have anything to say."

"But perhaps tomorrow?"

"Yes, maybe tomorrow. Tests. They're going to do tests," Madelyn said as she lifted food on her fork and brought it to her mouth.

Billie watched her carefully.

"He's been coughing for weeks... I just didn't... I did think, but I would have never thought... "

Billie covered her wrist with her carefully manicured hand. Comforting.

Warm.

Warm when everything seemed so awfully cold.

Madelyn clasped Billie's hand tightly in her own.

"What is it?" Billie asked, leaning forward, covering Madelyn's hand with her own.

"I don't want to be alone. Tonight," Madelyn whispered.

The words fragile.

Because she was always so alone, and she should know how to be alone...

Billie patted her hand. "I'll call Pete. I won't go anywhere." She smiled in reassurance, slipping away from Madelyn so that she could go to the phone, lifting it from its cradle and dialing the number to the house just across the yard.

He picked up on the third ring. Madelyn could hear his voice, hear him asking about her. She listened as Billie spoke to him candidly. She would stay the night and no, there wasn't anything he could do just then. A few words and then she hung up and looked at Madelyn. "He sends his well wishes."

Madelyn smiled faintly.

Billie stepped outside to smoke.

Madelyn thought she heard another voice outside and when Billie came back, she had a little night bag in hand.

Pete had been there.

Billie looked down at Madelyn's half-eaten plate. "Is that all you can manage?"

Madelyn nodded.

Billie went about putting away the food – despite Madelyn's protests - cleaning the counters and pans and utensils until everything was sparkly and clean and tidy as it never quite was under Madelyn's watch.

"Do you want a drink?" Billie asked when she was finished.

Madelyn stood from the table. "Why not." And she went to the cupboard where she kept a few bottles of liquor for special occasions.

Billie found two tumblers in the cabinet above.

"Come on." Madelyn took a bottle of whiskey and motioned for Billie to follow.

She turned off the overhead lights in the kitchen and they walked through the dimly lit house, to the stairs. Billie followed close behind her, up the stairs.

Her heart pounded, her head on the verge of a migraine.

But the smell of Billie's cigarettes and perfume was a strange, arousing comfort.

She led the woman to her bedroom, turning on the bedside lamp.

Billie stood awkwardly for a moment at the doorstep, tumblers in one hand, night bag in the other.

"Come here." Madelyn sat on the edge of the bed.

Billie came, settling on the edge next to Madelyn. She put the tumblers between them, and Madelyn poured carefully, a finger in each.

Billie watched her as they drank.

Madelyn stared into the auburn liquid. "We don't even share a bedroom and yet it still feels different without him here."

"It's understandable." Billie nodded, glancing around the room. "It's nice here, though. You have this all to yourself," she marveled, standing to scan the bookshelf in the corner.

Madelyn watched as Billie moved on to the window that overlooked the yard and then out, out toward the house next door, to the bedroom window...

Billie lifted the tumbler to her lips and looked directly across the space between their homes.

She stood, as if in a daze.

A drop of sweat formed on Madelyn's brow.

Her heart was beating rapidly. The alcohol only served to amplify the sound in her ears.

Billie drank again.

"It's curious," she finally said.

"What?" Madelyn rasped.

She could see the shadow of a smile curl its way across Billie's red lips. "I can see right into my bedroom from here. I hadn't realized... " And she turned to look at Madelyn.

The smile did not slip from her lips.

Madelyn could not meet Billie's eyes. She sipped the whiskey instead.

"How about a bath?" Billie suggested.

As if the topic might just be swept under the rug. As if she might overlook what she had learned.

And Madelyn was thankful for the diversion.

Billie disappeared into the adjoining bathroom to run a bath.

Madelyn poured herself another drop of whiskey and then stood up.

Billie was leaning against the side of the tub, fingers skimming over the surface of the water. "It's a little warm."

"I like it that way," Madelyn assured her, slipping into the small bathroom.

Billie's perfume mingled with the steam from the water. Bits of her hair had slipped from her updo and curled about her face.

Billie moved to stand. "I'll give you some privacy... "

"No, it's all right." Madelyn kicked off her slippers, settling the whiskey tumbler on the edge of the sink so that she could remove her robe then her pajamas beneath.

Billie settled on the ground, leaning back against the tiled wall, sipping her whiskey. Watching.

The mirror light was soft and diffused.

She thought that perhaps she should feel self-conscious, but she did not.

Standing naked before Billie.

She picked up the whiskey tumbler and stepped into the heat of the water. An assault to her frozen body.

Carefully she lowered herself into the tub, the heat thawing her weary bones as she did so.

She hadn't a clue what time it was.

She felt exhausted and yet not tired at all.

Not with Billie sitting at the side of the tub, watching her. Or was she monitoring her?

Arthur would be all right, wouldn't he?

She had to assume that things would work out, that they would go on as they always had. That he would come home and be sitting at the kitchen table when she awoke the next morning. As he always was.

Billie's fingers skimmed over the surface of the water. Almost carelessly.

Madelyn settled her tumbler on the edge of the tub and slowly, slowly slid beneath the watery surface.

She scrubbed herself clean and then, when the water had gone cold, she stood, and Billie wrapped her up in a towel.

"Shall I... go to another room?" Billie asked as Madelyn dried herself.

"Don't be silly. Sleep in here. With me." Madelyn smiled a little.

Billie smiled.

They both changed into pajamas and then stood at the sink together brushing their teeth.

Madelyn did not remember having ever shared this bathroom with anyone.

She caught Billie's eyes in the mirror and then looked away. Shy.

They climbed into Madelyn's bed.

At first, they did not touch.

Madelyn lay staring up at the ceiling.

Billie finally turned in the bed. Her warm body enveloped Madelyn, and she held her in her arms until they both fell asleep.

Chapter Forty

The sun's bright, morning rays crawled through the cracks in the blinds, flooding the room with light.

A body was pressed against her.

Someone else in the bed.

The smell of her perfume lingered on the pillowcase and Madelyn's eyes came open at the realization that Billie was still asleep beside her. That her arm was draped across Madelyn still, that little puffs of warm air were steadily pulsing against her arm.

Madelyn's arm was around Billie, holding her close.

They had switched places in the night.

It felt divine.

She never wanted to move, and yet there were the usual morning urges, the growing numbness in her arm, that would force her away from the woman asleep at her side. Her red hair fanned out across the pillow. Wild and unkempt and gorgeous.

Billie shifted in her sleep. As if sensing Madelyn was awake.

Madelyn watched her eyes come open. She looked around until their eyes met.

A slow smile spread its way across Billie's lips.

"Morning." Her voice was rough and hoarse from sleep.

Madelyn smiled, marveling at the brilliance of Billie's eyes as they shone in the oncoming daylight. "Morning," she offered back. "I... " She did not want to leave the warmth of the bed. And yet the whiskeys had done her in. "I'll be right back." And she got out of the bed and was immediately cold as she made her way across the room, disappearing into the bathroom.

She relieved herself and washed out her mouth.

Billie was standing at the bathroom door and slid inside after Madelyn.

Madelyn listened to the noises of Billie in her bathroom as she sat on the edge of the bed.

The bed was warm from Billie's body.

The toilet flushed. The sink ran. Billie emerged with her hair pushed back into some semblance of order.

"Did I kick you in my sleep? Pete's always telling me that I'm a restless sleeper," Billie asked as she walked toward Madelyn, coming to stand between Madelyn's legs, placing her hands on either of Madelyn's shoulders, looking down at her.

Madelyn shook her head. "I was out like a light. But I don't have any bruises, so I think you were very well behaved."

Billie chuckled and ran a hand through Madelyn's lifeless hair. She'd let it dry while she slept so it hung in natural, shapeless waves.

"My God, you're gorgeous." Billie sighed.

Madelyn's arms went instinctively about Billie, pressing her cheek against Billie's soft stomach. She wanted to claim the other woman. To say mine, mine, mine. To never let her return to Pete, to the world outside.

And yet, there was no claim that she could make over her.

And no one would understand what Madelyn was feeling just then.

Women did not have affairs with other women.

Especially not esteemed and well-respected professors.

If it ever got out... no, it was only this morning's indulgence.

Billie's lips upon her lips, the way Billie's body pressed her back onto the bed.

It was not the right time to feel the way that she was feeling. It seemed inappropriate at best, but they were alone together and the feel of Billie so close to her all night had been intoxicating.

The phone started ringing somewhere downstairs.

Billie shifted away from Madelyn.

"Oh." Madelyn sighed, sitting up, running a hand through her tousled hair. She got up, reaching for her robe. "It may be the hospital." She pulled the garment about herself and opened the bedroom door.

She crossed the threshold and knew that the moment had been lost.

That they could not come back to it.

She made it to the phone in Arthur's study before the caller hung up. "Hello?"

"Why the hell didn't you call me last night? I had to learn from the goddamn newspaper that Daddy was in the hospital!" Rose's voice cried out too brightly on the other line.

"Darling, I would have called you, but I didn't have anything to tell you."

"What do you mean? What's the matter with him?" Rose demanded.

Always her father's daughter.

"I don't know, Rose." Madelyn sighed. She could hear Billie's soft footsteps on the stairs.

Would she leave?

"Well, what did they say at the hospital?"

"Nothing. They're doing tests. I'll... I'm going to the hospital. I'll call you later."

"I should... I should be there."

She did not want to see her daughter just then.

"No, I'll... I'll call. As soon as I know anything."

They hung up and Madelyn found anger welling deep inside of her at the thought of her daughter's concern for her father that was so lacking when it came to her own daughter...

"I started the coffee." Billie appeared in the doorway to the study.

Her dour mood lifted at the sight of the woman, wrapped up in one of her satin robes. Her hair cascading down about her face in careless, wild waves.

She held an unlit cigarette between her fingers and nodded toward the back door. "I'll go out to smoke, but I'll make you breakfast and then take you to get your car. I'm assuming it's at the college."

Madelyn marveled at the woman before her. Thought of how her hand had only earlier caressed the soft curve of her hip, her lips...

She nodded.

Billie disappeared and Madelyn went up the stairs to put herself together.

She smelled something delicious cooking when she returned to the kitchen.

She stood in the doorway and watched as Billie turned down the heat of the stove and then looked up to meet her gaze.

Billie's smile was mesmerizing.

"You look beautiful today," Billie said cheerfully.

They looked at one another. The sun streaming in the window. Just any other day, just an ordinary day. And yet Arthur was in the hospital and Billie was making breakfast in her kitchen.

They found one another.

Billie's hand coming to rest on Madelyn's hip, their lips brushing delicately. The smoky, coffee taste of her unpainted lips was somehow intoxicating.

"I'll go change." Billie moved past Madelyn.

They ate across the table from one another, Billie scanning the newspaper Madelyn had retrieved from the front lawn.

Domestic.

Billie's eyes flashed upward and caught Madelyn's overt gaze.

Their eyes held.

Billie's lip twisted upward as she lifted the coffee cup to her mouth, eyebrow quirking upward before looking back at the newspaper and Madelyn continued to gaze.

Unafraid, unashamed.

They got into Billie's car – Pete's already missing from the driveway next door. Madelyn watched as Billie lit a cigarette and then started up the engine.

The drive to the college was not long enough.

The moment was dwindling, and Madelyn did not want to let go.

She pointed the way to the faculty lot. Her car was where she had left it, but she would need to retrieve her things from her office. She would have to face the worried looks of her students and colleagues.

She sighed as the car idled.

Billie's fingers found hers in the space between their seats. Hidden from view.

Fingertips danced together, middle fingers twining together, held.

"It will be okay," Billie said, looking out across the campus.

Madelyn did not believe her.

Chapter Forty-One

Rose was at the hospital when Madelyn arrived. She was pacing restlessly about in the waiting room, a cigarette dangling from her fingers. She looked older than her thirty-six years. She was being too hard on her body. Her body that Madelyn had created, had once held inside herself.

She hated that she was relieved to see her.

"I haven't heard a thing!" she exclaimed when she saw Madelyn.

Madelyn moved past her and went to the reception desk.

The woman seated behind it looked up at her with an annoyed smile. "How can I help you?"

"My husband, Arthur Turner, was admitted here yesterday and I haven't heard a word about what's going on. Is there a doctor or someone I can talk to? Can I see my husband?" Madelyn spoke evenly, but sternly.

The woman before her looked down at her notes. "One moment." She picked up a phone and called somewhere else in the hospital.

Madelyn tapped her fingers against the counter. Fingers that had caressed another woman.

No, it was inappropriate.

They had only shared a bed together. Nothing had... well, it was simply transient. It was not a permanent affliction, surely.

"Ma'am?" The woman was trying to get her attention.

She had spaced out.

"What the hell's the matter with you?" Rose was standing beside her.

"Ma'am, your husband has just been released to room 204. You can take the elevator there. Is she related?"

"She's my daughter." Madelyn sighed.

They took the elevator together.

"Don't smoke in the room." Madelyn smoothed out her jacket. "You know how that makes his migraines worse."

"Don't talk to me like I'm a child," Rose shot back.

Madelyn felt another migraine coming on.

They got off the elevator and walked down the hallway, heels clicking in tandem.

Arthur was sitting up in the bed connected to an oxygen tank.

He looked weak. Weaker than Madelyn ever remembered him looking.

Had he wasted away before her eyes? Without her ever having noticed?

His eyes lit up at the sight of them and she felt an ache in her chest.

"Arthur. Are you all right?" She took hold of his hand.

He squeezed it gently.

Rose took his other hand, and he looked at her.

She was crying.

"Daddy, are you feeling all right?" Rose asked.

He nodded, patted her hand gently.

She leaned down and kissed his cheek.

"Ah, you must be Mrs. Turner."

Madelyn turned to see a young man in a white lab coat standing at the door.

"Professor." She held out her hand.

"Professor, I see." He smiled. "I am Dr. Roberts."

"Well, Dr. Roberts, it would be nice to know just what is going on with my husband. I haven't heard a word since he came here yesterday."

The doctor smiled at her again. She did not like his smile. "As you know, these things take time to diagnose. Might we step outside in the hall?"

"Whatever you have to say, you can say in front of him and our daughter." Madelyn crossed her arms. The pain in her head only intensifying.

The doctor looked from one face to another and then nodded.

"It is my medical opinion that there may be a tumor growing in Mr. Turner's lungs that is causing him to have difficulty breathing."

Madelyn felt her pulse quicken, a ringing in her ears. "But he... he... how is that possible?"

"Was he an army man?"

"Well, he... yes, he served in the first war, but he had a... he had a... it was brain trauma, it wasn't... anything to do with his lungs... "

The doctor was nodding. "I've noticed this in a few other men. It was mustard gas used back then. Even a small amount could have caused issues, especially over time. We're waiting for the X-Rays to see what they show."

Madelyn felt her knees going weak and reached for the side of the bed where Arthur lay to steady herself. "What... what happens now?"

The doctor gave her a sad smile. "We'll see how far along things have progressed. There is chemotherapy for this sort of thing, but it will depend on how far it's spread in his system."

"Why didn't... but I should have... "

She felt Arthur's hand find hers on the side of the bed.

"You're welcome to stay here. We'll have the X-Rays processed soon and then I'll know more," the doctor assured her. He nodded to Rose and then took his leave.

Madelyn sank into a chair near the bed.

"Daddy, you're going to be okay, though." Rose bent over her father, putting her arms around him.

Arthur looked stoically from his daughter to his wife.

Madelyn met his eyes for the briefest of moments and saw some strange resolve in his gaze.

It was the calmness in his eyes that made her own begin to water.

Chapter Forty-Two

Around lunchtime she went to the pay phones in the lobby and called Alfred Mannes, the head of the art department. He assured her not to worry about her seminars, that the assistant professor would cover her classes until she was able to return. She let Alfred know that there were detailed notes and slides in the closet of her office and that Ms. Langley should have a key.

They disconnected the call, and she stood staring at the phone receiver in her hands.

The dial tone drone on.

She hung up the phone and found Rose anxiously smoking a cigarette near the window of the waiting room.

Tears clung to her lashes.

Madelyn went to the cafeteria. She purchased two sandwiches – neither of which looked very appetizing – and then returned to take the seat beside her daughter.

"You should eat something." Madelyn handed her the sandwich.

"I'm not hungry." Rose sighed. The anger had dissolved into exhaustion.

"Neither am I." Madelyn sat back in the chair, surveying the other hospital patrons. All waiting anxiously as they were.

She toyed with the wax paper around the sandwich.

Rose brought the cigarette to her lips with a shaky hand.

"He'll be all right, won't he?" Rose wiped at her cheek.

Madelyn tapped her foot to some unheard rhythm.

"I haven't a clue." Madelyn rubbed her forehead.

"How could you not have known that he was so sick?" Rose was looking at her.

Madelyn took a deep breath.

The past months fluttered through her memory.

She had been with Arthur, but she had not been with him. She had been a million miles away, preoccupied with the couple across the yard.

How could she have not known? Well, perhaps she had known, but she hadn't guessed, had not fathomed that it could be this.

"I didn't think... well, I certainly didn't think... " Madelyn shook her head.

No, the doctor would tell them it was something else. Some other affliction. Perhaps give him some pills and send him home.

A nurse appeared in the doorway; her eyes came to rest on them.

They were escorted back to Arthur's room.

He was sitting up a little more in the bed.

Madelyn kissed his forehead.

Dr. Roberts returned with a large envelope in hand. His face did not betray the news he was about to give.

He flipped a switch that illuminated a white board and placed two black sheets over the illuminated surface, the light filtering through to outline the internal structure of Arthur's body.

Dr. Roberts stood looking at the images for a moment before turning to look at Madelyn and then Arthur, glancing briefly at Rose. "If you'll look here," He pointed to the middle of the image. Madelyn saw nothing but the outlines of bones and blackness. "If you see here, there is a considerable sized tumor growing. Yes, it's quite large."

"What... what does that mean?" Rose's small voice inquired. She sounded just as she had as a young girl.

"What that means is that there is a tumor growing inside your father's lungs and we're going to have to get it out if he wants to be able to breathe properly again."

"Then he'll be all right?" Madelyn felt a wave of relief wash over her. That there was something that could be *done*. Something that could help, that would make everything all right again. That Arthur would come home with her healed. That it would only be his ongoing migraines that plagued him and nothing more.

But Dr. Roberts looked at her with a sad sort of smile. "Let's see how the surgery goes."

Dr. Roberts left and Madelyn sank down into the chair in the corner of the room. Rose paced restlessly until she left them to go to the lobby to smoke and Madelyn was left alone with Arthur.

His body looked so small in the hospital bed. As if he were slowly shrinking, withering right before her eyes.

She went to him, sat on the edge of the bed. She reached out and stroked his cheek.

He caught her hand and held it tightly.

She looked into his eyes and saw a calmness. Perhaps the added oxygen from the mask, going right to his brain. She wondered if his head hurt then or if he felt good.

His fingers tightened about hers.

She felt the threat of tears but did not look away from him.

Knowing what he meant.

"I'm afraid... " she whispered. "Because I've always had you."

He looked as if he were smiling at her, his eyes wrinkled pleasurably.

"Oh, I love you, you know." She laughed a little. "No matter what, no matter who... I am proud to be your wife."

He closed his eyes.

She held his hand tighter.

Tear drops slid from her eyes, seeping into the hospital blanket.

Madelyn did not want to leave when the nurse informed them that visiting hours were over for the day.

She left with Rose. They walked side-by-side to the parking lot.

"You should come for dinner," Rose said when they came to stand near her parked car.

"No." Madelyn shook her head. "Not tonight."

"But you're all alone... "

"I'll be all right," Madelyn insisted.

Rose shook her head. On the verge of tears again.

Madelyn took her in her arms and held her close.

She could almost smell that scent that she remembered when she'd pressed Rose close to her as a young child. An innocence, a nakedness.

"I love you," Madelyn whispered into her daughter's ear.

And then they untangled from one another, and Rose stood crying.

Madelyn gave her a little smile and began walking to her own car. "You say hello to Charlotte and Russell for me."

Rose nodded up and down. "I will."

And Madelyn walked to her car, got inside, and drove herself home. As if it were any other day. As if she had not just learned that Arthur had cancer and that he was resolved to die and leave her. The road ending just like that. A life built together. Forty years with him at her side. Finished.

Had she done it all wrong? Could she have done better? Been better for him?

She pulled into her driveway, glancing at the house next door. It did not appear that anyone was home at that early hour.

And she wanted to be alone.

She needed to be alone to process, to think, to allow her mind to catch up with reality.

She went inside and pulled a beer out of the fridge and sat at the kitchen table drinking, staring idly out the window.

She watched the sun fade in the horizon.

Darkness surrounded her.

The house was silent except for the ticking of the clock.

The beer was empty, and she felt light-headed from having not eaten that day.

She got up to stare into the brightly lit refrigerator but was not hungry.

She closed the refrigerator door, and the kitchen was thrown back into blackness.

She moved through the house. Quietly.

Looking at the pieces of her life as if it were a museum. A monument to a marriage.

She was lonely and spooked so she went to Arthur's study and turned on the lamp. She sat down in the chair in the corner, staring at Arthur's shelves of books.

She inhaled the scent of Arthur that clung to every crevice of his space.

She felt an intense swell of love for him and then a pain that splintered in her chest.

She picked up the phone and dialed the number she knew so well.

The phone rang and she thought she might cry if the person on the other end did not pick up.

Finally there was a click and then a voice. "Hello?"

"Carole," Madelyn exhaled shakily. And she realized then that she was crying, that she had been crying perhaps for some time.

"My God, Madelyn. What's the matter?"

Madelyn inhaled, tried to pull herself together. "It's Arthur."

"Arthur?"

Madelyn found the words and told Carole.

And Carole resolutely said, "I'll be on the next flight out."

Chapter Forty-Three

It was the sound of an unfamiliar engine idling in the street that caught her attention.

She looked at her watch, stomach fluttering at the prospect...

She sipped her coffee and stood from the kitchen table where the newspaper was laid out beside an untouched piece of toast with jam and butter.

She felt dizzy as she moved toward the front of the house. Light pouring in through the windows, illuminating everything. A perfect day had it not been for everything else.

She peeked out the front window just as the back door of the taxicab was pulled open by the cabbie and out stepped a sensible black heel followed by the line of a nylon encased calf. And then the woman appeared in total. A simple burgundy traveling suit. A neat hat pinned in her soft honey blonde hair. She was laughing with the cabbie as he got her bags from the trunk.

Not looking any different and yet she had changed.

And then the woman was looking up at the house, wistfully.

And Madelyn wanted to put her arms about her.

She went to the door, heart racing, at the prospect of coming face-to-face with her again.

Madelyn wondered if she was still cross with her. About Pete...Billie...

Her stomach knotted.

Her hand clasped the doorknob and in seconds she was looking directly at Carole's surprised face. Up close. Her violet eyes shone in the light of the sun. At first her eyes looked startled and then a tender, happy smile crawled its way over her burgundy lips.

Madelyn was wrapped up in Carole's arms in a matter of seconds, enveloped in the forgotten scent of her perfume that mingled with the unfamiliar hint of tobacco.

"My God," Carole breathed against her ear, and Madelyn felt a strange thrill race through her at their closeness, at having Carole in the flesh, standing right there before her.

"Excuse me," the cabbie cleared his throat.

They stepped apart to find the man holding Carole's bags, waiting for his pay.

"Can you put the bags just in the door there?" Carole asked as she opened her purse to pay him.

The bags were left by the door and Madelyn let Carole in as the cabbie drove off down the street.

Carole unpinned her hat and looked about the foyer, drinking it all in. "It's as if nothing's changed and yet..."

Madelyn looked with fresh eyes on the same things she saw every day. The same wallpaper. The same stairs, the same wooden banister, the same doorway into the living room, the dining room, down the hall to the kitchen. She could not see anything different and yet Carole looked as if she had never seen it before.

Then Carole was looking at Madelyn, studying her intensely as if she had never seen her before.

Could Madelyn have changed so much? It had nearly been

a year since they'd last seen one another. Certainly, she could not be so different.

"You look well. Very well," Carole said, giving her that curiously charming little smile that she thought she might never see again.

"You don't look so bad yourself." Madelyn smiled. "Are you hungry? I just made some toast and I have a fresh pot of coffee going."

"I'm famished," Carole conceded and unbuttoned her jacket as she followed Madelyn into the kitchen.

And there was Carole, in her kitchen again. Sitting across from her at the table, sipping coffee as if she had just stopped by before running out to the grocery store. Only this time she had flown half-way across the country to drop in on Madelyn.

"But what do they say?" Carole toyed with the crust of her toast.

Madelyn shook her head. "They'll do the surgery as soon as they can, but there's no way to know just how invasive it will be."

Carole took a deep breath. "God."

"I know." Madelyn did not want to talk about this. About Arthur who was in the hospital instead of teaching at the college across town.

Madelyn should be teaching her Renaissance art seminar at the college across town just now.

Instead, she was sitting across from Carole, sipping her second cup of coffee.

"It's awful." Carole sat back in the chair.

Her eyes traveled from Madelyn's face toward the window over the kitchen sink.

At first Madelyn did not notice the shift in her gaze.

But soon she realized where the woman was looking.

The house that had once been hers. Hers and Frank's.

"The new neighbors have been... helpful?" Carole asked without meeting Madelyn's eyes.

"Oh, sure." Madelyn felt guarded speaking of the Coopers with Carole. Carole had prodded her and now the mere mention of them made her go rigid.

Carole had never minded her stories before.

When there had been Wes, Carole had listened as if living it all vicariously.

Wes.

She rarely allowed herself to think of Wes, Arthur's dearest friend who had lived out of town with his wife. Who came to visit them at least once a year. And somehow Wes and Madelyn had always ended up in bed together at the hotel near the airport before he went home to his wife. She suspected he had always known the score between her and Arthur. Madelyn had thought Wes might be her last affair. Their last coupling the weekend after her fiftieth birthday.

She had felt strangely bereft at his funeral some months later. A heart attack.

Stuck somewhere between friend and widow.

Oh God, she didn't want to think of funerals just then.

"I think you'd like them if you met them," Madelyn said as she settled her coffee cup down.

"I'm sure." Carole fussed with her hair, not meeting Madelyn's eyes.

So, it was a sore subject between them.

Madelyn supposed she could understand it. The strange queerness of the whole thing. She had thought Carole might accept it... understand it, but...

"I'm glad you're here," Madelyn said, letting it drop.

Carole met her gaze. A shy little smile played on her lips.

Madelyn smiled at the sight of her. Lost for a moment.

Carole held her gaze as they marveled at one another.

There was something that made Madelyn look away, catching sight of the clock on the wall. "You can sleep in Rose's old room. I've put fresh sheets on the bed. I'll go to the hospital now to check in on Arthur. I'll leave the keys to his car if you need to get out for anything," Madelyn said as she stood up to clear away the dishes.

"I can help with that." Carole stood with her. "Go on upstairs and get yourself together."

Madelyn was surprised by their nearness, Carole taking the plates from her and pushing her toward the doorway.

They were both startled when Madelyn clasped Carole's slender wrist.

There was a surprised inhale, Carole's eyes dropping before meeting Madelyn's gaze.

Madelyn released Carole and they stepped away from one another. "Sorry," she whispered, suddenly shy in Carole's presence.

She had thought that it might be the same as it had always been, but it was not.

The tension was dispelled when Carole shifted the dishes to one hand and reached out to touch Madelyn's cheek. "You've had an awful shock this week. I'm happy I can be here."

Madelyn clasped her hand. "Thank you."

Carole smiled at her and shooed her away from the kitchen.

As Madelyn drove to the hospital she tried to put her finger on just what was different about Carole.

It was a heaviness that clung to her, she decided. It was something in the way she looked at Madelyn. Different now. Did she find her repulsive? Vile? Because she had done what she had done with the new neighbors?

They would have the evening together. Perhaps Madelyn would uncover what it was then.

Arthur was sleepily laying in the hospital bed when she came. His cheeks were sunken, but he was not on the oxygen now.

How had it all changed so quickly? One moment he had been vibrant and alive – or had he been fading for some time?

His eyes smiled at her arrival.

Madelyn went to him, leaned down to kiss his forehead. "You're better today?"

Arthur tried to laugh at that. "I'm afraid there is no better here, but they're letting me breathe on my own for a bit." His speech was labored.

She stroked his hand clasped between her own. "Carole is here."

"Ah, I'm glad." He nodded.

"Has the doctor said anymore?" Madelyn asked, unbuttoning the top buttons of her coat. The hospital room was warm.

Arthur shook his head. "Not much of anything. They're scheduling the surgery. Soon I presume." He sounded neither relieved nor afraid of it.

Madelyn pulled a chair up next to the bed, sitting at his side. "I had no idea... "

"It wasn't your fault."

Madelyn shook her head, felt the tears sting her eyes. She did not want to cry just then. She sniffed. "You feel all right? You're comfortable?"

Arthur shrugged. "They bring me something passable to eat every now and again. The bed is comfortable enough." He had never been one to complain about things. She thought that he had learned discomfort in the war so that everything else had always been a luxury. And she liked that about him. That he had never complained.

"I want you to know that Mitch and I worked out a trust fund for Betsy, so that she'll be taken care of for as long as she needs. No matter what. And there is money for Charlotte and Russell, for college. You'll have the house, of course, and a little more should you need."

"Darling, don't speak as if you're dying." Madelyn could not look at him.

They were silent. The beeping of a machine counted out his heartbeats. Steady, even. Alive.

"Madelyn," he said her name as he had all those years ago.

She closed her eyes.

"You've been a good wife to me. Better than could be expected after everything... Don't you want to be free?"

A tear slid its way down her cheek.

Chapter Forty-Four

Carole had made her special chicken amandine and there was a chocolate cream pie chilling in the fridge. "Well, we don't have to eat it all today," she said as she removed Madelyn's apron from about her waist.

She had changed from her traveling suit into a black turtleneck and fitted tartan pants. She looked relaxed, as if some of the heaviness had dissipated in the refuge of Madelyn's home that day. When Madelyn happened past Carole, she smelled the faint hint of tobacco again mixed with her fading perfume.

She was not yet used to this new habit of Carole's. It felt like a secret, hidden away from her. Imperceptible, but present between them.

"You didn't have to... " Madelyn tried to protest but Carole hushed her.

The table was already set.

They sat across from one another, Carole serving each of them.

"I didn't call you here to be my wife."

"You were never any good at letting someone else take care of you." Carole half-smiled.

They ate and it was as good, if not better, than it had always been.

"How was Arthur?" Carole asked.

Madelyn looked down at her plate. She shook her head. "It's as if he… "

Carole's hand found hers atop the table.

"They'll perform the surgery, but it's as if he's… given up."

She wiped at a stubborn tear that slipped from the corner of her eye.

Carole squeezed her hand and then got up. Madelyn watched her graceful motions as she moved to the cabinet where she knew Madelyn kept the liquor and pulled it down to pour them each a finger of whiskey. She added a splash of water to each and then brought them back to the table.

The drinks relaxed the evening around them, and they wound up laughing together, after their second glass of whiskey. Carole insisted that she clean up the kitchen and told Madelyn to go put a record on. Madelyn gazed hazily over their vast record collection, thinking of just how many of the albums Arthur had purchased.

She did not want to listen to music that he liked that evening. It felt a strange betrayal to do so.

So, she pulled out a Doris Day album and put it on the player. It crackled and then the instruments started up.

Carole was standing in the doorway, watching her, when she turned.

She brought a fresh tumbler of whiskey to her lips and drank it back.

Madelyn laughed and moved toward the couch.

They ended up sitting on the floor in front of the couch. Their knees touching.

"What's the matter with us?" Madelyn giggled, stealing Carole's tumbler away from her to have a sip since her own was now empty.

"What do you mean?" Carole asked, fighting for her glass back.

"We're stiff." Madelyn sighed. "Off."

Carole drank back the rest of her whiskey and settled the glass on the coffee table before them. "You're right," she agreed.

"What is it?" Madelyn turned to look at Carole. Drunk.

Carole looked beautiful but sad.

Had she always been sad like this, and Madelyn had never noticed?

"Is everything all right?" Madelyn asked, thrilled by their proximity. That she could actually look at Carole and know that things were not right instead of guessing from the sound of her voice.

Carole was smiling, but there was sorrow in her gaze. "No, I don't suppose everything is all right, but I'm... I'm here for you."

"I don't want to think about all of that right now. Let me worry about something else." Madelyn insisted.

"Fine," Carole conceded.

"You're unhappy," Madelyn said.

Carole laughed without mirth. "Oh God, am I ever."

Madelyn frowned. "I wish you'd tell me about it." And she shoved at Carole because she wanted to touch her and because she was angry with her for not telling her about these things over the phone. "It's Frank, isn't it?"

Carole rolled her head slowly back and forth where it rested on the seat of the couch. "He's not cruel, you know. I'm just... bored. Dreadfully bored there. You know my sons have their wives and children and jobs and lives and there's an occasional phone call, we saw them for Christmas, but it hardly feels like a family anymore. And where Frank's taken us... I have nothing in common with those women and he's off doing God knows what all day. I almost suspect that he's taken up with one of the neighbor women – they're always off together talking at parties. But I know him. I know he's a creature of habit and he comes crawling back to me every Wednesday night. On the dot. Whether I want to or not." She stared idly at the ceiling.

Madelyn couldn't look away from the contour of her face, her gentle forehead, her angular nose, the soft curve of her lips, her shapely chin.

"It's really nothing. Just, perhaps a bit of melancholy." Carole shrugged, turning to look at Madelyn.

Madelyn's head was resting against the seat cushion so that their faces were near the other's.

Carole's vibrant eyes scanned Madelyn's face.

The phone was ringing.

Madelyn startled.

Carole sat up.

Madelyn moved to try and stand up but ended up falling against Carole and they laughed, and Carole braced her, helping her up.

"Just a minute... just a minute!" Madelyn cried to no one as she went to the phone in Arthur's study. She was certainly high when she picked it up. "The Turner residence," she said into the receiver.

"What a formal greeting," Billie's voice said on the other end.

A strange twist lodged its way into her chest.

"I meant to stop over, but I noticed you might have company, and I didn't want to intrude." Billie went on.

Madelyn could hear said company moving about in the living room. "Oh, you wouldn't have been. It's my dearest friend Carole. She used to live in your house."

"Ah, I see. That's nice of her to come."

"Yes. She's my dearest friend." Madelyn laughed, listening as Carole moved about. The sound of a door opening, closing. Where had she gone?

"Sounds as if I couldn't compete," Billie flirted.

"Oh." Madelyn felt her cheeks flush red.

Billie asked after Arthur, asked if there was anything she could do. Madelyn assured her she was all right, that things were taken care of, but that she would keep her updated.

And before they hung up, Billie said, "But I do hope we'll get to meet her. This dear friend of yours."

"Oh, yes."

"You'll both come to dinner," Billie insisted.

Madelyn's stomach knotted at the prospect. She noncommittally agreed.

They disconnected and Madelyn listened to the silence of the air around her. The house was quiet. The record had ended.

She moved into the living room again, reaching for a Stan Kenton record that she replaced Doris Day with and then went to the kitchen. It was there, in the darkened room, that she looked out to find Carole wrapped up in her coat, looking out at the pitch-black lawn.

Madelyn watched from her spot in the kitchen as Carole lifted her hand and brought a little dot of glowing ember upward. An inhale made the cherry glow and then a stream of smoke escaped from between parted lips.

The image felt too intimate, too shocking for her to be watching as she was.

She moved toward the backdoor. Opening it, she was accosted by the frigid chill of the night and the smell of approaching winter mixed with the tobacco of Carole's cigarette.

Carole turned at the interruption but did not try to hide what it was she was doing.

"It's freezing out here. You'd better come inside and do that."

"But..."

"Arthur's the one who's sensitive to it." Madelyn held the door open.

"If you're sure…"

"Come inside."

Madelyn fetched an ashtray from the kitchen cabinet and moved back to the living room. Carole had extinguished her cigarette and rid herself of the coat when she wandered back to join her. She looked chilled, albeit refreshed. The sadness had gone from her eyes.

"Well, it's not something I'm proud of, but it helps," Carole said, as if in response to an unasked question.

She let a pack of cigarettes drop on the coffee table, a silver lighter next to it.

"I'm not one to judge." Madelyn patted the spot on the couch beside her.

Carole sat down. "Was that your new neighbor on the phone?"

Madelyn nodded. "She was checking up on me."

"How thoughtful of her."

Madelyn rested her elbow against the back of the couch and pushed her head against her hand. "I don't know what your animosity is toward them, but it's completely out of proportion."

"I don't… I don't have any animosity toward them," Carole shot back. "I don't even know them. Don't be ridiculous."

Madelyn sighed and leaned back on the couch. "You're right. You don't know them."

"Well, can you blame me? It's not so easy knowing that they live in my old house or that they're right next door to you…"

Madelyn turned back to Carole, seeming to understand something. She smiled at her.

"What?" Carole eyed her cautiously.

Madelyn moved closer to Carole, putting her arm about the other woman, holding her close. "So, you have missed me."

"Terribly." Carole allowed herself to sink into Madelyn's side. The closest they had been since her arrival.

"How long can you stay?"

"For as long as you need."

The orchestra swelled to a crescendo and then died out and it was the scratch of the needle against PVC.

They let the static play itself out, winding again and again until the needle stopped.

Carole's perfume was intoxicating, so near her. The feel of her in her arms – perhaps as they had never been together – felt strangely comfortable. Comforting.

Carole's breathing was even, almost as if she'd fallen asleep.

"It's late," Madelyn said then. "You're probably exhausted from traveling. We should get up to bed."

Carole did not protest.

They went around turning off the lights and then Carole followed Madelyn up the stairs. It was on the landing that they paused.

In the dark hallway they stood together, looking at one another.

Carole's eyes were laughing, and Madelyn could not help her own smile. Together again. At last. Only a room away from the other, occupying the same house. No husbands about to interrupt or need anything from them.

Carole clasped Madelyn's elbow and pulled her close. "Sleep well," she whispered and pressed her lips to Madelyn's cheek.

Once inside her own room, Madelyn pressed herself against the closed door and shut her eyes.

Something had overcome her.

The scent of Carole so near her, clinging to every surface, made her warm and aroused.

She held her breath, wanting it to pass, but the feeling did not abate.

She went to the window and saw that the light was still on in the room across the yard.

She willed Billie to appear, but it was only the glow of yellow light that she could see. What would they be doing?

She sat on the edge of her bed and found herself imagining Carole in Rose's room, crawling beneath the floral bedcover, between the blush-colored sheets. And how would she sleep? In a nightgown or flannels or...

She stood up and went about putting herself together for bed.

She heard the flush of the toilet in the hall and knew that Carole was still awake.

She stood at her door, listening, but there was only silence on the other side.

So, she went back to the bed and laid down beneath the sheets and stared at the ceiling.

Until an insatiable urge, wholly inappropriate just then, tugged at her and she gave in, embarrassed by the images she conjured that led her over the edge.

Chapter Forty-Five

There were parts of it that she remembered and parts that were a blur.

It was like some sort of sick joke. That he had known it would happen the way it had.

The surgery had gone well enough, but his body did not recover.

He died the following Tuesday.

There were people who needed things from her. Signatures, funeral arrangements, Rose's tears, the lawyer, the accountant, the college calling her to let her know that they would handle his classes and that she could take the remainder of the semester, if she needed it.

She focused on each task as it crossed her path.

She held Rose in her arms at the side of Arthur's bed after his being had left his body.

She had gone to see the accountant to settle his affairs.

She had chosen a coffin. They already had a burial plot.

Richard had said he would clean out Arthur's office, so not to worry.

And there was Carole at the end of every day to make her eat and put her to bed.

The sun was shining the day they put Arthur in the ground. It was a frigid bright day. She did not cry as Rose did at her side.

And after the ceremony there was a potluck dinner where everyone came to her home, and they all spoke their condolences to her and told her what a wonderful man Arthur had been. And she still did not cry.

And there was Billie and Pete who came and brought her flowers and she wanted to bury herself in Pete's strong arms and melt into Billie's embrace, but she greeted them the same as anyone else.

And Carole happened to pass by at the moment of their arrival so that they were all introduced casually.

There were more people waiting. Billie and Pete moved along into the room, lost in the sea of people.

It was only sometime later when Madelyn got away from the well-wishers that she happened to glance out the window and caught sight of Billie and Carole smoking on the back porch together.

Carole had an unreadable expression on her face as she regarded Billie, something guarded and thoughtful.

It was strange to see them together. Both so very different from the other.

It was wholly inappropriate when her mind shifted to that night, all those weeks before, and the image of Billie between her legs. Then it was thoughts of that morning when she had seen the outline of Carole's naked body in the shower. The pinkness of her nipples.

Madelyn was startled from her reverie when she felt two small arms go about her and she looked down to find Russell wrapped about her.

"Are you sad like my mother is?" He tugged gently at her.

Madelyn bent down to look him in the eyes. "Of course, I'm sad."

"But you're not crying," he stated.

"Sometimes people can't show what they're feeling on the inside." She ran her fingers through his soft hair.

He was so young yet.

He ran off and she was left to circulate again. Allowing everyone to express their exhausting sympathy and praise of the man she had been married to.

And finally, it dwindled down, slowly, slowly. Billie and Pete came to wish her well.

Billie pressed her crimson lips to Madelyn's cheek. "We'll have you to dinner some night soon. When you're up to it."

Madelyn nodded.

Pete kissed her gently on the other cheek. "You bring Carole, too, if she's still around."

"Yes. Yes, I will."

And they left her, and the other guests slowly filtered out until it was only her and Carole in the silence of the big old house.

They sank onto the couch together and Carole took her in her arms and finally the tears that had not materialized arrived. Carole held her until the tears dried up and she had nothing left.

Chapter Forty-Six

Madelyn came down the stairs fumbling to clasp an earring, when she heard the soft sound of Carole's voice coming from Arthur's study.

She paused on the stairs, straining to hear.

"... no... well, you certainly can handle it... I don't know, dear... of course, I – but... I know that you're.... just give me more time... Frank, please... "

Madelyn continued down the stairs, moving toward the kitchen. Away from the study. She pulled down a glass and poured herself some water from the faucet while staring out the kitchen window.

It still felt surreal. All of it.

Arthur's study untouched.

Richard had come to collect the student's assignments from Arthur's desk. They'd had a drink with Carole in the living room and it felt as if Arthur might come through the kitchen door at any moment and join them.

But Richard had taken the papers and had gone away, and Arthur had not come home.

She had not yet had the courage to go into his room so that she knew it was the same as it had been since the morning he'd left. She knew it would be neat and tidy with everything in its place – as her own room never quite seemed to be.

She did not want to disturb it.

So, she left it for the time being.

She drank the water and looked out into the already fading evening, out to the lighted window of the kitchen next door.

She thought that she should not be looking forward to the dinner that Billie and Pete were hosting for her and Carole that evening, and yet she was.

She heard the creak of the floorboards and half expected Arthur to appear in the kitchen doorway.

But it was Carole.

She looked carefully pieced together, eyes alighting when Madelyn turned to look at her.

"Everything all right?" Madelyn asked.

"Hmm?" Carole demurred.

"If you need to go on back to Frank…"

Carole laughed darkly. "Do you want me gone so soon?" Her eyes lacked humor.

Madelyn shook her head. "Of course I don't, but if you…"

"Frank can fend for himself for a while. The neighbors love hosting him for dinner. He'll be just fine without me."

Madelyn was relieved that Carole would not leave her so soon.

"Shall we go then?" Madelyn settled the glass in the sink.

Carole took a deep breath and nodded. "I could always stay here if you…"

"Don't be ridiculous. They want you along." Madelyn went for her coat in the kitchen vestibule. "You made quite the impression on them."

"All right." Carole followed Madelyn, tucking her cigarettes into her own coat pocket, slipping into her heels.

"I'm not sure you'll like what she's done with the place, but it's certainly… interesting." Madelyn commented as they buttoned up together.

Carole rolled her eyes.

Madelyn laughed and then caught Carole's arm. "I am very glad you're staying. Thank you."

Carole's face softened.

After checking that she had her keys, they went out and walked the short distance down the drive and over to the house next door.

It was Pete who answered the door. He looked very handsome that evening. He kissed Madelyn gently on the cheek and then shook Carole's hand, welcoming them both inside.

There was big band music playing on a record somewhere, and the aroma of a roast floated out from the kitchen.

"Well, Carole, have we ruined the place?" Pete playfully goaded.

Madelyn and Pete watched as Carole took in the changes around her.

She finally offered a small smile. "No, no. It's... lovely."

And then Billie appeared from the kitchen, stunning in a simple green dress that complimented her hair.

"We've ruined it, haven't we?" She laughed. "Oh! It's so wonderful to see you again." And she wrapped Madelyn up in her arms and then turned to Carole, kissing her cheek in greeting. "The food is nearly ready. Pete, won't you get our guests a drink?"

And they ended up in the living room with highballs, Carole seated properly on one end of the couch, Madelyn near her and Pete perched on his chair, picking Carole's mind about the house. If she remembered having any water in the basement or if the floorboards had always creaked in the hallway upstairs, and Carole indulged him.

Madelyn could not read her expression. Whether she was annoyed or relaxed.

She fumbled with her cigarettes and Pete sat forward to light one for her.

Madelyn watched the exchange, the way that Carole was

now comfortable with the motions of the habit. She knew just how to draw on the cigarette and hold it with a certain poise.

"It's strange." Carole smirked. "To be smoking in what once was my home." She shook her head. "If anyone had ever smoked here... Frank would have had a fit." She laughed on an exhale, smoke streaming from her lips.

"I'm afraid Frank wouldn't like us very much then." Billie appeared again from the kitchen. "Shall we eat?"

They sat around the table and the food was as delicious as always.

Carole seemed to relax as they ate. She became more animated as she spoke, more comfortable with Pete and Billie, and Madelyn felt herself relax. She realized she had wanted Carole to like them.

Carole offered to help clear the dishes with Billie. Madelyn tried to help, but they both insisted that she go have another drink.

She retired to the living room with Pete, feeling as if Billie and Carole's concern was rather unwarranted. Arthur had died, but she was still capable of living.

Pete handed her a refreshed highball and settled on the couch beside her.

His frame was warm, his arm went about her, and she felt a wave of emotions wash over her. The prickly sensations of want fluttered to the surface.

She wanted to sink into his embrace, to kiss him, but Carole was so near just then and it seemed inappropriate to seek out physical intimacy with anyone. Not so soon... certainly.

"She's real wonderful," Pete said.

"Hmm?" Madelyn turned to look at him.

"Carole."

"Yes," Madelyn agreed.

Pete sipped his drink. "It may not be my place to say it, but she seems to like you a great deal."

Madelyn laughed. "Of course she likes me."

Pete shook his head with a knowing smile on his lips. "I take it she knows... "

Madelyn felt her cheeks flush.

She bowed her head and looked into the amber liquid that was slowly melting ice cubes.

"I suppose that explains it."

"Explains what?" Madelyn shot back.

"... I can't believe I never thought of it," Carole was saying as she and Billie came into the living room together.

Carole paused in her tracks, looking at Madelyn and Pete sitting so near one another on the couch.

Pete stood to refresh everyone's drinks.

"It just made sense to have it there. It saves so much more room in the overhead cabinets." Billie did not seem to notice this exchange. She stopped at a bureau to lift the top of a cigarette box. She reached for two, offering one to Carole.

Carole accepted and Billie held a light for her. Their faces close as fire erupted and then extinguished into smoke.

Billie's eyelashes fluttered as she took Carole in.

Madelyn felt a knot in her stomach, uncertain of which she was envious of.

Pete returned, handing Carole and then Billie a freshened drink. He sat in his chair and Billie sat on the arm of his chair.

He put his hand on his wife's back. She handed him her cigarette.

He was asking Carole something, but Madelyn was in a daze.

Carole came to sit beside Madelyn on the couch, not as close as she had been before. Their eyes met for the briefest of moments before Carole turned ever so to address Pete.

"Oh, many people might find it a wonderful retreat to have sun and the ocean nearby every day, but for me it's rather like being on an extended vacation that I wish would end."

Carole laughed, but her voice lacked humor. He had asked what she thought of her new home.

Billie asked something then.

The conversation flowed cautiously, carefully.

They spoke topically, avoiding the tension that had settled over them.

Madelyn watched as Billie regarded Carole. And when Billie happened to glance at Madelyn, their eyes met, and Billie gave her a knowing smile.

Madelyn was not sure she understood.

They were all tipsy by the time Madelyn and Carole left that evening.

Carole leaned up against Madelyn, their arms linked together as they walked in the chilly night back to Madelyn's house.

Madelyn hung up their coats neatly and Carole poured them each a glass of water as they stood in the kitchen together, looking at one another without looking at the other.

"I hope it wasn't... "

"I can't believe they painted the living room blue. I never would have imagined it, but... well, it's certainly different. Quite bold of them." Carole rubbed her forehead.

Madelyn worried her lip. Madelyn could not read Carole's mood, and wanted to know more of what Carole thought, but felt afraid to ask. "Would you care for a nightcap?"

Carole shook her head. "No. It's late. We should get to bed."

Madelyn nodded.

They left the glasses on the drainboard and climbed the stairs together.

They stood on the landing. Something awkward had settled between them.

Madelyn wanted to reach for Carole, but she did not.

"Sleep well," Carole said as she went off to her room.

Chapter Forty-Seven

The house was quiet when Carole went out to meet her friend, Judy, for lunch. She had invited Madelyn along, but Madelyn had declined. Having never felt all that close with Judy, and she supposed that she was supposed to be in mourning to the outside world still.

But the house's walls were beginning to close in around her.

She was restless at home, walking around with Arthur's ghost.

She slipped into her moccasins and wrapped her coat about herself and went out into the frigid, rainy day.

She hadn't a clue if she would be welcomed, but she rang the doorbell to the house next door and waited, shivering as the northern winds picked up.

The door opened and Billie - tousled red hair piled up atop her head, wearing pants and what looked to be one of Pete's oversized sweaters with her dark-rimmed glasses slipping down her nose – answered the door.

"Madelyn! What a pleasant surprise! Get in here, it's freezing out." And she pulled her in and helped her out of her coat. "I was just about to give up writing for the day. It's not working."

"What's the problem?" Madelyn asked as they walked through to the kitchen.

Billie put a kettle of water on the stove. "I don't want Edith to give into Max too soon. You see Edith is a proper woman from a certain set and she must appear to not want or know what Max is doing to her."

"And Max is a... "

"Female of course." Billie laughed.

"How does Max know that Edith is interested in her?" Madelyn twirled her wedding band about her finger.

She wondered if she should leave it on or if she should take it off. She was not sure what a widow should do.

"Well," Billie placed tea bags into mugs. "Edith always gives into Max's every whim. If Max invites her out to dinner at the last moment – and her husband is otherwise occupied – " Here Billie winked, "Then she goes. And she's always inviting Max over when she has any moment alone. To chat. And now Edith has asked Max along to her vacation home because her husband can't join her, and she doesn't want to go alone."

Madelyn nodded. "I see."

"But how can I keep them apart if they're sharing a house together?" Billie removed her glasses and rubbed her forehead. The kettle was whistling. She lifted it from the heat.

"Well, I'm sure there are separate bedrooms."

Billie thought about this. "And Max is a real gentleman. She'd never cross a line when it came to Edith. She's crazy for her, but she'd respect her wishes to not share a room."

"It could be very erotic," Madelyn found herself saying. "To be so near to one another and yet not... cross that line."

Billie settled down in the seat across from her, a big smile crossing her features. "I think you might have a future in pulp fiction."

Madelyn rolled her eyes and accepted her cup of tea.

"What brought you over here anyway?" Billie reached out and brushed an errant strand of hair away from Madelyn's cheek, tucking it safely behind her ear.

Madelyn felt herself blush. "Carole's having lunch with an old friend." She looked into the steaming black liquid.

Billie twirled the tea bag about in her cup. "You've known one another a long time."

Madelyn nodded. "It feels... somehow... different. Strained. I can't figure it out."

Billie sipped her tea.

"We were always so close."

"You've changed." Billie mused.

Madelyn huffed. "I haven't... I haven't changed. I'm the same as I've always been."

Billie shook her head. "No one stays the same."

Madelyn toyed with the handle of the teacup.

Was she really so different from who she had been before?

She feared that she was changed. It was how she felt now in Billie's presence, how she was beginning to feel toward Carole. A world opening up to her. Something she could not yet grasp and yet felt tangibly.

"She's been your confidant for some time, hasn't she?" Billie guessed as she fumbled with her pack of cigarettes on the kitchen table.

"Sure. I told her... I told her everything. And she never... " Madelyn shrugged. "She never thought less of me for it."

Billie nodded as she lit a cigarette. "I take it she knows... "

Madelyn nodded up and down.

"Well, that can certainly change people's attitudes."

"No, she isn't like other people. She's not... conservative in that way." At least Madelyn had never thought her to be. The details she used to share with Carole had never been tame or reserved and Carole had readily, openly accepted them and had needled her for more. "Am I really so different?"

Billie laughed and shook her head. "No." And she tapped off ash. "But perhaps you feel differently than you did... Before our little tryst."

Madelyn felt a thrill at the mention of it. That Billie should still think of it and could refer to it so easily.

Billie was smiling at her. "You never explored that side of yourself before. Perhaps you didn't recognize that it was even there."

Madelyn felt a shy blush creep its way up her neck. "I... "

"It's all right. You can speak freely here." Billie's hand covered Madelyn's.

Billie's hand thrilled and frightened her. "Does it make me... queer to feel this way?"

"It depends."

Madelyn exhaled a shaky breath. "On what?"

"Well, how you feel about the word queer." Billie managed a laugh.

Madelyn did not feel relieved at having voiced it. "I've never thought anything of it before. I have known a... a homosexual a time or two as a college professor. I can always tell the young men who aren't interested in the opposite sex and there have been young women who pay me special attention. Especially in the art department. It is not shocking to me, only I never... "

"... would have thought of yourself as a part of it?" Billie offered helpfully.

"Yes," Madelyn nearly whispered.

"It's perfectly natural to feel this way. Beautiful even, but society wants to tell us that we should marry someone of the opposite sex and produce children left and right. But that's not exactly how it is, is it? Here I am married but without a child and you were in a marriage of friendship. So, how could that be the only way?"

Madelyn took a deep breath. "But if anyone were to know... "

"Is it different from what you had before?" Billie asked pointedly.

Madelyn felt hurt well in her chest at the thought that someone could see her marriage to Arthur so clearly.

But Billie was not wrong.

"Don't you deserve to have some happiness now?"

Madelyn laughed. "I was... happy. I was... "

"But now you see what could be."

"Oh." Madelyn huffed and sipped her tea. "She's not... "

"How do you know?" Billie seemed to know just who she was talking about.

They both heard the engine that grew ever closer on the street outside, crawling to a stop in the driveway next door.

Madelyn felt her heart pounding. "She's back." She stood. "I... I should go... "

Billie put out her cigarette and rose to walk Madelyn to the door. "Thanks."

"For what?" Madelyn asked as she slid her arms into her coat that Billie held for her, slipping her feet into her shoes.

"Your plot advice. I think I've been reinspired." Billie was smiling at Madelyn when she looked at her again.

Madelyn found herself smiling. "Well, thank you. For listening."

"Any time." Billie leaned in and kissed Madelyn chastely on the lips. "Enjoy it."

Madelyn felt the blush return to her cheeks.

Billie saw her out.

She walked the short distance back to her house, going through the kitchen door.

Carole's shoes were already neatly placed beside the door, her coat hung on the rack, smelling of cigarettes and her perfume.

The woman was absent from the kitchen. She was also absent from the living room and Arthur's study, and the dining room, so Madelyn climbed the stairs.

"Carole?"

She found Rose's old bedroom door slightly ajar.

It was the smell of tobacco – different from Billie's – that accosted her senses, reminding her of when she had caught Rose smoking all those years ago. How she'd hated it, how she'd tried everything to stop it to no avail.

Carole was halfway out of her dress. It hung from her waist, revealing the cream straps of her bra and smooth, tanned skin.

She turned at Madelyn's footsteps.

The front of her revealed. The freckled spans of skin that covered her chest, dipping between her breasts and the soft skin that covered her abdomen.

She did not try to cover herself, but she stood self-consciously. "I didn't hear you come in," she said, reaching for a cigarette burning in an ashtray on the bureau.

"How was Judy?" Madelyn asked, hovering in the doorway.

"Oh." Carole opened a drawer that Madelyn had emptied for her. She reached for a sweater. "The same as always. But it was nice to catch up. She asked about you."

"Did she." Madelyn crossed her arms, watching as Carole pulled the sweater over her head and then slid the dress the rest of the way from her body. Madelyn averted her gaze to the window so as not to see the blush pink satin of Carole's underwear.

"And you," Carole spoke as she slipped into trousers. "You were at the Coopers."

"Yes." Madelyn felt a strange knot in her stomach. That Carole could be displeased with her. "I just wanted to... get out. Get some fresh air."

Carole closed the dresser drawer and lifted the cigarette to inhale delicately at it again.

They looked at one another.

"I see," Carole said coolly. "Perhaps I've outstayed my welcome."

Chapter Forty-Eight

Madelyn stared at Carole as if she had never seen her before.

A stranger standing before her.

Had she ever known this woman?

They used to laugh together, but now there was no laughter.

"What the hell is the matter with you?" Madelyn snapped.

"What's the matter with me?" Carole laughed sardonically. "What's the matter? Nothing is the matter."

"Then why are you running away?" Madelyn insisted.

Carole's eyebrow rose. "Madelyn, I have a husband. I have a life..."

"That you were all too willing to get away from only a few days ago. You can't stand that life, so what changed? I'm not forcing you away. I like you here. I want you here." Madelyn felt anger coursing through her body, suddenly afraid that Carole might slip past her and never come back.

Carole smoked and ran a finger over her brow. She could not look Madelyn in the eyes. "The things you... is that what you..."

Madelyn frowned at Carole's incoherent words.

"You don't *need* me." Carole sighed, settling on the edge of the bed.

Madelyn felt tension release from her shoulders. She moved to the bed, settling atop its surface near, but not too near Carole. "What are you talking about?"

"Billie. And Pete." Carole inhaled shakily.

Madelyn watched as the cherry of the cigarette glowed fiery red. "They haven't replaced you. You're my oldest... my dearest friend. I can't... I can't imagine losing you. Especially if you can't accept... "

Carole stared at her perfectly manicured fingernails. She twirled her wedding band around her finger. "I'm not a bigot."

"I certainly never thought you were."

"It's just one thing to hear about it, but to know them... " Carole's hand was shaking ever so slightly. "Is that what you were up to today?" she asked without looking at Madelyn.

"No," Madelyn said resolutely. "I went to... to talk to Billie." She thought of their passing kiss as she had left, but it was not a passionate embrace. It was familiar, comforting at best.

"But you want... "

"I don't know what I want." Madelyn sighed.

Carole nodded, standing up to put out her cigarette.

"But I do know that I don't want you to leave."

She watched as Carole's shoulders sank.

"A drink sounds good just about now," her voice came out low and defeated.

They made their way down the stairs. Madelyn glanced out the window in the dining room and saw that snow had begun to fall.

Madelyn pulled out the tumblers and Carole fished out the whiskey bottle.

They went to the living room.

Madelyn put a Glenn Miller record on low as Carole poured liquor into each glass.

They sat on the ground together. Only a lamp was on in the corner, casting a warm glow across the room.

They watched as the snow fell outside the window.

"What you did... you enjoyed it?" Carole swirled the liquid about in her glass.

Madelyn sipped the whiskey, feeling warm. "Yes."

Carole nodded.

Madelyn did not turn to look at her. The memory of it flooded her mind as it had not for some days.

Carole sipped at her whiskey, considering something. "I don't... well, you know most women would be happy if their husbands didn't have an interest in it."

Madelyn chanced a glance in Carole's direction. "You've never liked..."

Carole exhaled a held breath of air, an incredulous laugh. "Maybe I'm not like you." She shrugged.

Madelyn could not comprehend that the woman beside her had never felt anything. "Surely you..."

Carole looked down at her lap. "Perhaps in the beginning I wanted to like it." She sipped the whiskey again. Still not looking at Madelyn. "It was never proper for women our age to want *that*. I didn't know what to expect, but it certainly was not what happened."

Madelyn did not speak a word, having never heard Carole speak so frankly with her.

"And then it just... never really got any better." She shrugged. "Perhaps I'm broken."

"No." Madelyn shook her head.

"No?" Carole laughed.

Her glass was empty. The whiskey made her loose and wistful.

Carole reached for the bottle and topped off her glass,

holding it out for Madelyn. Madelyn allowed her to pour a drop more into her glass.

They drank in silence, Madelyn's mind racing a mile a minute. Warm from the alcohol. Warm from Carole's presence beside her, telling her these things about herself.

So intimate and different from before.

Madelyn felt as if she could tell her anything and she would receive it and volley the conversation back.

She tested the theory. "You've never... done it yourself?"

Carole went still for a second. Her head shook. "No. I... I, sure, I tried. But I couldn't... " She toyed with the edge of a book on the coffee table. "You see? I am broken," she finally concluded.

Madelyn laughed. "No, you just haven't had the right experience."

Carole raised her eyebrow. "And it's always so pleasurable and wonderful for you? You certainly make it sound that way, anyway."

"I wouldn't say it's always pleasurable. It depends on the person."

"But you can... "

Madelyn tilted her head. "Yes. I can, but not always. Not always with someone else anyway. I've gotten quite adept at handling myself, though." She was on the verge of being drunk.

Carole marveled at her then looked away again. "Well."

They drank.

Madelyn looked out the window and saw that it had grown darker.

"We should eat something instead of drinking the night away," Madelyn suggested.

Carole agreed, swaying as they went to the kitchen.

Madelyn made them coffee, telling Carole to not fuss and to take a seat at the table. Carole lit a cigarette as Madelyn set to work on a simple stew.

She could feel Carole's eyes trained on her back as she cooked. They spoke of mundane things, but she could feel a question on the tip of Carole's tongue. There was something more she wanted to know.

And it was thrilling and disheartening to know that Carole had never felt what Madelyn had felt. It set her on edge at the idea that she might be able to show Carole what it was to have enjoyment...

No.

Nothing about Carole's demeanor had hinted that she might...

They sat across from one another at the table eating, sobering up. Carole's glances had returned to just ordinary looks. Her questions and answers had returned to friendly chaste comments. Nothing more was spoken of what they had spoken of.

They washed up after they ate and then retreated to the living room with refilled cups of coffee.

"I can hardly have more than one drink anymore," Carole lamented. "All they do down there is drink and I end up with an awful headache the next day. Perhaps I have been drinking a bit more than I used to, but... " She sighed.

"You're unhappy there," Madelyn said from her corner of the couch, her feet tucked up beside Carole's thigh, Carole's feet tucked up beside Madelyn's thigh.

Carole rolled her eyes. "You don't say."

"Stay here," Madelyn said playfully but meant it.

"Don't tempt me," Carole said flatly, not serious.

The Charlie Parker record petered out. They listened as the needle whirled about before coming to a stop.

Madelyn nudged at Carole's foot and maneuvered herself up to flip the record. "It's nice, having you here," she said, back turned to Carole.

When she turned, she found Carole sitting up, rubbing at her shoulder.

"Are you all right?"

Carole rolled her neck. "Fine, fine. Just a little tight."

"Here." Madelyn sat beside her and let her hand replace Carole's, digging carefully into Carole's lithe frame through her sweater. She could feel a knot that she soothed over with her thumb.

"It's all right… " Carole tried to protest but seemed to melt under Madelyn's touch. Her rigid posture slackened. Her pink lips parted and her eyes closed.

It was hardly perceptible over Charlie Parker's saxophone, the little moan that escaped from somewhere deep inside Carole's throat.

Her eyes blinked open, and she moved ever so slightly away from Madelyn, patting her hand. "That's… that's better. Thank you."

Madelyn felt as if she couldn't move. Arousal had overwhelmed her, and she wanted…

But Carole was reaching forward for her coffee, was not the slightest bit concerned with what had transpired between them in that moment.

And then the doorbell rang.

Madelyn's heart leapt in her chest. "Who could that be?" And on a night like this. The snow had only continued to fall.

She hadn't heard a car go by, or perhaps the pounding of her heart in her ears had made her deaf to the world outside her living room in that moment.

She uncurled herself from the couch and walked to the door, flipping on the hallway light as she did so.

She opened the door and found her granddaughter shivering and crying on her front porch.

"Charlotte?"

Chapter Forty-Nine

Charlotte's arms went about her, face burying in Madelyn's chest.

"What's the matter?" Madelyn pulled her inside, closing the door to the frigid night. A car slowly moved down the street. Someone had brought her there.

"I couldn't... I couldn't stay there... she's out... out of her mind." Charlotte sobbed.

"Shh." Madelyn held her close and then helped her out of her coat. It was in this motion that she caught sight of the ugly red welt on Charlotte's cheek. She caught her chin between her thumb and forefinger and examined the girl's face. "She did this?"

Charlotte's eyes watered again, and she looked away from Madelyn.

"I'm going to call her..."

"What's the use? She's sloshed out of her mind," Charlotte whimpered and then looked over Madelyn's shoulder with wide, momentarily frightened eyes.

Madelyn turned to find Carole standing nearby.

Charlotte tried to hide her tears and face by looking down. "Oh, hello, Aunt Carole."

Carole looked with worry at the young woman before her. "Charlotte," she acknowledged the girl. "Perhaps... I should go on to bed."

Madelyn felt something twist in her stomach. A frustrated yearning at Carole's abrupt departure from their evening. Something still not quite right between them, and yet some sort of new awareness of the other.

"You don't have to... , " Madelyn tried to protest, but Carole touched her arm gently.

"It's all right. I have a novel waiting for me," Carole insisted, looking at Charlotte. "I'm glad you've come here. Your grandmother will take good care of you." She kissed Charlotte on the forehead and went up the stairs.

Madelyn took Charlotte to the kitchen, stopping to grab a blanket from the couch to wrap the girl with, and then settled her in the kitchen chair Carole had occupied only hours before.

She went to the phone. "I'm going to at least let your father know where you are."

Charlotte sulked as she wrapped herself up in the blanket.

Madelyn dialed the familiar number, and it only rang twice before Mitch picked up. "Hello?" His voice was tense.

"It's Madelyn. I have Charlotte with me."

He seemed only somewhat relieved at the news. After she hung up with him, she went to the fridge for a bag of frozen peas.

"Grandma?" Charlotte asked.

"Hmm?" Madelyn wrapped the sack of peas in a dish towel and wetted the side of it a bit under the faucet.

"Do you smoke?"

Madelyn turned to find the ashtray that Carole had been using.

"No, darling." And she brought the makeshift ice pack to the girl and pressed it against her cheek. "Hold this here."

Charlotte did as she was told and Madelyn removed the

ashtray to toss the ashes in the trash can, placing it in the sink to wash out.

"Is Russell all right?" Madelyn stopped the water in the sink. Afraid.

Charlotte laughed darkly. "She'd never touch him. Daddy wouldn't allow it."

Madelyn pursed her lips. Displeased.

She reached for the tea kettle on the stove and filled it with water.

"How did you get here? The roads are getting dangerous," Madelyn asked as she put the tea kettle on the stove and lit it.

"Johnny drove me. I-I called him to come after she... ," Charlotte's voice wavered.

Madelyn turned to find the girl shivering, a tear slipping down her good cheek.

"Johnny McMillian?"

Charlotte nodded. "We've been... you know... going steady for a while now."

Madelyn knew his older brother who was at the college. The family was prominent in the community, their father was head of the town's bank. "That was very nice of him. To do that in this weather."

"Oh, he's a very good driver. He was very careful," Charlotte assured Madelyn.

"Well, you got here in one piece," she agreed.

Both avoiding the real issue.

The tea kettle whistled.

Madelyn poured the steaming water over two tea bags and then picked up the mugs. "Come into the living room. It's warmer."

Charlotte gathered up her ice pack and the blanket around her then followed Madelyn to the couch. Where only moments before she had been so close to Carole. Carole who was now upstairs. Would she be reading? Listening? Asleep?

Charlotte snuggled into the cushions, tears slipping down

her cheeks. She took the offered warm mug in her free hand, cradling it against her chest as she held the icepack to her angry red cheek.

Madelyn leaned forward and tucked a strand of dark hair behind Charlotte's ear. "Tell me what happened," she whispered.

Charlotte sobbed. "We got into another fight. Ever since... ever since Grandpa's funeral she's been drinking more. And I... I told her I didn't like it. And she... she got really angry and she... she called me a slut because she thinks I've done things with Johnny, but he'd never... he'd never... he's a real gentleman and I... I wouldn't... and she said I was going to turn out just like her and it got me really upset and I just... lashed out and called her a drunk and then she slapped me."

Madelyn wrapped Charlotte up in her arms. "It's okay," she soothed the girl who cried into her chest. "I'm so sorry."

She wished she could change it. She wished she could make it different, that she could change Rose. She felt disgusted, totally upset that her own daughter could do this to *her* own daughter.

"She's awful," Charlotte hissed.

"She's hurt. But it doesn't excuse... it doesn't make it all right for her to take it out on you. Do you understand?" Madelyn looked into the girl's dark, red eyes. "She really does loves you so much."

"She doesn't," Charlotte insisted.

"She does."

"Then she has an awfully strange way of showing it," Charlotte huffed.

"Sometimes we hurt the people we love the most," Madelyn said and thought she'd heard it somewhere before. But over the course of her life, she supposed she had come to know it was true.

Charlotte looked away from her. "I can't wait to get out of here."

And Madelyn understood the wish. "One day you will. And you can be your own person and make your own decisions and live the life you want. And hopefully you can learn to forgive yourself for your mistakes so that you and others don't have to needlessly suffer," she said wistfully.

Charlotte was looking at her. "Is it... is it really so hard?"

"What, darling?" Madelyn stroked her cheek again, wishing she could hold Charlotte like a baby and keep her locked away from the world and from the pain that came with it. But she was nearly grown, and she knew.

"To be grown up?" Charlotte stared at her warily.

Madelyn half-smiled. "I'm afraid so. But it also depends on how hard you make it for yourself."

Charlotte lowered her eyes. Her body relaxing as she warmed on the couch. Safe. Away from her mother and her drunken tirades. "It's all right that I came here?"

"Of course, darling." Madelyn massaged her shoulders. "I'm glad you came here. You know you're always welcome here."

Charlotte nodded. "I'm so tired."

"Let's get you up to bed," Madelyn insisted. Then remembered that Carole was in the guest room. And Arthur's bedroom was too morose. "You can sleep with me."

Charlotte warmed at the offer.

They went up the stairs and Madelyn glanced to Carole's room. It was silent, but she could see the light was still on through the thin slit beneath the door.

She offered Charlotte some flannel pajamas and an extra toothbrush.

They took turns in the bathroom and then they climbed into bed together, Charlotte moving close to Madelyn, Madelyn taking her in her arms.

The girl was seeking comfort, solace.

"Thank you," Charlotte whispered. Her body was long

and lean. And Madelyn wondered when she had grown taller than her.

She kissed her forehead. "I'll talk to her tomorrow, all right?" she promised.

Charlotte nodded against her chest.

The girl, comforted and protected, fell asleep easily.

Madelyn stayed awake, staring at the ceiling.

and later. And Madelyn wondered what she had given to in that bed.

She loved this girl and... "I'll talk to her tomorrow night," she promised.

She hummed, nodding against her chest.

The girl, comforted and protected, fell asleep while Madelyn stayed awake, staring at the ceiling.

Chapter Fifty

Madelyn could smell coffee brewing downstairs when she slipped silently out from beneath Charlotte's warm body. The girl had claimed her in the night, as if hungry for a body's nearness. Her cheek had looked better in the light of morning. The angry redness had receded.

Madelyn went to the bathroom and then down the stairs to find Carole pouring coffee and smoking a cigarette.

She smiled at Madelyn, a bashfulness warming her cheeks. "How is she?"

"Asleep still," Madelyn said. "She was very upset. And rightfully so. I just... " Madelyn raked a hand through her wrecked curls. "I hope it's not... a pattern. For Charlotte's sake."

Carole frowned, pouring the coffee into another cup for Madelyn. "Here." She handed it to Madelyn, and they stood sipping the dark liquid together. "Rose has never been easy, has she?"

Madelyn shook her head. "No. I just wish... I wish I could have done something. Said something. Anything... "

Carole let her hand fall over Madelyn's. "You did what you

thought best at the time. How she turned out has nothing to do with you."

Madelyn's eyebrow rose in disbelief at the statement. "I need to talk to her." But she had no desire to do so.

Carole squeezed her hand and then turned away to take a final drag of her cigarette before putting it out with tap water and tossing it in the trash beneath the sink. "Shall I make breakfast?"

It felt deliciously domestic.

She was growing far too comfortable with Carole's presence in her home. As if she had forgotten how to make her own breakfast because Carole was an early-riser and usually had the table set and ready by the time she came down the stairs.

"If you'll let me help," Madelyn said guiltily.

Carole laughed. "Get the eggs."

They moved about the kitchen deftly. A dance they both knew well.

Carole seemed more relaxed, but her inner thoughts were concealed behind flipping omelets.

Charlotte's presence had altered whatever they had been on the precipice of the night before.

And Madelyn did not know how to reach inside again, or if they would have a chance to come close to it again.

Perhaps those inner confessions were reserved for the darkness of evening and not the light of morning.

They moved together without the need for words.

Madelyn was laying out the plates when she happened to look up and saw Charlotte standing in the kitchen doorway, wrapped up in a blanket, sleepy-eyed. "Good morning, sleepyhead." Madelyn smiled at the girl.

Charlotte smiled bashfully.

"Hope you're hungry," Carole said as she brought a plate of omelets and toast to the table.

Charlotte stared at the food uncertainly.

She picked at a little of everything but did not seem to have much of an appetite.

"I spoke to Hugh yesterday," Carole said as she bit into a piece of toast and then brushed the crumbs with her long, elegant fingers into a pile.

"Oh?" Madelyn had forgotten that Carole's son lived in the city. Her other son, Morris, had moved to the east coast.

"He invited me to dinner tonight. I forgot to mention it." She seemed, for some reason, to look guilty about this admission. Perhaps regretful.

Madelyn felt her stomach sink. "I see. Well, that's... perfectly all right. I'm glad you'll get to see him and your grandchildren."

Carole smiled somewhat at that. "Yes, I suppose it will be nice." She sipped her coffee.

Charlotte was looking at Madelyn, a question in her gaze.

Madelyn avoided the look, feeling heat creeping across the back of her neck.

The girl looked at Carole and then continued picking at her food in silence.

"The roads seem clear enough," Carole said, not seeming to notice the way that Charlotte was regarding her and Madelyn.

"Then I'll be fine to take Charlotte to school. Would you like to go home first to get your things?" Madelyn glanced at the girl.

Charlotte visibly flinched at the thought of going home.

"Don't worry, I'll talk to your mother later," Madelyn assured her. Inwardly hating the day that was being laid out before her. First, she would have to talk to Rose and then Carole would be off to the city to see her son and their time together would diminish.

How many more days could Carole feasibly stay? Madelyn heard the phone conversations with Frank. He was getting more and more impatient.

And Madelyn was sure it looked a certain way that Carole was still there over a week after the funeral.

"All right. Let me go change." Charlotte took her plate dutifully to the sink and then raced off to change into her clothes.

"I suppose I'll have to go put myself together, then. I haven't had a school run in ages." Madelyn laughed and wiped at her lips with a napkin.

Carole leaned back in her chair. "Don't worry about cleaning up."

Madelyn stood from the table.

She let her hand come to rest on Carole's shoulder.

"Thank you," she whispered.

Carole's whole being went still beneath her touch.

They stayed like that for what seemed an eternity but was perhaps three ticks of the second hand on the wall clock.

Carole patted Madelyn's hand with her own and then rose from the table, leaning down to collect up the plates.

Madelyn looked down at the ground, strangely embarrassed.

Had Carole not felt what she had?

She thought, as she went up the stairs to change, that it might be just fine that Carole went away from her that evening. Perhaps she was hallucinating something that didn't actually exist between them. She needed a night alone.

The drive to her daughter's home was quiet. Charlotte's arms were crossed over her chest, and she stared listlessly out the window.

When they pulled into the drive, Madelyn reached over and took the girl by the shoulders, turning her to face her. "You don't have to forgive her or talk to her right now. Just go and get your things and then I'll take you to school."

Charlotte nodded. They both got out of the car and walked up the snowy path to the front door.

It opened and Rose was standing disheveled and red-faced in the doorway.

"Oh, baby! Oh, honey. I'm so sorry." She tried to reach for Charlotte, but Charlotte slithered out of her grasp and went up the stairs.

Madelyn stood staring at her daughter. She was so angry at her and yet loved her so terribly.

Rose did not look at her. "I don't want to talk to you."

"Well, you're going to, after I take Charlotte to school." Madelyn said firmly.

Charlotte raced back down the stairs in a fresh dress and back-pack over her shoulder. She avoided her mother the best she could.

Madelyn took her the few blocks to the school and then drove back to the large suburban home. That to the outside looked so terribly calm and normal but was horribly broken on the inside.

Rose was smoking a cigarette when she opened the door for her mother.

"I don't want to hear it," she started.

Madelyn closed the door behind her, slipping from her heels, hanging her own coat on the nearby rack. "Have you had coffee?"

Rose trailed her to her kitchen and watched as Madelyn went about working the machine that Mitch had recently purchased.

Rose sat at the counter in her bathrobe, smoking.

When Madelyn turned to look at her, there were tears in her eyes.

"I'm awful." Rose raked her fingers through her hair, rubbing her forehead.

"Do you need an Aspirin?" Madelyn asked, knowing just where she kept the pills.

Rose scowled at her but shyly nodded.

Madelyn went to the cabinet and looked through the

bottles of prescription drugs and wondered just how many Rose could possibly need. She found the bottle of Aspirin and shook two out, taking it back to Rose with a glass of water.

The coffee machine sputtered its ready signal, and Madelyn went about pouring the liquid into two cups. She stirred in a dash of milk for Rose.

She stood in the kitchen, looking at Rose.

Rose smoked the last of her cigarette and butted it out in a nearby, full ashtray. "Aren't you going to say something?"

Madelyn sipped the coffee. "I think you've beaten yourself up enough."

A fresh tear slipped from Rose's eyes. "I didn't mean... I never mean... I just get so... so goddamn... an-angry." She sighed, hands balling into fists.

Madelyn nodded. "You shouldn't take it out on your daughter."

"I know that!" Rose shot off and then wilted again. "She's so... infuriating. She knows too much; she sees too much."

"She made you face yourself." Madelyn leaned against the countertop.

Rose sneered, wiped at her nose. "I'm not... I'm not a drunk. I-I... sure, I like a drink, but I'm not... "

Madelyn looked at her hands wrapped about the mug. "Can you stop it whenever you want?"

Rose cowered. "Sure... I... sure I can."

Madelyn shook her head. "So, all those times I've come to save you from that dingy, awful bar and find you with some man hanging all over you... you could have stopped it?"

Rose flushed and looked away.

"Rose, honey, I'm worried about you. We're all worried about you. We love you. We want you to be okay."

"Bullshit." Rose clasped her ears as if she didn't want to hear it. "Bullshit." She looked at Madelyn and then reached for her cigarettes. "Charlotte can't wait to get away from me and Russell is... is terrified... " She put a cigarette between her lips and lit it. "Mitch would leave me if he didn't already have a girl on the side." She wrinkled her nose in distaste.

"Rose, you push people away," Madelyn held firm.

Tears filled her eyes again.

"You push and push and push."

"Stop it," Rose whispered. "Don't you... don't you think I already hate myself enough?" She looked up at Madelyn. All the sadness in the world in her eyes. "I failed. I'm a f-failure."

Madelyn shook her head. "Perhaps you did. Perhaps you failed, but it doesn't mean you have to fail everyone else around you. The children love you. They *want* to love you. If you went to Betsy, I know she would... "

"Don't. Let's not talk about her." Rose shook her head.

"I think we need to talk about her. She is your daughter, and I know somewhere deep inside you do love her."

"No." Rose was crying again. "No."

"There is nothing wrong with her, darling. She is perfect in her own way. You didn't fail. You did not fail her."

Rose broke into tears.

Madelyn moved toward her, put her arms about her weeping child, holding her as she used to when she was little and came to Madelyn to bandage her up and fix her sadness.

Rose clung to her, held her close as if she wanted to melt their bodies together.

"Shh." Madelyn rubbed a soothing hand over her back, holding her close until the tears subsided.

She kissed the top of Rose's head.

"I love you, Rose."

Rose held her tighter, wanting to believe it.

Chapter Fifty-One

Carole was reading in the living room when Madelyn returned.

Madelyn wondered if she could mask her red eyes, having allowed the tears to fall after she'd left her daughter.

But Carole seemed to notice, never one to miss a thing.

"Is everything all right?" Carole settled her book on the coffee table and removed her legs from the couch, giving Madelyn room to sit down.

Madelyn collapsed on the couch beside her, seeking something in the ceiling above. "I told her she should consider going to an addiction center, you know a facility, and she almost agreed. So, I suppose that's progress. And I encouraged her to come with me on Saturday to see Betsy."

"Do you think she will?" Carole asked.

Madelyn shrugged. "Your guess is as good as mine."

They sat back on the couch together.

Carole's leg was warm near her own.

"God, I miss teaching. Perhaps I shouldn't have agreed to sit out the end of this term." Madelyn rubbed at her forehead. "I need something to... to do."

Carole laughed. "I like that about you. You're never afraid to work hard."

Madelyn eyed her. "You would have made an excellent teacher, you know."

Carole took a deep breath. "Frank never wanted me to work."

The conversation ended because it was fruitless to persist. That Carole had always been smart and wise. Had always delighted in reading an essay or two when Madelyn was short on time, that she had helped to streamline one of Madelyn's courses, that her mind had not been put to good enough use. And it angered her.

Madelyn wanted to say, "Don't go back to him," but she couldn't.

Carole suggested some lunch.

They made sandwiches in the kitchen and then ate with the radio playing in the background.

"When will you go?" Madelyn stared at the clock and saw that the day had worn on. That it was nearing three.

"Oh, perhaps around five." Carole shrugged, wiping her hands on a napkin.

"Do you think the roads will stay clear tonight?"

"Well, if they get bad, I'm sure I could stay in Hugh's extra bedroom," Carole decided. "It didn't look like any snow would be coming tonight though. Perhaps tomorrow."

And Madelyn smiled at the thought of being trapped inside with Carole for another snowy evening. How she wanted to go back to before Charlotte had come knocking on her door the previous night.

They cleaned up after their late lunch and then Carole went up the stairs to put herself together.

Madelyn picked up the novel Carole had been reading. *Women in Love.*

It was from her own shelf.

She smiled to herself at Carole's choice.

The day was growing dim when Carole descended the stairs, smelling of perfume and the faint aroma of her cigarettes, in a proper dress, hair sprayed into place, pearls in her ears. One would think she was going on a date with a man.

"What will you do?" Carole asked, opening her purse to check for her things.

"Oh." Madelyn shrugged. "Perhaps I should start looking over Arthur's things. See if I come up with a hidden stash of money or something," she joked but was distracted by Carole's presence.

Carole gave her a funny look. "There's a roast in the fridge if you're hungry."

"You make it sound as if I'm your incapable husband," Madelyn huffed.

Carole laughed at herself then. "If the roads become too much, I'll call. But I should be back before eleven."

Madelyn went to her to see her out. They made their way to the front door and Madelyn helped her into her coat. Then they stood facing one another.

"Drive safe," Madelyn said to fill the silence.

Carole smiled.

Their eyes danced before Carole looked away, reaching for the doorknob.

She was out the door in a matter of seconds.

Madelyn could hardly breathe. She leaned against the closed door; the wind knocked out of her lungs.

She listened as Arthur's car started up and then faded away down the street.

She could not stay cooped up in the house all night feeling the way she felt. Or perhaps she could. Perhaps she should walk up those stairs and into her bedroom and then...

She caught sight, through the dining room window, of the house next door.

She could tell, through the dimming evening, that someone was home next door. A light was on in the kitchen.

Billie.

She pulled on her coat and boots and went out the kitchen door and across the driveway to the sidewalk that connected to the driveway next door.

She rang the doorbell and waited, anxious.

Billie appeared on the other side, a curious smile pulling her lips upward. "Well, well, well. Get in here!" She pulled Madelyn inside and almost instantly Madelyn's lips were on Billie's, kissing her.

She realized what she was doing and bashfully pulled away.

"I'm sorry. I'm so... I'm so sorry." Madelyn fell against the wall in the hallway, breathless and embarrassed.

But Billie was just smiling at her. Amused. "What a welcome," she finally quipped and turned to lead Madelyn into the living room. "I think you might be the inspiration for my current little writing project. Edith just gave over to Max's gentlemanly seduction. Their second night alone in the country house."

"How did she do it?" Madelyn asked, glad that Billie would not humiliate her for her untoward, frustrated behavior.

"Well, would you like a drink?" Billie eyed her as she stood at the minibar.

Madelyn acquiesced as she sat on the couch.

Billie pulled out two tumblers and went to work making highballs. "Edith, curious, sneaks across the hall in the middle of the night and finds Max half-naked in her room. You know, getting undressed to go to bed, and the image of it so overwhelms her that she goes into the room and closes the door and then she goes to Max." Billie turned back to Madelyn, passing off a tumbler before collapsing on the couch next to her.

"And then what?" Madelyn felt her heart beating wildly, thankful for the alcohol that might cause it to slow.

"And then I haven't written a thing. But I would suspect that they might kiss and then... " Billie smiled demurely.

"Ah." Madelyn nodded.

And then... as simple as that. A kiss, and then...

"How are things?" Billie's foot toyed at Madelyn's thigh.

Madelyn covered her sock clad ankle with her hand. "Oh, fine. Just fine."

"Trouble in paradise, I take it?"

"What? No, nothing like... nothing like that... "

"Where is she tonight?" Billie asked and sipped her drink.

Madelyn rolled her ankle about in her hand, as if nervously. "Her son's. He lives in the city. She's having dinner. With him and his family."

Billie continued to look at her, as if waiting for something more.

"What?" Madelyn whispered.

"I... certainly enjoyed your kiss. Surprising as it may have been, I think, well," Billie placed her finger in her drink and swirled the ice around. "I don't think it was intended for me."

"Oh." Madelyn rolled her eyes. "I am sorry... I... "

"There's no need to apologize, Madelyn," Billie stopped the useless apology.

Madelyn took a deep breath. "It's not so simple."

Billie waited.

"She's not... like me... us. People like... us."

"Are you so sure?" Billie prodded, sipping her drink again.

Madelyn was not.

So, she drank more of her highball.

They both heard the door opening and Madelyn sat up a bit straighter.

"Darling, I'm home!" Pete's voice bellowed through the house.

Billie had not moved from her spot, her foot still pressed to Madelyn's thigh, her eyes not straying from Madelyn's face. "We're in here, darling!" She called back.

"We?" Pete asked when he came around the corner, cigarette dangling from his lips, jacket removed, rolling up his sleeves. "Madelyn, what a pleasant surprise." He leaned down to kiss her cheek and then he moved to cover Billie's lips with his own.

She took his cigarette, and he went to the minibar to fix himself a drink.

"I'm sorry... I'm intruding on your evening." Madelyn felt as if she should be going. Because she liked the comfortable feeling they gave her, and yet it now felt like some sort of a betrayal to Carole.

"No," Billie simply stated, smoke billowing from her lips. "You'll stay for dinner. Won't you?"

"Oh, I... " But Carole was in the city with her son. And it was only dinner, after all.

"We insist," Pete added.

"Well, if you'll... if you'll let me help."

Billie smiled.

"I'm going up to bathe." Pete kissed Billie again, touched Madelyn's shoulder, and then was off.

The dinner was nearly already made. A roast that Billie had had going all afternoon. It smelled heavenly.

Madelyn helped to set the table and made a salad.

They moved about as if a family, bodies comfortable with one another, and yet Billie was not Carole.

But Carole was not Billie, either.

Pete came down fresh and took his seat at the head of the table.

They sat down and spoke of the Korean War. Of an optimistic outlook. That perhaps General MacArthur would have the United States in and out in no time. And Pete wondered why the United States need be involved at all. "Well, we're a part of the UN, are we not?" Billie had countered.

And so, their conversation went on until Pete thought to ask after Carole. "Has she gone home?"

"No." Madelyn shook her head. "To her son's in the city for the evening."

Pete nodded. "It's awfully nice of her to stay on like this. Hasn't she got a husband?"

"Oh, yes." Madelyn felt as if he could see through her.

Pete was smiling at her. As if he were joking her. "She doesn't want to go home to her husband."

"Well, she... sure, but... " Madelyn was tongue-tied.

Pete winked at her and then Billie kicked him with her foot beneath the table. "You stop that. We haven't any idea how Carole is in that regard. You know these prim and proper ladies never show themselves. Not so easily, anyway."

Madelyn stared at them, mortified. "You make it sound as if... as if you want me to... " But she couldn't finish her thought.

"She likes you an awful lot. I told you that," Pete reiterated.

"But that doesn't mean... we are very close friends... as I said... and she wouldn't... " But the wheels were rolling about in Madelyn's head again.

She wanted another drink.

They cleared the dishes and Billie smoked and dried as Madelyn washed.

They returned to the living room where Pete fixed them all a drink.

Madelyn ventured a glance at the clock on the wall. It was nearing nine. She felt a panic that she might not be home if Carole were to call, to say she wouldn't be coming home, that the roads were too bad.

No, Madelyn was being silly. The roads were clear.

But there was an eagerness, a knowledge that if Carole were coming back, she would be there soon.

"You're restless." Billie noted from her place on the couch.

Madelyn pressed a hand to her forehead. "Perhaps I should be going. She'll be back soon, I'm sure."

Billie nodded. She walked Madelyn to the front door, helping her into her coat. "She'd be lucky to have you, you know."

"Oh, stop... stop putting these crazy notions into my head." Madelyn felt her cheeks grow red.

She was glad when she left the Coopers and made her way back to her own drive, her own home.

It was dark.

She went about turning on the lights.

In anticipation of Carole's return.

A want tugged at her, made her tempted to climb the stairs and fall into her bed...

But Carole would be back soon, wouldn't she?

So, she sat on the couch and picked up the D. H. Lawrence novel that Carole had been reading, and took solace in the words Carole had seen.

Chapter Fifty-Two

I t was sometime after ten that the sound of Arthur's car in the drive alerted Madelyn to Carole's return.

Madelyn was suddenly struck nervous at the idea of seeing Carole. As if Carole was suddenly a stranger to her.

She listened as the car door shut and then silence until there was a key in the lock.

Madelyn sat up a bit straighter, letting *Women in Love* fall back atop the coffee table.

The back door opened. There was the sound of heels on the linoleum before they were discarded, and the rustle of a coat being removed.

"Madelyn?" Carole's voice called out, lower and darker than Madelyn had ever remembered it being.

Madelyn got up and went to the kitchen, stomach knotting, anxious.

Carole looked up from her purse, catching Madelyn staring, standing in the doorway to the living room.

Carole smiled.

"You made it all right?" Madelyn found the courage to ask.

"Oh, yes. The roads were just fine." Carole rubbed at her neck, then reached to unbutton her jacket.

"And Hugh... how... how was Hugh and the children?" Madelyn thought then to ask.

Carole had gone back to rummaging in her purse for her cigarettes. "Oh, just as pleasant as always. He kept asking why his father wasn't here, and when I would be going back. As if I'm not allowed to travel by myself." She sank into the kitchen seat and used a match to light the end of her cigarette. Madelyn could tell she'd been nervously smoking the entire way home.

"Tea?" Madelyn suggested.

"Yes, thank you." Carole coughed and sat back in her chair. "And his wife, God, she is insufferable. I can't understand it. I've done nothing to her since they were married and yet she can't stand me. Am I so awful?" She smoked irritably.

"No." Madelyn shook her head as she started the tea kettle.

Carole was eyeing her curiously. "What's the matter with you?" she asked as she tapped off her cigarette.

Madelyn felt her cheeks flush. Was she being so different? "Nothing. Nothing at all."

"Did you eat the leftover casserole?"

Madelyn did not look at Carole when she responded. "No, I had dinner with Billie and Pete."

There was silence for what felt an eternity.

The tea kettle whistled.

Madelyn removed it from the stove and poured it over the waiting tea bags.

"I see." Carole exhaled.

Madelyn took the cups to the table, passing one to Carole before settling down across from her.

She watched Carole's lips wrap around the cigarette. Her lipstick had faded, but still left a mark on the white paper.

Madelyn was being ridiculous. Carole was the same as always, wasn't she? Nothing had changed, nor would change between them. So why was she so anxious?

"It was dinner," Madelyn found herself saying, as if clarification was needed.

Carole held up her hand in mock surrender.

They let it drop.

There was the clicking of the clock in the silence around them.

The burning of Carole's cigarette paper.

Carole scratched at her forehead. "Perhaps Hugh is right."

"About what?" Madelyn looked startled at the woman across from her.

"Perhaps I should be going on back to Frank."

Madelyn shook her head. "No."

"But it does look a certain way. You must admit." Carole tapped off her cigarette, lifting the teacup to her lips to drink.

"Who cares," Madelyn uttered. "Who cares if it does."

Carole looked at her with an unreadable, almost startled expression. It teetered on amusement. "You know these things could get out."

"What things?" Madelyn hissed.

Carole leaned forward. "Two women holed up together."

Madelyn felt her pulse quicken, anger overtaking her. "Well, if that's what you're so worried about then perhaps... " But she did not want her to leave, so she did not finish the sentence.

"Oh, Madelyn." Carole puffed at the last of her cigarette and then crushed it in the ashtray on the table. "It's late. Maybe we should... "

Madelyn felt frustration and disappointment swirl about inside of her, making her dizzy and delirious. "Right," she agreed and reached for the cups and the ashtray.

"I can do that," Carole muttered but allowed Madelyn to open the trash bin and toss the butts and ash inside before rinsing out the tray along with the two half-drunk cups of tea.

"I never thought... well I never thought you were so close-minded." Madelyn knew it was the late hour, knew it was the one too many drinks she'd had at Billie and Pete's.

But she could feel Carole growing further and further from her and soon she would end up leaving.

Carole laughed darkly. "I'm not close-minded."

Madelyn hummed as she went about putting out the lights.

Carole stood in the kitchen doorway until Madelyn brushed past her and went toward the stairs.

Carole followed her.

"What's the matter with you?" Carole demanded as they reached the top of the staircase. Her hand reached out and her fingers clasped Madelyn's wrist, stopping her dead in her tracks.

"Let me go," Madelyn whispered.

But Carole did not.

Her lips tasted like tobacco and wine.

It happened so suddenly that Madelyn wasn't sure how it had happened in the first place.

She'd turned and Carole's face had been there, and Madelyn had cupped her cheek and Carole had leaned into her touch and then their lips had met.

Then met again.

They stood, touching yet not touching. Breath labored. Madelyn afraid to look at Carole, thankful for the darkness of the hallway.

Carole's head fell back against the wall that Madelyn had inadvertently pushed her against.

She sighed, licked her lips. "I think I need a drink."

They reclined on Rose's old bed. Side-by-side, drinks in hand moments later.

It was funny that they should be in Rose's old room. There was something about it that felt terribly wrong, inappropriate, yet fitting.

Madelyn could feel her heart pounding away in her chest.

Her hand was shaking so that she held the hand that was holding the tumbler in place with the other.

Carole was stoic.

But soon Madelyn realized that it was not stoicism, it was fear and elation flowing through the woman beside her.

"How does it even work?" Carole wondered aloud as she brought the tumbler of whiskey to her lips.

Madelyn turned to look at her and thought she looked more beautiful than she ever had. Her nice shirt crumpled and half-pulled from her skirt. Her hair falling from its previously perfect style. Lips red and not from her lipstick. Her eyes were glassy from the alcohol and yet they looked right at Madelyn.

"Do you… " Madelyn was afraid that if she pushed too hard the other woman might disappear before her eyes.

"I don't think I'd be very good at it." Carole swirled the liquid around, not looking at Madelyn.

"But you… " Madelyn felt her heart racing.

"I liked… kissing you," Carole continued to avoid her gaze.

Madelyn felt a small smile upturn the corners of her lips at the admission. Carole always so closed off about herself, was cracking open.

Slowly, slowly.

"We could… kiss again… "

"But then what?" Carole hummed.

"There doesn't have to be a 'then'… " Madelyn sat her tumbler down on the bedside table and turned back to take Carole's from her slightly shaking hand. She reached over Carole's body to settle the glass atop the other bedside table, next to the whiskey bottle, and then straightened again to look at Carole.

There was trepidation mixed with curiosity in her eyes.

"I won't be anything like your neighbors, you know. If you'd rather… ," Carole demurred.

Madelyn traced the side of her face with her trembling hand. "Shut up," she commanded.

Carole closed her mouth and swallowed.

Madelyn's finger trailed down the side of her neck, across her shapely shoulder, down her silk clad arm.

Carole shivered. "I wouldn't know... "

Madelyn leaned forward to press her lips to Carole's neck, inhaling the scent of her skin. There was a hint of her perfume, cigarettes, and soap and then something that was all Carole. It was overwhelming.

She heard Carole's breathing catch in her throat. "Oh, Madelyn." Carole sighed, hands that had been rigid at her sides came up to embrace Madelyn.

Carole sought out her mouth and kissed her, tentatively, almost hesitantly at first.

But the kisses grew bolder, hands tightening at Madelyn's back.

They clasped each other, rolled together, explored with hands and mouths and tongues and teeth. Clothing wrinkled, coming dislodged from where it was intended to rest on the human form.

It was the moment that Madelyn let her fingers glide up the nylon clad inside of Carole's thigh that Carole reached for her hand and stopped its path.

Madelyn rolled away and Carole sat up, twisting for her cigarettes. She hit one out of the pack and placed it between her lips as she sought out her lighter.

"I'm... I'm sorry. Are you all right?" Madelyn asked as she smoothed down her hair, righted her twisted shirt about her torso.

She left the top buttons undone.

"Mmm," Carole hummed around the cigarette. She laid back on the bed and exhaled a decadent cloud of smoke. She looked up at Madelyn, expression unreadable. Then her hand came up, tracing down Madelyn's sternum lazily, pausing right between her breasts. "I've never felt this way."

And Madelyn smiled, lifting Carole's hand to her lips to kiss her palm and each of her fingertips.

Carole's wide, brilliant eyes stared up at her. "I don't... I don't think I can... "

"Darling, I'm not asking you... "

Carole toyed with the hem of Madelyn's shirt, not meeting her eyes. "I'm not... queer," she said it with no conviction. "I can't... "

Madelyn laid down beside her "Would it be so awful?"

Carole inhaled deeply on her cigarette. Madelyn watched the smoke billow from her lips, then watched as they moved to form the word "yes."

Madelyn had never been more turned on before in her life. She pressed her legs together.

Carole sat up to put out her cigarette and to turn out the lamp on the bedside table.

She laid back again.

They stared at the ceiling in darkness.

Carole did not ask her to leave.

Chapter Fifty-Three

She awoke fully clothed. The sun shining in through a slit in the blinds.

At first, she did not recognize where she was and then saw the soft pink of the walls, the floral print of the drapes, and realized.

Carole was turned away from her on her side. Still dressed in her twisted skirt and silk top.

Madelyn could only see her back, the rise and fall of her ribcage, the sound of her open-mouthed breaths. She was still asleep.

Madelyn squinted toward the bedside table to see the time and felt a wave of panic overcome her.

She sat up, startling Carole from her sleep so that she sucked in a deep breath, coughed, before turning on her back. Disoriented.

Madelyn apologized.

Carole stared at her with furrowed brow, a lack of recognition.

"I'm sorry. I... I have to go."

"Go?" Carole's voice was hoarse.

"Betsy... " Madelyn straightened her shirt back around.

"Oh," Carole just said.

"It's a... a big day. The state is coming to access her," Madelyn explained sheepishly. "I'm late. I'm going to be late."

Carole's eyes were wide-awake then. She sat up slowly and Madelyn could tell her head was pounding from the night before. "I'll... uh, I'll change and make us some coffee." Carole rubbed her temples.

Madelyn did not want to leave her like this. But time was clicking away.

She left Carole to change, moving to her own bedroom. She showered quickly, made herself up – though her hand shook – fluffed her hair, and put on a fresh dress.

Carole was in a robe in the kitchen, smoking a cigarette and drinking coffee, when Madelyn emerged.

She poured herself coffee from the pot and took a few sips to calm herself.

She would be late for certain at this point.

"It won't be long... I'll be back before two," Madelyn explained.

Carole did not respond, just continued to smoke and stare at the empty table before her.

Madelyn felt the strangest urge to cry.

Carole was miles away from her.

Had they spoiled it all the night before?

But now was not the time to figure it all out. They would have time. Later.

"There's Aspirin in my bathroom medicine cabinet," Madelyn said.

"Thank you," Carole said as she tapped off ash.

"I'll... I'll be back," Madelyn said as she took her last sip of coffee and then moved to collect up her purse and her coat, to slip her feet into her heels.

She looked back to Carole, but only saw the same unreadable expression on her face.

Something felt horribly wrong as she went out the door, started up her car, and drove away from Carole.

But she could not think about it. Because there was Betsy to deal with.

Mitch would be there.

The state would be there.

Would Betsy be scared?

Madelyn needed to be there for her.

She drove faster than was allowed and was only ten minutes late.

She was surprised, however, when she pulled into the parking lot and saw a handsome couple standing near the foot of the stairs that led to the gloomy institution. A couple she recognized.

She parked the car and reached for her purse. Her heart pounding at the sight of them.

Her heels clicked on the pavement as she walked toward them.

"Rose?" Madelyn was surprised by her appearance.

Rose looked up at her. Fear in her eyes. She stood smoking nervously.

Mitch looked relieved at Madelyn's arrival.

Rose put out her cigarette beneath her heel.

Madelyn led them inside. The nurse greeted her kindly and Madelyn introduced her daughter and son-in-law. They were led down the hall, informed that the men from the state were waiting in the corridor.

Madelyn could not look back at her daughter as they made their way to the second floor.

The men were in dark suits. Waiting.

Everyone shook hands, cordially.

Madelyn could feel Rose hanging back.

A nurse opened the door, and they went inside.

Betsy was in a new dress, her hair done up neatly, her face wiped clean. She looked beautiful.

She bounced at their arrival, as if she knew who had come to see her. As if she could sense it.

Madelyn smiled at the sight of her. "Hello, Betsy. How are you my darling girl?"

Betsy clapped.

"These nice men are going to have a little conversation with you, is that all right?"

Betsy looked everywhere about the room but did not seem to focus on anyone. But her head tilted, turned toward the corner. Where Rose stood.

The men were talking mostly amongst themselves. Not even addressing Betsy. They tried to get close, but a nurse cautioned them that Betsy did not like touch.

It was an inhuman cry that made Madelyn turn.

Rose's eyes were wide, a hand clamped over her mouth.

Rose turned, racing from the room.

Mitch had the same bewildered look in his eyes, but he did not follow after his wife. He looked at Madelyn, as if pleading with her.

Madelyn excused herself and went out, walking quickly down the hall, following her daughter's retreating form all the way back down the stairs and out the front door.

"Rose!" Madelyn cried, trying to keep up with her daughter as she raced through the leaf covered grounds of the facility, finally falling to her knees, burying her face in her hands, bending forward.

So that Madelyn caught up to her, kneeling down beside her in the soft grass. "Rose, what's the matter?"

"I wish... I wish... I wish... " Rose gasped between sobs, tears wracking her whole being as she cried.

"Shh." Madelyn stroked her back.

"I wish she'd died. I wish she'd died, and the other one had lived." Rose gasped into the ground.

"Stop it!" Madelyn hushed those words.

"I wish she'd died. I should have killed her, not the other one," Rose repeated the words more loudly, more defiantly.

"You do not wish that, Rose. You do not," Madelyn insisted.

"I do, oh God, I do." Rose was breathing heavily.

Madelyn pulled her upward, wrapping her up in her arms. "You were so young, Rose. You were so young."

"I don't care," Rose sputtered. "She shouldn't be alive. She shouldn't... she shouldn't have to suffer... like this... " Rose gasped, grasping at Madelyn.

"Oh, darling." Madelyn held her closer. "Darling. She's not suffering. She has a lovely life here. If only you could... "

"What kind of life can she have? She can't even... she can't even talk!" Rose cried. "You can't even... you can't even hold her! She screams and cries. She's not... she's not human, Mama. She's not human." Rose sobbed.

"She is a human. She is a person. And she deserves the same respect as any other human, Rose. She's just... different. She has different needs," Madelyn soothed her hand over Rose's back, rocking her as if she were a child again. "She's beautiful, Rose."

"No." Rose shook her head. "She's a monster. I... I... "

"Stop this!" Madelyn shook her daughter, pulling her away so that she could look into her red eyes. "Stop this, right now! You're just guilty that you couldn't be there for her, but you can be here now. I need you to be here now. I can't... I can't take care of her forever, darling. She has a long road ahead of her and she needs *you*. She needs her mother. Even if she can't express it, even if she can't talk or touch you, she needs you. She's always needed you."

"Stop it." Rose couldn't look her in the eyes.

She shook her again. "You can be here for her now," Madelyn reiterated.

"Oh, God." Rose looked to the overcast sky, as if seeking escape heavenwards.

"She'll forgive you. She's very forgiving." Madelyn stroked her daughter's tearstained cheek. "You just have to talk to her. That's all she really wants. To be spoken to, like she matters. Sometimes she gets upset, sometimes she lashes out, like anyone else. But she loves art, she loves painting, she loves the colors purple and orange and green. She's very intelligent. Like you, darling. She has a bit of you in her."

Rose shook her head.

"Did you see... " Madelyn asked as she sat down on the ground beside her daughter, "... did you see when she looked at you? She knows you. She wanted to see you."

Tears slipped down Rose's cheeks. She rummaged about in her purse for a cigarette. She lit it with shaking hands, inhaling deeply.

"She did." Rose exhaled a cloud of smoke. "She looked at me like she... "

"She knows you. She will always know you." Madelyn patted her daughter's knee.

When she looked up, she saw the men in the dark suits leaving.

"Why don't we go in and just talk to her. She would like that," Madelyn suggested.

Rose kept smoking in her undignified state on the front lawn of the institution. Finally, after the men had driven away, she put out her cigarette and wiped her eyes and nodded.

They helped one another up, brushing leaves from their crumbled coats and skirts, and walked arm-in-arm back to the building.

Madelyn did not let her go as they ascended the stairs, making their way back into the room.

Betsy stilled when they entered the room.

She seemed to look toward her mother as they approached.

"Betsy, this is your mother," Madelyn said as they came closer.

Rose held tight to Madelyn.

Madelyn turned an encouraging look to Rose, and Rose looked at her daughter. "Hello, Betsy."

Chapter Fifty-Four

The house was spotless when she stepped inside.

Her heart sank into her chest as she slipped from her heels, removing her coat to hang it on the tidied rack.

Not a thing out of place, the kitchen sparkling in the dim daylight.

Something was terribly wrong.

"Carole?" Madelyn called out as she walked through the kitchen, afraid that it might already be too late.

But as she rounded the corner into the living room, she found Carole dressed in her traveling suit, suitcase packed and settled beside her, cigarette dangling from her fingers as she stared vacantly through the freshly cleaned windows.

The lights were all off. Only the overcast day illuminated the room, the cherry of Carole's cigarette glowing bright as she inhaled.

"No," Madelyn said loudly.

Carole did not look at her, simply exhaled her protest in a cloud of smoke.

"No, you're not going back there."

"I've already called a cab," Carole spoke listlessly.

Madelyn shook her head, anger curling in her arms and chest, tears stinging at her eyes. Anger and fear that Carole really would leave. Just walk out and leave it unfinished.

"Don't go back there. You're miserable there."

"And I'm miserable here so what... "

"No." Madelyn stopped her. "No... "

"Madelyn, I have to go back," Carole's voice was barely audible. She flicked at a piece of ash that had fallen on her skirt. "Frank called today. He needs me. And I fear that I've... outstayed my welcome here."

Madelyn shook with rage and fear. "Bullshit."

Carole flicked her cigarette in the ashtray and lifted it to her lips again, barely even flinching at Madelyn's outburst.

So, she was resolved to leave. Just like that.

No.

Madelyn could see the shake of her hand in its motion.

She was barely holding herself together.

"Stay with me," Madelyn whispered, heart racing at the thought of Carole walking out the front door.

Carole's lips parted as if she might say something, but no words came.

"You don't have to go back there."

Carole nearly laughed.

"We could... we could sell this house. We could move to the city, I could keep my job, no one would... no one would have to know."

"And what?" Carole's voice was low when she spoke. "I'd be a kept woman again?"

Madelyn's brow furrowed. "I would never... You could get a job if you'd like. Anything you want. I'd help you."

Carole exhaled a cloud of smoke, as if in thought, as if she were picturing it. "I'm afraid I wouldn't... " She looked down at her lap, examined the wedding ring on her left hand. Her head shook its protest. "What if I couldn't give you what you wanted?"

Madelyn inhaled sharply. She moved forward, forward until she was kneeling before Carole, forcing her gaze to land upon her. "What do you want?"

Carole looked away. Madelyn could not be certain in the ever-darkening room, but she could sense tears in the other woman's eyes.

Carole smoked, her hand completely unsteady.

Madelyn took the nearly spent cigarette from her fingers and crushed it in the ashtray as Carole crumbled before her. Her fingers combed through her neatly curled hair as she leaned over, tears overtaking her.

Madelyn ran a soothing hand across her back. Warm and boney. She had lost weight, her unhappiness eating away at her.

She cried in practiced silence.

"Oh God," she finally gasped. "What do *I* want? What... what can I want?"

"Anything," Madelyn encouraged her, heart hammering away in her chest, but she did not let on. Because she realized that she loved Carole.

She moved to sit beside her on the couch, taking her hands in her own.

Carole was half-laughing half-crying. "I want... oh." She sat up and Madelyn offered her a tissue. "I want to divorce him. I never want to see him again. I never want to go back there. I want... but it would be impossible... "

"It's not impossible," Madelyn whispered.

"But I'm... I don't even know... " Carole sighed.

"If you're afraid that I would... expect things, I wouldn't. Only what you're willing to give. Do you understand? We could simply... be." Madelyn felt pain in her chest as she spoke. Because she would do that for Carole. She would live with her as she had with Arthur, if that was all she could give.

Carole was looking at her.

The room was growing darker and darker.

But Carole's violet eyes remained fixed upon Madelyn.

Lights flashed through the front blinds. A car on the street.

"Madelyn," Carole whispered. "I love you and I'm scared."

The words hardly spoken above a whisper.

Madelyn's chest burst deliciously in a myriad of pain and pleasure.

She clasped Carole's cheek in her hand.

Carole's eyes widened.

Madelyn leaned in to press her lips against Carole's.

Her lips were waxy from lipstick, and they tasted ashy with a hint of whiskey and the mint of toothpaste.

"I love you so..." Madelyn whispered.

There was a honk outside that startled them apart.

"Oh!" Carole cried. Her body shaking, a nervous laugh surprising them both. "It's the cab."

"You really called for one?" Madelyn reached for a tissue to wipe Carole's lipstick from her lips.

Carole took the tissue from Madelyn and tilted her chin upwards to help clean away the mess. "Of course, I did... "

"You would have... if I hadn't come home... " Madelyn felt furious and elated all at once.

"No... I don't know... " Carole wavered.

"I'm sending him away." Madelyn ducked out from Carole's focused cleaning and stood to go to the door. She checked her reflection in the mirrored surface of a vase. Her lips looked unkissed.

She opened the door and took care of the cabby, offering him some cash for his trouble and then went back inside to find Carole standing in the living room as if she did not know what to do.

Madelyn felt a smile lift the corner of her lips. "Why don't we turn on some lights?"

Carole cowered, as if the light might reveal something.

Madelyn moved to turn on the lamp near the couch. Its

warm light flooded about them, and Carole stood - tear-streaked face, hair undone - before her. And she had never looked more beautiful.

She was still trembling.

"It's all right." Madelyn moved carefully toward her, afraid to startle her.

But Carole allowed her to put her arms about her, allowed her to pull her into her embrace and they stood swaying to an invisible song.

Carole's head rested on her shoulder. "What do we do now?" Her arms slowly went about Madelyn, clinging to her.

"Now?" Madelyn whispered and kissed the top of her head. "Now, we should eat something."

Carole's grasp loosened and she began to laugh. As if it were the simplest thing. As if she'd been holding her breath, afraid of what else they might do now that they were on the same page.

"One thing at a time," Madelyn said, knowingly. "Go unpack and change out of those clothes. I'll make that soup you like."

Carole obeyed, as if she needed the instruction to keep herself together.

Madelyn put on a Bing Crosby record and went to the kitchen. She began slicing vegetables, putting them to simmer in vegetable broth. The motions soothing as the day melted away from her.

She listened to Carole's footsteps above her. The sound of a sink, and then her feet on the staircase.

Madelyn's heart raced in her chest.

Carole had washed her face clean. She'd put on pants and a sweater, her hair tied up.

She looked uncertain and startled, as if she no longer knew how to fit into their domestic routine.

Madelyn told her to set the table, and the motion cut through the tension. Plates on the table, slices of bread warmed in the oven, the soup brought to the table, drinks made, dinnerware placed atop napkins. The work they knew so well.

And then they sat across from one another.

Carole looked down into her soup and shook her head. "I'm being silly." She toyed with the spoon in her hand. "It's as if I... I know you. I've known you for years and... "

"Now it's different," Madelyn agreed.

Carole looked up and offered her a soft smile. As if to prove that she was not afraid. "Yes. It is different."

"It doesn't have to be... so different." Madelyn settled her spoon down beside her bowl. "I'm still me and you're still you."

Carole shook her head, not able to meet Madelyn's gaze. "I don't feel so much like myself anymore." She flipped the spoon over on the table. "I feel foolish around you."

"Foolish?"

"No... perhaps not foolish, but... maybe more like I want something that I'm not sure I can have."

"You can have anything you want," Madelyn insisted.

Carole shook her head. "It couldn't be that easy, could it?"

"Maybe it can be."

Chapter Fifty-Five

Chapter Fifty-Five

They sat, reclining on the couch.

The dishes done. Tumblers half-full of whiskey. Smoke swirling from Carole's cigarette, Glenn Miller playing on the record, a candle dancing lazily in the otherwise dimly lit room.

They sat near one another and yet they hardly touched.

They spoke of Rose and Betsy's reunion, of nothing.

Madelyn felt her heart pounding in her chest, could feel the tense way in which Carole was holding herself on the couch beside her.

They had lapsed into silence.

The moment only punctuated by the lifting of Carole's cigarette to her lips followed by a stream of smoke.

"I'm smoking too much," she commented, carelessly.

Madelyn glanced at her profile. Her perfectly rounded nose, her deep-set eyes, the curve of her pert, pink lips, the wrinkles that had grown deeper since their first meeting all those years before.

"I suppose I'm nervous." She sat forward to tap off ashes. Her red fingernails elegant in the motion, the gleam of her wedding band catching the light as she moved.

Madelyn realized she was still wearing her own wedding band. A reminder of the men they belonged to.

But the men were not there anymore.

It was only the two of them.

She reached out and found Carole's hand. "Don't be."

Carole laughed deeply, letting their hands fold together, fingers lacing between fingers.

Silence. The record started up its next number.

Carole was looking at their hands, resting comfortably on the couch between them.

"What is it that two women... do... together, exactly?" Carole tilted her cigarette upwards to inhale after she asked. The words sounded hesitant and foreign.

Madelyn also had her eyes trained on their combined hands. "Whatever they'd like to do together."

Carole squeezed her hand. "Madelyn." She groaned.

Madelyn laughed then. "Well, it's... it's... " She thought of Billie's hands on her, of Billie's mouth, the pleasurable sensation that had overcome her. "It's, I suppose, a bit like touching yourself, but you're touching someone else."

Carole shifted, crossing her legs toward Madelyn. "I see." She considered as she smoked again. Her hand was shaking.

Madelyn sipped her whiskey. "If I'm honest, I don't even know if I'll be any good at it," she admitted, as if it might level their situation.

Carole glanced at her. "Didn't you... "

"Well, yes... but, I was rather... passive," Madelyn decided.

Carole smoked again. Her eyes wide. She leaned forward to put out her cigarette. "Oh," she simply said after a moment. "At least," she sipped her whiskey, "at least you've... " Her sentence trailed off.

Madelyn turned to look at the woman at her side.

Carole did not look at her, but also continued to hold her hand. As if it were a life preserver. "I feel different. Thinking about it with you. With Frank it's awful. I just lay there. I could be anyone or anything for all he cares." Carole sighed. "Year after year. He just... and I just... take it... " She sniffed and Madelyn thought she might be crying. But she looked at her face and saw anger in her eyes. "It's terribly uncomfortable, not that he'd care."

Madelyn lifted their hands and kissed Carole's palm. "You deserve more than that."

"Oh, I don't even know if I can... " Carole inhaled as Madelyn's lips covered her wrist. She sucked gently at the flesh there and Carole inhaled sharply.

Carole shifted again. Their faces close. Madelyn let her hand cup at Carole's cheek, her thumb skimming the soft flesh of her lips, Carole leaning into her. Their lips met, bodies hovering close to one another.

Carole was shaking in her embrace.

They parted; Carole's eyes sought Madelyn's before she was kissing her again. As if she couldn't get enough of her lips. A part of her coming to life, and Madelyn basked in the yearning way in which Carole kissed her. Lips hungry, starving to be kissed.

Carole pulled back after a moment, reaching for her tumbler of whiskey that had been abandoned. She sipped the amber liquid, Madelyn resting back against the couch, heart pounding, heat building between her legs.

Carole. Carole aroused before her was almost more than she could stand, but she did not want to frighten her away. So, she watched her as she drank, as she sat forward and put her arms on her knees, ran a hand through her hair that had slipped from its barrette that held it back.

"I've never... I'm sorry." Carole tried to pull herself together.

"There's nothing to be sorry about." Madelyn smiled as she let her hand trail down Carole's back.

"I feel... oh, I feel like I could just... explode. I... I need, but I'm... " Carole was very far gone.

Madelyn took her tumbler from her and lifted her cheek upward. "Whatever you want... whatever you need... "

She wanted to give to her everything she had felt herself. She wanted Carole to know what it was to love and be loved and to fall into the abyss.

Carole hummed low in her throat. "I need... but I don't know... "

"I can show you." Madelyn stood up, went about the room putting out the lights, stopping the record on the record player, blowing out the candle.

Carole sat in the darkness, hugging herself.

Madelyn held out her hand to her. "Let's go upstairs."

Carole stared at her hand. Afraid to accept, but she allowed Madelyn to take her hand and pull her up. They went up the stairs together and Madelyn led her into her bedroom.

She moved to turn on the bedside lamp, but Carole stopped her.

They stood, in the dark, staring at one another.

Carole's shoulders rose and fell with her breathing. Her hair was falling messily around her face. She had never looked more beautiful than in that moment, basked in the dim moonlight that shone through the blinds.

"What now?" Carole asked, a willing, nervous student.

Madelyn wanted to see her naked again. Wanted to see her pert, pink nipples and the long naked spans of the body that she had held and touched the night before.

But the woman had her arms wrapped around herself.

Madelyn stepped toward her, placing her hands on Carole's hips. The other woman opened her arms to pull Madelyn against her.

"It's just me," Madelyn whispered.

Carole smiled a little, but the worried line was still etched in her brow.

Madelyn kissed her, little kisses at first and then their lips opened to the other and Carole's grasp on her tightened. A sigh. A strangled sob.

Madelyn's fingers went to the hem of Carole's sweater, nudging it upward. Carole stepped back, helping her to take the article off. Carole's fingers toyed with the buttons on Madelyn's shirt and Madelyn eased her shirt off so that she stood in her bra and Carole stepped back to look at her, to marvel at this exposed skin. Her fingers shook, afraid to reach out.

Madelyn took her hands and pressed them against her body.

Carole inhaled sharply.

Madelyn reached behind her back and unclasped her bra, pulling it away to expose her own breasts, watching Carole's eyes follow the motion. Then her hands, tentatively, explored the freshly revealed spans of skin, fingers stroking over hardened nipples.

"Beautiful," Carole whispered.

Madelyn sought her consent and then reached about Carole to unclasp her bra, pulling the material away from her skin so that she could see, in the dim light, her two pink, hardened nipples. She met Carole's eyes and then let her hand pass over one breast, bending her head to kiss at Carole's neck, to kiss a path downward until her lips covered the left nipple. Carole's hands threaded in her hair, holding her close, head thrown back, an audible sigh emitted from between her lips. "Oh, God," whispered like a prayer.

Madelyn's hands found the zipper on the side of Carole's slim pants. She pulled it downward and the other woman helped her discard it quickly, the material rolling away from her skin.

Madelyn unclasped her skirt and let it fall to the ground, ridding herself of her pantyhose and they stood together in their underwear.

Carole panted, eyes wide and aroused in the dim light.

Madelyn took her in her arms, turning her about so that they were both facing the long mirror in the corner, and they could see one another together. Their varying shades of blonde hair, ruffled and mused, the flush of their cheeks.

And at first Carole was startled at the image. Afraid of it, but Madelyn held her close, wanting to admire and wanting her to admire her own beauty. "Gorgeous," Madelyn whispered, running her hand down the side of Carole's taut body.

Carole watched the motion, lips parted.

Their hands met and Madelyn pressed Carole's hand against her own skin, guiding it upward to cover her pink nipple, to grasp at her own breast.

Carole whimpered, leaning against Madelyn.

She was soft and taut. Madelyn could feel her muscles contracting as their hands glided down Carole's torso, pressing over her center to touch the soft flesh of her thighs.

Her legs parted, she swallowed, head rolling back against Madelyn's shoulder, gasping ever so when their hands finally came to rest between her legs.

She was far, far gone.

Her hips moved against their hands, wanting, her knees going weak.

"The bed... " Madelyn whispered, finding that she could no longer support the crumbling woman in her embrace.

Carole groaned in protest at the lost contact.

Underwear was discarded.

Madelyn took Carole in her arms, her back against her chest. She kissed at her neck, taking her hand in her own. "I want you to touch yourself," Madelyn whispered and Carole whimpered again.

Carole's legs came apart and Madelyn guided their hands to press against Carole's arousal. She was warm, her hips moved against their stilled hands. Madelyn could feel the touch in her own center.

Madelyn stroked Carole's fingers against herself. The woman twitched in her embrace and then relaxed again.

Carole was fully stimulated. Madelyn could feel her as their fingers moved in tandem.

"Oh... I never... oh... " Carole whimpered as they alternated tempos and pressures. Her hips came alive, matching the motion of their hands.

Madelyn guided their fingers downward, so that they dipped inside of Carole. Her hips pressed forward to try and reclaim the sensation from before, until Madelyn led their hands back upward. And then Carole seemed to take over, to touch in a new way, the same place again and again, rubbing against the sensitive area and Madelyn could barely breathe at how erotic it was to feel and hear Carole fall apart.

The spasm started beneath their fingers. Madelyn could feel the sensation of it as if she were experiencing it herself.

Carole's cry was deep and throaty. She gasped, catching Madelyn's hand and pressing it against her swollen, pulsating center until the waves subsided and she fell back limp and breathless.

As if all the life had gone out of her.

Her slackened body grew rigid as she became aware of the world again, of her surroundings, of Madelyn's arms around her, holding her close.

She covered her face with her hands as if embarrassed and Madelyn kissed her shoulder. "It's all right, darling."

Carole was sobbing.

Madelyn shifted their bodies so that she could take Carole into her arms and hold her close until the crying subsided into a sleepy silence.

Chapter Fifty-Six

Madelyn sat on the edge of the bed drying her hair with a towel.

The lamp was on.

Carole stood in a robe at the window, cigarette dangling from her fingers, face soft as she stared out into the night.

She was even more beautiful undone as she was.

They had awoken from their dreamy slumber and Carole had reached for her. They had explored one another more intimately and then Madelyn had drawn them a bath and Carole brought the last of the whiskey and they'd laid in one another's arms in the warm, aromatic water, a candle dancing on the wall. Washed clean, made new for one another.

It was late and yet Madelyn hadn't a clue of the time. Time was elusive and inconsequential because there was Carole standing before her, robe open at the front as she stood unashamed of her nakedness. Or perhaps not even aware of it.

"My son lives in the city," Carole said wistfully.

Madelyn met her gaze.

"If we moved to the city..." Carole had been thinking.

Madelyn smiled. "He wouldn't think anything of it, would he?"

360

Carole shrugged and went back to looking out the window. She inhaled on her cigarette, slow and leisurely and relaxed. "I don't think I'd give a damn anymore. I can't... I can't imagine... " She turned to Madelyn and smiled, lifting the cigarette to her lips. Lost.

Madelyn laid back against the headboard of the bed, her arousal returning at the sight of Carole's flushed cheeks. There was a hint of her pink nipple exposed when she moved her hand to tap off ash.

A painting come to life before her.

Her eyes watched, inhaling the sight before her.

Carole stared at the night sky before her gaze caught on something across the way.

She smoked and stared.

"It's curious."

"Hmm?" Madelyn reached for her hand lotion.

"In all those years that we lived next door to one another... I never realized that our bedroom windows faced one another."

Madelyn sat up.

She went to the window, to stand beside Carole, and looked out into the dark night.

She could see that the light was on in the window across the yard.

The Gallery

Pablo Picasso,
Homme nu assis, 1908-09

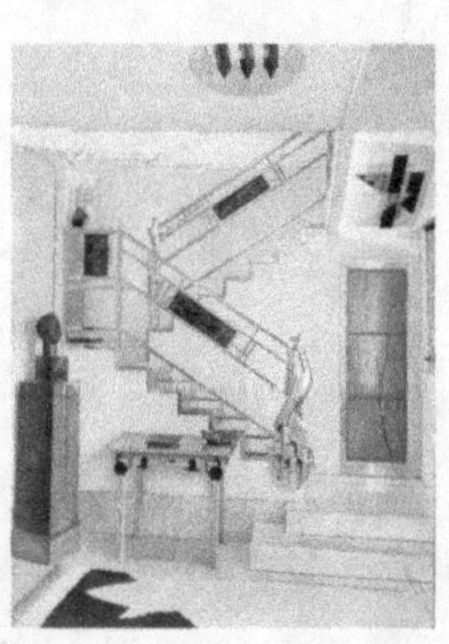

Jacques Doucet's hôtel
particulier staircase,
design by Joseph Csaky,
1929

*Edwin Bower Hesser's
Arts Monthly*, Griffith
Park in Los Angeles in
1929, subject: Jean
Harlow

Henri Matisse
Young Woman at the
Window, Sunset, 1921

John Singer Sargent,
Portrait of Madame X,
1884

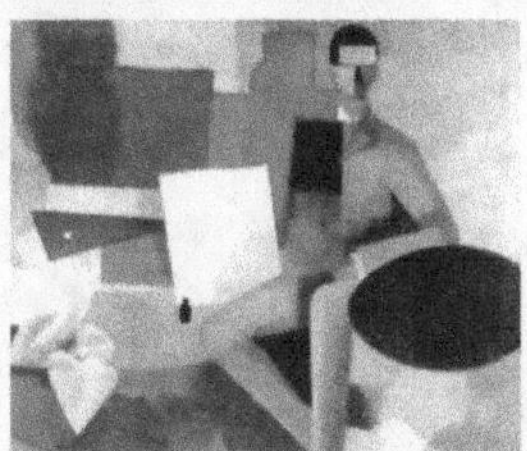

Roger de La Fresnaye,
Homme assis,
1913 - 1914

Édouard-Henri Avril,
from De Figuris Veneris,
1824

The Seed of the Areoi,
Paul Gauguin
1892

Acknowledgments

Thank you to my bestest reader friend ever, Lorrie. I love that you keep me going and help me process what comes next.

Thank you to Linda for editing - your comma lessons were revelatory!

To all the wonderful people I've met since publishing my first novel - you all motivate me to keep going and to get more books out! I appreciate all of my readers and book friends so much!

About the Author

Anna Woiwood is a writer of mid-century Sapphic stories. Her debut novel, The Veracity of Lies, was a finalist for a 2023 Golden Crown Literary Award in historical fiction and A Tiger in Suburbia was a 2024 Golden Crown Literary Ann Bannon Popular Choice finalist. She lives in Kansas City with her small cat son, Walter. Find her on Instagram @anna.w.writes